BY MANY
OR BY FEW
FEW

BY MANY
OR BY FEW

WALKER BUCKALEW

Providence House Publishers
PROVIDENCE PUBLISHING CORPORATION
FRANKLIN, TENNESSEE

Printed in the United States of America

10   09   08   07   06   1   2   3   4   5

Library of Congress Control Number: 2006901019

13-Digit ISBN: 978-1-57736-360-6
10-Digit ISBN: 1-57736-360-4

Cover illustration by Jeff Whitlock, Whitlock Graphics

Cover design by Joey McNair

This is a work of fiction. Names, characters, places, and incidents are products of the author's imagination or are used fictitiously.

PROVIDENCE HOUSE PUBLISHERS
an imprint of
Providence Publishing Corporation
238 Seaboard Lane • Franklin, Tennessee 37067
www.providence-publishing.com
800-321-5692

This book is dedicated to Linda,
without whose encouragement and inspiration
The Rebecca Series *would not have been formulated nor,*
once formulated, carried through to completion.

PREFACE

This story can be read by itself, but it is also a sequel to *The Face of the Enemy*. In this episode, exactly one year has passed since the conclusion of the first book in The Rebecca Series.

Readers are reminded that these stories are set in the 1970s, and that being the case:

- airport security will not resemble what we experience now in the twenty-first century,
- telephones will be encumbered with rotary dials,
- long-distance phone calls will often be made "collect," and will involve conversations with telephone operators,
- there will be no Internet, and
- the twin towers of New York City's World Trade Center will still preside over the skyline of lower Manhattan.

Chapter One

LIKE A YOUNG ANIMAL WITH AN OLD WOUND, THE gentleman, aged twenty-eight years and one day, just over six feet four straight-backed inches in height, and physically asymmetrical in a disconcerting way, paced in front of the British Airways gate. In fifteen minutes, if her plane were on schedule, he would see her for the first time since the previous June. Yes, certainly, they had corresponded weekly during that time, but he had found it impossible to translate their long-distance relationship into a language of actual encounter.

He took a deep breath as he paced, and tried again to be analytical about the uncharacteristic anxiety that had dogged him in the weeks since she had arranged her flights and informed him of her arrival day and time in New York. When last he had been with her, in a Welsh hospital, he had been so groggy from anesthesia and pain medication that he had scarcely been coherent. But he could still see her face with absolute clarity. He could see her leaning toward his hospital bed, her thick, straight, dark tresses falling in a hypnotic cascade down the front of her borrowed medical gown, framing her cheekbones, highlighting the elegance of her face. That face with the deepest, most penetrating gray eyes he had ever seen, before or since. And he still had the clearest of memories of the frenetic violence just thirty-six hours before that hospital moment, shortly before his left shoulder and upper arm had been shredded by automatic weapons fire and his skull fractured within a centimeter of his life.

He could see in his mind and feel on his face and lips the hours-earlier encounter, perhaps forty-five minutes before the gunfire had begun. He studied once more in memory that encounter's uncanny foreshadowing of their hospital farewell. They had leaned toward each other then, not in the seclusion of the medical sanctuary soon to come, but in the midnight wildness and driving rain outside the perimeter wall of St. David's Cathedral on the Pembrokeshire coast. He could frame in his mind, even now, the trembling intensity of her face as the two of them had crouched there together, and he could sense, his fingertips now rising to his mouth, the kiss they had shared in the utter desperation of that moment, minutes before they were to expose themselves to capture and likely death at the hands of the greatest Evil he had ever known or imagined.

Beyond all that, he could feel somehow with even greater force and clarity, if that were possible, the otherworldly sensations that had passed through him as he had knelt with her at the rear of the cathedral in the eerie, explosive silence that presaged their final lunging, climbing, sprinting escape. And he thought, as he paced back and forth through JFK's European terminal, of the woman's near-incomprehensible feat of carrying his inert two-hundred-pound body for more than a mile along the twisting coast path to Porth Clais, from which the two of them were finally evacuated. He stopped pacing and drank in the wonder of it for the hundredth time. All in one seemingly endless, terror-laden night, they had savored their only kiss, shared in the cathedral the most riveting of supernatural encounters, and in sequence, saved each other's life.

He began to pace again. Oh yes, they had corresponded since then. She had written him faithfully from her small flat in London in the deteriorating neighborhood in which she taught at a junior school for girls. He had written with equal regularity and, he acknowledged to himself, with more fervor than she, from his even smaller apartment near the Hudson River from which he daily walked to Columbia University or Union Theological Seminary for graduate classes. But a shyness played through their letters. A hesitancy. His love for her had sprung from such a cauldron of violence and emotion, and his separation from her had been so chaotic and precipitous, that he had no settled confidence in their relationship, if, indeed, there could be said to be a relationship.

He knew that his own letters were as uncertain in their tone as his thoughts were now, familiar but superficial, filled with news of his graduate studies and of his internship, teaching history in a tough Bronx high school.

He stopped pacing again. He forced himself to face squarely the truth that had clamored for admission to his mind for the entire year of separation from her. It was a truth that was exposed at this moment, surely, because of the imminence of her arrival. And so, standing in the crowded airport, he confronted the fact that the uncertainties were all his; there were none on her part. There never had been. She was *not* in love with him. She would not allow herself to be. She had simply accepted his love for her. That was all.

He continued to stride rapidly, if aimlessly, through the broad, tightly peopled corridor. Why could he not just relax and look forward to the moment of their reunion? He stopped again. Why indeed? And he knew. He moved his long-fingered, thick-muscled right hand to his forehead and covered his eyes with the pain of the acknowledgement: he was, quite simply, afraid of her. She, after all, was younger than he in age only. In every other way, she was his senior. It had been only during their danger-laced forays in England and Wales that he had become her near equal and had grown confident enough to think himself as even remotely worthy of her as a suitor. But now, so much time had passed.

Yet here she was. Arriving in New York City. And to see him. What more could he possibly want or expect? He smiled. She had given him permission to court her. That was enough.

He looked down at the delicate gold ring on the small finger of his right hand. His parents had elected to remain in England after the chaos of the previous summer, and before he had left them for New York, his mother had asked him to wear the ring, her own mother's engagement band. Her mother had wanted the band to pass down through generations of daughters, but he was an only child. He knew to whom his mother hoped the ring would be given.

Suddenly the voice in the loudspeaker bleated at its anxious listeners: "British Airways Flight Seventy-six from London Heathrow is now on the runway and will be at the gate in approximately ten minutes. Those awaiting the flight may meet arriving passengers just outside the customs area. Thank you."

"Welcome to New York's John F. Kennedy International Airport. The local time is 3:35 P.M. The captain asks that you keep your seat belts fastened while we taxi to the gate. The captain will inform you when you may unfasten your seat belt and stand. Please use caution when opening the overhead bins, as your belongings may have shifted in flight. We appreciate your selecting British Airways for your journey, and we look forward to serving you in the future."

The young woman, twenty-seven years old and six feet tall, with the sinewy hands and rangy build of a two-fisted tennis player, stretched her sculptured legs under her long, dark blue skirt as far as the Boeing 747's cramped seating would allow, and thought again of the man who awaited her. A year had passed since they had been thrown together in a battle from which, at times, it seemed neither could emerge alive. She knew he had been in love with her from the moment he had seen her and had said as much to him in a forthright conversation that she hoped he still remembered. With Ecclesiastes, she had noted that there was indeed a time to love. For her, that was not the time.

And then, she thought again to herself in wonder, after a few days and nights of nearly continual action, the battle had been over. He had been critically wounded while shielding her from gunfire. And she had immediately saved his life in return by carrying his unconscious form on her shoulders for more than a mile through the violence and darkness along the Pembrokeshire cliffs, by far the most difficult physical effort of her athletics-filled life. More than difficult. Impossible, actually. And yet it had happened. He was living proof of that.

And he loved her, she acknowledged again. Yes. But she would not permit herself to fall in love with him in return under those emotion-charged circumstances. For her, vocation was primary. And despite a year of correspondence, she still felt that same constraint. Quaint though the notion seemed in the English and American cultures of the day, she viewed the situation simply as courtship. She was required to know him much better than she could possibly know him after a few days of intense action followed by a year of letter writing. And so she had come to the United States to see him as soon as their academy years had ended. Now she declined to draw conclusions in advance or to guess the outcome of what she knew in the man's mind was romance. She was secure in the rightness of her vocation as a teacher. She would need to become equally secure in the rightness of her suitor. Her fondness for him was genuine and deeply felt. But it was, in itself, not enough.

As the lumbering aircraft made its way slowly to the arrival gate, she removed her small, dark blue Church of England prayer book from her pack, switched on her reading lamp, and opened the book to a well-marked page.

And she read, softly speaking the words aloud in a whisper, as was her habit:

> Almighty God, Father of all mercies . . . We bless thee for our creation, preservation, and all the blessings of this life; but above all for thine inestimable love in the redemption of the world by our Lord Jesus Christ, for the means of grace, and for the hope of glory. And we beseech thee, give us that due sense of all thy mercies, that our hearts may be unfeignedly thankful, and that we shew forth thy praise, not only with our lips, but in our lives; by giving up ourselves to thy service, and by walking before thee in holiness and righteousness all our days. . . .

Then she continued her prayer, eyes closed, giving thanks for the safe flight across the Atlantic, for her parents' and her brother's love, and for the man who awaited her. And she asked God's help in her approach to this man: to show the affection she truly felt, but no more; to present her life's priorities candidly, but with compassion and tenderness; and, above all, to allow herself to be guided by Him in this and in all things, whether that meant carrying the relationship forward to a lifetime commitment, or reducing it to the simplest and plainest of long-distance friendships.

She finished her prayer and looked up. The plane was at the gate.

Matthew Clark now stood impatiently behind the roped-off corridor through which the flight's 350-odd passengers would walk after they had cleared U.S. Customs. The first cluster of those passengers, probably those traveling in the first-class cabin, had already begun to come through the wide-swinging doors that separated the newly arrived from those that waited for them. The woman might actually emerge from behind those doors at any second. Hers might, in fact, be the next face to appear. Or the one just after. Or the next.

Minutes passed. Dozens of passengers walked through. Each time the doors swung open, Matt peered first at the face of the person who pushed upon the door, then beyond that face into the interior of the customs area. His heart was in his throat. He moved his right hand to his forehead—his habitual movement in seeking composure—and he closed his eyes and tried to steady himself as well as he could. He remained in that position, oblivious to the crowd around him, for what must have been several minutes. And then, his eyes still closed, suddenly he knew that she was there. Gradually he lowered his hand from his face and raised his eyes.

She stood facing him, ten feet away, looking into his eyes just as she had in a moment twelve months before when he had first beheld her. It had been a stunning, shattering experience then, just seeing her for the first time. And now the experience recreated itself. The tall, powerful, feminine stature; the long, dark, straight hair falling over her shoulders and down her back; and the grayest of eyes . . . always the eyes. And now, too, the obvious strength in her shoulders, her bare arms exposed beyond the white sleeveless blouse, and the power in her hands, as she held her book-crammed backpack in her left and a well-traveled, nondescript piece of luggage in her right. Then, suddenly, he saw that she was striding rapidly toward him, her eyes not leaving his face. As she neared him, she opened each of her hands without stooping and allowed her burdens to drop haphazardly to the floor. And when she reached the barrier rope, she simply ignored it, pushed it forward with her body, raised her now empty hands to his face, and turned her face up to his. He stood transfixed. Then she pulled his lips to hers just as he had once done with her, an eternity ago.

Her lips remained on his for some time. He felt as though his heart might actually burst, and he realized, but without embarrassment, that tears were rolling down his cheeks and onto her face. And he knew also that he was trembling, shivering uncontrollably.

She drew her face back from his, but just by inches. Her hands remained on his face. He saw that, without conscious effort, he had moved his right hand to her face, his thumb moving slowly back and forth, wiping the wetness of his own tears from the taut, soft skin of her left cheek, a movement that mirrored her hands' actions on his own face. Then he saw her eyes move from his face to his left shoulder. And he watched her eyes follow the sleeved shape of his atrophied left arm, all the way down to his hand, hanging limply at his side.

She reached for that hand with her right and raised it slowly, tenderly to her lips. She closed her eyes and held his shattered limb against her chest with both hands. And now the tears flowed from her eyes, too, falling in swift rivulets onto his nearly lifeless left hand.

Then, still hugging the limb tightly against herself, she leaned into his chest, and he held her there with his strong right hand and arm, his lips now buried in the sweet-smelling blackness of her hair. And so they stood in the midst of the airport throng, silent, still, remembering. . . .

When finally they emerged at the terminal's curbside waiting and loading area, Matt gestured toward an ancient, faded black Buick sedan, and guided her toward it. A distinguished, carefully dressed gentleman emerged quickly from behind the wheel and circled the front of the car, both hands extended in greeting to the visitor. He took her right hand in both his own as Matt spoke his words of introduction.

"Dr. Cameron Stafford," he was saying in a husky voice, but with a glad, almost giddy formality, "may I present Miss Rebecca Manguson."

The gentleman, still holding her right hand in both of his, bowed gracefully in the playful spirit of the moment and, smiling with undisguised pleasure, said to her in a surprisingly deep voice, "Miss Manguson, if you turn out to be one quarter the person Matthew believes you to be, I shall recall this meeting as a true milestone in my eventful life. I welcome you to the United States of America."

The woman, completely unembarrassed by such flourishes, laughed aloud in her musical contralto, and replied in what she quickly realized was to be regarded in this country as her "Oxford accent." Looking over her shoulder at Matt, she said, "Dr. Stafford, Matt has been confused about many things in his life. You'll find this to be just one more of them."

At this all three joined in the genuine, relaxed laughter of those who like the feel of a first meeting, and they busied themselves placing Rebecca's suitcase in the vintage auto's trunk and arranging themselves within its ample interior. Dr. Stafford, who never allowed anyone else behind the wheel of his faux antique car, held the right front door for Rebecca while she took her seat, her backpack on the floorboard at her feet. Matt placed himself in the left rear position so that he might converse with Rebecca without her needing to turn all the way around in her seat to see him.

Their distinguished chauffeur walked around to the driver's door. Cameron Stafford was not yet fifty. He stood an inch under six feet in height, and wore a nicely tailored, light-color, summer-weight suit on his medium frame. Although he was trim from a lifetime of disciplined eating and exercise, his neat, graying mustache and completely white temples led some to think him older. Nothing in his movements suggested age, however. He was quick and athletic as he slipped behind the wheel of his treasured Buick, closed the door, removed his suit coat, and tossed it onto the rear seat beside Matt.

Matt was silently berating himself at that moment for having no driver's license. During five years on sea duty with the United States Navy, he had not needed one; and when he had returned the previous summer from his near-fatal adventure with Rebecca in England and Wales, he still held out hope that further reconstructive surgeries and rehabilitation would restore his damaged limb to at least partial use. As the school year had begun and his life had become filled with his master's degree work and, later, with the duties and challenge of his teaching internship, Matt had slowly begun to accept the likelihood that his left arm and hand would be forever useless to him.

What remained now was to apply for a New York state "disabled" driver's license. He recoiled from the thought. Yet he intensely disliked being dependent upon others, or upon public transportation, to move around the city beyond reasonable walking distance from his Morningside Heights apartment. He irritably shook the thought from his mind and looked up at Rebecca, now in partial profile as she engaged Dr. Stafford in conversation. And gradually, joy began to build again in the center of Matt's being. He was enthralled with her mere presence. She fully consumed him. He watched and listened quietly and happily as the dialogue moved steadily beyond its opening questions and answers.

As the Buick doggedly plodded toward the city, Stafford had begun to carry the conversation, essentially because, Matt thought to himself, Rebecca was the better question-asker and the better listener. And Cameron Stafford was certainly accustomed to talking. He was Matt's advisor in his master of arts in teaching program, and held a dual senior professorship both at Columbia and at Union Theological Seminary, just across Broadway from the university. Stafford's name was well known in the fields of academic theology and the psychology of learning, placing him in the rarified atmosphere of a mere handful of twentieth century scholars with genuine achievement in two such disparate areas. Matt knew how fortunate he was to have such a mentor, and had been gratified and flattered when Stafford had acceded to his request to become an advisee. Then, at Stafford's prompting, Matt had enrolled each semester in his popular contemporary theology course, a difficult two-semester sequence required of all Union's divinity students, and one that Columbia allowed as an elective within the philosophy requirement in its M.A.T. program.

Now Matt listened as his advisor, in response to Rebecca's questions, developed for her the details of a project in which he had begun to involve Matt. "Yes," Stafford was just saying to her, "I do think there is a really fine possibility that by this time next year the six states carrying the most political weight in this effort—New York, Massachusetts, Illinois, Florida, Texas, and California—will all have adopted the new textbook series. And if they have, we may well have the remaining forty-four in short order. It's quite exciting, Rebecca. And most gratifying, I must admit.

"Matt may have written you that I brought him in on the project early in the year. He's been a great help, a marvelous organizer, and I hope he'll be willing to assist our group with some of the presentations that we've tentatively scheduled for late summer in each of those key states. Even in this state, of course, we'll need to drive up to Albany to deal with the legislature."

Rebecca's eyes moved to Matt's, and he dropped his immediately, smiled, and actually blushed. It was not the first time she had seen his face redden under her gaze. When they had first met, it had seemed to him that he had virtually no other response to the sight of her for days on end. Now, as he lifted his eyes again to hers, prepared to lodge a mild protest out of routine courtesy, he saw her jaw suddenly tense, saw her frown briefly—a devastating sight to Matt—and watched her cover her eyes quickly with both hands. After a moment, she looked up and dropped her hands. Her face became impassive.

In a flash, his right hand reached for her left arm as it returned to its relaxed position on the back of the front seat, and alarmed, he asked, "Rebecca? What is it?"

She covered his hand with her right, and without smiling, shook her head at him. "I'm not sure, Matt." Then, seeing Stafford glancing at her as he came to a stop at a traffic signal, she smiled her reassurance at him. "I'm quite all right," she added simply, though not quite convincingly.

Both men assumed that she would have said more if she had been in Matt's company alone, and that her guarded response was the result of being in a stranger's presence, even one who was known and trusted by Matt. Both men were correct.

After a pause, the conversation moved on, and so did the Buick. It was a Friday afternoon, and rush hour—roughly a three-hour span of time in New York City—was at its worst. As the growling, twenty-five-year-old General Motors engine labored to drag the monstrously heavy, tank-like chassis and body along the streets of Brooklyn, Matt saw Rebecca, some fifteen minutes after the first episode, repeat the swift, inexplicable movement of her hands to her face. Cameron Stafford, finding himself in the midst of a left turn, did not observe this second occurrence. And this time Matt said nothing. But their eyes met and lingered. Rebecca was disturbed by something, and it was clear to him that she could not, or would not, speak about it in their host's presence.

Traffic slowed once more to a painful creep. The old Buick had no air conditioning. Its windows were down, but little air moved through the car. Stafford was apologetic, and noted that, in just two more blocks, there was a shortcut that he intended to take, one that would move them toward the Brooklyn-Queens Expressway more rapidly and, he hoped, allow them to get into a swifter flow of traffic in preparation for crossing the East River into Manhattan.

At last, having inched the full length of the two blocks, the Buick, engine roaring, launched itself majestically into another left turn. Matt saw that they were entering an apparently abandoned heavy industrial area, with huge warehouses lining each side of a wide, deserted street. Matt looked hopefully ahead in the direction of the river, trying to gauge the time that might be needed to gain access to an expressway entry ramp, when his eyes were again distracted by a movement from Rebecca. She did not repeat her earlier action; this time she turned her head quickly all the way to the rear and looked behind Matt, out the Buick's rear window. And again, he saw her jaw muscles tense. Before he could turn to the rear to follow her gaze, his attention was caught by the sight of a dilapidated flatbed truck pulling out of one of the defunct warehouses about a half block away, directly into their path. The truck stopped in the center of the roadway, blocking the entire width of the street, warehouse to warehouse, and a half dozen men followed the decrepit vehicle out of the warehouse and onto the pavement. Several of them carried orange road-marker cones in their hands. As Stafford, muttering something under his breath, slowed the Buick in response to this new obstacle, Rebecca turned her head to the front and observed the obstruction at the same time that Matt turned to the rear to see what had seized her attention seconds earlier.

He saw two things. A mere three car lengths behind them, and moving into position to pass them, he saw a gray limousine, a stretched Cadillac, with, he thought, four passenger doors on the right side of its elongated body. And some distance behind the Cadillac, he saw several other men blocking off the street at the intersection they had just cleared, using rubber cones like those that were now beginning to dot the roadway in front of them, set in a line parallel to the flatbed truck's mottled carcass.

Stafford brought the Buick to a stop. "Looks like my shortcut may not work out quite so well," he said miserably to his companions, shaking his head slowly. Then, forcing a tone of cheerfulness into his voice, he leaned out the window and called to two of the men who approached the Buick, both of them carrying several of the road markers in each hand, "Good afternoon, gentlemen! Have we made a mistake on our route?"

The two men continued to approach without replying. Matt saw at least four other men were behind these two, and that they, too, were advancing toward them. Turning his head back to the rear, he saw that the limousine had now pulled up almost to the Buick's bumper and just to one side of it, and had stopped, and that, behind the Cadillac, another half dozen men were approaching the two cars from that direction. He turned his head once more to the front and saw Stafford reach toward the ignition key to turn off the engine.

Later, Matt was to remind himself that a full year had passed since he had last seen Rebecca Manguson in action. But in the next few seconds the full range of her warrior personality and her astonishing strength and coordination overwhelmed him and, indeed, the entire field of play. His repeated efforts in the upcoming days to reconstruct the scene in his mind brought him at least this much: in an eyeblink she had seized Cameron Stafford's right wrist in her iron grip, preventing his turning off the ignition key. Then she had thrown her body across the bench seat of the old Buick, slamming Matt's venerable mentor into the door with such force that he appeared from the rear seat to crumple into nothing. Pinning Stafford against the door with her left arm and shoulder, she then flipped the transmission shift lever into the drive position as she jammed her foot onto the accelerator. The Buick's actual response was so sluggish that, Matt decided later, the workmen's terrified reaction could only have been in response to the preternatural roar of its engine.

In any case, the men's first movements were to scatter in every direction away from the car as Rebecca, using the palm of her right hand, spun the steering wheel all the way to the left and steered the ponderous vehicle into a swinging, screeching turn that took the right wheels well up onto the opposite curb, nearly scraping the right side of the Buick against the warehouse walls. The entire visible length of the street was deserted except for the combatants, and Matt saw that Rebecca apparently intended to keep the car halfway on the sidewalk in the expectation of reentering, in that position, the thoroughfare from which they had just come. He glanced behind them and saw the limousine beginning a laborious Y-turn, while the men who had initially scattered at the Buick's first movements were now running after the aging, thundering vehicle as it approached thirty-five miles per hour in its stately flight.

When Matt turned again to the front, his eyes widened. At least two of the men who had closed off their escape route had moved directly in their path, on the sidewalk, and were standing with their hands raised, imploring the Buick's driver to stop. The driver did not stop, nor did she slow the automobile. Instead, continuing to accelerate, Rebecca wrenched the wheel to the left, flew to the extreme opposite side of the street, scattered the remaining workmen on either side and, clearing both the men and the road markers, wheeled back to the right and braked sharply as she approached the intersection. Without stopping, she whipped the tired auto into the line of traffic, maneuvered forward for a half block, and pulled violently into a loading zone in front of a neighborhood grocery store. Halting the Buick with a squeal of rubber, she flipped the shift lever into park, slid quickly back across the seat, opened the right front door, paused to remove her low-heeled shoes, tossed them onto the floorboard, and, in stocking feet, her thick, black tresses streaming behind her as she ran, flew back down the sidewalk in the direction from which they had just come.

Matt sat stock still, watching her disappear through the crowds that parted to allow her swift passage. Then, recovering himself, he turned to attend to Cameron Stafford.

Stafford, middle-aged though he might be, was not physically delicate. He brushed off Matt's solicitous questions and gestures in a fury of exclamations and questions of his own. "What the devil was that all about? Is that woman crazy? You told me something about her exploits, Matthew, but what on *earth* could have justified the stunt she just pulled? And what's she doing now? Yes, yes, I'm just fine, thank you. What I'd like now is to have a few words with this Rebecca Manguson of yours. What's she *doing*, I said? Just get out of the car and *find that woman*, young man!"

Rebecca Manguson and Matthew Clark, sitting side by side on a park bench overlooking the Hudson River, faced each other in the sudden coolness of late evening. Cameron Stafford, nonplussed and obviously furious at Rebecca, had dropped the two of them at the seminary. Stafford had gone to some lengths in the previous weeks, working with seminary housing officials, to arrange for her to stay for ten days in one of the briefly unoccupied married student apartments. Accompanied by Matt, but not by Stafford, she had quickly checked in with the residence hall supervisor, received her key, and tossed her backpack and suitcase inside the door. Then she and Matt had walked across Riverside Drive at 120th Street, found the empty bench, and sat down to discuss what had happened a very long ninety minutes earlier.

It was now after midnight, London time, and Rebecca was tired and hungry. Matt was neither. He was confused and upset after seeing Cameron Stafford's outrage and experiencing, eventually, his mentor's sullen, punishing silence after Rebecca had returned to the car, having conducted her swift inspection of the industrial street from which she had just extricated them. When she had sat down again in the Buick, she had reported simply that there had been no sign of anyone on the street. The limousine was gone. The street markers, moved into place seconds earlier, had been swiftly removed. Only the old flatbed truck, still straddling the street about five hundred feet away in the direction of the river, remained. She had seemed to think that that should end the matter. No explanation or apology had been forthcoming. So, in Matt's mind, Stafford's anger and silence were altogether justified. Rebecca's corresponding appearance of regal aplomb had seemed callous to the point of rudeness. Matt was determined to say so to Rebecca when the right time came. But he also knew that, in the privacy afforded by the park bench, she would first offer at least some explanation to him.

Matt held his silence, knowing that she would begin as soon as she could. Rebecca sat with her eyes closed, breathing deeply. He did not know whether or not she was praying, but her posture reminded him that he had not prayed once since the start of the day. Not at the airport, awaiting her arrival in anguish, not during the wildness of the "escape" in Brooklyn, not during the long, silent drive to the Morningside Heights area of Manhattan. He shook his head. In some ways he was no different than he had been two years previous: a skeptic, a materialist, even, in some ways, a hedonist. At least now he knew his deficits. And that was something, he guessed. But he was sitting beside someone who . . .

"Matt," she began, "I know you remember the dreams that were sent to me a year ago."

He nodded.

"Do you also remember that strange 'vision,' if that's what it could be called, when I was in the midst of a twenty-minute run around the perimeter and, with my eyes wide open, I 'saw' you and me—the two of us—sitting in a reading room at the mansion, engaged in serious conversation?"

He nodded again. "I'm not likely to forget much that happened that week, Rebecca, if I live to be a hundred."

"You remember, then," she continued, unsmiling, "that I told you later that same morning that I could not conceive of the idea that the Supernatural would toy with us by giving me some sort of vision, a *real* vision, about something as frivolous as two people's chatting about the English weather. And so, because of that vision, you and I entered into conversation about you as a new Christian, and about what that might mean. The vision had actually served as a prompt, of sorts, to a certain kind of action. Do you remember, Matt?"

"Every word," he affirmed, nodding again.

"In the car this afternoon, when you saw me cover my face twice . . . both times, a vision like that one had just come to me."

He stared at her, his mouth open. It had not occurred to him, and perhaps not even to her, that her dreams and visions were anything other than transitory phenomena delivered to her in the specific crisis that they and their elders had faced in England and Wales the previous summer. The idea that any of those divine messages, as they had all learned to think of them . . . would recur, once that crisis had ended, was foreign to him and, he had assumed, to her as well.

She looked at him and nodded her head. "The exact phenomenon. Images with sharp outlines. My eyes wide open. In the midst of conversation with Dr. Stafford. Perfectly conscious, and mentally and emotionally engaged.

"And there it was. The same vision both times, Matt. I saw the deserted street in Brooklyn, long before we arrived there . . . the gray limousine behind us, long before it actually materialized . . . the men with their orange roadway markers, long before any of them appeared . . . and one more thing, Matt." Here she paused and looked away, through the trees, at the blue-green of the Hudson far below them. "I saw Dr. Stafford as . . . as . . . as Evil. I don't think I can explain how. But the vision was unequivocal . . . and absolutely unambiguous on this point. He was the Enemy. And he was clearly in league with those men on the Brooklyn street. That was no coincidental turning into a shortcut that happened to be clogged by a sudden flurry of warehouse activity. That was a trap. And we were the victims. And Dr. Stafford was . . . in charge."

Matt did not move. He sat silent, shaken.

Rebecca looked down at her hands. "I don't know why I thought it was all over, Matt. Just because bad men died last year in Wales does not mean that their colleagues in America are not ready now to do their worst. Your parents, after all, were accosted right here in New York by men that, to the best of our knowledge, we never confronted last summer at all. As far as we know, in point of fact, Dr. Stafford himself, and the men we saw this afternoon, may have been the very people who . . ."

"Rebecca!" Matt cried. "Stop! Please! Listen to yourself!

"Dr. Stafford is the finest man I know . . . the most learned . . . the most committed . . . revered by the students and the faculty . . . involved in dozens of Christian projects here and around the world. And you had a daytime 'vision' that he was Evil? Rebecca, what are you talking about?

"He took a shortcut. People were moving a truck and arranging for some shipments, I suppose, to come in or go out of those warehouses. No one threatened us at any point. The limousine turned behind us either with the same shortcut in mind or just in hopes that we knew how to remove ourselves from the traffic jam. No one did anything in the least bit strange,

Rebecca . . . except you! You slammed Dr. Stafford into the door, commandeered his car, drove it like a crazy woman, endangered us and those poor
workmen. What has happened to you? You're raving, Rebecca! Just stop!
Please. Just stop."

Desperately, Matt covered her hands with his good right hand.

"Let's go up to the corner and get something to eat," he continued
hopefully. "Then let me get you back to your suite so you can turn on the
air conditioner and just sleep for twelve hours or so. Tomorrow we'll find
Dr. Stafford and plead exhaustion. You'll find he'll be very understanding.
So far, you've given him nothing to understand."

He looked down for a moment, weighing whether or not to speak aloud
the thought that pressed on him. Then he sighed and continued. "Rebecca,
Dr. Stafford is my mentor and my advisor and my professor and my counselor . . . and, I must add, my 'meal ticket,' if you'll forgive the vulgar
expression, to whatever opportunities I may have for entrance into a
doctoral program at Columbia, and a graduate research assistantship that
would set me up financially.

"I haven't mentioned this in my letters, and I really did like my internship
teaching in the Bronx. But this project that Dr. Stafford is heading, and that
he wants my increasing involvement with, is a tremendous thing, Rebecca. If
I can finish my M.A.T. degree by December, move into a doctoral program
with him, and take on more and more responsibility and visibility in the
national project . . . why, there's no telling what kind of opportunities will
open up for me . . . for us, Rebecca. There are so many teaching opportunities for you here in the U.S., and regardless of whether or not I end up with
Dr. Stafford here in New York, or heading up one of his regional projects,
there would certainly be teaching vacancies that would fit you perfectly. Your
vocation would be intact. And we could be together."

He stopped, nearly breathless from the exertion of this emotional
disclosure, and moved closer to her, removing his right hand from her lap
and placing his arm around her shoulders. "Rebecca, I have so much to tell
you . . . so much to ask you . . . let's walk up to the corner and get something to eat. I'll save the rest until tomorrow."

Less than an hour later, having consumed sandwiches without much
more conversation, they returned to her apartment at the seminary, and
Matt said good night to her. He leaned toward her to kiss her, but she put
her hand up to his lips and stopped him. Her hand still on his mouth, her

face enigmatic, she looked long into his eyes, then turned, unlocked the door to her suite, and was gone.

Rebecca listened to Matt's footsteps as they echoed down the wooden hallway. She heard the heavy outside door open and close. She turned, opened her backpack, removed her prayer book, and dropped to her knees at the small writing desk that served the room's occupants as a nightstand as well. Turning purposefully to a page near the back of the small volume, she spoke the words aloud, softly: " . . . Stir up thy strength, O Lord, and come and help us; for thou givest not alway the battle to the strong, but canst save by many or by few. . . ."

Fifteen minutes later she picked up her still unopened suitcase and her backpack, placed the room key on the writing desk, exited her room, strode out of the building, walked back to Riverside Drive, and hailed a taxi. She asked the driver to take her to the Greenwich Village area. While she rode, she scrutinized her New York City guidebook. At length she spoke again to the driver: "Would you take me to the Washington Square Hotel on Waverly Place, please?"

As nightfall completed its occupation of the city, Rebecca Manguson checked into a tiny second-floor room just marginally larger than the single bed that awaited her tired body. She washed her face, brushed her teeth, prayed her evening thanksgiving for her deliverance from the day's danger, and, exhausted, fell into deep, uninterrupted sleep.

She awoke late on Saturday morning. Immediately, she unpacked her suitcase, donned her running clothes, and went for a fifty-minute run around lower Manhattan. She relished the cooling June breeze from the harbor and delighted in the views of the colorful ferries, the majesty of the Statue of Liberty, and the symmetry of the distant span of the Verrazano Bridge.

Near her hotel, in the midst of New York University's teeming campus, she stopped at a public telephone and placed two calls. The first was an international collect call to London.

The second was local. It was not to Matthew Clark.

CHAPTER TWO

REBECCA SAT ALONE ON A WOODEN BENCH IN THE CHURCH'S intimate courtyard, savoring both the shade of its young trees and the bracing warmth of a summer Sunday morning. Having just attended the eight o'clock service at the Church of St. Luke in the Fields, Rebecca smiled as she thought about this, her first Episcopal service, and how closely it mirrored her familiar Church of England's rhythmic ebb and flow of scripture, prayer, and sacrament. She knew that such was historically implied, given the outcome of a certain war some two hundred years earlier. But she had been pleased actually to immerse herself in the American application of things originally—and still—Anglican. The church service's obvious genealogy had been a delight to her from the moment it had begun.

Idly, she considered staying for the 10:30 service, which she expected to be filled with families and, in wonderful consequence, the bustling of children's young energy, but knew that her 9:30 appointment could easily extend longer than a single hour. She looked at her watch. It showed 9:25. She had no doubt that the gentleman would be on time, and perhaps early. So she was not surprised to look up and see him entering the compound.

Spontaneously, she was on her feet and running to him, clapping her hands like an excited ten-year-old and opening her arms wide to him. The tiny, grizzled object of her attention seemed momentarily to disappear within her concussive embrace. They hugged each other long and gladly, she laughing aloud in the sheer pleasure of the reunion. "Come. Sit with me," she said after an impromptu kiss on the gnome-like creature's forehead, now pulling him by one hand toward a different bench than the one she had just vacated. This one was removed from the impending flow of parishioners to and from the church's main doors, which opened toward the interior of the courtyard rather than onto Hudson Street. Rebecca and the gentleman sat down, deep within the landscaped confines of the walled and gated church and its attached school.

Placing herself on his right and patting his knee with her left hand, Rebecca said with unrestrained joy in her voice, "You are *wonderful* to meet me on such short notice, Mr. Belton. Simply *wonderful*. I don't know how to thank you. I have missed you so much!"

The rumpled policeman, looking up at her through dark, shaggy eyebrows with his deep-set, childlike black eyes, smiled his lopsided smile and replied, "Now, Miss Manguson, you know I woulda dropped everything I had on my plate to get to you, and a lot quicker than this, if you'd asked me."

She patted him again, maternally, this time on the shoulder. "I do know that, Detective. I had *no* doubt you would come. Did you have a chance to attend mass earlier this morning?"

"Oh, yes, ma'am," replied Sidney Belton in his familiar guttural Brooklynese. "St. Patrick's starts its masses real early, every day, not just Sunday, so I'm always able to get to a service.

"You know me, Miss Manguson. I'm not a good enough Christian to miss church. There's just too much awful stuff I gotta deal with every day. Y'know what I mean by that, ma'am, I'm pretty sure."

Rebecca laughed again, warmed as always by the genuineness of the odd little man's self-deprecation. With some she had known, such self-effacing commentary could ring terribly false. With Sid Belton, a certain shambling humility had always struck her as inbred, a rich, revealing expression of his unsparing assessment of himself.

"And your injury, Detective?" she asked, her expression now somber, the character of her sculptured face restored instantly to its familiar, queenly aspect. "Are you well?"

"I'm not sick, ma'am," he replied, "but I don't expect I'll ever be much use again jumpin' over walls after bad guys. Not that I was ever great at that part of the job. But the hard part for me has been gettin' used to bein' on disability. I'm able to get plenty of work as a private detective, and some of it is pretty good, but I miss workin' with my buddies, Miss Manguson. It's not the same.

"But I hafta say, my injury has come around just fine. It's been about six months, y'know, since that guy blew himself up over in the Bowery and I took all that shrapnel in my legs and chest. At least it missed my face, so I'm still as handsome as ever." His lopsided smile returned. "Know what I mean?"

She nodded and smiled. She had corresponded with him periodically since he had left her in England the previous June. They had worked there together after he had clandestinely trailed Matt Clark to her country in search of Matt's parents, Martha and Paul, who had been kidnapped in plain daylight while walking in Central Park. The detective had written her reluctantly of his midwinter accident, and of his having been forced into early retirement by his cherished New York City Police Department.

"Ma'am, I'd like to ask how your parents and brother are doin', but I don't want to keep us from gettin' to the point. You said on the phone that there was an urgent problem you needed my help with, and then you wouldn't answer my question about the kid." This last was, out of long habit, Sid Belton's only name for Matt Clark. The detective looked at her sharply. "Tell me what's goin' on."

Rebecca sat back on the bench, looked up briefly at the trees overhead, and then down at the sun's soft rays as they fell in oddly configured patches on the brick walkways of the courtyard. After a moment she faced him again, and then began to trace for him the events of Friday afternoon, placing greatest emphasis upon details of the twice-seen vision, and then of its perfect correspondence with the subsequent developments in the deserted warehouse street. She skimmed rapidly over the drama of her own actions in sending the Buick careening through its escape maneuvers, but recounted in minute detail her Friday evening conversation with Matt. At Belton's studied request to hear Matt's exact words still again, she repeated, slowly and as near verbatim as possible, his impassioned summary of his relationship with Dr. Cameron Stafford.

They fell silent. A few families were already beginning to arrive for the 10:30 service. As Rebecca had anticipated, they followed the more direct walkway into the church, well away from the bench where she and her confidant huddled, deep in thought.

"Can you say more, ma'am," the detective asked, "about *how* this Stafford character looked evil to you? What was there in his appearance that led you to that . . . don't misunderstand me, ma'am . . . to that kind of extreme conclusion?"

"Certainly, the conclusion is extreme, Detective," she replied. "But I don't think I know the answer. I don't think I can say. His evil nature was the primary impression . . . and the dominant message . . . but, trying to explain *how* . . ."

"Then it was, in that way, like the dreams you had in London last year, miss, when the face that was shown to you during those dreams showed, you said then, 'lethal intent,' even though you never could explain exactly how?"

"Yes. Precisely. We haven't any words for some things, Mr. Belton. We haven't words even for some *natural* things, to say nothing of *supernatural* things. We are forced to say that some things are 'like' other things, knowing full well that they are also 'unlike' those very same things. Our Lord Himself spoke to us about wineskins and mustard seeds and . . ."

She saw him shaking his head slowly and she stopped. His lopsided grin had reappeared. "I don't know, ma'am," he said slowly. "I just know I gotta have some words to help me get a sense of what you saw. You ended up doing that pretty well for us last summer, seems to me."

"Yes," she acknowledged immediately at this pointed reminder of an earlier effort to speak of things unseen by others. "Yes, and it did help, didn't it?" She nodded her head in answer to her own question. "All right, then, I'll try it, Detective, even though it all seems . . . well . . . so . . . beyond language."

She thought for a moment, then spoke, slowly and softly. "The two evil faces, last summer's and this Friday's, were, of course, those of two different men. But, in each vision, the color . . . no, the *colors* . . . of the visage . . . and its contour . . . no . . . no . . . its *contours* . . . and its . . . its . . . its fibrillation . . . and . . . and its alternating opaqueness and . . . transparency . . . and . . . no, there's more . . . and . . . the frozen, hardened, ice-like *emanations* that seemed to spiral from each face . . . all of that combined to send over-whelming messages into my mind, Detective: that this was Evil incarnate. Not just another routinely bad person, you understand. The message to me on Friday was that Dr. Cameron Stafford represented . . . no . . . no . . . he fundamentally *was* Evil. And he was taking us into a cul de sac of death . . . a trap of his own careful devising."

She paused again, thinking.

The detective waited, then leaned toward her. "Are you sayin' this guy is the Devil himself, ma'am?" His tone was matter-of-fact, as though he were asking if Cameron Stafford wore reading glasses or had a receding hairline.

"No," she replied quickly, "although I can't imagine that the Devil could look any *more* grotesquely satanic than Dr. Stafford did in these two brief visions, Detective. No, I am saying that this man was shown to me as *invested* with Evil . . . *consumed* by Evil . . . *saturated* with Evil . . . to such an extent that there was absolutely no trace of goodness left in him. If, indeed, there ever had been."

Again, the detective waited, now leaning well forward on the bench, staring straight down at his feet as was his long habit. Then he looked up at her and, his lopsided smile just visible, again shook his head at her.

She looked at him and nodded. "You're right, of course. 'Incarnate' was too strong, wasn't it? 'Invested' and 'consumed' and 'saturated' do not equal 'incarnate.'" And she nodded again. "But if we take that word out, I think the remaining words do work. They fit quite tightly, Detective. Quite tightly.

"Thank you for making me do that. It's not the same as showing you a picture of what I saw in this man. But it's *something*, isn't it, Detective?"

He nodded, and both were silent again.

Finally Rebecca continued. "Please understand, Mr. Belton, it's not that I saw him as Evil *because* he was taking us into the trap. It's that I saw him as Evil *and* he was taking us into the trap. His Evil was shown me in the visions as integral to his very being, as though he might not be able to exist without it. And, you must understand, his Evil was shown to be of vast consequence. Murdering me, if that was his plan, would have been no more than a quick afternoon's work in a lifetime of infinitely more insidious and widespread devilry than the no doubt brutal elimination of one trouble-some British woman."

Silence resumed. Finally Belton spoke again. "Miss Manguson, what do you think the kid knew about the trap . . . or anything else?"

"I think he knew, and knows, nothing whatever," she replied immediately. "What stunned me, Detective, then and now, was Matt's out-of-hand rejection of the possibility that Dr. Stafford could be anything other than what Matt has found him to be thus far in their relationship. After all, Matt's own mother, twice in her lifetime, experienced this extraordinary . . . this truly *extraordinary* . . . kind of dreamed statement of and by Supernature, in serial fashion each time. And she experienced it by means of this very vehicle—a certain kind of dream or vision. And you'll certainly remember, Detective, that Matt was himself brought to Christianity a year ago, in part, because he rather dramatically came to understand and believe that."

"Yes, ma'am," responded the detective, nodding his head and continuing to gaze down at his feet, "but could it have been just one of those quick denials that most people resort to when they don't wanna hear somethin'?

Y'know. One of those this-can't-possibly-be-the-truth-about-this-person statements and reactions without any thought behind it?"

"Yes, certainly, insofar as my allegations—actually, my two visions' allegations—regarding Dr. Stafford's *fundamental* Evil are concerned." Rebecca emphasized the adjective so strongly, and with such a powerful, slicing movement of both of her graceful, muscular hands, that the detective turned his head quickly to watch her. She continued animatedly, her hands now working against each other in front of her chest. "I would, and did, expect utter incredulity from Matt on first reaction. But his response, you see, was accompanied by an out-of-hand rejection of the possibility of any sort of supernatural intervention as the most *rational* explanation of the things that I had just reported to him, Detective. An *out-of-hand* dismissal, sir.

"I had known, of course, that he would be staggered by these completely incompatible 'truths': one of them grounded in his year-long experience with this man whom he has come to admire so greatly; the second delivered via familiar, if extraordinary, phenomena—dreams and visions—the validity of which he has witnessed previously . . . and repeatedly.

"And this second truth, I must emphasize, was presented to him by a Christian woman whom he professes to love . . . whom he does love.

"I had expected him to be torn, Detective." She paused again. Then, sighing deeply and shaking her head, she continued, her voice now very soft, her eyes following her hands into her lap, her lustrous, raven hair falling forward over the front of her lightweight summer dress and nearly to her waist.

"He was not torn. He was clear. He displayed no hesitation in labeling the twin visions mere nonsense. And there were other portions of his response, you'll agree if you'll think about them again, that revealed an individual I hardly knew. An individual caught up in political ambition and power of the worst sort. He showed me in just a few sentences, spoken in no more than fifteen seconds, Detective, that he has been captured by them." She paused still again, looked away from him, and nodded her head slowly. And he knew she had begun to cry.

Still looking away, she added, "All of that told me instantly Matt would be an impossible encumbrance under the immediate demands of the situation." And now her voice took on the harder, deeper, subtly threatening pitch and timbre that the detective knew well. *"For demands there will be, sir."*

More silence. The detective continued now to look in the woman's direction. And she continued to look away from him.

Finally, again, the detective's guttural rumble. "Whad'ya think he's been doin', ma'am, since he realized yesterday mornin' that you were gone?"

Her hands continuing to rest in her lap, she turned a tear-streaked face toward him. "I've thought about that quite a lot, Detective. I fear he's torturing himself. The full range of recriminations, I'd expect. It's almost more than I can bear, you understand, not to go to him, and not to contact him. But this is one of those times when *almost* is a thousand miles from what it points to, Mr. Belton. I cannot go to him now. He is a willing captive. In fact, he may be so thoroughly 'gone' that he has shrugged off my absence as good riddance.

"Regardless . . . I cannot go to him." And here her voice changed again. "There will be demands on me . . . and on you. We know that."

After a moment, she continued. "Detective? What are you thinking? How do you think I should respond to all this?"

Sidney Belton did not hesitate. He spoke rapidly in his rumbling voice, turning his face from her to look again at his scuffed brown shoes. "I'd like to take you to a safe house for the rest of the day and night, ma'am, and then put you on a flight to London in the morning.

"That's the first thing, I think.

"The second thing is this. You said that you expect there'll be demands on us. I assume, miss, that you mean more messages . . . visions . . . dreams . . . and . . . ah . . . *orders*?" He glanced up and saw her nod, then looked away again. "Yes. I expect the same thing, ma'am, and have expected it from your first mention of the Friday afternoon events. I have no doubt at all that you'll get more supernatural messages than this first one, Miss Manguson. That one you did get—twice—on Friday afternoon . . . *that* one probably saved your life . . . and maybe the kid's, too. But you and I have learned, if we've learned anything at all, that we can expect somethin' more . . . somethin' bigger . . . somethin' harder . . .

"It'll come, but we can't know when or how. And so I just wanna get you outta here right now. I wanna get you back across the Atlantic to your brother, and then wait to see what happens . . .

"Meanwhile, I'll start a little research project on Dr. Cameron Stafford. See what I can turn up over the next few days. Try to get a line on what he's tryin' to accomplish with this project he started tellin' you about. This project he's got the kid so excited about. And I wanna see what else he's been up to. I think it's gonna be pretty interesting, ma'am.

"If I just don't have to worry about you while I'm doin' that, Miss Manguson, I'll be a happy detective. And I'll do a better job, too. Y'know what I mean, miss?"

When the detective finished, he looked up into her face and was taken aback by what he saw there. What he saw was an angry woman. And he knew Rebecca Manguson. He did not relish proximity to *this* angry woman.

She reached for the detective's near arm. Clasping his small, bony right hand in both her immensely strong ones, she moved her face near his and stared into his eyes. He did not flinch or blink.

"Mr. Belton," she began evenly, her voice low in volume and in pitch, "am I to understand that you expect me to flee to safety under this threat, and beyond that, to abandon Matthew Clark to the Enemy merely because he has been secured by them for now? That is your advice to me? That is how you believe my gifts should be utilized in the face of this unspeakable Evil?"

He did not move his eyes from hers, nor attempt to extricate his hand. After a pause, he replied, "Ma'am, I care about you too much to give any other advice. If I had a daughter, it's what I'd say to her, and for the same reason I said it to you. No apologies, Miss Manguson. Nope. Not one."

Unsmiling, she lifted his hand slowly to her lips and kissed the roughened skin. Then, her steel gray eyes still fastened on his, she spoke to him in a soft, impassioned voice that filled his ears and stung his heart. "It's the most terrible advice I have ever heard, Mr. Belton. I reject it fully, completely, absolutely.

"And," she added, without changing any aspect of her demeanor, "you're the dearest, loveliest man, other than my father, I've ever known. I cherish you."

Late Saturday morning, at roughly the same time Rebecca Manguson dialed Sid Belton's unlisted home number from a public telephone near Washington Square to request the Sunday morning rendezvous, Matt Clark tapped lightly on her apartment door at the seminary. Hearing no answer, he tapped louder and called her name.

Thoughtfully, he turned away, walked several steps down the hallway, and then, an indistinct cloud passing through his mind, he turned back. Approaching her door again, he placed his right hand on the doorknob. He hesitated, then turned it slowly, soundlessly, and, hesitating yet again, pushed gently. The door readily yielded.

He created a two-inch seam in the doorway and moved his face near the opening. His stomach tightening with every passing second, he called quietly, "Rebecca?" The silence was complete. Telling himself that she had gone for her morning run and foolishly left the door unlocked, but, at the same time, fearing another explanation more likely, he pushed the door far enough to lean in and view the foot of her bed. Then the whole bed. And then the whole room. It was clearly unoccupied. He saw a room key on the nightstand.

He stepped back and looked at the room number to confirm his certainty, then entered and looked hopelessly for a message from her. He found none. Closing the door from inside, he crossed the room and sat down on the small sofa. He forced himself to breathe, and to consider rationally what could have happened. Was violence actually to become part of his life again? He thought about everything Rebecca had said to him regarding the previous afternoon's escapade and the two visions that preceded it. The question forced itself upon him: what if she had been right about Cameron Stafford?

Certainly, Stafford knew where her seminary apartment was; he had made the arrangements himself. Matt shook his head at this absurdity. No, that was exactly the preposterous, hysterical line that she herself had followed, and he would have none of it. Yet his mind continued to entertain doubts. He acknowledged, grudgingly, that the points she had made about Matt's parents' abduction from Central Park a year ago were anything but hysterical. He raised his right hand to his forehead and rubbed his temples with thumb and fingers. Why had he not been more circumspect, he asked himself, a sudden bitterness beginning to overtake him. Merely because Rebecca had gone off the deep end about Cameron Stafford . . . that should certainly not have led him to reject everything else she had said. She could have been wrong about Stafford, yet right about their facing real danger in that warehouse street. There had certainly been nothing amicable in the demeanor of the men who had advanced upon them. He had not thought them menacing, but . . .

He thought back. He remembered with a shudder that, during their struggles in England, there had even been an enemy intelligence report on

Rebecca, targeting her for recruitment to the other side. . . . Matt let his head fall slowly back onto the headrest of the cheap, battered sofa. The more he allowed his mind to dwell on the events of a year ago, the less improbable Rebecca's entire presentation came to seem. Why not a new set of visions, dreams, divine premonitions? He harbored no doubts whatever about the validity and the source of the dreams and visions that his mother and Rebecca had experienced before. Why had he rejected her new ones so absolutely?

And he knew.

Cameron Stafford could not be what she had asserted. That part was impossible. The rest could, in theory, be correct. That could have been a trap in the warehouse district. Those men in the street and following them in the limousine could have been . . . But wait . . . for that to be the case, Cameron Stafford would have had to be complicit. They would not have set a trap in that deserted Brooklyn street on the infinitesimal chance that the old Buick might materialize that Friday afternoon, with dozens—actually, hundreds—of choices of routes between the airport and Manhattan's Morningside Heights district. He shook his head. Rebecca was wrong. Plain and simply and completely wrong. And if she were indeed completely wrong, then obviously no shadowy figures had come to the apartment to abduct her: there were no kidnappers or murderers trying to ensnare her. It was fantasy.

And then, just as obviously, the explanation of her absence from the apartment could only be . . .

She had decided to leave *him*.

The color drained from his face. She had simply walked away from him. She had presented a wild story he could not accept, and when he had told her that he could not . . . How could she do that to him?

Instantly, having faced and accepted her abandonment of him as the only possible reality, he rejected forthwith every component part of his previous speculation. In a heartbeat, his new conviction took on all the solidity and indestructible certainty of the recently completed World Trade Center, its massive twin towers looming in the distance over lower Manhattan. His first reaction to Rebecca's ravings had been the right reaction. Nothing in her diatribe held any relationship to reality. His mistake—if it could be said to have been a mistake—had been simply to say so, and to say it bluntly. Why could he not have looked at her ramblings through her eyes?

He should have realized that she was exhausted and confused. If he had reacted considerately and prudently, he would simply have comforted her as they sat together on the park bench. Then, after dinner, she would have let him kiss her good night. And she would have slept soundly in her suite and awakened well rested. And, in the light of a new day, he could gingerly have broached the subject. In fact, he told himself, he would not have needed to broach the subject at all. She, finally refreshed, would have opened the apartment door, smiled her radiant smile, captivated him inevitably with her astonishing gray eyes, and apologized to him for her inexplicable, inexcusable behavior. Then she would have asked to be taken to Dr. Stafford so that she could apologize to him as well, especially for smashing him into the door of the Buick and pinning him there throughout their reeling "escape" from the warehouse street.

What a fool he had been. And now she had left him in disgust at his ham-handed fumbling of the whole situation. He groaned audibly. How could he have been such a . . . He sat up. Stop it, he said to himself. Stop wallowing in your own self-recriminations and think. Where would she have gone? She might have walked somewhere to find lodging, but, he thought, more likely she hailed a cab and selected something downtown from her guidebook. Well, there was nothing for it now but to return to his own flat and await her call. And she would call. No doubt about that. Rebecca Manguson was not petty. She wouldn't go off in a sulk and decide not to get in touch merely because she had made such a mess of things, embarrassed herself in the process, and incited him to confront her about it. He'd done badly . . . could hardly, in fact, have behaved more clumsily had he devised a plan to do so . . . but she'd done far worse. She'd see that.

He jumped up, happy in his new certainty, left the room, and jogged down the hallway and out into the June sunlight. Continuing in his easy loping run, his disabled left arm pinned across his waist by his right hand, he did not stop running until he reached his apartment. And there he waited, confident. Soon she would call. And soon he would be given the chance to forgive her.

Matt looked at his watch. Four o'clock. His stomach churned while his mind fought against the truth. Rebecca had not telephoned. And she was not going to. He picked up the phone with his good hand, tucked the receiver between his chin and left shoulder, and, struggling with the rotary dial's infuriating mechanical resistance, finally dialed the correct number on the third attempt.

"Yes?" said the familiar voice.

"Dr. Stafford, this is Matt. I'm so sorry to disturb you on a Saturday afternoon, but I need your advice, sir. Is there a chance you could give me a few minutes of your time?"

There was a pause during which Matt had a sense that his mentor was weighing a number of responses, not just a direct yes or no to a simple request from a desperate-sounding advisee. Finally, he replied, his voice cold. "I'll be at my office in twenty minutes. I can give you about fifteen, but I'll need to be back home within the hour. I must allow time to dress for dinner." Then he hung up without awaiting a reply from Matt.

Matt was at Stafford's Columbia office in five minutes, pacing anxiously in the hallway as he waited. He tried to remain focused on what he knew. He knew that this man could be trusted. He knew that this man held every key to his future except one. And that key was held by the woman he had just managed to alienate. Cameron Stafford had advised him throughout the academic year, concerning almost every significant element in Matt's life: graduate studies in teaching; graduate studies in theology; Matt's vocational future; his relationship, short-term and long-term, with Rebecca Manguson. He would ask for counsel just once more, in this emergency. It was all he could do.

Near one end of the hallway, as he reversed course again in his incessant pacing, he realized with a start that Stafford was there in the hallway with him, his hand extended toward his office door. Matt had heard nothing of his approach and had prepared no introduction. He stopped, uncertain.

Stafford brusquely inserted his key in the door, swept it open with one hand, and, as the door began to close, called out curtly behind him. "Come in, Mr. Clark. What is the nature of your emergency?"

By the time Matt reached the door and stepped into the anteroom, Stafford had already exited that space and was just seating himself within the spacious confines of his extravagant office. Nestling into his high-backed swivel chair, one chosen thoughtfully to match the scale of his ornate, glass-topped mahogany desk, Stafford gestured carelessly in the direction of one of the three dark leather chairs that faced the massive desk, waited for Matt to take his seat, and then simply elevated his eyebrows.

Matt knew his cue and began speaking nervously, knowing he should have spent the last few minutes rehearsing this presentation rather than fulminating about his misfortune. "Thank you for meeting me, sir. I'll just take a few minutes. I . . . ah . . . want to ask your advice about Rebecca."

"My advice would be to send her back to London tonight."

Matt laughed aloud, then quickly withdrew the residue of a smile from his face. Stafford had a fine sense of humor when he chose to use it. His statement had been delivered without so much as a trace of that humor. Matt tried again. "I know she behaved strangely and rudely on our ride from the airport yesterday, sir, but I think she was simply exhausted and on edge about being in New York City for the first time in her life. Our reputation abroad is not exactly pristine, you know." Matt tried to give this last a light touch, but knew the remark was doomed even before it had passed his lips.

Stafford said nothing. He stared at Matt, unsmiling and unmoved.

Matt shifted in his seat. Swallowing hard, he blurted, "She's gone, sir."

With a suddenness that simultaneously surprised and confused Matt, Stafford's expression changed from a mixture of sullen resentment and studied disinterest to something he could not read. If he had been asked to name it, he would have wrestled with words like excitement, anticipation, and, perhaps . . . just perhaps . . . arousal. Physical arousal. His nostrils flared, his face flushed, and, after a moment, he pushed the chair back away from the desk, stood, and began to patrol the room restlessly, still not speaking. Finally he stopped at one of the two high windows that towered behind his desk. His back to Matt, he said, his voice a hoarse whisper, "Tell me exactly what happened—and exactly what was said—from the moment I dropped the two of you off last night until this moment."

"Well, sir," Matt began, "I know you don't have much time. . . ."

"Take all the time you need, Matthew," replied Cameron Stafford, his voice returning to its normal rich baritone. "This is important . . . to you and to Rebecca." He resumed his seat. "I want very much to be as helpful as I can. Please . . . continue, Matt . . . and leave out nothing . . . nothing at all."

Chapter Three

AT ALMOST THE SAME MOMENT THAT REBECCA MANGUSON and Detective Sidney Belton drew their churchyard conversation to a close and rose to enter the Church of St. Luke in the Fields, Matthew Clark, nearly six miles of New York City street and sidewalk to their north, was entering famed Riverside Church, a five-minute walk from his third-floor 112th Street apartment. At his side as he stepped through the church doorway was Dr. Cameron Stafford.

Matt scarcely heard or participated in the service. Afterward, he would have been able to say that the sermon had been delivered by a guest minister who spoke on issues of gender equity in America, and that the choir had been its spectacular self throughout. But even those impressions were hazy. He had spent the entire time in an agony of doubt and indecision, much of it stemming from his meeting with Stafford at Columbia the previous afternoon.

He had not expected his advisor to take any genuine interest in Rebecca's disappearance, especially after her rudeness to him on Friday. The most he had hoped for was a word of grudging advice regarding how he might proceed to find her, or, perhaps more useful to him in the long run, how he might frame the larger problem for himself: her whereabouts; her erratic behavior; her role in his future; and that future itself, with or without Rebecca. Instead, Stafford had evinced a consuming interest from the second Matt had reported her absence to him. In response, he had made three telephone calls from his desk while they were still together, and Matt had the strong impression, as Stafford dismissed him nearly an hour into their meeting, that he intended to return to his desk to make still further contacts on her behalf.

Stafford had taken the line, both with Matt and with those whom he telephoned, that this was not a matter for the New York City police, but for a private firm that he and at least two of those whom he telephoned had used with success to find individuals discreetly. "You must understand, Matt," he had explained patiently, "that there is no reason to suspect criminal activity against Rebecca, and we certainly do not want her, especially in her confused and excitable state, hunted down as though she were some sort of fugitive. We'll just alert the principals at the private agency we use regularly to give us some informal help. They're quite good, and they've got enough people to canvass even a city of this size effectively. They'll have little trouble, and you'll be face to face with her again within just a few days. Really, my young friend. There's nothing to it." And here he smiled his kindest, most comforting smile.

When Matt had protested timidly that he wasn't sure he wanted her searched out in quite this way, and that he wasn't even certain that he himself should try to find her, in view of the fact that she clearly didn't want to see him, his mentor had brushed him off deftly. "This is the sort of thing any responsible person would do for a lost daughter, student, or friend, Matt, and without the slightest hesitation. This way, we'll just get a sense of where she's staying, and gain a measure of confidence that she hasn't stumbled into any . . . difficulties that she can't manage. After all, as you said, this is New York City."

After the service, the two of them exited the church, turned south, and strolled along the same tree-lined walkway that Matt had traced, side by side with Rebecca, just two nights before. When Stafford gestured to a particular bench where the two of them might sit, presumably to resume the previous afternoon's conversation, Matt realized with a start that it was the same bench on which he and Rebecca had sat on Friday evening.

Instead of opening the conversation with further perspective on the missing person, Stafford began by introducing an entirely new topic. "Matt," he said thoughtfully, looking out over the river and stroking his chin idly with his left hand, "a number of things have begun to come together more quickly than I had expected, regarding our project. Friday morning I received calls from Austin and Sacramento. Texas and California are ready. It's time to move forward. Now. This very week." Here he turned to face Matt. "Can I count on you to travel with us? Will you be able to make the commitment on short notice?"

Matt blanched. Forgetting his usual automatic assent to any request Cameron Stafford might make, he protested immediately, his voice taking on a faintly whining quality that he had despised in himself since early adolescence. "But Dr. Stafford . . . what about Rebecca? You said that I might actually be face to face with her in a few days. . . ."

Stafford raised his hand to silence the objection. "We'll probably have you two together by dinnertime tomorrow evening, Matt, but even if not, the Texas trip, which is slated first, will take no more than twelve hours: to Austin at midday Tuesday on one of our charter jets, afternoon meetings followed by a dinner session, then back to New York before midnight." Here he looked pointedly into Matt's eyes. "I need you on this, Matt. I need you very much. We've prepared you well, and you've been instrumental from the first. The long-term impact for good is incalculable, and as a platform for your career, this is critical. You know that."

"Yes, sir," Matt replied more quickly and easily than he would have expected of himself, at the same time forcing all thoughts of Rebecca into a mysteriously available crevasse near the back of his mind. "Yes, sir. I'll be ready to go. You know you can count on me, Dr. Stafford."

Matt turned his face back toward the river and grimaced. There were times when he disliked himself very much.

Rebecca and her diminutive companion entered the church five minutes after the 10:30 family service was underway at St. Luke in the Fields. They found a place on a back pew and knelt quietly, each thanking God for the other, and for the chance to worship again in His house. After the Scripture readings, the brief sermon on the Holy Spirit's continuous activity in individual lives, and the prayers, the two of them stood in line as the congregation filed to the altar rail to receive Holy Communion. Since both of them had already taken the bread and wine earlier that same morning, they each chose simply to receive the minister's blessing, kneeling in the midst of a long row of children and their parents.

As Rebecca knelt, her elbows resting on the altar rail and her hands folded under her chin, she listened attentively, smiling to herself, as the minister voiced his blessing on the young children and offered the sacrament to their parents. Then, just seconds after she had begun to attend to him in a more focused way as his words of blessing and sacrament slowly approached her down the line of worshippers, she felt something begin to happen to her. And suddenly the minister's voice, though it steadily neared her, seemed supremely distant, removed from her like a whispered prayer from a pulpit as it might sound in the very back of a large and silent cathedral. Although her eyes were open, resting unfocused on the floor just beyond the altar rail, the outline of a vision began rapidly to form itself, and she knew instantly, her heart racing in spontaneous response, that she was to be the recipient, at that moment, of another message from Truth's only Source. She caught her breath and waited, gray eyes wide, muscles taut. . . .

As the minister reached the child on Rebecca's immediate right and began his spoken blessing for the youngster, the vision completed itself with startling clarity directly in front of her line of sight, outlines sharp and bright as on other occasions. She looked intently, knowing the importance of remembering every detail. First she saw the interior of a spacious outdoor arena of some kind, with an expanse of rich, textured grass spreading before her. The arena's walls, vast and high and distant, seemed to her to display a series of messages that she could not decipher, not because the words were formed in an unknown language, but because the emerging centerpiece of the vision forced her mental focus away from the background and toward the immediate center. And at the center of her adjusted focus were children by the hundreds . . . no, she corrected herself quickly . . . children certainly by the thousands. Children of many ages and of every ethnicity. And each child, as far into the dreamed distance as she could see, held a book from which it read, silent and intent.

And as the children read, she saw the children themselves begin to change. Over this sea of healthy, vigorous, alert children came gradually but steadily a low cloud . . . no . . . a thick bank of fog . . . and as it blew itself into the arena and through and among the children, each child, one by one, became immediately weak, fragile, ill, almost granular. Decomposing. And although she neither saw nor heard a command, visual or auditory, from the vision's Source, she knew with utter certainty and finality that a command was attendant. And with the same certainty and finality she knew precisely the nature of that command as it painted itself into her brain. It held but two words: *Prevent this.*

The vision of arena and fog and children remained before her eyes, unwavering, as the minister stepped in front of her and, leaning down to her and placing his hand firmly on her head, administered his blessing. Then his hand lifted, he stepped to her left to give his blessing to the detective kneeling beside her, and the vision was gone. Rebecca's heart continued to race, and she closed her eyes to gather herself. Then she opened her eyes and looked down at the altar rail, gripped the rail with both hands, and, struggling, tried to rise. She failed, her normally powerful legs seemingly unable to respond. She took a deep breath, pushed down on the rail as hard as she could, her sleekly muscled forearms and hands straining, and tried again. Unsteadily, she willed herself to her feet. Turning and stepping cautiously, she passed behind Sid Belton, who had already risen and was turning to follow her to the rear of the church. She sensed his hand on her elbow as she moved past him and felt his small, determined presence at her side, as together they moved to the side aisle. Then she heard his whispered voice, an undefined urgency communicated both from his touch and from the force of his rasping, persistent query. "You okay, ma'am? What is it? What is it? You okay? Are you okay, ma'am?"

She nodded, squeezed his hand, and, the disorienting force and weight of Supernature's impact slowly lifting from her mind and muscles, strode, still unsteadily, toward their pew. Now gradually coming erect again, her shoulders braced, her carriage restored, she sensed as she walked an unexpected infusion of clarity and vitality flowing into mind and body. A charge had been given her . . . again. And she knew that such a charge was simply to be obeyed. Issues of probable success or failure were not hers to weigh. There had been a command. And she would respond.

Her gifts were to be used, again, to intervene in something that she as yet understood not at all. As she knelt at her pew, she gave thanks to the Source for this, His commission. No outcome was assured, only a duty to be undertaken. But it was a godly duty, and it was *her* duty. And she knew that His selection of her implied that her gifts could somehow be made commensurate with the presumed enormity of the commission. Neither success nor failure nor life nor death was hers to consider.

She folded her hands under her chin and looked down, a faint smile on her lips. Then she realized that her companion, now kneeling beside her, was still looking into her face anxiously. She turned to him, looked into his eyes, and nodded. He understood. And she saw the veteran policeman draw a deep breath, turn his eyes back to the front of the church, and nod his head once in response. And a grim, lopsided smile spread slowly across the crinkled face.

Wearing her dark blue, long-sleeved tennis warm-up suit despite an overnight low temperature in the seventies, Rebecca Manguson, her nearly waist-length tresses drawn into a tight ponytail, stepped out the door of the Washington Square Hotel promptly at five o'clock. The Monday morning blackness still clung to the awakening city, but the detective had extracted a promise from her that she would not do her daily two- and four-mile runs in daylight. He was desperately concerned about her safety, and although he had seen that he had absolutely no chance to get her to return immediately to London, he had grappled with her like a terrier on this one issue. He had insisted that she acknowledge the reality: her own vision, the first, on the trip from the airport, had forecast imminent danger; her second, at the altar rail, had reinforced the suggestion of a broader threat, not yet clear in detail. He had pounded home their sure knowledge that this newly received commission obligated her not to the kind of recklessness that might accompany an endeavor the success of which had been divinely *promised*, but to the thoughtful weighing of opportunity and risk implicit in action divinely *commissioned*. She had listened. She knew she was not considering the advice of a novice or a coward when Sid Belton spoke of opportunity and risk. And so, in the end, she had acquiesced.

The detective had noted that, for many women, running in the early morning New York City darkness would be far more dangerous than running at midday. But for Rebecca, with her great strength and when needed, blazing speed of foot, it was not so. The real danger to her was that she would, while running the streets of the city in daylight, be recognized by those who sought on Friday to capture or kill her. And she was that most easily recognized and remembered of women: exquisitely tall, surpassingly athletic, and, though completely unadorned by cosmetics and jewelry, strikingly beautiful. He wanted her on the streets, if she must run daily despite his preferences, in the hour before sunrise. At all other times, he wanted her in her hotel room or at his side, usually in his automobile. He did not have to explain to her the fact that he was licensed to carry weapons. She knew he was nearly always armed. And, despite his physical limitations, she knew also that he was highly skilled with any weapon he might choose to carry on his person.

So she stood for a moment on the dirty sidewalk, in the humid darkness, looking both ways along Waverly Place and, across the street, into the dimly lit confines of Washington Square. She could see no one, even on the park benches, though she felt certain that, as in London, the park sheltered homeless people by the dozens on every warm night. The only movement was vehicular, occasional taxis moving to and fro, and a single garbage truck already beginning its cacophonous rounds. She turned to her right, toward the Hudson, with the casual intention of following Waverly to Christopher Street, thence to Hudson Street, and then south to Battery Park on the tip of Manhattan Island as she had on her Saturday morning run. From there, she expected to move north on Broadway toward the approaches to the venerable Brooklyn Bridge, which she looked forward to crossing, over and back, or at least to midpoint, before returning to the hotel. She was excited to begin.

And so she did, running slowly as her muscles warmed to the task. Already she had begun to play again in her mind her altar-rail vision from the previous morning. She held more than a faint hope that the undecipherable writing, dimly apprehended on the distant walls of the visionary arena, might gradually take intelligible form in her memory if she focused sufficiently on it. And so it was that, after traveling a short distance northwest on Waverly, she swung absently onto Christopher Street, now moving directly toward the Hudson. Her eyes were down on the sidewalk in front of her, unfocused, rather than up, sharply focused, swinging left to right and back systematically, as the detective had instructed her. Thinking hard about the remembered vision at St. Luke in the Fields, Rebecca, thus absorbed, failed to notice the other runner. He had, as she approached him on Waverly, sheltered himself from her view behind a parked newspaper delivery truck. She passed by the truck, and he fell softly in behind her at a distance of forty yards. He carried something in his left hand, something which caught and reflected the weak light from occasional lampposts.

Rebecca, her pace gradually increasing as her body awakened more fully, hardly slowed at the several intersections along deserted Christopher Street as she approached the church corner. She reached Hudson Street, saw the church on her left, and swung south to pass in front of it. Just as she did, she heard a metallic, clattering noise behind her, a sound at once indeterminate and yet instantly suggestive of danger. In a heartbeat, she pivoted hard right, back into the center of the intersection, still running strongly, and prepared immediately to run harder and to run evasively. Looking back to her right, she saw something that brought her to a complete stop in the intersection. Fewer than thirty yards away, a stocky, muscular, uniformed man, presumably a police officer, appeared to have pinned a much taller man, dressed in running attire, to the granite façade of an apartment building. The policeman seemed to hold the tall man immobile, and apparently with great ease, in some kind of arm lock. Both of them, improbably, were looking in her direction. On the sidewalk beside them Rebecca saw, unmistakably, at the extreme edge of the circle of light provided by the corner lamppost, an outsized knife, its menacing blade extending out over the curb where it had fallen. She stared. The uniformed man had begun to speak into the ear of the runner, whose facial contortions bespoke considerable pain. She could see even at the thirty-yard distance between them that the policeman's grip bound the taller man so completely that he could move not at all. Then she saw the policeman step back, drawing the man with him, pivot to his right, and virtually hurl the other in the direction opposite her, back up Christopher Street in the direction of Seventh Avenue. The runner, recovering his balance after several stumbling strides, ran like a gangling, terrified giraffe into the distance. At no point did he look back. The uniformed man watched him until he was out of sight.

Something held Rebecca in place. She stood still, taut and alert, and watched the man closely as he turned again to face her. Slowly he strode to the curb, stooped, and lifted the knife. He seemed to examine it briefly, then managed somehow to sheath the weapon inside his uniform jacket, leading her to guess that he wore some sort of concealed shoulder apparatus designed to accept more than one kind of weapon. The man then raised his eyes to hers and, at the same moment, removed his cap.

Her gray eyes widened. She leaned forward. Her mouth fell open. And suddenly she was running again. Just as she had done on Sunday morning in the church courtyard, she ran toward a man whom she cherished, her arms wide.

Mirroring her movement, Royal Navy Lieutenant Luke Manguson opened his massive, muscular arms equally wide, and gratefully returned the embrace of his sister, his twin.

"You got here so fast!" she exclaimed delightedly, extricating herself from his grasp after several moments.

"And a jolly good thing, I'd say," he replied with a good natured reprimand layered into his tone. "After you phoned on Saturday, I checked around and got a Sunday night ride on United States Air Force transport, London to Washington. My reserve unit was good enough to make all the arrangements for me. Told me I'd have to wear the uniform on the flight, and I was glad to oblige. Nice chaps, those Yanks that brought me over.

"We landed at Andrews Air Force Base late last night, and I managed a Greyhound bus from Washington to New York. Arrived about an hour ago, a little after 0400. Didn't want to awaken you just then, so I thought I'd stroll down Seventh Avenue to your hotel. Very good directions, Rebecca."

"Luke, are you telling me you just happened to arrive on this street as I ran by? Are you telling me that that man was chasing me with that enormous knife, and you just happened to intercept him at the right moment? You're telling me that this is all a coincidence?"

"Nothing is coincidence."

"Yes, I know. I meant . . ."

"I know what you meant, dear. Yes. I was on Seventh Avenue, preparing to turn left toward Washington Square, when I saw you run past. I started to call out to you, but then I saw that bloke following along. Dropped my knapsack and ran him down after a couple of blocks. Good thing you were still moving pretty slowly. I'm not exactly dressed for a sprint."

"Luke, how could he have been waiting for me? How could anyone know where I am? I don't understand."

"Well, I don't know, Rebecca, but you probably went to church yesterday?"

"Yes, of course. Just across the street, in fact . . . over there."

"If I were looking for you, my dear, I'd certainly have enough data on you to know you're both a Christian and a daily runner. Then I'd consider the fact that you're a member of the Church of England, and so I'd send a scout to every Anglican or Episcopal church in Manhattan on Sunday morning. Then I'd have them follow you from the church to your quarters. I'd also make the assumption that you'd be going for a run before sunrise on Monday, because you would have been cautioned by someone not to run in the daylight. Then I'd place several men on the streets around your hotel by five o'clock on Monday morning, give them each a pair of running shoes and a long knife, and . . ."

"Oh, Luke, I'm so sorry. I didn't really take Mr. Belton's cautions very seriously. And I wasn't even thinking about danger when I started this run."

"Of course you weren't, Rebecca. Your job is to think about the big puzzles and how to solve them. The detective's job—and mine—is to keep you alive and well." And he laughed his good, big laugh and squeezed her hand. "I am so glad to be with you! Don't leave again like this. I don't do well with it."

They fell silent as they began to walk back toward Seventh Avenue to pick up the knapsack. After a few moments, Rebecca looked at her brother and asked, "Luke, why did you let the man go? Did you not want to question him? Did you not want the New York police to question him?"

Luke shook his head, the bill of his Royal Navy officer's cap casting intermittent shadow over his chiseled features. "He wasn't going to tell me anything, Rebecca, and we've nothing against him legally. Further to your questions, I wouldn't know what to say to police. We can't expect them to go to work on a case just on the basis of the vision you saw on Friday after your plane arrived here. I simply told the poor bloke to start running and that if I ever saw him again I'd not be quite so gentle with him." And he laughed again.

After a few more steps, Luke continued. "But you do realize, Rebecca, that there are probably at least two more of them waiting for you near the hotel. If I'd been in their shoes, I'd have stationed someone in the park, right across from the hotel, and another to the east, in addition to the fellow whose post you ran past."

She nodded. "Yes, I was just beginning to have that thought, Luke. I can't go back to the hotel at all."

In the next block, they picked up the knapsack, still resting where Luke had dropped it, and returned to the site of the altercation. Luke watched while Rebecca crossed the deserted intersection and scaled the wrought iron fence surrounding the churchyard at St. Luke in the Fields. He then walked briskly back to his sister's hotel, entered via the delivery garage, and slipping unobserved into the back stairwell, climbed the stairs to her floor.

Some fifteen minutes later, Rebecca's luggage and his own knapsack in the taxi's trunk, Luke instructed the driver to pull up to the church and stop. Over the fence in a graceful economy of maneuver came his sister, and, now momentarily safe in the darkened interior of the car, the two Londoners disappeared into the vastness of New York City.

Chapter Four

THE SENIOR PROFESSOR AND DEPARTMENT CHAIR OF OLD
Testament studies at Union Theological Seminary was hungry. Regardless of
the time of year on the academic calendar, Monday mornings were long and
slow. Even though the first summer term had not yet begun, the weekly
cycle of meetings included a 7:30 department meeting, a 9:30 faculty
meeting, and, for department chairs, an 11:30 administrative staff meeting.
It was now nearly one o'clock. Breakfast, cold cereal and orange juice, was a
distant memory.

The telephone's ring, as irresistible as it was irritating, came a scant ten
seconds before the distinguished-but-famished educator would have been
out the door and scurrying toward the neighborhood delicatessen.

"This is Dr. Chapel speaking. May I help you?" The courtesy of the
words themselves fit poorly with the obvious impatience in the tone of
voice, a tone adopted specifically to suggest interruption to the caller.

"Dr. Chapel, my name is Sid Belton. I'm formerly with the New York
City Police Department. I work now as a private investigator. Can you give
me a minute or two of your time?"

"I'm hungry, Mr. Belton."

"So am I. Can I take you to lunch?"

"Why?"

"So we'd both be less hungry."

"Very funny, Mr. Belton. I repeat my question. Why?"

"Well . . . I got a problem, Dr. Chapel. And, the thing is . . . I can't really
say much about it over the phone."

"Then I'll be going to lunch without you, Mr. Belton."

"Well . . . ah . . . I can tell you this much. It's got something to do with
one of your colleagues."

This induced the first pause in the conversation. Then, after a moment, "One of my colleagues? And which one of them might it be?"

"Well . . . do I hafta tell you now . . . on the phone?"

"Only if you're still looking for a two-person lunch."

It was Sid Belton's turn to pause. Finally, shrugging to himself, he went forward. "It's got something to do with Dr. Stafford. Dr. Cameron Stafford."

Still another pause followed. This one became lengthy.

"Dr. Chapel," Belton said finally, "you still there?"

"Where are you calling from, Mr. Belton?"

"I'm calling from the Columbia campus, near 120th Street. I can pick you up in ten minutes. I'll look for you in front of the seminary. Whad'ya wearing?"

"A gray suit. I'll wait outside on the steps. Make it five minutes."

Seven minutes later, Sid Belton pulled his dirty, faintly yellow Plymouth coupe into position at the seminary, double-parked the faded relic on Broadway, and turned off the engine. He stepped from the coupe and crossed to the passenger side, cheerily acknowledging the irritated taxi horns with a wave and a lopsided grin, and placing his hand on the passenger door, looked toward the seminary steps and waved again, this time at the gray-clad figure that peered, through lightly tinted sunglasses, in his direction from the top step. He held the door open while his luncheon guest marched briskly toward him and, pausing just long enough to inquire, "Mr. Belton?" slid into the Plymouth's torn passenger seat.

After Belton once more rounded the front of the car, still waving pleasantly to the taxi drivers, and took his position behind the wheel of the Plymouth, he extended his hand. "How you doin', doctor?"

Belton's hand was ignored. "Your identification, please?"

"Sure." He reached quickly to the inside pocket of his rumpled brown-and-black-checked sport coat. "Here y'go."

"Thank you, Mr. Belton. Your car is hideous."

He wrestled the steering-column-mounted shift lever into the drive position and pulled into the flow of traffic, oblivious to the taxis' chorus.

"Yeah, I know. I try to be inconspicuous, y'know what I mean?"

"Well, you've failed, Mr. Belton. Your car is dramatically conspicuous by its very hideousness."

He grinned, then laughed. "You sure know how to hurt a guy, ma'am."

"Yes, I do. Where are we going, Mr. Belton?"

"I'd like to drive a ways, ma'am, so we're not sittin' next to people that know you. You got time to go all the way down Broadway to the Columbus Circle area? I know the guy at the Mayflower Hotel's coffee shop. He'll give us some privacy. Whad'ya say?"

Sid Belton found Dr. Eleanor Chapel a formidable presence despite her stature. She was shorter than the slight detective by almost a foot, standing four feet and ten petite inches when wearing her trademark accessories, a bedraggled pair of once-white tennis shoes. She was almost fifteen years his senior, having moved vigorously into her early sixties and, as always, her light gray hair was pulled into a tight bun at the back of her head. Color was provided, against the gray suit, gray hair, and graying tennis shoes, by a cherished red silk scarf, and above all, by her startling blue-green eyes. Her shaded eyeglasses having been removed as soon as she sat down in the Plymouth, the bright eyes sparkled, centerpieces in an elfin face that displayed her engaging smile often. It was a smile she used to blunt the razor-sharp impact of much that she said. Thus, face to face, she struck the detective as a no-nonsense woman, but one without a trace of built-in hostility or cynicism. A good person steeped in the notion that life worked best without circumlocution. He liked her immediately.

At the Mayflower Hotel's coffee shop, two blocks from the southwest corner of Central Park, Eleanor Chapel, leaving her delicate, wire-framed reading glasses perched on her small nose after reviewing the menu, consumed her soup and sandwich with a certain inbred daintiness. She listened intently while Sid Belton explained his need to talk with her.

His voice rumbled at her from a depth consistent with the chest and lungs of a man much larger than he. "I've been on the phone for most of the last twenty-four hours, ma'am," he began. "When you've been in detective work as long as I have, you build up a lotta connections, y'know what I mean? I got connections that help me find people. I got connections that help me figure out why people are workin' on the stuff they're workin' on. I got connections that help me understand what people are tryin' to accomplish politically. I got connections that help me understand what people are tryin' to do when they use a lotta money to get somethin' they want. I got people who help me see how all those kinds of things sometimes go together into one thing. Know what I mean, ma'am?"

She shook her head. "I have no idea what you mean, but you might as well keep going, Mr. Belton."

The detective smiled. Then he continued. "And I got people, Dr. Chapel, who . . . ah . . . well . . . people who help me . . . understand the battle."

She looked up from her plate. "What battle is that?"

The detective's smile disappeared from his face. "Good against Evil, ma'am. The battle you've spent your life teachin' and writin' about. Angels and devils. Our Lord Jesus Christ."

She put her half-eaten sandwich down, wiped her hands on her napkin, and pushed her plate away. Then she removed her glasses and peered at him closely. The blue-green eyes no longer sparkled. They bored into him. He returned her gaze, his deep-set black eyes unblinking and with a trace of a smile returning to his face. Finally she spoke. "The only way for me to evaluate what you have just said, and to determine whether it is flippant sacrilege or reference to sacred truth is to ask you this: are you a believer?" She stared into his eyes.

"Yes, ma'am."

"How does your belief manifest itself?"

"In lots of ways, ma'am."

"Name one."

"Well, I go to mass every morning, seven days a week."

"A Roman Catholic," she mused. "And are you a good Roman Catholic, or one who thinks Christianity is nothing but ritual and rosary?"

Belton's engaging, lopsided grin suddenly reappeared fully. "I can't say whether or not I'm a *good* Catholic, Dr. Chapel. I can say that I'm weak and sinful and that, without daily worship, I can slip away from the center of the faith in a heartbeat. And since I deal with bad people a lot, I hafta be careful."

She started to ask him something else, but he raised his hand, extended his quirky grin still further, and continued. "Ritual and rosary, as you put it, ma'am, are important pieces of how I manage to keep to the center of the faith, but I don't confuse either one with the faith itself. And, Dr. Chapel, don't make light of ritual and rosary, or I just might decide to ask you if you're a *good* Southern Baptist, or one of those Baptists who thinks Christianity is nothin' but a list of things not to do . . . say, for example, like not dancin' or not drinkin'."

For the first time, the elfin face showed surprise, then, slowly, almost imperceptibly, something Belton could only interpret as a kind of delighted astonishment. After several additional moments, during which he maintained his enigmatic smile while she continued to register a sort of happy amazement, she finally composed herself to reply. "My *goodness*, Mr. Belton! You just grew into a person before my very eyes! My *goodness*!"

Then she laughed aloud. It was a tinkling laugh, Belton thought to himself, one you might associate with a teenage girl, rather than with a sixty-plus senior professor and academic department chair at one of the world's premier seminaries. Still smiling at him, she said, "And, to answer your last question—the one you didn't actually ask me—if you knew enough to consider inquiring about whether or not I'm a *good* Southern Baptist, I'm quite certain that you knew the answer before you raised the issue."

"Yes, ma'am, I did, and I do."

"Then, Detective, I would conclude that you and I, as Roman Catholic and Southern Baptist, are very much on the same Christian page, though looking at the page from somewhat different angles. And neither of us confuses our own church's popular image with the faith itself. Am I correct?"

"Yes, ma'am, I believe you are."

"Well . . . I'm . . . I'm suddenly quite intrigued, sir." Here she pushed her plate all the way to the edge of their table. She leaned toward him, still without replacing her spectacles. Her blue-green eyes had once again begun to sparkle. "All right. Tell me everything, Detective."

And so he began. He explained, over coffee, that he had learned from his sources that Cameron Stafford's gigantic project called for the placement of new reading textbooks in public schools throughout the nation, grades one through four. Given the fact that the states make their own decisions on texts, Stafford's focus from the start had been on six populous states, on the assumption that the other forty-four would follow the leaders. Huge sums of money had been committed consequently to lobbyists' efforts in the states of Massachusetts, New York, Florida, Illinois, Texas, and California.

The four-level reading series had a name: the Matheson Mental Health Curriculum for Children (MMHCC). Cameron Stafford, by throwing Columbia University's and his own prestige behind the project, had greatly enhanced the national visibility of the promotional effort.

The detective paused and stirred a little more cream into his second cup of coffee. He looked up. "What do you know about the MMHCC, Dr. Chapel?"

"You may call me Eleanor, Detective. You've earned it."

"Thank you, ma'am. I hope you won't think I'm rude to ask that you keep referring to me as 'Detective.' It's been a couple of decades since anybody called me by my first name, and so I don't know how to be anything else."

Eleanor Chapel laughed again. "All right, Detective. You'll just be 'Detective' to me. You've earned that, too.

"Insofar as the MMHCC is concerned . . . Cameron Stafford did his utmost to induce the seminary to grant its formal endorsement to his whole project. He lost. I was his main opposition. It was one of the toughest fights I've had in my forty years in education."

"And what is it about the MMHCC that makes it worth opposing, ma'am? 'Mental Health for Children' doesn't sound like a bad thing to me."

"Here's how it works, Detective. It teaches children that every statement regarding what you and I would call 'reality' is, in fact, merely a statement about ourselves. You or I might say, 'That's a nice tree.' Any of the reading texts produced by the MMHCC will teach children to think, 'I have nice feelings when I look at that tree.' There is no such thing as *objective* value, you see. There are only my own thoughts and feelings . . . no external reality to which I respond. No values except those arbitrarily acknowledged by me at a given moment. If I should find it meaningful and convenient to value, say, courage, at a given point, that's fine, if that's what I happen to wish. Nothing wrong with that, you understand. But I must not try to convince myself that there is some true and real, objectively determined value that places courage at a higher level than cowardice. I must not *demand* courage of myself, nor of anyone else. And you see, of course, that in the act of saying that, I have just violated my own precept? I have just said that there is an ultimate value, namely, the utter and complete validity of every conceivable value, premise, conclusion, decision, action.

"There is no reality out there. Children will be taught that there is only subjectivism. Thus, there is no Truth. There is only your truth and my truth. One truth is just as good as another. Your truth may be that you should not hurt me. Mine may be that I should hit you with a rock.

"Furthermore, no one is responsible for her or his own actions and decisions. All actions and decisions are explainable—and *defensible*—from the mere fact that you and I have differing basic assumptions, and consequently, differing premises, and consequently once more, differing decisions and differing actions. And none is correct and none is incorrect. Each one is equally defensible. Nothing is right. Nothing is wrong.

"And all this will be taught, you understand, in the context of instructing youngsters in *reading* skills, and under the broad heading of 'mental health.' And, if you can imagine, this will be done in the name of enhancing children's 'self-esteem.' The idea is that a child's self-esteem is strengthened when she comes to the realization that anything she ever thinks or does is perfectly legitimate, provided she does not 'impose her views' on anyone else, because that, of course, might suggest that one view could be right and the other wrong. Once the child becomes confident that all thoughts and actions are readily justifiable, she has nothing you or I would call a conscience. The moral law has been successfully liquidated in her. The foundation stone upon which the Lord built, first, Judaism, and, eventually, Christianity, is simply removed.

"I suppose it goes without saying . . . but perhaps not. I will add the obvious: tolerance of another person's right to hold a view different from one's own is indeed a real value. The MMHCC will teach children that tolerance is the *supreme* value . . . perhaps the *only* value."

She thought for a moment, looking down at her hands as they rested on the edge of the table, clasped together tightly in front of her chest. She looked up. "Have you ever read the works of the late C. S. Lewis, Detective?" she asked.

"Yes, ma'am," he replied, "I was actually reading one of them when he died . . . about fifteen years ago now, wasn't it . . . but I hafta admit, I haven't always understood what I read."

"In a book called *The Abolition of Man*," she continued, "he gave us these sentences. I committed them to memory the first time, many years ago, that I encountered them." She looked up and away from her companion momentarily, calling the words to memory, then fastened her gaze on him once more.

She spoke the Lewis sentences slowly and carefully, pausing at the end of every phrase so that Belton could feel the impact. *"In a sort of ghastly simplicity,"* she quoted in her measured rhythm, *"we remove the organ and demand the function. We make men without chests and expect of them virtue and enterprise. We laugh at honour and are shocked to find traitors in our midst. We castrate and bid the geldings be fruitful."*

She stopped and smiled. "He was writing about this very thing, Detective. He anticipated everything that my colleague hopes to achieve.

"And so I must tell you, if there has ever been a project worth opposing by a seminary, this was it. The MMHCC is as dangerous an idea as has ever been advanced, made doubly and triply so because it aims to corrupt its readers on behalf of ultimate Evil by the time they are not yet ten years old."

Belton thought for a moment, then asked, "The fact that the seminary did not endorse Stafford's proposal doesn't seem to have run the thing off the rails, though, I gather?"

"Oh no, Detective. Just a minor bump in Stafford's road. The project is, I'm certain, going on full steam ahead. I can only hope that the states will show their collective wisdom and decline to purchase the MMHCC texts for their children."

Then she looked at him sharply. She smiled. "Ah, but that's why you're here, isn't it? That's why you have tracked me down? It's going *too* smoothly?"

"Yes, ma'am . . . I believe it is."

"Does that mean there is criminal activity?"

"There's not much evidence either way right now. At least, there's not much evidence that I've been able to get. I have a long way to go."

There was a pause while each reviewed the insights provided by the other. Then Eleanor Chapel spoke. "Why me, Detective? Why seek me out?"

He replied immediately. "My sources say you're not corruptible, ma'am. . . . And they say you are intellectually the equal, or better, of Cameron Stafford. . . . And they say you are fearless. And they say, to put it simply, that you live your Christianity every day."

She did not respond to this. She neither blushed with embarrassment nor protested the effusiveness of the praise. Instead, she seemed hardly to notice, and immediately pursued a different tack. "And who is your client? You are a *private* detective. You've been hired by whom?"

"No one. But there is a client of sorts."

Here he seemed to hesitate a moment. He consumed the dregs of his second cup of coffee, placed the cup in its saucer, and looked up at her. "A young woman named Rebecca Manguson teaches in a school for girls in London. She's an extraordinary person. I got to know her last summer in England when I went there on a missing persons case. She was pretty well known, I understand, in her late teens and early twenties as an amateur tennis player."

He hesitated again, looked at his empty cup, then looked again into the blue-green eyes. "She's *chosen*, Eleanor. She's specially *chosen*."

She looked at him and nodded her head. "What is her gift?"

"She is the recipient, from time to time, of visions . . . dreams . . . messages. Some of the visions provide information in advance of the events they describe, and in that way, serve as warnings. Others . . ."

"Yes, Detective?"

"Others . . . are commands . . . orders. . . ."

She nodded again. "The orders are from whom?"

Belton smiled. "From your Old Testament authorities, Eleanor."

"Angels?"

"Well . . . last summer, some of her messages were from, we think, a certain kind of angel, yes. Other messages were not specified, as to their exact Source, in any way that became clear to us."

"Then . . . the Holy Spirit Himself? Providing warnings and commands?"

"Yes, ma'am. I'd say so. And, on two occasions, there was divine intervention that went beyond warnings and commands. Far beyond. And, in both cases, it was Miss Manguson who was the focus of the divine action."

"And it is she who is your unofficial client?"

He nodded. "Yes, she is here in the city now. I was with her yesterday at the Church of St. Luke in the Fields, down in Greenwich Village. I was beside her at the altar rail when she received her second . . . ah . . . message . . . in three days. The first had been a warning. The second was a command. She and I are on a war footing right now, so to speak. And that's why I've been on the phone for most of the last twenty-four hours, talking to my contacts around the country. And that's what has led me eventually to you, Dr. Chapel. I'm looking for your help in this."

They fell silent once more. A waiter came to them, conveyed compliments from the manager, told the detective that their lunch had been provided *gratis*, and retired. Belton grinned at his guest. "When I was NYPD, I had to turn down all these free lunches. Now I can just say, 'Thanks.'"

Eleanor Chapel wasn't listening just then. Leaning forward again, she asked, "Can you say anything to me now about yesterday's command?"

He described the vision, as reported by Rebecca, to his intense listener and, as he did, realized that he had come to understand at least some of the vision while his guest had been speaking to him about the nature of the MMHCC. "As you gave me that description of Dr. Stafford's project," he said, "I didn't have any doubt about those children that appeared in Miss Manguson's vision. They were reading, you know. And, as the vision went on, they began to . . . well . . . fall apart . . . almost dissolve . . . while they read. There was more in the vision than that, she said. But that seemed to be the main thing."

"And the command . . ."

"The command was simply: *Prevent this*."

"And Miss Manguson had—and still has—no knowledge whatever of the Matheson Mental Health Curriculum for Children?"

"Well, she's never been in the U.S. before, until Friday. We'd have to ask her if she'd heard of it, over in London. It's possible, of course, but I gotta admit I'd never heard of it until I started makin' my phone calls yesterday."

"She's an educator, though, Detective. And this proposal has international ramifications, especially for teachers of young children."

"Sure, but so what, ma'am? Are you thinkin' that Miss Manguson coulda just made up this vision to give herself an excuse to take some action on it? Or what? If you don't trust somebody as good and true as she is . . ."

Eleanor Chapel held up her hand to stop him. When she spoke, her voice was soft, her manner of speaking slower and gentler than before. "You must understand, I try to bring a healthy skepticism to many aspects of modern life, Detective, just as, I'm certain, you do. As a Christian, I have absolutely no reservations about divine intervention in our lives . . . divine intervention of all kinds: warnings, orders, direct action . . . and by any means at all: angelic creatures, acts of nature, our fellow human beings, even our animals . . . and, obviously, the Holy Spirit Himself.

"That is not the same as saying that when a stranger takes me to lunch and provides me a secondhand report of divine action, I uncritically accept it simply because I am certain of the ubiquitous presence and action of God in our lives, day to day, moment to moment.

"But I am intrigued enough—and the situation you've described is urgent enough—for me to follow up immediately . . . this very afternoon." She produced a notepad and pen, then looked up at the detective. "Give me your NYPD biography, in short form, Detective. And give me the names of your supervisors at each stage of your career. Phone them and ask them to take my call. Depending upon how my research on your background turns out, I'll get in touch with you. I'll want to meet your Miss Manguson . . . possibly tonight."

She wrote rapidly while Belton described the numerous NYPD posts he had held, referring to his own notebook to provide telephone numbers for each supervisory figure he named. At length, both put their notebooks away, and Eleanor Chapel sat back and posed a final question. "You haven't said exactly what you would ask of me, if I were willing to assist, Detective. What is it that I might contribute to your efforts?"

"The same thing you've given me this afternoon, ma'am. Information, insight, the capacity to influence others. We're gonna need a lot of all three."

It was Monday night, shortly before nine o'clock. Six hours had passed since the detective had returned Eleanor Chapel to her office at the seminary. Now he paced the floor in his modest apartment on 151st Street, near Broadway, about halfway between Columbia University and the George Washington Bridge. Like many people of modest means who wished or needed to live in Manhattan itself, Sid Belton had had to range far to the north of midtown in order to find an affordable spot. Subway access was good, and he could park his weathered Plymouth on the street, thereby avoiding the crushing garage fees that added to the already prohibitive expense of living nearer to the precincts in which he had served. Now as a private detective, his apartment was his office.

His own nervousness was obvious to him as he walked back and forth in the small living room. The nervousness had two sources. He was nervous, first, that he was about to act as host to three guests. He couldn't remember the last time he had had a visitor to his apartment. He had almost nothing for them to eat and drink, and he had had no time to clean or straighten the apartment. He acknowledged to himself that, at least, he was an orderly person. Maybe his visitors would not notice that he had not vacuumed in months, nor dusted . . . in his lifetime. He grinned his lopsided grin. Of course, they would notice. But they wouldn't care. They would just focus on the enormity of the issues and problems that faced them.

And that was the second source of his nervousness. As a rule, it was he who, on any project, was first to generate a set of hypotheses, first to lead his group in the direction of meaningful conclusions, first to grasp the over-arching relationships among disparate observations and findings. He was nearly always the one who formulated the road maps others could use to pass safely through uncharted terrain. But now . . . he wasn't sure. So much had happened, and it had happened so fast. He had been genuinely shocked by Luke Manguson's telephone call to him late that afternoon. Not that Luke's presence in New York was a surprise; he knew Rebecca had telephoned her brother Saturday morning, just before she had phoned the detective himself.

No, he was surprised by Luke's description of his apprehension of Rebecca's pursuer that morning in the darkness of Greenwich Village, and of his and Rebecca's subsequent move to a different hotel. He knew that he shouldn't have been surprised by the attempted kidnapping, or perhaps attempted murder, of Rebecca Manguson under these circumstances, but he had been. And the fact that Luke's arrival at exactly the right time and exactly the right place had been critical to her having escaped was unnerving to Sid Belton. How could he have allowed her to think that she could be safe going to church at St. Luke's, then going for a run the next morning? He had been proud of having talked her out of daylight running. Why had he not foreseen that her enemies could draw the obvious conclusion that he would have counseled her against the daylight run, and of course, then staked out the Washington Square Hotel well before daylight? He shook his head. He had failed her. What if she had . . .

He stopped and looked down at his feet. He forcibly reminded himself that, if Luke had not materialized when he did, that would not necessarily have meant that Rebecca would have been undone. Sending one man after this woman, he said to himself, carrying nothing but a knife, certainly did not assure her enemies of success. First, she could outrun *anybody* short of an Olympic sprinter. Second, if the man had overtaken her before she could accelerate, he'd probably have felt the force of those powerful legs driving a foot right through his ribs. But none of that meant that he had failed her any less . . .

Then he shook his head again, sighed, and tried to redirect his thoughts. He couldn't seem to get his failure out of his mind. He turned and sat down on the arm of his small sofa, actually groaning audibly as he did.

He slammed his right fist into his open left palm in anger and frustration, and at the same moment, heard footsteps at his door. A sharp knock followed immediately: two quick, assertive raps. He rose, took a breath, and put his eye to the tiny concave peephole in the door. He saw, looking up toward the peephole, the small, but magnified and distorted, face of

Dr. Eleanor Chapel. Belton unfastened the three locking mechanisms and opened the door.

"Come in, ma'am," he said, standing aside for her.

She had changed from her gray suit into a child-sized Columbia University sweat suit. Like the professorial suit she had worn to work, and then to lunch with the detective, the sweat suit was gray. She wore the same pair of tennis shoes that she had worn earlier, and her hair remained in the same tight bun at the back of her head. She stepped quickly into the living room and scanned it critically, her reading glasses in one hand, a thin, tan leather briefcase in the other. Still sweeping the room with her bright eyes, she asked, "When did you last dust and vacuum your apartment, Detective? This decade? Or last?"

He grinned at her over his shoulder as he refastened the three locks on the door. "I'm pretty sure I vacuumed in February or March of this year, Eleanor. But in regard to dusting: I've been here for almost twelve years, and I can assure you that the place hasn't been dusted in that period of time. You wanna have a seat? I got water and diet soda, if you want somethin' from the kitchen."

Ignoring both offers, she remained standing near the door and turned to him. "Your history with the NYPD is impressive, Detective. I am honored—truly honored, sir—to have been invited by someone of your calibre to participate in something of such enormous import. I am humbled, Detective. And I thank you."

He looked at his feet. "I guess my bosses must have been in pretty good moods when you talked to 'em this afternoon, ma'am."

"Actually, no. They were difficult persons, each one. But their admiration for you was undisguised. Your injury still distresses them, as does your forced retirement on that account. Your wisdom and energy are sorely missed, sir. Rarely have I heard such fulsome and varied praise under circumstances in which there was no incentive to provide such . . . except that it was the truth."

Belton continued to examine his feet. No response came to his mind.

She stepped toward him and patted his elbow reassuringly. "All right. I'll stop. Let's get to business now."

Seated across from each other in the small room, she on the sofa and he in his reading chair, the two reviewed other details of their afternoon telephone activity. At Belton's description of Luke Manguson's call, and at his summary of the early morning altercation in the darkened streets, Eleanor Chapel found herself leaning forward, astonished and stricken at Rebecca's brush with disaster. "I'm sorry, Eleanor," said the detective, seeing her response, "I didn't mean to scare you. I just needed you to know how much danger Miss Manguson is in, and how deadly her enemies can be. And I needed you to know that, if you get yourself hooked up with us, they'll put you in their sights just as fast."

"And who are 'they,' Detective? Are you saying that Cameron Stafford is behind this kind of thuggery? That my distinguished colleague intends not just the subversion of the Almighty's moral law and the corruption of the nation's children, but that he deals in kidnapping and murder, too, where it suits his purposes? Is that what you're telling me?"

Belton looked into her wide eyes. Then he simply said: "Yes."

The blue-green eyes narrowed. Then Eleanor Chapel sat back on the sofa and crossed her arms over the Columbia University letters emblazoned across her gray sweatshirt.

After a moment, Belton spoke again. "Maybe I shouldn't have involved you, ma'am. Or maybe I shoulda started my story at lunch with an account of what happened Friday afternoon, when Miss Manguson arrived in New York. They tried to get her then, almost as soon as she got here.

"This is probably going to get violent, Eleanor. I'm sorry. I shouldn't . . ."

"Stop!" she ordered, nearly at a shout. "What do you think I am, Mr. Belton? Some fragile little antique? Just because I'm in my sixties and not five feet tall, you think I'm afraid of my shadow, do you?

"Well, think for a minute, Detective. I am an *Old Testament* scholar. I teach *Old Testament*. Have you ever read the Old Testament carefully, sir? You want violence? Open the thing at random and read for about ten pages. You want subversion and deception and lying and stealing and adultery? You want visions and dreams and angels and direct divine intervention in human lives? Read the Old Testament, sir! It is life lived in its truest, rawest form."

"Ma'am, I didn't mean . . ."

"Or, for that matter, think about the *New* Testament for a moment. Do you remember that Christ instructed the disciples to arm themselves with swords, Detective? What do you suppose He intended them to do with those, shave their beards?"

"No, ma'am, but you'll bear in mind that when one member of His party actually *used* a sword . . ."

"He brought the action to a halt and repaired the damage. Of course, He did! My point is not that He advocated gratuitous violence, Detective, but that He acknowledged its possibility."

"Yes, ma'am, but . . ."

"And have you ever seriously pictured Jesus in the process of making a whip out of cords and driving the moneychangers out of the temple? Have you ever seriously pictured how it looked—and how *He* looked—when He overturned their tables? Have you seriously confronted those scenes and images, sir?

"A lot of people talk about Christianity as though it were all about sweetness and peace, Mr. Belton, and certainly God's peace is a dominant theme. I know that as well as anyone. But I'm still waiting for someone to show me how peace is a *larger* New Testament theme than is '*the battle*,' as you so succinctly put it at lunch today. Good *versus* Evil, Detective.

"So, yes, let's work and pray for peace. And while we do, let's bear in mind that we can either take Our Lord seriously when He speaks about the reality of Evil as an active force, or we can pretend that He is simply speaking in vivid first-century metaphor. . . ."

She paused for breath, her cheeks flushed and her blue-green eyes flashing. "You said this afternoon that your 'sources' referred to me as someone who lives her Christianity every day. Please understand, Detective, that means that I am ready to do battle with Evil every minute.

"In fact, Detective, it means almost nothing else."

She stopped. They looked at each other steadily, and for some time. It was Sid Belton who broke the silence when he said softly, in his New York City guttural growl, "I know, Dr. Chapel."

There was a pause. And then he added, "I know who you are, ma'am."

Exactly on cue, as his words died away, footsteps again neared the doorway. Belton stood before the heavy knock came, saying as he did, "This will be the Mangusons, ma'am."

CHAPTER FIVE

AT FIVE O'CLOCK ON MONDAY MORNING, JUST AS REBECCA Manguson stepped from the Washington Square Hotel to begin her short-lived run through the darkness, and at the precise moment at which Luke Manguson had swung into view of the intersection across which his sister would run momentarily, Matt Clark awoke. Provoked into consciousness by something he could not at once identify, his eyelids fluttered briefly, then opened wide in surprise. Instantly, he jerked his head sharply to the right, an automatic response to the tightly focused beam of light that shone directly into his eyes, glancing first off of something on his writing desk. Rubbing his eyes with his right thumb and index finger, he maneuvered himself into an upright position in bed, muttering unintelligible syllables from the effort.

Struggling, he leaned to his right and, extending his arm, switched on the reading lamp. Then he turned, still dazed, back to the left, in the direction from which the intrusive beam had materialized, and saw that it had apparently reflected off the small, framed print of St. David's Cathedral, the eight-centuries old church occupying the "holiest ground in Great Britain." The print sat on the far side of his writing desk; on the near side was a photograph of Rebecca, taken the previous fall by the mother of one of her students, as the beloved Miss Manguson had led her girls on a hike into the countryside south of London. The expressions on the faces of the girls who trailed her and fought to hold each of her hands conveyed Rebecca's essence to him at a glance, each time he looked at the picture.

Still sitting up in bed, Matt stared numbly at the cathedral print, wondering mildly about the strange illumination that seemed to have visited him . . . or had it? He then allowed his eyes to fall obliquely on the photo of Rebecca. His gaze rested there only for a moment. Then he turned, leaned over grumpily in the direction opposite, and reached again for the reading lamp. He switched it off, and turning back toward the writing desk and his bedroom's only window, lay down. He composed himself in the approximate position in which he had slept, closed his eyes, and, within seconds, encountered a shattering repetition of the same phenomenon, this one even more optically violent than the first.

Disbelieving, but now fully awake and on high alert, he found his heart racing, every system within him preparing for fight or flight. He sat up again, and in the moderate darkness, stared hard in the direction of the cathedral print. There was no trace of the shaft that had now twice attacked him. In the early morning grayness, he could see the outline of the cathedral print only dimly, aided by the indirect illumination provided by a street lamp near the intersection below.

Fighting for an explanation, he searched his brain and found only confusion, fury, and fear. He forced himself to breathe more slowly in an effort to restore normal rhythms to his body.

Minutes passed.

Arriving finally at a semblance of physiological control, he decided to initiate a test of sorts. Slowly, very slowly, his good arm across his chest, right hand pressing against the mattress surface, eyes open but eyelids held tense in defensive anticipation, he lowered his head inch by inch toward the pillow, all the while squinting intently toward the darkened outline of the St. David's print.

As his left cheekbone made tentative contact with the pillow, the tightly compressed, unnaturally brilliant beam of golden light smote his eyes for the third time. It bore in through the window, deflected off the frame of the cathedral print, or perhaps off the center of the glass itself—he could not tell which in the unendurable brightness—and then drove itself directly into and seemingly through his eyes into the depths of his brain and soul. His head again jerked involuntarily to the right, away from the window, else to risk blindness from the devastating force and otherworldly density of the golden shaft. Stunned briefly, he recovered almost instantly and surged into action. He tossed the covering sheet away, sprang to his feet, and crossed to the window. He looked out and up. He saw nothing. He turned his head and stared at the darkened cathedral print, then, tracing with his eyes the remembered beam of light, followed its path outward and upward.

Still nothing.

Taking a slow breath, he now stood erect, his right hand on his hip in the grayness of the room, his useless left arm hanging straight down, his brow furrowed. Despite the warmth of the June night, a shudder suddenly passed through him, head to toe. His mind by now was racing in a direction toward which it had not ventured for perhaps six months. He turned, his stomach wall tight and tense, and crept hesitantly to his writing desk. He stood for moments, then pulled out the straight-backed chair and, stepping around it, eased himself lightly into it.

He began to replay the last five minutes in his mind. The thing had happened *three times*, he said to himself. He demanded that the fact be verified in his memory. And so he recreated the sequence, carefully, actually speaking softly to himself, as though explaining what had occurred to an incredulous visitor. And he noted aloud that, in the third instance, he had been wide awake, his eyes open throughout the entire trial. Now leaning forward and to his left in the chair, he reached with his good hand to the left rear of his desk where a small, metal-shaded, flexible-necked writing lamp curled over the photograph of Rebecca with her students. He turned the switch on the lamp's circular base, and suddenly Rebecca's face shone radiant before him. After a moment, he pulled his eyes from the athletic figure, the dazzling face, and the dark, thick mane blowing partially across the gray eyes in the English breeze, and looked still again to the right side of the desk, to the St. David's print. Despite its small size, the print conveyed with considerable success both the mass and the ancient grandeur of the cathedral. Now drawing his left hand into his lap with his right, he propped his right elbow on the edge of the desk, rested his chin on top of the loose fist formed by his curled fingers, and forced himself to confront as objectively as possible what had just occurred.

And, as he expected, he found himself struggling with rising fear. Involuntarily, he twisted in his chair and looked over his right shoulder toward the window. Then he turned and faced the St. David's print once more.

Three times . . . three times . . . *three times* . . . the golden beam had arrowed into his eyes, the third under conditions framed by the informal test that he had contrived impromptu. There simply was no explanation for this, as desperately as he wished one. Something had . . . come for him . . . actually, had seemed to come *after* him. And, each time, he sensed in retrospect that the shaft had instantly begun to *damage* his eyes, not merely to irritate them. He had felt, certainly on the second and third times, as though actual blindness were at hand in the fraction of a second between the supernatural thrust of the golden dagger and his reflexive twist in the opposite direction.

The fear grew greater. Perspiration had begun to collect across his forehead and now began to form itself into small rivulets that descended past the bridge of his nose and down onto his tongue as he licked his lips absently. He stared now at the cathedral's looming eminence. Although he did not move his eyes from its image, with its fierce, fortress-like tower dominating the Welsh landscape, he felt Rebecca's eyes following him from the center of her photograph, under the glare of the desk lamp. And he felt his mind being steadily forced back to the night, a year previous, when the two of them had knelt together in the rear of the darkened cathedral. Another shudder ran through him, this one more insistent than the first.

He grasped the edge of the desk with his good hand. What was happening to him? No answer came, as he felt his mind again forced back to the cathedral and to the experience on that June midnight. They had known then that in moments both their lives were likely to be taken. And the sensations that had passed through him in those quiet moments had been so obviously supernatural in their origins that to account for them in some other fashion had been, and forever would remain, out of the question.

And still the fear grew. He groaned and leaned forward, letting his forehead fall onto his right forearm as it now rested flat on the desktop. After a moment, he raised his head, reached across the desk for Rebecca's picture, and drew it to the center of the desk, inches from his face. He stared into the gray eyes. And he groaned again. He knew dimly that his heart was breaking. He knew less dimly that that was not even the most important thing that was happening to him as he sat there in the predawn, now alternating between sweat and chill. No, this went beyond falling in love with a woman, and then having the beloved walk straight out of one's life without explanation or apology. This went to the *reason* for her rejection of him. And he knew the reason exactly. He, Matthew Clark, three days before, had dismissed her report of a divine action that, he now knew beyond question, had saved at least her life, and perhaps his, as well. A *divine* action. A *divine* warning. This he had dismissed, out of hand, with a majestic, materialistic casualness, simply because . . . and he groaned once more and again let his forehead fall to the desk . . . simply because he had had . . . *career aspirations.*

Humiliated, appalled, he began to feel sick.

His thoughts were forced now in the direction of his revered mentor. For a moment, he held Rebecca Manguson and Dr. Cameron Stafford juxtaposed in his mind's eye. Suddenly he spun around, grabbed the metal trash basket from its place to the right of his desk, and was sick, vomiting into a tiny void, struggling to control his body as it convulsed repeatedly.

Minutes passed. The nausea subsided reluctantly. He slumped to the floor beside the soiled trash can and rolled onto his back, his right hand moving to his temples in his habitual gesture of bewilderment, distress, and despair. And there, in the darkness, he confronted himself and what he had allowed himself to become in the months of his meticulous tutelage under Cameron Stafford. He had become the old Matthew Clark, full blown, the one that had developed itself so carefully during twenty-six years of life, prior to the emergency that had taken him to England, to Wales, and to Rebecca Manguson. Matt Clark, the educated man. The materialist. The skeptic. The naval officer without compass.

He had not noticed his slide back into the pit; he suddenly saw, because the slope on which he had descended comprised things allegedly Christian: the earnest lectures on spirituality; the titillating courses in contemporary theology; the erudite and socially responsible sermons on everything *except* sin, Satan, hell, heaven, the resurrected Christ, the Second Coming. Under the guise of an intellectually sophisticated Christianity, he had gradually, but altogether willingly, let it all go. He had let it all go to such an extent that, when Rebecca, a woman so obviously chosen by God that it was impossible not to see the bloom of Christianity in her every action, had presented the details of her vision to him, he had thrown out the whole thing, and the woman besides. The only surprise, in retrospect, was that she had ever shown any interest in him at all. How could he ever have hoped . . .

His shame suddenly overwhelmed him, and sobs wracked his muscular body. And her name came to his lips repeatedly as he cried in the darkness: "Rebecca . . . Rebecca . . . I'm so sorry."

How long he lay on the floor he did not know. But a moment arrived when the tears no longer flowed, when his breath no longer came in ragged gasps, and when he felt something like a sense of confidence—of renewed well-being—beginning to return to him. He sat up, propping himself awkwardly on his good hand and arm, and looked toward the window. First light had arrived, the harbinger of freshness and of new chance.

Rising first to one knee, then to his feet, his eyes returned to the woman's photograph on his desk. He moved to his chair, sat down quickly, and brought Rebecca's picture to the near edge, just under his gaze. He let his mind go free, indulging in the renewed feeling of tight proximity to this woman who had secured him without gesture, captured him without pursuit. Closing his eyes, he let his head fall slowly back, reveling in the sensations that poured through him, sensations of strength, of certainty in his capacities, of excitement about his future . . . about *their* future.

The events of the past three days seemed oddly indistinct now. The elusive images tumbled together, starting with his nerve-wracking wait for Rebecca's arrival and culminating in the strange, utterly preposterous confusion of this morning's awakening and brief illness. Why, after all that, did he suddenly feel so well? And then he knew.

The last three days had comprised some sort of aberration that now, after having made himself literally sick, he was somehow able to cast aside as if nothing had actually transpired. He saw that, truly, he could start over . . . could cancel the three days and simply reconnect to the Matt Clark that he had become prior to these three days . . . three days filled so strangely with nonsensical events.

Yes. Nonsensical.

For he now acknowledged forthrightly to himself that he would be a fool to turn his life 180 degrees from its course in response to some temporary . . . some momentary . . . what? Some momentary illness . . . or perhaps delusion . . . or whatever that might have been . . . that optical apparition that had so mysteriously beset him in the morning darkness, hardly more than an hour ago. He had, after all, been under enormous stress in the days just before Rebecca's arrival, planning the details of his approach to her, always in a swirl of confused hopes and fears regarding her imagined attitude toward him. And then the extraordinary disaster that she had managed to precipitate within minutes of having been introduced to the individual who held his future—and hers, as well, if she could but understand—in his two hands. Given all that, could it really be any surprise that he had been rousted from sleep by some neurological anomaly laced with optical manifestations . . . that he had briefly begun to feel such inexplicable and wrenching guilt . . . that he had actually vomited in response to this choking, intolerable tangle of physical and psychological snares? Should he not, in fact, just go right ahead and name what he had experienced? Was it not, at bottom, a sort of transitory madness?

Yes. Yes, it was. But now he felt immensely better . . . stronger . . . clearer . . . unencumbered . . . sane!

His eyes still closed, his face still upturned, neck muscles relaxed, head back, he realized finally, and above all, the nature of the supreme gift he'd been given by the morning's circus of phenomena. Somehow he had come out of the experience with the certainty that he was still in love with Rebecca Manguson. After all the emotional and psychological detours and entrapments were stripped away, that remained, clear and true. And now he felt confident at last that he would, in fact, somehow get her back. The fact that he knew this, and knew it with certainty, induced in him a calm assurance that further lifted his spirits.

Slowly he let his head come forward again. He opened his eyes and fixed them purposefully once more on the elegant face framed before him on his desk. He then moved the photograph carefully back to its place under the small lamp and made as if to rise. As he did, something drew his eye to the small red book on the corner of the desk, just behind the lamp. And he paused.

For this was his mother's prayer book, the one she had used daily in the Manhattan apartment in which she and Paul Clark had lived before they decided to move back to England after the electrifying events of the last summer. This was the book she had insisted that Matt retain in his possession after he had supervised, in his parents' absence, the shipment of their possessions across the Atlantic to their new home in a Birmingham suburb.

He stared at the book, his eyes somehow unable or unwilling to shift elsewhere. He made again to rise from his chair. Yet he did not rise.

That book . . . that very book . . . had been his starting point a year ago . . . when he had traveled in such haste from Norfolk to New York . . . when he had yielded to Detective Sidney Belton's insistence that he inspect his parents' apartment in response to their disappearance.

He remembered how, after the detective had left him alone in the silence of the apartment, he had crept to the door of his mother's study and had stood in the doorway desperately searching for some indication of what might have transpired. And it had been the sight of this very prayer book, resting in its regular place on her orderly desk, that had convinced him beyond doubt that sinister forces were behind his parents' disappearance. Martha and Paul Clark had not departed of their own volition; his mother never traveled overnight without this compact red volume in her hands.

Shaking his head to remove the memory so as to restore the marvelous sense of well-being that had consumed him since he had, just moments earlier, recovered from his early-morning, madness-induced sickness, he set himself once more to rise from his desk. But he could not rise.

Grimly, feeling himself helpless to do otherwise, and sensing a vague nausea beginning again to rise from somewhere deep, deep inside him, he reached warily across the desk for the prayer book and lifted it from the dusty surface. A year ago, in his mother's study, he had cradled the book in his left hand while he had turned its pages with his right. Now he had but one hand to use, and so, placing the prayer book flat on the desk surface just in front of his chest, he pushed the book open with his good hand and let his eyes fall to the page. He scanned the line that met his gaze: "*. . . you are sealed by the Holy Spirit in Baptism and marked as Christ's own forever. . . .*"

Matt saw that he had turned to a page used in baptism ceremonies. Near the bottom of the page he read: "*. . . We receive you into the household of God. Confess the faith of Christ crucified, proclaim his resurrection. . . .*"

The words sprang from the page and into his brain with none of the optical violence with which the golden beam had attacked him in the predawn darkness, and yet, somehow, with no less force . . . with no less intensity . . . and, yes, with no less sense of threat . . . What was happening *now*, he asked himself desperately?

Why . . . *why* . . . could he not simply be allowed—even for just a few hours—to retain those riotous feelings of well-being, of matchless self-esteem, of unsurpassed confidence? Why . . . exactly *why* . . . would it be asking too much simply to be allowed to be content . . . to be *happy* . . . with this splendid and heartfelt affirmation of his love for the woman? What more did there need to be, beyond this colossal . . . this *stupendous* truth?

Slowly he lowered his face toward the open prayer book, allowing his head to drop lower and lower until finally his forehead rested heavily on its delicate pages. He moaned softly. The sense of renewed strength with which he had awakened from his early morning *angst* had departed completely. Now an angry perplexity overwhelmed him. Confusion surged through his mind and body, chasing before it every vestige of the blessed confidence and self-assurance that had so filled him just moments earlier.

Again he moaned softly.

What was happening? How could he go from one extreme perspective to another, and then, metronome-like, to still another in the space of just minutes? Suddenly a violent convulsion passed through him as a memory thrust itself like a medieval lance into his tortured chest.

The memory was of Rebecca's experience in what they had learned to conceive as "enemy headquarters" in England, near Cambridge, a year ago. There, in the very lair of the Enemy, she had been attacked . . . physically attacked . . . by a force that was unambiguously identified with Evil. And the attack had come, she reported later, at the very instant that she had weakened . . . had allowed her mind to fondle, however briefly, the international fame that was unexpectedly proffered her in open recognition of her beauty, her brilliance, her versatility. And there, in that horrible solitude, she had found herself overpowered . . . utterly unable to resist this force . . . until she had finally, *in extremis*, called . . . called aloud . . . upon the name of the Lord.

Now that very memory smote Matthew Clark with shattering effect. Rebecca Manguson herself, in a moment of triumph . . . in a moment of high accomplishment . . . in a moment during which she must have experienced immense satisfaction within herself . . . in a moment, surely, in which a sense of expansive well-being, self-confidence, and self-assurance had predominated . . . even Rebecca Manguson had found herself overwhelmed by Evil.

And, presumably in light of her extraordinary gifts and unmatched resourcefulness, the attack had been by main force . . . physically unstoppable.

His mind reeled.

Had he just suffered a *petite* attack of the same sort, and yet, perversely, from within the confines of his own home? An attack from the same source, approaching from the side of self-congratulation and self-assurance? A seduction in the guise of a proud certainty that his previous course—followed unerringly for the last six months under Cameron Stafford's guidance—had been, or so he had been convinced, in the direction of true north, while the morning's mysterious interruption was nothing but an aberrant thrust toward some incomprehensible typhoon of madness and destruction?

Was he—insignificant soul that he was—serving somehow as a conse-quential and especially brittle bone of contention between primal opponents? *Could* it be?

What label, he wondered briefly, would the psychiatrists select to account for these phenomena? In lay terms, at least, he would be pronounced "disturbed." And he was, he knew, certainly that.

But disturbed how? Disturbed why? And then he knew, though he was aware that this knowing was in the direction opposite that of his equally certain knowing of just seconds before . . . that this knowing, if it were a true knowing, could only mean that the last ten minutes' fresh surge of self-assurance and self-confidence had been grounded in a lie . . . that his true condition admitted of no self-congratulation whatsoever . . . that his true condition was, in fact, desperate beyond measure.

And so it was that Matthew Clark turned once more, and for the final time, back toward home.

He now understood.

The source of the golden shaft could not be bought by half measures. A recommitment to the woman without a recommitment to the faith was Hell's invitation to place second things first. A sense of well-being and self-confidence and self-satisfaction in conjunction with love for the woman was a lure in the direction of that most treacherous of snares, toward a pathway both comfortable and tranquil, deep into a seductive and luxuriant forest. It was a pathway whose opening was situated so very near to that of The Way that at first glance they appeared to be one and the same. Yet the adjacent pathway would lead by degrees further and further from the Christian path, separating the traveler step-by-step from truth. And it would call itself the good life.

And it would indeed look like the good life, especially from a distance. And it might even feel like the good life, especially at first.

And it would lead the traveler gradually further from The Way in the most subtle of progressions, with no dramatic twists or turns, so that, not long after that route had been selected, the traveler would find himself yards, then miles, then continents, then a universe away from God's own path. So far away that the traveler would be lost forever unless Supernature itself came to his rescue.

And suddenly, to his astonishment, Matthew Clark rose to his full six-foot and four-inch height, turned his face upward toward the low ceiling of his diminutive bedroom, and shouted in his full naval command voice, "No! I'll not do it! I *will NOT go that way again!*"

And then, his voice dropping to a whisper, eyes closed: "Christ Jesus, my Lord and Savior, I am yours . . . please . . . let me finally be yours . . . please. . . ."

Shocked, he stood motionless for some time. Then, slowly, tentatively, he resumed his seat.

As he felt his senses returning cautiously to him, he sought hesitant counsel in his sense of self . . . and, looking within, he found that he was . . . angry. Yes. Angry at the violation. Angry at the trespass. Angry at his own naïveté. Angry that he could still be so infantile as a Christian so as to think that, simply because he had been led to refocus himself on his faith and on the woman, there would be no assault—no counterattack—launched against that redirection.

And for the moment he cared nothing for attribution. For the moment, he cared not at all about the counterattack's being attributed to the voice of materialism, or to the counsel of cynicism, or to the whisper of skepticism, or to every devil whom Christ Himself ever called forth from first-century human beings. At the moment, they all seemed to him to be one and the same.

Of course there would have been an immediate effort by the enemy, by any name, to retake the territory just lost. *Of course* it would have come, by any name, from an unexpected direction. *Of course* he would have misinterpreted the threat and would have fallen into the trap, to be saved from recapture only at the last moment, the moment at which his Rescuer had forced him back to the only foundation on which a relationship with Rebecca Manguson could ever be permanently established. Of course . . . of course . . . of course . . .

His eyes fell once more to the prayer book, still resting open on his desk. ". . . *You are sealed by the Holy Spirit in Baptism and marked as Christ's own forever*. . . ."

That New York City Monday grew rapidly into a day fearsome in its heat. As noon approached, Matthew Clark, his shirt soaked with perspiration from the nine-block walk, his black briefcase swinging heavily from his right hand, climbed the steps to the main doors of the Church of Corpus

Christi on 121st Street. Seven hours had passed since a supernaturally blinding shaft had routed him first from sleep and then completely out of himself and back into something he had once started to become.

Corpus Christi, a red brick Catholic church of unimposing design, located just to the east of Broadway in the shadows of Columbia University, was one Matt had visited the previous fall when he had first moved to the Morningside Heights section of Manhattan. That initial visit had been prompted by his close, then-regular reading of his mother's copy of Thomas Merton's autobiography. In it, Merton, once a staunch atheist, had described his first mass as having taken place at Corpus Christi in the 1930s. Matt had seen much of himself in the young Merton, as the latter had described his spiritual journey from Cambridge debauchee to, eventually, Cistercian monk. Matt had visited the church the fall previous simply to view for himself what the young Merton had seen some forty years before.

He knew that Corpus Christi held daily masses at noon and that the church would be open beforehand for prayer. He entered, glanced around the bright interior with its slender white columns, and slipped into a rear pew. Kneeling, covering his eyes and cradling his forehead in his good hand, he prayed, moving his lips silently. "Almighty God, Heavenly Father, please give me the strength and the wisdom to do Thy will in this crisis of my own making. Please give me the courage to do what must be done to stop the Evil, whatever form it may take. Please prevent my doing anything unknowingly that would endanger Rebecca. And please help her to understand that I am coming back. . . ."

He continued in prayer for some time, long after the priest had begun the mass for the surprisingly large number of worshippers who had assembled for the midday service. When his prayer was finished, Matt sat quietly, waiting for the mass to conclude. When it did, most of the worshippers departed quickly, though several remained seated or kneeling in prayer. A clean peace now seeming to envelop him, Matt finally rose, lifted his briefcase, and walked slowly out through the double doors and into the oppressive heat. He descended the church steps, walked to the corner, and looked to the south, across Broadway in the direction of the compact gothic structures of Union Theological Seminary.

His mentor, he knew, awaited him. Matt breathed deeply. And then, as he had a number of times throughout that terrible and wonderful morning, he smiled to himself, a quick, fleeting smile. He was ready.

Cameron Stafford was impatient. His greeting was perfunctory. It was obvious to Matt that Stafford felt he must feign a decent level of concern regarding Rebecca Manguson's well-being.

Stafford reported that the "location agency," as he called it, had had no trouble finding her on Sunday morning, confident as it was that she would turn up at an Anglican or Episcopal church somewhere in the city. There had been some sort of complication, however, and she had since then apparently changed hotels. They would find her once more in short order, he assured his protégé, probably before the Texas trip got underway next day, or, if not, later in the week. Nothing to worry about. Things would be fine.

Matt, now wary of anything Stafford might choose to report to him, played the role of the anxious suitor, purposely going far enough to irritate Stafford into a display of temper. "Enough!" the distinguished scholar finally snapped, showing Matt two emphatically upraised palms. "I told you that you'll see her soon enough. And you will. Concentrate on the work at hand, Matthew. That's what has real importance right now, you know. Mend things with your girlfriend later."

With that, he headed out the door, Matt following. The two of them stepped into a waiting taxi, and Stafford gave the driver a Manhattan address just north of the seminary. Nearly twenty minutes later, after a silent, halting, stifling drive in noon-hour traffic, they stepped from the taxi in front of the Aristotelian Bookstore and Lending Library on the corner of Broadway and 130th Street. The bookstore, co-owned by Stafford with several of his university and seminary colleagues, offered used books, cold tea and hot coffee, and more than two dozen nooks and crannies into which undergraduate and graduate students regularly inserted themselves to read, write, study, and procrastinate. The store was nearly always filled with a rich mixture of academic humanity. The area around the bookstore, with its plethora of green grocers, inexpensive clothiers, and ethnic restaurants jumbled together amid small, mostly nondescript apartment buildings, had gradually, in the late 1960s and early 1970s, become a teeming residential haven both for students and young faculty members.

They stopped at a street vendor's mobile wagon and bought pretzels—fat, salty pastries constituting a small meal in themselves—and soft drinks to serve as a makeshift lunch. Stafford thoughtfully held Matt's briefcase for him while Matt's good hand was occupied in the transaction with the vendor, then managed to carry both drinks and both pretzels when Matt's right hand became again occupied carrying the briefcase. Once inside the air-conditioned store, the two men put their burdens down and breathed deeply, relieved to be out of the sweltering heat. They paused to survey the bookstore and its customers.

Stafford had informed him by telephone that morning that Matt's Monday afternoon would necessarily be devoted to a careful review of Texas's current political conditions, of the state's power brokers' histories, and of Stafford's tentative business agenda for the trip. Their charter flight to the state capital was booked for Tuesday noon out of LaGuardia. The first meeting in Austin was scheduled for midafternoon, and a second meeting was to be held over an informal dinner with the legislative and corporate leadership of Texas's highly organized and well-financed effort in support of the Matheson Mental Health Curriculum for Children. They expected to return to New York by midnight.

Concerning Rebecca, Stafford had said on the phone that morning only that he would have news about her when they met at noon. Matt was certain that there was, in fact, much more "news" in Cameron Stafford's possession than Stafford had just provided so irritably upon Matt's arrival at his seminary office. But Matt also suspected that Stafford's "location agency" really did not, in fact, know where she was now. He wondered what the "complication" might have been. And he smiled at the thought.

This was not Matt's first visit to the Aristotelian Bookstore. He had lounged in its cozy quarters many times during the school year just ended and had even been invited upstairs to the MMHCC lobbying headquarters proper on several occasions. In addition, he had been present for one memorable public event, a midwinter debate, arranged and sponsored by the seminary and by the university's college of education, a debate in which Cameron Stafford had been opposed by a senior professor of Old Testament, a Dr. Eleanor Chapel. The debate had been conducted in the bookstore's "amphitheater," as the cluttered northeast corner of the store was euphemistically called whenever it was cleared for any sort of group activity, most commonly a book signing.

Now, while his mentor engaged several students in conversation, Matt chewed his pretzel and recalled that disturbing evening. The Chapel-Stafford debate was an occasion he had called to mind more than once before. He had, in fact, spent some time thinking about the debate that very morning, as he had, in his apartment, worked agonizingly through the implications of his precipitous reversal of course.

There in his room, Matt had recalled how the debate had profoundly, though temporarily, weakened his sense of discipleship to his graduate program advisor. The Chapel-Stafford confrontation had been attended by perhaps eighty faculty and graduate students who had packed the amphitheater long before the 8:00 P.M. starting time. Public announcements for the event, couched in the tortured language of dissertation and thesis titles, had suggested just another esoteric argument between out-of-touch scholars, an argument with no importance to anyone other than the debaters themselves and their closest colleagues. But these debaters' own students, particularly those who had studied under both teachers, had known from the start that this debate would be different. It would be different not because of the announced topic—"The Ramifications of the *Matheson Mental Health Curriculum for Children* for America's Educational, Ethical and Cultural Substrata"—but because of the debaters themselves.

Dr. Cameron Stafford was known widely beyond the university and the seminary as one of the very few in academia whose name commanded attention not only in two scholarly fields, but in the political arena as well. His opponent, Dr. Eleanor Chapel, a graying, energetic slip of a woman, was less well known than he, especially politically, but was, in some ways, an even more intriguing figure than Stafford himself. She was an Old Testament scholar with impeccable research and publication credentials. She was a Southern Baptist, who, though herself Caucasian, was a prominent member of the famed Abyssinian Baptist Church in Harlem. And she was a woman. This last was in itself interesting, given the traditionally male battlegrounds on which Eleanor Chapel seemed to wage much of her scholarly warfare.

And the debate itself, two hours of intense, riveting exchange, had been a revelation to Matt. All the fine-sounding descriptors which he associated with the MMHCC—the "enhancement" of children's self-esteem, the "broadening" of children's perspectives, the "enrichment" of children's philosophies and worldviews, the "expanding" of children's horizons— Eleanor Chapel had systematically destroyed, given the context in which they were advanced, with the subtlety of a high-speed locomotive. The over-powering, straight-line rationale that she advanced in her opposition to the MMHCC was far simpler, more forceful, and more arresting than her opponent's arguments in favor. She established a core premise and built so massive an argument upon it that not even the brilliant Cameron Stafford could find a means of assailing it. Her premise was that Judaism and Christianity were rooted in a moral law that served to underwrite all specific divine revelation. And, she continued, the systematic introduction into the nation's classrooms of material that, in its daily repetition, was designed to replace children's innate sense of objective truth, moral structure, and ethical boundary with a virulent subjectivism—"myself as ultimate referent"—comprised an antitheistic, antimoral, counterethical dogma that was the worse because it was embedded in children's *reading* texts. At times during the debate, Dr. Chapel had unapologetically advanced the notion that the MMHCC was not merely a well-intended, but misguided, form of moral subversion. It was evil, and its advocates knew it to be evil.

In response to Stafford's challenges, she had made clear that Jewish and Christian children, and, certainly, children raised within the framework of most major religions, did indeed develop a strong sense of self-esteem, but it was self-esteem of a different and infinitely higher order than that which animated the texts of the MMHCC. Judeo-Christian-based self-esteem, she showed her audience, generated and regenerated itself in children as they came to understand that they were "sealed" as God's own. Each Judeo-Christian child, she demonstrated, could come to see herself as being of eternal value, precisely due to the fact of being treasured by Almighty God Himself, infused with His Spirit, and for Christians, redeemed by His action.

Then, in response to questions from her audience, Eleanor Chapel had applied a gentle overlay to her quietly masterful performance by noting that children, rightly taught in church and temple, would come readily to see that all who worship—all who acknowledge God's sovereignty—share a mystical, not merely a psychological, sense of self-esteem that cannot be subtracted from them. And then she had added simply and softly that, for her, Christianity . . . specifically, the Incarnation, the Christ event . . . comprised the pinnacle of the Almighty's long, increasingly complex yet divinely simple, record of revelation to His creatures on earth, and that Christianity would always stand foursquare with Judaism—

her Old Testament expertise reinforcing her inclusion of the Mosaic history—against the materialism, subjectivity, and corruption spawned by the atheistic and materialistic forces of this, or any other, era. She would oppose with every ounce of her strength her seminary's endorsement of the wolf in sheep's clothing that stood before them in the guise of the Matheson Mental Health Curriculum for Children. If it were destined to succeed in legislatures throughout the United States, let it do so without the support of Christian or Jewish institutions and their leaders.

Matt swallowed the last bite of the huge, pulpy pretzel and found himself smiling, just as he had been inexplicably smiling to himself throughout the day. But during and after the Chapel-Stafford debate, he had not smiled. He had been stunned that his idol, increasingly as the debate continued, had had less and less to say in response to his opponent's onslaught. His only tactics during the second hour of the debate had been technical and stylistic. He had used everything from bombast to condescension to sarcasm to humor. Nothing had worked for him. And Eleanor Chapel's own disregard for anything tactical or stylistic had simply strengthened her hand in the eyes of her audience. She had the stronger position. She seemed smarter. She seemed better prepared. And, importantly to most of the onlookers, she was so obviously a Christian *believer*.

Now, his food and drink finished, Matt wondered idly where Dr. Eleanor Chapel might be now, and what she might be doing. He regretted now that he had not followed up on his decision, taken privately just after the debate, to enroll in one of her Old Testament courses as an elective in the spring. He had let that decision go almost immediately, immersed in his day-to-day regimen of serving Cameron Stafford as admiring student, grateful graduate program advisee, and eager assistant to him in the burgeoning MMHCC project.

Matt looked up. His mentor was returning to him after his chat with his fawning students. "Ready?" Stafford inquired.

"Yes, sir," Matt replied, lifting his briefcase again.

The two meandered slowly through the bookstore's convoluted aisles. Everything about the homey, eccentric establishment seemed to Matt to reflect Cameron Stafford's penchant for good literature and serious, prolonged academic engagement with it. They stopped briefly to chat with a young seminarian whom they found buried deep in Sartre's *No Exit*, required reading in Stafford's contemporary theology classes. They then ambled through the maze of irregular shelves, unmatched furniture, and wobbly study desks, through a door at the rear that led them into a cluttered office. They passed quickly through the office, noisy with the rapid staccato of three secretaries pounding dutifully away at their big, black Royal typewriters.

Electric typewriters, still novelties in academe, were just now replacing the ancient manual machines both at Columbia and at the seminary, and Stafford had acquired a dozen of the old typewriters for the cost of carting them away to his store. It occurred to Matt to ask himself why a small bookstore would require extensive secretarial support, and he answered himself as soon as he formed the question. The MMHCC lobbying project needed such support, not the bookstore. The Aristotelian Bookstore's mission was not fundamentally to sell and lend books. It was to serve as the heartbeat of something of much more widespread significance, at least in the eyes of one of its owners.

Although this was not to be Matt's first visit to the second floor, he paid much closer attention to the route than on earlier visits. He followed Stafford to the obscure stairwell at the extreme rear of the store, one that led to the second floor by way of a landing. The landing provided access, on the left, to the store's employee bathrooms; on the right, a good view, over the top of the façade that formed one wall of the small office, of the bookstore proper. Above the landing, at the top of the stairway, Stafford fumbled briefly for his keys, then unlocked a heavy fire door. He stepped into a hallway and bade Matt follow. The metal door closed itself very slowly, as Matt had remembered, making a small hissing sound as it crept toward its door frame, then traveling the last several inches to full closure with a rush and a slam. Stafford walked several steps along a short, dimly lighted hallway and repeated the entire procedure at a second door. Matt stepped through again and confirmed that the second door performed the same slow-motion automatic closure that its twin had, taking a very long time to pass through its range of motion from full open to complete, emphatic closure. He had begun to count off the seconds as Stafford had pushed the second door open.

Matt noted, as he counted, that plush carpet now lay under his feet and that they now traversed a capacious hallway, one with expensively framed artwork lining the walls. He paused to examine the first painting. After a moment, he heard the second fire door close. He had counted fifteen seconds exactly.

Stafford led him down the right-hand hallway. Thirty feet from the second door, they turned into a spacious office on the left, one that contained nearly as much floor space as the entire bookstore below it. They entered through a decorative archway fit for a ballroom. There was no door. Although he had not attended to the fact before, Matt saw on this visit that the immaculate, well-appointed office space was dominated by rows of shoulder-height file cabinets and by a long table with built-in telephone stations lining each side. At a glance, it seemed to Matt that perhaps a half dozen or more of its phone stations were occupied, mostly by young, bright-faced men and women each of whom held a phone receiver in one hand and jotted notes or wrestled with the rotary dial with the other. He had no time to look more carefully at this arrangement because Stafford was already leading him briskly between rows of file cabinets toward the rear of the office. Matt did, however, make a point of looking across the top of the file cabinets toward the row of windows that, he knew, overlooked 130th Street. He saw that the windows were high and traditional in design and appeared to have been untouched by the remodeling that the office itself had undergone when Stafford and his colleagues had purchased the bookstore.

Stafford used his keys to access still another locked door and drew Matt inside. As they stepped through the doorway, the heavy door, as with the two fire doors at the top of the rear stairway, closed itself slowly behind them and appeared to lock itself automatically.

This final room, one which Matt had not seen before, was clearly a board conference room. The room was empty. Its original ambience had been maintained in the remodeling project. Tall, elegant windows allowed natural light into the room in abundance. Its carpet was actually deeper than any of that over which they had just passed, its framed art more elegant, its artificial lighting more elaborately soft and indirect, and its long, rectangular table, which seemed to take up most of the floor space, was of fine, polished wood, perhaps mahogany. There were a dozen upholstered swivel chairs placed evenly around the conference table. Two smaller worktables occupied each of the far corners, a straight-backed chair placed under each. It was to one of these that Stafford took Matt and gestured for him to seat himself.

Despite its old look, the room had the feel of a vault. An almost eerie silence seemed to call for Matt's attention, even as Stafford moved noiselessly to the only other door in the boardroom, and reaching into an inside pocket of his light silk sport coat, pulled out a single key. He unlocked and opened the door, a metal fire door apparently set up mechanically exactly like the other three, and stepped inside what appeared to be a large storage room. He wheeled from it a three-drawer file cabinet. The heavy door slammed shut behind him as he returned the key to his inside pocket. He rolled the file to Matt's table.

"Try to get all the way through the Texas files by four o'clock this afternoon," Stafford said brusquely, indicating the middle file. "Here's a legal pad for your notes. You have a pen in your briefcase?"

With that, Cameron Stafford walked quickly to the boardroom's only exit and was gone. The door closed itself inexorably and with grim precision.

Matt opened his briefcase and removed a pen and a wooden pencil. He pulled open the middle file drawer and lifted from it the first set of folders. He organized himself for work, then sat back and looked around the room with apparent purpose. Taking the pencil in his right hand, he rose from his chair and strode swiftly to the window nearest the entrance to the boardroom, at the opposite end from his worktable. He looked down. Traffic on 130th Street below him moved easily, although by placing his face near the window and looking obliquely to his right, he could see that Broadway's traffic flow was still constricted even as the noon rush eased. He laid the pencil on the windowsill and, placing his right hand against the window frame, he leaned even closer to the glass pane and, standing on tiptoe, looked directly downward. His gaze was rewarded; he could see a portion of a ledge that appeared to run continuously along the side of the building, perhaps three feet below the lower ledge of the window, and protruding, he guessed, eighteen to twenty inches from the side of the building.

Next he examined the window mechanism. He was gratified to find that, not only had the original windows been retained through the renovation, their locking devices were also unchanged. These windows had been designed many decades ago to be opened and closed easily on hot summer days. He fingered the antique locking mechanism with his right hand, applied torque with his thumb, and felt it yield. He lifted the window several inches by pressing upward at the top of the frame with his good hand. Then he moved his hand under the window and raised it another fifteen inches. Stooping low, he leaned out through the partially open window and, looking to the left, saw the black, iron outline of the building's south fire escape near the southeast corner of the building. The ledge just below him led directly to it. Withdrawing his head into the boardroom, he stood erect, inserted the wooden pencil into the opening at the base of the window, then gently lowered the window until it rested on the slender implement.

Satisfied, he walked to the boardroom door, bent over, and examined the doorknob, its bolt, and its lock. The mechanism could be locked and unlocked only from the office side, and apparently only with its key. He placed his hand on the heavy metal knob, turned it cautiously, and heard the bolt slide in response. He pushed the solid metal door slowly, created an opening sufficient to accept his head and shoulders, and leaned through the doorway. The physical layout of the second-floor office was as he remembered from previous visits and from his quick walk-through with Stafford minutes earlier. The rows of file cabinets hid this doorway from those seated and working with the telephones at the other end of the office. He looked down at the bolt, turned the knob again to observe its action, and, holding the door in position with his foot, pushed directly on the bolt to test the strength of its spring.

Finally, after closing the door as carefully and noiselessly as he had opened it, he walked back to his worktable. He stood for a moment looking down at his open briefcase, then, reaching into it with his good hand, he rummaged in it briefly, lifted from it a roll of maximum-adhesive commercial-strength strapping tape, and placed the tape on the desk beside the briefcase. Then he reached into his right-hand trousers pocket and removed his six-bladed Swiss Army knife. He placed the knife on the table next to the roll of tape.

Matt stepped back from the table, turned, and looked down the length of the long table toward the boardroom door. He stood now on the precipice. Over the course of the next few hours, he would move from that morning's strictly internal activities of prayer, decision, and planning . . . to action. These actions carried the gravest of risks. Should Cameron Stafford return to the boardroom at any time during the next several minutes, Matt would have no explanation for his actions. And should that happen, he knew the consequences were incalculable.

Still facing the boardroom door, he brought the morning's final decision before his mind once more. The evidence that formed the basis for that decision was, he knew, of an order so strange that he would not know how to begin to explain it to anyone else. But there it was, clear and final, in three parts. First, Rebecca Manguson had reported to him her twice-seen vision in which Cameron Stafford was shown to her as unequivocally Evil. Acting on that, she had extricated the two of them from a lethal trap, one that had presented itself to his eyes as benign or, at worst, ambiguous.

Second, three days later, Matt himself had been the recipient of a different kind of vision, one with, at first, no intelligible message other than threat. Divine threat. The blinding shaft, ricocheting from the framed print depicting the site of the most powerful divine reassurance he had ever received, had told him simply to return to that Source . . . to Jesus Christ Himself . . . or else become a blind man, literally and figuratively, forever. And that had been supplemented shortly thereafter by the strange compulsion to pick up his mother's prayer book, and to open the book, and to read the words that there presented themselves to him. He had felt at that moment that he was being offered his final chance.

And third, complementing the two supernatural interventions had been the image, still strong in his mind after six months, of Dr. Eleanor Chapel's indictment of the MMHCC and of its leading proponent . . . and her unabashed linking of the project and its progenitor with evil. That linkage comforted him now, as he continued to stand facing the door of the boardroom. It was the single completely earthly, ordinary, and rational piece of his decision. The other two components in the decision traced themselves either to Rebecca's vision or to his own. Without Eleanor Chapel's overwhelming argument in opposition to the MMHCC project and its leadership, Matt knew he would not, in all likelihood, have had the faith or the courage to move into action on the basis solely of his own or anyone else's interpretation of Supernature's messages. And, in fact, even now, still standing completely motionless and alone in the boardroom, he hesitated. How could he be sure that he was not on the verge of throwing away a lucrative and high-profile career in education and politics for something illusory?

He looked down at the floor and raised his right hand to his face in his habitual motion of uncertainty, massaging his temples with thumb and fingers. How could he be sure? How could he *ever* be sure? And his eyes seemed to move automatically toward his left hand, hanging limp at his side. And there his eyes remained, focused on the sight of his own inert fingers.

And he knew finally that he was answered. The answer was grounded in Rebecca, in his mother's diaries, in the certainties that had developed in him as Christianity had forced itself upon him the year previous, and in the hail of bullets that had destroyed his shoulder and his arm, and but for Rebecca's heroism, would have taken his life. This was no abstract miracle-and-theology-and-ethics problem to be sorted out in a seminar conversation among pompous, disengaged, self-important religious philosophers. This was revelation. This was life and death. And this was Jesus Christ Himself: *my life for yours.*

He drew a deep breath and looked up at the door. And suddenly he knew, and with a certainty he would not have been able to verbalize, that neither Cameron Stafford nor anyone else would be coming through that door in the next half hour, while he began to translate revelation and prayer and concept and plan into uncompromising, irretrievable action.

He turned to his worktable and picked up the knife.

CHAPTER SIX

IT WAS NEARLY EIGHT O'CLOCK, AN HOUR BEFORE MONDAY night's closing time. The Aristotelian Bookstore was still filled with students, albeit less so than during its 4:00-7:00 P.M. peak hours. Matt Clark, carrying nothing in his right hand and wearing his short-sleeved cotton shirt untucked, entered the store casually and moved to the Contemporary Theology section. His shirt, the largest and loosest-fitting in his wardrobe, hung to his hips and successfully concealed, he hoped, the long, heavy, four-battery flashlight that was secured horizontally by its two clips to the belt loops in the back of his khaki trousers.

He began to browse through the offerings. He removed a two-volume set of Paul Tillich's works, carried the set to a favorite chair situated behind a pillar along the north wall of the store, and leafed through the pages. His mind was elsewhere. He began to review his afternoon's work. While things had not gone perfectly, he felt that they had gone well enough.

Commercial-strength strapping tape, he had known in advance, was hard enough to tear and manipulate by a person with two good hands. Working with just one that afternoon in the boardroom, Matt's ingenuity had been tested considerably just by the act of trying to cut several strips from the roll. He had finally hit upon the expedient of raising one corner of the worktable with his shoulder and inserting the table leg down through the center of the roll of tape. Then, using the table leg as a spindle around which the roll of tape could turn, he had laboriously pulled from the roll various lengths of tape and, holding the tape with his teeth, had cut the lengths with the small scissor-blade mechanism that formed one component in the pocketknife's versatile armament. He had used several strips to replace the too-visible pencil as a placeholder to prevent the previously opened boardroom window from closing itself by its own weight. And he had successfully arranged for several short lengths of tape to protrude beyond the now paper-thin opening to facilitate the window's being raised from the outside by a person standing on the ledge that ran continuously under the row of windows. The thing had been clumsily done, he knew. But it was a serviceable arrangement, and he had confidence that, if necessary, he would be able to raise the window and enter the boardroom from the ledge. He was also confident that he could exit the boardroom by the same means, and that he would then be able to reach the building's fire escape by traversing the ledge to its southeast extremity.

The riskiest moments had come after Cameron Stafford had arrived at four o'clock to terminate Matt's afternoon of study of the Texas files. Since Matt could not open the storage room door from the boardroom side without a key, he could prepare the door for later reentry only in Stafford's presence. And he had.

When Stafford had rolled the file drawers to the storage room and unlocked the door, Matt had followed quickly, then had graciously held the door open while his mentor had wheeled the files into the storage area. With Stafford's back to the doorway, Matt, holding the door open with his foot, had surreptitiously applied two previously cut strips of the strapping tape—each strip having been affixed lightly to the right seam of his trousers—to the bolt mechanism, preventing the bolt from responding to its spring-loaded push into locking position. The two men had then walked briskly away from the door as it passed through its slow-motion closing routine, and Matt had made a point of being in loud mid-sentence at the moment the door finally slammed itself shut, lest a slight alteration in the metallic locking sound attract Stafford's attention and lead him to investigate.

Matt's effort to fix the boardroom's entry/exit door in the same fashion had failed, since Stafford had insisted on holding the door himself, and Matt's elaborate ruse of returning to his desk to retrieve his pencil had not led Stafford to abandon the door to walk ahead of him through the office. But Matt had anticipated that this ploy might fail. He had unlocked and prepared the boardroom window with the strapping tape specifically to serve in that eventuality. He was sure that, if he could successfully return to the second floor at all, he would be able to exit the office window nearest to the boardroom, traverse the ledge, and reach the boardroom window that he had prepared for reentry. It was the storage room door, not the boardroom door, that would have to be navigated directly, else he would be forced to shatter a storage room window in order to enter from the ledge. He wanted to leave no trace of his reentry that night. Stafford must continue to regard Matt as part of his team, and the storage area for the MMHCC's most secret files as inviolate.

Matt knew from his previous visits to the second-floor office, and from earlier conversations with the part-time staffers there, that the closing procedure for all bookstore personnel, including the MMHCC staff, was rigid. The second-floor office's telephone lobbying effort stopped on weeknights at 8:45. The office was then tidied and prepared for the next day's work, and at 8:55, the staff supervisor always turned off the lights behind the staff members and followed them through the two automatically locking fire doors down to the landing and on to the first floor. The bookstore manager expected all upstairs staff, including the supervisor, to be out of the front door by 9:00 sharp, and customers were shepherded out before that, between 8:45 and 8:55. The front door was always locked at 9:00, with only the bookstore manager remaining in the building.

The manager then, working alone, totaled the cash receipts for the day, arranged the records for the bookkeeper's review, which would begin at seven o'clock the next morning, and, usually by half past ten, left the building. Cameron Stafford was a stickler for orderliness, and his bookstore ran like clockwork.

This night, Matt put down his Tillich at exactly 8:30, stood, and quickly adjusted the flashlight so that it fit as snugly as possible across the small of his back and under his ample shirttail. Then, acting on an impulse that had come to him during the long morning fight within himself, he walked purposefully to the New Bibles section of the store. Although the array was comprehensive, it tended toward fat, hardcover, scholarly editions based upon the latest translations. On this occasion, Matt was searching for something quite different from these, and, after several minutes, he reached down and fingered the very book he sought. He pulled it from the shelf and smiled. It was a peculiarly shaped little volume, very thin, measuring perhaps 4x2 inches in height and width. Bound in maroon softcover, its title read simply: *The New Testament.*

Matt crossed to the cash register, paid for his new book, and returned to his same seat along the north wall. Using his right hand, he leafed through the pages of his purchase. Passing through Luke's Gospel, his eyes fell on the passage in the twenty-first chapter in which Jesus explains to the disciples that, while terrible trials most certainly awaited them, and although they would be brought before kings and rulers in His name, they should make up their minds beforehand not to worry about what they should say in their defense, for, when those times arose, *"I will give you words and wisdom that none of your adversaries will be able to resist or contradict."*

He stared at the passage for several minutes, thinking. Then he closed the little volume and looked at his watch. It was 8:45.

Matt placed his new book in the left breast pocket of his shirt, stood, adjusted the flashlight once more, and walked quietly along the north wall, moving so that shelving and pillars formed a continuous visual screen between himself and the bookstore manager, who stood near the front door bidding good night to students and other customers. He slipped softly around the back office to the stairs, out of sight of the manager, and moved quickly up to the landing, stooping to keep his head and shoulders below the line-of-sight from the front door. Near the south side of the landing, he opened the door to the men's room and stepped inside. He did not turn on the light.

Matt took a deep breath. He estimated that he had taken two minutes to move from his seat to the employees' bathroom on the landing. He fought his nervousness, consciously relaxing muscles and trying to force his breathing into a more regular pattern than his systems were demanding of him. He tried to say a prayer and failed completely. He could not pray. He relied instead on the prayers he had said, on and off, throughout this long day. Those would have to serve, for he could bring himself to do no more. His hand moved involuntarily to his left chest, where his New Testament lodged quietly. And he smiled again.

Then he simply listened.

One minute later, he heard the clatter of footsteps coming down from the second floor toward the landing. Holding the men's room door open the width of a finger, Matt could see through the slit in the doorway a fragmentary, vertical slice of each staff member as a half dozen young men and women filed down the first set of steps to the landing. Then he saw nothing more, but listened as their footsteps traversed the landing and began to descend the second flight of steps toward the main floor.

Afraid to blink, he peered through the doorway's slit at the first fire door as it closed itself slowly at the top of the flight of stairs, now halfway, now three-quarters. Then, just before the door began its rush to its fully closed position, he heard the second, interior fire door open again noisily, and instantly he began to count off the seconds. His heart pounding nearly uncontrollably now, he listened to the quick footsteps of the MMHCC staff supervisor in the corridor above, and then saw and heard the first door swing open. The supervisor descended the first flight of steps swiftly, conscious of the fact that the bookstore manager was waiting impatiently for her at the front door.

Matt waited, counting steadily. He knew he could not move until the supervisor began her descent of the second flight of steps. Three seconds . . . she had begun her descent of the first flight. Six seconds . . . she had reached the landing. Nine seconds . . . she had completed her crossing of the landing. Ten seconds . . . she began her second descent. Matt slipped through the men's room door and, taking two steps at a time, glided as fast as possible up the stairway. He passed through the slowly closing first door without needing to push it open, just brushing it with his left shoulder. As he passed through the first door, his count reached thirteen. He lunged toward the second door, his six-foot-four-inch frame extended, right hand straining toward the diminishing opening.

On the second lunging step, he hurled himself full-length toward the door just as it reached the end of its range of resistance and snapped itself toward the doorframe. He was too late to get his hand into the crack as it disappeared, and in the final millisecond he turned his desperately extended fingers into a fist and drove his knuckles into the base of the metal door. Tumbling to the floor, he could not at first tell whether the concussions reaching his ears came from the door's slam or his own body's frantic, full-length crash to the floor.

He looked up. The door, wedged against his fist, appeared closed. But was it? He rolled his knuckles forward against the heavy metal base plate. Groaning from the whole-body effort, every muscle fiber still straining, he drove a knee into the floor and thrust his body forward. He felt movement, and the fact confused him. Looking up toward the locking mechanism, he saw what must have happened. The door had been closed, but his fist, in the final fraction of time and distance, had prevented its settling deeply enough into the frame for the bolt to spring into its locking cavity.

Inching forward from his knees, not daring to relax a single muscle, he strained against the door's base, groaning softly with the effort. Grudgingly, it began to yield. He slid his fist across the base of the door, reaching for the opening that had begun to appear. Finally, his hand reached the small space he had doggedly created between door and frame, and, extending his hand fully, he grasped the door's lower corner with long, strong fingers, and relaxed, the corner of the door now fully in his grasp, his hand and wrist firmly wedged into the three-inch space he had fought to win. He breathed, listening. He knew that his dive to the floor had created sounds that, if they had reached the ears of the departing supervisor or of the manager, still standing at the front door, could lead either person to investigate. The seconds passed. Then the minutes. No footsteps advanced up the stairway.

Gathering himself again, he inched further into the widening opening, then moved slowly through it on his knees. Finally, holding the door firmly in his good hand, he moved it carefully toward the doorframe. He allowed the door to slip into the frame, heard the bolt slide into its cavity, and leaned back against the wall. Looking up at the door, he read with new eyes its block-lettered sign:

EXIT

MMHCC

Information Storage, Retrieval, and Telephone Education Center

With his good hand, he felt his left chest for his New Testament. And he smiled yet again.

Detective Sid Belton paused in mid-sentence and looked long into the face of Luke Manguson. Then he turned his head and looked over his shoulder at the clock that sat on his living-room bookcase. Luke's eyes were closed in sleep, and the clock indicated five minutes after midnight. The detective turned again and looked at his other two guests. He smiled, first at Rebecca Manguson and then at Eleanor Chapel. "Luke's still running on London time, ladies. He's been awake for about forty-eight hours. Let's call it a night."

As Rebecca gently began to awaken her brother and as Eleanor Chapel started the process of collecting her notes and other materials, the telephone rang from the apartment's only bedroom. Frowning at the idea of a midnight phone call, the detective disappeared quickly and answered on the third ring.

The women, materials and belongings in hand, stood chatting quietly while Luke washed his face and Sid Belton spoke to his telephone caller, his guttural voice heard as an indistinct murmur by those in the living room. After several minutes, the detective and Luke returned from opposite directions, and it was Sid Belton to whom the other three faces turned inquisitively. His lopsided smile was broader than usual, and his deep-set black eyes actually danced with amusement or excitement . . . perhaps both, thought Rebecca.

And then she saw with surprise that he turned to address her specifically. "Well, Miss Manguson," he said slowly, "wanna guess who that was?" The detective did not pause for an answer. "That was the kid himself . . . our long lost Matt. Called from a pay phone two blocks from here. Sounds like he's had a pretty interesting day, ma'am. Sounds like he's had a day that's made him . . . ah . . . different from who he was when you were with him Friday. Know what I mean, ma'am? Says he's got stuff that he's got to tell me. I didn't tell him that anybody else was here. He's on his way over right now. I can send all three of you out the back way. Or you can stick around to see what the kid's got for me."

Fewer than three minutes later, Matt Clark knocked on Sid Belton's apartment door. Throughout the long walk from 130th Street, Matt had rehearsed what he would say to the detective. He wanted to get everything laid out in a fashion that was as orderly as he could make it, and he wanted to do it quickly, before anything that he had read in the storage room by flashlight during the previous two-plus hours began to slip from his memory.

He rapped three times on the door and looked down at the floor, arranging his opening sentences in his mind. The door opened and he looked up, opening his mouth to speak. But he uttered no sound. He simply stared at the face in the doorway. His jaw sagged further, and all color drained from his face. Still in the hallway, his right hand grasping at the doorframe for support, he sank to his knees, eyes brimming. His voice caught in his throat. Yet he forced the words from his lips. "I'm sorry," he whispered. "Rebecca . . . I'm so sorry."

Kneeling, he closed his eyes, and his head dropped forward to his chest. He slowly moved his right hand from the doorframe to his forehead. He thought for a moment that he might actually faint. Then, after what seemed a very long time, he heard soft footsteps. As he lowered his hand from his temples, he actually felt her against him.

She pressed the side of his face, while he remained kneeling, into her taut stomach. He felt the coolness of light cotton fabric against his face, and under the fabric, the flat muscular wall of her abdomen. And he felt strong hands cradling his head, pressing his face against her.

And there she held him.

In response to Matt's knock on the apartment door and, to their mild surprise, Rebecca's quick movement to answer it, the others had moved discreetly into the tiny kitchen, ostensibly to prepare a fresh pot of coffee for what was now obviously to become a second late-night session. And there they waited until, after minutes, the sound of the front door closing and Rebecca's cheery summons brought Eleanor Chapel and Sid Belton back into the living room carrying their coffee cups. Rebecca spoke to the pair immediately: "Matt and I have much to discuss, as you can imagine. But we'll defer our conversation until tonight's business is complete. Oh . . . I'm sorry . . . Dr. Chapel." Pulling the still-dazed Matt along behind her, she moved quickly to the gray-clad professor, who had crossed the room to the sofa. "Dr. Eleanor Chapel," said Rebecca, "may I present Matthew Clark."

They completed a comical handshake, the six-foot-four man towering over the four-foot-ten woman, his long fingers and huge palm completely enveloping her tiny right hand. As he tried to say something intelligible to her about how much her midwinter debate against Cameron Stafford had affected him, not just at the time, but, indeed, that very morning, he suddenly felt himself lifted bodily off the floor from behind. A gruff voice spoke from somewhere behind and beneath him: "Hey, mate! Stand at attention when the Royal Navy enters the room! I'll throw your bloody carcass over the side, I will!"

Released and dropped to the floor after a moment to stand on his own feet again, Matt spun around, feigning outrage at being thus manhandled. "If you try again to sneak up abaft the United States Navy, mister, I'll have you keelhauled on the quarter hour 'til you turn to seaweed!"

The two young men grappled in a rough, laughter-filled embrace, Luke Manguson carefully avoiding pressure on Matt's atrophied limb. Taking in the unruly scene, Rebecca turned and rolled her gray eyes at Eleanor Chapel's blue-green ones. "Ignore them if you can, Dr. Chapel. I think there must be an eleventh commandment that requires former naval officers to behave like twelve-year-olds whenever they come across each other. You'll find they each have a certain capacity to behave as civilized persons. You must just give them time."

Eleanor Chapel laughed her tinkling laugh and replied, "We must simply indulge them, Rebecca. They're painfully aware, you understand, that they can't do that with you or me. They know we'd toss them overboard in a flash . . . figuratively speaking, in my case . . . perhaps literally, in yours."

The happy commotion gradually subsiding, the group members, balancing their coffee cups, began to arrange themselves for the next session. The detective placed Matt in his personal reading chair, stage center. Eleanor Chapel and Luke Manguson shared the sofa directly across from Matt. Sid Belton sat in the straight-backed chair at his writing desk. And Rebecca chose one of the kitchen chairs that the detective had brought in, moving it carefully off to one side of Matt, and well out of his line of vision. She knew that this was not the time for him to be looking into her eyes. This was business.

"Kid," said the detective when all were seated, "we've spent most of the last three hours just gettin' everybody on the same page. Dr. Chapel has covered the MMHCC's immediate and long-range dangers for the benefit of Rebecca and Luke. She already did that for me, at lunch today. And, if I understood what you were just sayin' to her before Luke jumped you a couple of minutes ago, you've heard Dr. Chapel make a presentation on that subject? Yes? Good.

"In any case, when Eleanor had finished with her overview of the MMHCC, Rebecca, Luke, and I covered last summer's events for her pretty thoroughly. We tried to emphasize what may be the connections between your parents' bein' kidnapped out of Central Park last summer and taken to England, and some of what may be goin' on right now.

"And then I tried to bring all three of 'em up to speed on my telephone research over the last day and a half. Like I mentioned to you on the phone a few minutes ago, kid, I got nothin' solid from any of my contacts. But there sure are a lot of rumors out there, y'know what I mean? Big publishin' money tied up with what could turn out to be a fifty-state textbook project. I got rumors of blackmail, extortion, insider trading on the stock market . . . but not a single piece of hard evidence. There's not one thing that I've got so far that I could go to my police buddies with. Their bosses would just tell 'em to quit chasin' their tails and get after somethin' with real evidence behind it.

"Now, all I said to Eleanor and the Mangusons after your call fifteen minutes ago was that you said you'd been the biggest fool in history . . . and that you just had your head turned around 180 degrees this mornin' by the angels themselves . . . and that you'd just spent more than two hours readin' MMHCC memoranda with a flashlight . . . and that you had stuff you had to tell me. You wanna fill us in from there, kid?"

Matt then launched the explanation that he had rehearsed on his way to the detective's apartment. He began with the predawn shaft of light that had forced him back toward the path he had abandoned earlier in the year. He covered briefly his noon visit to Corpus Christi, his afternoon in the MMHCC's second-floor boardroom reviewing the Texas files, and his reentry at closing time. Then he turned to his review of the secreted materials.

"I didn't want to turn on the storage room lights," he continued, "and that's why I brought the flashlight. I expected the batteries to give me two hours, and they gave me that and a little more. I started reading from the 'internal memoranda' file at about 9:15, and the batteries died about an hour ago."

Matt then described a burgeoning network of extortion threats and outright bribes being prepared to influence decision-makers, state-by-state. The monies appeared to come from selected corporate sources, though several other allusions made him think that money from the sale of illegal drugs was also part of the MMHCC lobby's treasury. He had also come across a series of memos that suggested that, although the research evidence in support of the MMHCC's alleged enhancement of children's "self-esteem" might be technically legitimate, given the relativistic premises of the research projects, the evidence suggesting that children could actually read better as a result of exposure to the materials was probably fraudulent.

There were, in addition, hints that the next series of texts generated by the MMHCC's umbrella organization—an organization studiously *not* named—would be pastoral counseling texts for use in seminaries. These texts would operate from the same premise: that subjectivism in all its forms would reliably enhance the self-esteem both of seminarians, and once they became ministers, the members of their flocks. And for the same reasons. Once an individual—child or adult—could be induced to regard all statements of value as generated entirely from his own arbitrary assumptions and premises, he would be free to regard himself as "right" and "good" under all circumstances, always provided he remained careful not to push his own assumptions and premises on anyone else.

And finally, Matt carefully described a series of references to an upcoming meeting on Friday in "Oxford." For the longest time he had been unable to ascertain which Oxford, since, it seemed to him, the name dotted the American landscape like sparrows in summer. He had actually given up when, just before the flashlight batteries expired, he saw a reference to Oxford as "located just a few miles south of the Chesapeake Bay Bridge's eastern approaches."

And he had also noted with great interest that, while he and Cameron Stafford and others were to be in Texas on Tuesday, leaving at noon and returning at midnight, all of the key files in the storage room were to be loaded into trucks for transport on Wednesday and Thursday from New York to this same Oxford, in preparation for the Friday sessions there. It was obvious to him from these and other memoranda that the core players in the MMHCC project were to be in attendance, and that the files were to be on hand in advance for ready reference before and during the conference.

Matt paused. He leaned forward in his chair and turned his head so that he could see Rebecca's face. "And Rebecca," he added, "I saw a copy of . . . of what I think was the very same 'Confidential Report' that you read last summer . . . the one that led you to . . ." And here he stopped, looking at her closely.

Uncharacteristically and involuntarily, her hand flew to her mouth and she looked down and quickly closed her eyes. Her brother rose and moved to her immediately, his powerful hands on her shoulders. Matt, uncertain as to how he should comport himself with Rebecca, sat looking down at his feet, his good hand urgently massaging his forehead.

In response to Eleanor Chapel's inquiring look, Sid Belton said quietly, "Ma'am, when Miss Manguson was in a tough spot last year in England, she came across a 'Confidential Report' on herself. The Enemy—and it's beginnin' to look as if there is just one Enemy—had put together a report on the importance of recruitin' her to their side. The report described her as beautiful, articulate, brilliant . . . and pictured a future for her in service to the Enemy . . . television . . . movies . . . worldwide recognition . . . She told us that she found herself actually thinkin' about that, imaginin' how it might be, and when she did, she fell into the Enemy's grip in more ways than one. When she came out of it, with some 'special assistance,' she was ashamed. She was, y'know, humiliated to have been tempted—and seriously tempted—by all of that. She has a tough time with the memory of it. I don't think she's ever failed in quite that way, Eleanor."

Eleanor Chapel smiled knowingly at the detective and nodded her head. "Those with the greatest gifts," she murmured, "must endure the greatest temptations." And she turned and looked toward Rebecca, who sat covering her eyes with both hands, still comforted by her brother. "Our Lord Himself. . . ."

At that moment, Rebecca dropped her hands, looked up, squeezed Luke's arm, and rose to her feet. As Luke moved away toward the sofa where Eleanor Chapel still sat, Rebecca, standing at her chair, raised her hands to her face again and pressed both palms into her cheeks, unashamedly wiping away the matching streaks of tears. And then she began to walk deliberately across the floor. Her brother recognized immediately what he was seeing. His sister, when locked in deepest concentration, habitually paced, whether alone or in company.

Now, beginning to roam the narrow confines of the detective's living room like a contemplative tigress, she worked her sinewy hands against each other in front of her chest, thick, black tresses falling over high cheekbones and down over the front of her dark blue tennis warm-up suit. Her colleagues waited patiently. She would speak to them, they knew, as soon as she was ready.

Without pause in her measured, catlike movements around and among her seated companions, she finally began, her voice low in pitch and moderate in volume. "Matt," she said, without turning to face him, "I've had a second vision since I last saw you. The vision was presented to me at the family service I attended on Sunday morning . . . with the detective."

She described the vision for him briefly, still patrolling the room, then added, "And the message that accompanied those bright images of arena and children was simple. Just two words: *Prevent this.*"

She continued, still moving steadily about, now addressing all four of her colleagues. "Tonight, when I heard the detective describe his contacts' references to bribes and threats and other criminal acts . . . and when I heard Matt describe some of the memoranda, with their references to drugs and fraud . . . and when Matt told us a moment ago that he even found a copy of that unspeakable 'report' about me . . . I knew without the smallest doubt that our new Enemy is our old Enemy . . . the ancient Enemy."

Now she fell briefly silent, still padding softly and deliberately up and down and around the tiny room. And then she continued, speaking in the same low-pitched voice, the elegant vowels of her English accent washing like wisdom over the ears of the three Americans and her brother. "Yes . . . the new Enemy is certainly the ancient Enemy . . . and that means to me . . .

"That means to me that we can expect Dr. Stafford and his colleagues to enlist the aid of any corruptible individuals of influence that they can solicit, certainly including legislators in key states, and perhaps also including selected law enforcement officials. And that we can expect those corrupt individuals to threaten otherwise innocent people in every way they can. And that we can expect them to be physically violent whenever it suits them. And, finally, that we can expect them to tread just inside the technical letter of the law . . . or, where not, to threaten those who could act against them legally. . . .

"And all of this means to me that we will lose—we shall fail to *prevent this*, as we have been ordered—unless we go around and behind and above the corrupt power brokers . . . ultimately to the people themselves."

When she spoke these last words, three faces quickly turned to look up at her. The fourth had never stopped looking at her from the moment she had stood to begin her incessant pacing. That face was Matt Clark's, and it was he who spoke. "How . . . where . . . in what way can we reach the people, Rebecca? I . . . I don't think I know what you mean."

"Through Christian news media, Matt," she replied, still walking, still not looking in any direction except down at her hands as they continued to work vigorously against each other. "And once Christian media have published the full story, then the national and international wire services, I should think, will eventually want to get involved, as well."

After a moment, Sid Belton shook his head. "Ma'am," he said, now looking thoughtfully down at his shoes, "seems to me this whole thing is too . . . well . . . *complicated* . . . too . . . ah . . . too subtle . . . for newspapers or television. I mean, when we're tryin' to say somethin' that's psychological . . . y'know . . . that self-esteem for kids is a terrible thing when the self-esteem is created in the way they're gonna create it, and when we're gonna go in opposition to a label . . . a title . . . ah . . . a slogan . . . that's as warm and fuzzy as this one—'mental health for children,' for goodness' sake—I just don't see how we're gonna win against somethin' that will sound to everybody so . . . well . . . so doggone *good.* Y'know what I mean, ma'am? I know I didn't say it too well, but do y'know what I mean?"

Rebecca, approaching the detective from behind his chair as part of her regular pathway around and through the room, stopped and placed a hand on his shoulder. He looked up at her. Smiling down at him, she shook her head. "No, Detective. Actually, I don't mean we ought to try to teach some-thing so . . . so counterintuitive . . . as this certainly is, by means of the media. I mean that we should make it possible for the media to expose this evil's *modus operandi.*

"We can begin to teach the horror of this particular self-esteem concept . . . this subversion of the moral law and its ethical superstructure . . . by letting the public see what these vicious human beings are truly like . . . by introducing these horrible people, stripped of their disguises, to the public . . . by demonstrating not just to Christians everywhere, but to *everybody* everywhere, that these people are ghastly, beastly creatures doing ghastly, beastly things . . . stopping at nothing . . . stopping at absolutely nothing. . . .

"We can, I think, most effectively lead people to question the MMHCC's main theme, a theme that does have, I agree, a certain subtlety to it, by showing people exactly who this theme's chief advocate actually is. Dr. Stafford and his minions will do the hard work for us just by continuing to be themselves."

Rebecca continued to stand completely still, her hand resting lightly on the detective's shoulder. The room was silent now. Suddenly Rebecca seemed to awaken. She turned to face Eleanor Chapel.

"Dr. Chapel," she said. "You have thoughts for us, I believe?"

The small, studious face looked up in surprise, the bright eyes dancing even in the weak artificial light of Sid Belton's dusty quarters. "Why, yes . . . actually, I do. I think the idea is perfect, Rebecca. And the more I think on it, the more I think it is, when you consider the whole problem, the *only* idea. We mightn't be able to get the attention of the regular news media so quickly. But when I consider the Christian media . . .

"As I've sat here thinking," she continued, "three editors' names have already popped into my mind. I would trust each of them completely . . . I would trust each, in fact, with my life, which is a good thing, it would appear. And I could get in touch with any one of them tomorrow." She glanced at the detective's clock and corrected herself. "I mean . . . today."

Luke sat forward. "Rebecca . . . do you think this session coming up on Friday in Oxford . . . what state is it, Detective? Maryland? Do you think this Friday session that Matt has uncovered offers a chance to get at the thing you've proposed? Or is it too soon? Would we need more time?"

The detective glanced up at Rebecca, saw her turn the question over to him with a nod of her head, and replied, the lopsided grin again materializing and then widening as he spoke, "Well . . . those MMHCC folks aren't gonna sit down with a Christian editor or reporter and tell 'em all about how ruthless and rotten and violent they are. The thing we'd need would be a way to arrange for an editor to have a look at some of the files the kid just examined over at the bookstore. And if the kid's right about all this, those very documents are gonna be on their way tomorrow to Maryland, and are gonna be there for maybe a full day before the Friday conference gets underway.

"So, Luke, seems to me that we might be able to come up with a way to get a Christian editor or reporter face-to-face with some of those documents while the files are down there in Oxford." He nodded his head thoughtfully. "I like it, Luke. Seems to me we've got a lot better chance to get to those files while they're in some temporary small-town storage place or hotel room than up in that second floor vault on 130th Street.

"Let me get some information from the sheriff down in Easton, Maryland. I've worked with him before. He's a fine constable—a good man."

After another moment, with Rebecca still standing quietly at his side, Belton began to propose next steps. He suggested that they rendezvous again the following night, Wednesday, at eleven o'clock, there in his apartment. In the intervening hours, he continued, Matt would go forward as planned with his Texas trip, leaving by charter at noon that same day—

Tuesday—and returning to LaGuardia around midnight, as scheduled. Eleanor Chapel would select one of her editor friends and begin arrangements for the editor or a top reporter to join them on Thursday in Maryland. And the detective himself would find out all he could about the MMHCC's Oxford arrangements. Thus, Belton observed, in the Wednesday night session, nearly forty-eight hours away, Matt could enlighten them further about the MMHCC's Texas strategies. Eleanor Chapel could report on the success of her media arrangements. And Belton could provide an analysis of the logistical and security plans that were being put into place in the town of Oxford.

"And what about us, Detective?" asked Luke Manguson. "What can Rebecca and I begin to work on between now and tomorrow night?"

The detective's face changed. He stood and turned to Rebecca, looking grimly up into her face as he replied to her brother. "You can stay alive, son. I'm sure as I can be that Rebecca's death is an MMHCC objective in itself. Their brothers-in-crime tried to kill her last year in Wales. And you said that guy chasin' her this morning had a knife the size of the Empire State Building. Get her in your new hotel room tonight and keep her there for the next forty-five hours. She's by now just one thing to these people, and one thing only. She's a target. A target for murder. I want you both here in one piece Wednesday night."

Then he looked away from Rebecca to address the whole group. "I'm gonna phone for taxis in a few minutes. I'm gonna have 'em come to the 150th Street alleyway instead of to the front entrance on 151st. We'll go out the back way, through the alley. Use the same alleyway to get here tomorrow night."

On that somber note, the meeting dissolved and phone numbers were exchanged, the two young men, their military habits still strong in them, committing the numbers to memory rather than recording them in writing. Eleanor Chapel agreed to telephone the detective at eleven o'clock that morning to report on her preliminary success, or not, with the editors whom she was to contact. While the detective went to his bedroom to call for the taxis, Luke and Eleanor Chapel engaged each other studiously, so as to allow Rebecca and Matt a moment for a private good-bye. Matt was not altogether sure he wanted one, but it was obvious that Rebecca intended to speak to him before they left the apartment. He took a deep breath and followed her into the kitchen.

She faced him quickly, standing close, but not touching him, and looking up into his eyes. Her expression was enigmatic, her voice flat. "Matt," she said, "I am still badly disturbed by what you said to me Friday night. I can only hope that what happened to you in your room Monday morning has shaken you in the core of your soul. God came to you and ripped you away from something that had you in its talons and would have devoured you. And still might.

"Our relationship, yours and mine, is of *no* importance in comparison to that, or in comparison to the visions we have been given. But . . ."

Here she looked down. When she looked up again, her face and voice had changed. He actually thought he could read love in her eyes. It was more than just her beauty. She could transmit the universe to him with her eyes and with the expression on her face. He needed no words from her to know what she was thinking and feeling about him. That was how it had been from the first.

"Matt," she began again, "when I look at you, and . . . don't misunderstand this . . . when I look at your shoulder and arm and hand . . ." and here her eyes followed her words and traced the length of the atrophied left limb, "I feel a oneness with you that I've never felt with anyone else. Even with my family.

"And please be clear. It isn't pity. It's a statement of a fact that transforms whatever our relationship might otherwise have been. That night in Wales we saved each other. *Your life for mine. My life for yours.* God was present with us on that spot. Neither of us could have saved the other's life, had not God saved us both from what we faced.

"And so, my dear"—at those words, and at the smile that accompanied them, Matt felt his knees weaken—"I am convinced that we are expected to explore a meaningful . . . yes . . . romantic relationship with each other. And so we shall. But Matt, you have seen the faces that evil can wear. And you have seen that some of those faces come in the guise of kind, helpful, solicitous mentors. You are about to spend the better part of a day with some of the worst people on earth, each one of whom commands widespread respect throughout your country and in some cases beyond. Be ready for them, Matt.

"And when you get back, be ready for me." She stepped to him, raised herself on tiptoe, and kissed him just to one side of his mouth as he stood motionless, dumbfounded, and thrilled. His heart thudded against his ribs with such force that he felt certain she could actually hear it. She reached up, placed a hand on his cheek for a moment, and then left the kitchen.

Five minutes later, he watched her step into a taxi with her brother and Eleanor Chapel. They would ride together, since Dr. Chapel lived north of the detective's apartment, and the twins' new hotel was near her flat. He watched their taxi turn north at the end of the block and then he moved to step into his own. "Good night, Detective," he said. "Thank you for letting me come tonight."

"Sleep fast, kid," Belton replied. "You got another big day comin'."

Matt sat down wearily on the rear seat of the taxi and opened his window. He chatted with the detective for a moment more, and then, at a word from Sid Belton, the taxi pulled away from the curb. Matt turned around and waved.

As they approached the corner, he looked to the right and froze. His eyes widened. He saw a gray limousine racing toward the intersection. Recognition instantly consumed him. The limousine, moving at right angles to the taxi, screamed straight for their front bumper. Lurching and braking, tires squealing, the ungainly vehicle came skidding to a halt inches from the front of the taxi, completely blocking their exit from 150th Street. The doors of the limousine began to open. Shapes began to emerge.

Matt had but one immediate thought. "You've missed her, you miserable devils. You've missed her again."

Chapter Seven

HE KNEW THAT HIS EYES WERE CLOSED, THAT HIS EARS WERE open, that his head hurt, and that he was seated uncomfortably in a metal chair. Those things he knew right away. As consciousness began to return more fully, he found he knew also that he was slumped forward, his chin actually resting on his muscular chest, and that he was bound somehow to the chair in which he sat. And he knew that there was something peculiar about the sounds that came to him.

The sounds were those of voices, yes, but they seemed to reach his ears as echoes, as though they traveled through and over cavernous distances and confines to find him. Further, though he knew the sounds formed themselves into groupings of words, and though he sensed the language was his own, nothing was intelligible to his brain. He seemed to lie awash in a vast and profoundly alien sea of incoherence.

Then a memory began to form itself, and, as it did, the pain from his headache increased abruptly. Yes. He remembered. The gray limousine screeching to a stop in front of his taxi. Men running toward him from the limousine. Handguns glinting under the street lamps. An automatic rifle or machine gun visible in the dim background. Rough hands pulling at him. A blow to the head from something heavy and metallic. Then, while he lay on the asphalt, some sort of cloth quickly covering his face and a cloying, medicinal scent infiltrating his nostrils and respiratory system. Then the plunging, inevitable onset of blackness.

And now this.

"Hey! This guy's comin' around." The low, male voice was raspy and close. "Want me to put 'im out again?"

A murmured response from the void.

The sound of footsteps, several men. Now coming closer. Whispered conversations, near or far from him . . . he could not determine.

Then nothing. Renewed silence in his immediate surround. Distant murmuring again reverberating through and around him, unintelligible.

And now his head cleared further, and yet again the headache increased in its severity. He found he could answer none of the questions that swarmed through his mind. Where was he? Who had attacked and captured him? Was he hurt and how badly? How serious was the danger? What options did he have? How could he escape? And, if no escape could be attempted, how could he prepare for . . . for what?

He tried to lift his head from his chest and found that he could not. There seemed no strength in him. After a moment, he resumed his efforts to induce his brain to function, even if his muscles refused.

And somehow, to his surprise, a curtain parted and, in a flash of clarity, he was suddenly, miraculously lucid. The headache paused in its escalation, then began to diminish. True, he found that he still could not answer the array of questions that continued to pour through his mind. But, in this abrupt clarity, he knew also that this did not mean there could be no response to them. And so he reached immediately back to the session in the detective's apartment, perhaps just several hours earlier. Or could it have been twenty-four hours? Or forty-eight? Or several days? He shook his head and reminded himself that he had not merely been rendered unconscious by blows to the head; he had certainly been drugged, as well, and no doubt repeatedly. Any conceivable length of time might have passed since those hours in the detective's apartment.

After a moment's thought, he turned his head to the right and shrugged his right shoulder upward. He scraped his stubble of beard against his knit-shirted shoulder and guessed from the whiskers' length and texture that his Monday morning shave was closer to forty-eight hours previous than twenty-four or seventy-two. And that suggested that the session in Belton's apartment might have transpired the previous night and early morning, and that the present moment was—at least more likely than not—the small hours of Wednesday morning.

No matter. He was seeing and hearing in his mind Rebecca Manguson. She was striding again through the small living room, answering in advance the very questions he now asked himself. Who? The *ancient*

Enemy, she had said. How serious? Physically violent *whenever* it might suit them, she had asserted.

Yes. The same people who had kidnapped his parents the previous summer . . . who certainly would have killed his mother and father if not for Sid Belton's astonishing rescue of them . . . the same people who then had intended to corrupt the faith by such ingenious means . . . and who now intended to corrupt the children by coming at them from the other side of the mountain . . . from the undefended side of the battlement . . . *Those* people.

Yes, some of their leaders were dead or incarcerated, but what did that matter? This was the *ancient* Enemy.

There would never be any shortage of human beings eager to enact some particular program of hellish destruction. Of course not. And that being the case, he noted ruefully, most of the questions he had just asked himself were unimportant, unanswerable, or both.

But what of that final question? If no escape could be attempted, how should he prepare? And then came the answer to that, also. His eyes suddenly fluttered open, although his chin continued to loll heavily against his chest. In that position, looking straight down at himself, he saw, though his vision remained strangely unfocused, the shape of the petite *New Testament* that had remained firmly lodged, throughout the fracas, in his left breast pocket.

Yes, there was an answer to that final question. The answer had presented itself to him in the bookstore, as soon as he had purchased the small volume and seated himself. There, his eyes had fallen almost immediately on words from the twenty-first chapter of Luke's Gospel. *You will be brought before kings and governors, and all on account of my name . . . make up your mind not to worry beforehand . . . For I will give you words and wisdom. . . .*

And then slowly, reluctantly, yet inevitably, his eyes closed themselves again. As consciousness left him once more, there rose a stirring, a warmth, a comfort deep inside him. And, in what seemed both warning and benediction, rising inexorably from the heart of this interior movement, an initially indistinct form shaped itself within his dreaming mind into a huge, looming iron cross, formidable, overarching, reassuring, threatening. . . .

The emerging dream proceeded quickly to transform itself . . . the enormous cross faded and in its place there came an unsettling blend of fantasy and memory. Through his own eyes, he saw, just as he had lived, a year earlier, Rebecca and himself moving away from the doorway of the massive Welsh cathedral during a pause in the violence of the midnight storm. Through his own eyes, he saw, just as he had lived, the two of them staring across the cathedral grounds and directly into the face of the Enemy. Through his own eyes, he saw Rebecca and himself turn in response to race in the direction opposite, flying on foot over walls and through narrow streets and down open roadways, sprinting through the darkness toward the cliffs that towered over the surf hundreds of feet below them. Through his own eyes, he saw in his dream that which he could not have seen in reality as he had pounded over the rocky ground in Rebecca's wake, placing himself between her and their pursuers. And that sight—that which he could never have observed in reality—was the sight of rapid-fire muzzle flashes in the darkness, each flash signaling the explosive launch of clusters of large-calibre rifle projectiles, each individual bullet intended specifically for Rebecca. And now he saw what he had then only felt in the instant before unconsciousness: one hollow-point automatic-rifle round after another slamming into his left upper back and shoulder and arm.

And he then saw in his dream that which he also could not possibly have viewed before: himself, Matthew Clark, unconscious, his life's blood coursing into the seams in the Pembrokeshire granite, while, in the midnight distance, the madman screamed imprecations toward them through the deafening crashes of continuously descending thunderbolts, his mighty weapon held at the vertical, high above his head, the barrel pointed directly toward the eye of the menacing cloud that swirled above them . . .

And through his own eyes, he now saw in his dream, magnified dozens of times, the detail of the madman's face as he called upon every devil in hell to destroy them both. And finally, as the dream mercifully began to deteriorate, he saw that by degrees the face began slowly to transform itself until, as he watched in horror, it was no longer that of the Pembrokeshire madman at all. It had become, in fact, a face that was intimately familiar to him . . . a face almost as familiar to him as his own.

Matt awakened suddenly to a harsh pressure on his right shoulder, and immediately he opened his eyes and snapped his head up, muscles surging against their prolonged lassitude. And there, sitting before him on a high stool, Cameron Stafford leered drunkenly at him. The scholar leaned precariously forward, prodding Matt roughly with the hooked end of an iron crowbar. Matt stared at the ghastly countenance, scarcely able to believe what he saw.

Stafford's face, while unquestionably his own, had dramatically changed. The eyes were deeply bloodshot, their latticework of veins so thick that little of the whites of his eyes was visible. The handsome, sharply defined features appeared horribly distorted, bloated and distended. A stubble of mostly gray beard cluttered the hideous visage. Saliva crept unchecked from one corner of the sneering mouth.

Stafford was wearing some sort of dark leather jacket despite the June heat. His breath reeked of alcohol . . . no . . . of something else . . . something acidic . . . toxic . . . nauseating . . . And then the apparition spoke, its voice unnatural, a croaking whisper. "Where is she?" it said. *"Tell me where she is."*

Then Matt saw that they were not alone. They were in some narrowly confined space, yet there seemed to be a number of people in the room, crowded around the two of them as they sat facing each other at close range.

For a second time, the black crowbar thudded into his shoulder. "I said, *where is she? Tell me where she is."* The voice was frighteningly otherworldly, rank and coarse.

Curiously, the question raced through Matt's mind as to whether or not Stafford had, in fact, made the Texas trip. If this were indeed Wednesday morning, Stafford could have completed his flights and arrived back in New York several hours earlier, assuming the original schedule had been kept. But could the man have transformed his appearance—no, more than his appearance—from the condition in which he must have presented himself in Texas to . . . to . . . *this* . . . in just hours? The thing seemed impossible.

And then those thoughts fled and somehow words came to him, and he spoke them without processing them in advance, surprised at the confidence in his voice and at the fluency of his statements. "Rebecca has protection, sir. She is protected from you. If you and your . . . your forces . . . could possibly get her, you would have been permitted to do so long before now. She is chosen, Dr. Stafford. She is, quite simply, chosen. I do not think that Almighty God will allow you to get at her."

Matt paused and then continued. "Or, if He does, I think it will be on His terms and in His own time, not yours."

Stafford's face flushed crimson. He stood, drew the crowbar back behind his head, and initiated an overhead swing designed to crush Matthew Clark's skull, to split his cranium down its exact center. Matt called upon his right arm to block the assault, but his constraints bound him, preventing the movement. He saw in an instant that Stafford's blow would fall unobstructed. He watched the iron implement reach its apogee and begin its descent. He seemed to observe the weapon's approach dispassionately, even analytically, and so he saw that, as the crowbar moved downward, not one but several hands reached from the side and from behind the enraged professor, bringing the crowbar's movement to a fumbling, confused halt, just inches from its target. The iron bar, wrenched from Stafford's grasp, clattered loudly to the raw cement floor at Matt's feet.

A confusion of rough breathing and noisy scuffling ensued. This quickly subsided as the men who had disarmed their leader faded back into Matt's periphery, leaving Cameron Stafford once again front and center. As the others moved back and to each side, an uncertain silence grew slowly, punctuated only by Stafford's fitful mutterings and scoldings, his furious, blood-engorged eyes moving around the room and then back to his captive.

Matt stared into his mentor's face. It seemed ready to explode in rage and frustration, but he saw at the same time another man's face in profile, whispering into Stafford's ear, while others' hands now seemed to be moving him gently, slowly away from Matt. And then, uttering unintelligible oaths, Stafford was led off to the side of Matt's field of vision, and apparently out of the small room. After several seconds of quiet shuffling and maneuvering, the room had emptied itself except for Matt and the whisperer.

The man, youthful and slender, clad in a dark pinstriped suit, pale blue shirt, and yellow silk tie marked by a subtle diagonal pattern, looked fresh and meticulously pressed and dressed. The man watched the silent knot of observers departing the room behind Cameron Stafford, then sighed audibly and sat down on Stafford's vacated stool. After a moment, he turned his head and looked fully and forthrightly into Matt's eyes, not unkindly, perhaps entertaining some speculation about the captive's state of mind after so harrowing a moment.

The face was narrow and angular, with high forehead and disarmingly soft eyes, rich brown in color. The impression given was that of precise intellect mixed with a generous, natural compassion and courtesy. After yet another moment, he smiled at Matt, then turned and looked once more in the direction of the retreating throng. Then he turned again to Matt and shook his head slowly.

"I am truly sorry you had to deal with that, Mr. Clark. Dr. Stafford has his spells now and then, and all we can do when they come is minister to him until he feels better. I knew he'd been drinking this evening . . . this morning . . . but had no idea he might turn violent. Please accept my apology on his behalf. I've no question he will want to deliver an apology in person, once he's able."

The young man leaned forward solicitously. "How are you feeling? Can I get you anything?"

Matt shook his head.

"But you'll let me know if I can?"

Matt said nothing.

"Well," the man resumed, "I can certainly understand your reticence. But, please, allow me to introduce myself. I'm Edward Jamieson. I've been involved in the MMHCC project almost from the first, but I have not often been here, in New York, and I do not as yet know Dr. Stafford as well as most of the others do.

"Again, I must apologize for everything that just transpired."

Jamieson rose from the stool and strode away from Matt, turning again to face him from one corner of the cramped, unappointed room. He looked down, cleared his throat, and began what was clearly to be a difficult statement.

"I want to speak plainly, Mr. Clark. We certainly owe you at least that. And in that spirit . . . I must ask you to consider . . . if only for a moment . . . how Rebecca Manguson, her brother, and, yes, even you and Detective Belton must of necessity appear through the eyes of the MMHCC leadership." He paused, looked down, and then up again, engaging Matt's brown eyes with his own, a gentleness and sympathy both in his expression and in his soft voice.

"Through our eyes, although doubtless not at all through your own, you and Rebecca . . . and the others . . . are, directly or indirectly, responsible for the deaths, last summer, of at least four of our colleagues in England."

He paused again.

"Can you appreciate *that* perspective, Mr. Clark, even a little?"

At this unabashed confession of the heretofore merely assumed linkage between the previous year's attack on Christianity itself and this year's public-education-focused assault, Matt sat up straighter in his chair, now more aware than before of the physical constraints that held him roughly in position. And then he heard his response . . . immediate, dispassionate, unflinching. "If you mean by that that four men lost their lives a year ago before they were able to complete their murderous agenda, and that Rebecca and I had been among their targets, I find I can appreciate that perspective without difficulty, Mr. Jamieson."

The young man smiled, nodded, then turned and walked thoughtfully across the front of the small room to the corner opposite. Once there, he turned again and faced Matt. His smile now grave, he spoke again. "You and I are Christians, Mr. Clark. Yes. Members of the Body of Christ. *Christians*, both of us."

He paused and dropped his eyes, seeming to lose himself in a closely held reflection. Without engaging Matt's eyes again, still looking down and away from the prisoner, he spoke again, choosing his words with great care.

"You and I are Christians, as is, of course, Dr. Stafford himself. And we are, therefore, as Christians, required to look at the world in a certain way."

Jamieson paused again, looked up at Matt, then down again. He sighed deeply, squared his shoulders, and resumed.

"The MMHCC project, while nominally grounded in educational psychological research, is, if you'll consider it rightly, a Christianity-rooted endeavor, from start to finish. Yes. Christianity-rooted. And so there is some irony—in addition to great tragedy—in our being forced into a position that is actually opposed by Rebecca Manguson, or by you, yourself, Mr. Clark, or—perhaps most ironic and most tragic of all—by Dr. Eleanor Chapel.

"One simply cannot responsibly argue that a project designed to build reading skills and self-esteem in children is somehow diabolical, Mr. Clark. The notion is too fantastic even to be entertained seriously by thoughtful individuals. You, of all people, must know that. You've been successful in your lifetime, quite obviously, as a student, as a leader, and now—or, at least, until quite recently—as one of the bright stars in a project of immense value to the nation and, eventually, to and for the entire human race. You've experienced personally the research-derived truth of this project: that as your own self-esteem was built stronger and higher, stone by stone, so grew, stronger and higher, your academic and leadership successes. The relationship between the two, encapsulated in your own personal and professional history, is simply self-evident. There is no need, really, for educational and psychological research to establish something that is so clear from one's personal, *direct* experience.

"Please! Please, Mr. Clark. Please do not allow your . . . your infatuation with a marvelously talented and beautiful woman, however deeply felt, to cloud your theological and ethical capacity to judge correctly . . . not now . . . not ever.

"A career awaits you. First, in the MMHCC itself. And then in the field of your choice, Matt: politics, education, government service, the private sector. You can name your field. You can write your position description. You can pencil in your own salary and perquisites. It all awaits you . . . and Rebecca, as well, if she wishes . . . if you'll simply accept the transparent validity of this project . . . a validity which is, if you'll just come to think of it from a common sense perspective, virtually *prima facie.*"

He smiled. "This does not need to be *so hard*, Matt. Really. It doesn't."

While he had been speaking this last, Jamieson had been advancing in small, almost imperceptible steps toward Matt's chair. And as he proceeded, he had gradually lowered the volume of his speech until, when he concluded, he was so near to Matt as actually to whisper the final words. And so now he stood over the prisoner, smiling compassionately, and in a gesture intended to underscore and reinforce the generosity of his words, he reached out and touched Matt's good shoulder with a gentle hand.

And in that position, he awaited a reply.

Matt did not keep him waiting.

Shrugging the young man's hand from his shoulder, Matt looked up fiercely into the smiling face, his eyes hard. "You've just recited my 'direct experience,' Mr. Jamieson. I might ask you this. In what condition do you think my well-educated soul was, just one year ago? What do you suppose my priorities were then? Do you think Christianity had any role at all in my goals and hopes and plans?

"And what evidence have you that, had my education and leadership development been grounded in something quite different . . . grounded, let's say, in the conviction that I was a child of God . . . grounded in the conviction that my 'self-esteem' was a product of that very fact, and of no other . . . grounded in the conviction that I should therefore conceive my life's work as *vocation* . . . What evidence have you that, had that been the case, my intellectual and leadership development would not have been *at least* the equal of everything you now propose to claim for it?"

Matt paused. He found himself breathing heavily and became aware that he had begun, while speaking, to push forward heavily against his restraints.

He also realized that Jamieson, who now struck Matt as a much smaller man than he had at first perceived him to be, had begun a hasty retreat, a look of surprise and acute disappointment on his face, and had by now shuffled backward all the way into the corner from which he had begun his cautious advance just moments before. Seconds passed, both men silent, each staring hard at the other.

And suddenly Matt continued, jaw muscles rippling under the skin of his tense face, his speech now exhibiting a controlled fury that, both for him and for his listener, was wholly unexpected. "You've introduced yourself as Edward Jamieson. Who are you, Mr. Jamieson? You pose as my friend and confidant, politely noting the irrationality of my opposition to your alleged *children's reading* project . . . a project with colossal financial and political rewards for all involved . . . a project in which the actual ends—eradication of the moral law, elimination of all innate conception of right and wrong, reduction of all commitment to, or even awareness of, the notion of 'objective value' in the minds of the country's and the world's children—are so encompassing that they readily justify whatever means you and your colleagues find it convenient to imagine: fraud, extortion, bribery, and it goes without saying, violence . . . some of that violence, such as that in which you engage at this very moment, in this very room, linked obviously to your damnable goals . . . and some of it, as we saw last summer, simply and monstrously gratuitous."

Matt hardly knew what he had just said, but he knew that he had spoken truth and that his adversary seemed unable or unwilling to attempt an answer. And so, he found himself continuing, his voice rising, his words coming faster and faster, now tumbling over each other in their eagerness to be spoken. "What do you say for yourself, Mr. Jamieson, other than to assert what you claim to be your 'Christianity' and the righteousness of your 'self-esteem' project? What do you say for yourself to excuse the violence your colleagues attempted against my family and others a year ago in England?

"Your theory is ludicrous. Your methods are unspeakable. Your long-term goals are diabolical. And so I ask again, Mr. Jamieson. *Who are you?*"

Jamieson's youthful face had gradually altered itself while Matt spoke these last words. Even as he hovered uncertainly in the corner before his outraged captive, for the moment unable to formulate a response to the mountain of accusation, Jamieson's empathic smile had been replaced in small increments by what could only be deemed a snarl. And now, after several moments of silence, he spoke, having first crossed his arms in front of his chest. Matt noted that he chose to ignore the counterargument entirely, addressing himself to Matt's concluding question, and to that only.

"Who am I?" he began slowly, his face now contorted in fresh anger.

Matt watched while Jamieson turned, his arms still crossed, his face twisting itself in grotesque response to mounting fury, and began to prowl menacingly, the uncertainty now gone, across the front of the cubicle, eyes on the concrete floor. "Who am I?" he said again, very softly, nearly whispering to himself.

And suddenly he wheeled toward Matt and covered the short distance between them in four long, rapid strides. He halted in front of the captive, and uncrossing his arms, bent toward him, placing his hands on his knees.

In the tense silence, Jamieson moved his face closer, and then still closer, to Matt's. As the distance between the two faces diminished gradually to mere inches, Jamieson's brown eyes began to widen, and then to widen still further, until the dark orbs were at length surrounded completely, above and below, by white. At the same time the snarling upper lip curled higher to reveal fully an upper row of bright teeth, incisors now exposed as enamel daggers that seemed to Matt more fang than tooth. And Matt saw that the face before him, in its concentrated rage, evinced none of the distortion and distension that had so dominated Cameron Stafford's engorged countenance as it had presented itself to him just moments earlier in the same room.

Yet this face showed the greater Evil. It was Evil more elegantly rendered. It was Evil somehow less contaminated by goodness in any form. And hatred bespoke itself in every contour, in every nuance. And it said nothing.

It simply exhaled foully into Matt's protesting nostrils, filling them with an odor indescribable, one simultaneously repellant and curiously seductive, as though the scent itself communicated an evil that bore the capacity to turn even Satan into an object as desirable to Matthew Clark as was Rebecca Manguson herself. His mind reeled. He tried to shut his eyes and could not. He tried to turn his face away and could not. He brought his right hand and arm up hard against the constraints, to no avail.

And then he felt the impossible. He felt a weight—invisible and irresistible—beginning to build on his head and shoulders. He knew "nothing" was there, and yet the force mounted in implacable defiance of its own impossibility. His head began to drop perceptibly toward his chest, although his eyes remained irretrievably locked into Jamieson's, his nostrils filling themselves over and over with the disgusting, arresting scent that spewed from the twisted and quivering mouth.

Sweat burst from pores all over Matt's body, and he sensed the perspiration beginning to trickle from his forehead, his neck, his arms, his torso. He groaned involuntarily against the supernatural weight that bore relentlessly down, knowing somehow that his puny muscular resistance would be of no consequence, that he would be driven gradually down and down into the insubstantial chair in which he sat, and then . . . who could know? Then down into a crumpled and intermingled pillar of blood, muscle and metal. And then an image flashed through his brain.

As the rapidly increasing weight upon his head and shoulders grew swiftly to intolerable proportion, and while his eyes remained fixed, unblinking, on the fiendish orbs that transfixed him, the image returned to him of Rebecca, a year previous, pounded into the floor in her Enemy's sanctuary, helpless to resist the inevitable . . . until she had spoken.

And grasping in his soul the imperative, Matt held Rebecca's image before his mind's eye and forced himself to speak. His voice strained against the whole-body muscular effort . . . strained to fight through the vocal paralysis that gripped him . . . strained against the mixture of stench and aroma that poured into his nose, mouth, and lungs from his adversary's wet exhalations. And Matt heard his own voice indistinctly, a frail, wheedling cry against the roar of freight trains passing within inches of his soul: *"Father . . . help me! Father, Father . . . help me! Father . . . please . . ."*

And instantly, without Matt's being able to sense how it had happened, his eyes dropped freely from the hypnotic violence of Jamieson's ferocious stare. In the same instant, the invisible, insufferable weight flew from his head and shoulders. And he found himself gasping in breathless relief at the sudden and blessed freedom from burning eyes, from crushing weight, and from consuming odor that had saturated every muscle, every nerve.

Eyes now gratefully closed, head down, chin once more resting on his chest, Matt drew one long, relief-filled breath after another, as though he had finally surfaced after long minutes of watery submersion. And as his breathing gradually restored itself, he became aware of a fresh quietness in the room. Raising his head cautiously, Matt opened his eyes. He saw that Edward Jamieson stood now in the corner from whence he had advanced upon Matt just seconds—or had it been minutes—before. And now Matt heard again the alien voice, seeming to come toward him from a great distance.

"Who am I, Mr. Clark?" he was once more saying slowly, his voice now hardly louder than the whisper with which he had earlier intoned the question. "Who am I?"

And now he smiled . . . a hatred-laden smile hardly distinguishable from the snarl that had displayed itself earlier. "I am your *nightmare*, Mr. Clark."

He leaned slightly forward, rocking onto the balls of his feet, his voice returning again to its sinister whisper. *"And . . . perhaps of even greater interest to you . . . I am soon to become Miss Manguson's nightmare, as well."*

He paused, leering, and then continued, his voice still a whisper. *"Though you will not live to see it, we will have her killed publicly, Mr. Clark. . . . Yes. . . . If she lives long enough, and she may or may not live long enough, we will execute her before tens of thousands of pathetically helpless faces . . . And that is all you need to know about me, Mr. Clark. The rest will become clear . . . and sooner than you will like."*

He then turned his head and appeared to listen for a moment. Then he returned his eyes to Matt's, smiled again, and said simply, "What do you suppose those sounds might be, Mr. Clark?"

And Matt became newly aware of muffled noises, indistinct echoes that perhaps had been knocking for admission to his awareness for several minutes. As before, the sounds seemed to travel over large, enclosed distances, reverberating off of high walls and roofs, following convoluted pathways to the two listeners' ears. And then he knew. These were the sounds of a person being beaten to death . . . crushing, horrifying blows administered by rod, staff, and fist. The percussive thuds, at times followed by guttural groans, and twice punctuated by garbled but defiant shouts, told Matt two things immediately.

First, that Sid Belton had been captured, too.

And second, that the method of torture and execution selected for the detective had already been the method chosen, as well, for Matthew Clark.

He then endured thirty minutes of solitude, a half hour that moved past him in slow motion. Edward Jamieson had left him quickly after their exchange, doubtless to encourage Matt thoughtfully to consider his future while listening to the remote sounds of Sid Belton's murder by bludgeon. As the excruciating minutes passed, seemingly interminable, Matt had heard the detective repeat his shouted challenge to his torturers only once. After that, not only were there no more shouts, but even the detective's unwilling, semiconscious groans had become gradually less frequent and less audible to Matt. And for at least the last ten minutes, Matt had in fact heard nothing other than the sound of the endlessly repeating, stunningly heavy blows as they fell uninterrupted on the detective's small, defenseless body. The sickening force of the blows put him strangely in mind of an occasion, while still an undergraduate in college, on which he had stood and watched draft horses—Clydesdales or Percherons, he could not remember which—being led to their stables at a horse farm near Charlottesville. He still remembered how the pavement had trembled under the thudding impact of their hooves. Now, some quality in the incessant drumbeat against Sid Belton's senseless form put Matt in mind of that experience. But the draft horses' rolling, driving gait had been glorious . . . awe-inspiring as a demonstration of mammalian size, strength, power, and uncorrupted service to a Creator whose design they fulfilled faithfully. This, by way of absolute contrast, was sickening . . . brute force pummeling and battering a helpless blood-and-bone-and-brain creature until nothing remained of it.

Matt tried to pray and, to his surprise, found that he could. Almost as soon as he began, in fact, the thought was given him that Christ's promise—to give him the words he would need at the time that he would need them—was not limited to face-to-face exchanges of the sort he had just endured with Edward Jamieson, but could apply equally to the solitary act of prayer. And so he prayed, enveloped in a strange, palpably fortifying, comfortingly layered certainty that God both prompted and received this prayer.

And in this utterly unfamiliar state—exhausted beyond measure and yet supernaturally alert, choking against the looming terror that now stalked him and yet bathed in the glory of the Holy Spirit's transcendent but immanent presence—Matt Clark prayed for Sid Belton's body and soul, knowing that both lay in God's hands and in no other's. He found himself praying in a sort of desperate, hopeful excitement, certain that the words were received, simply because they had been demanded.

And when the blows finally became less frequent and, at length, stopped altogether, he was not surprised at their cessation. Yet, at the same time, he found that he had no confidence within him that the detective still lived. The command had been to pray for Sid Belton's body and soul, and Matt's prayer had simply asked for eternity . . . eternity for Sid Belton's body . . . and eternity for Sid Belton's soul.

And now he sighed deeply, his eyes still closed.

After a lengthy, peace-filled prayer of simple gratitude for prayer itself, he turned unashamedly, in a still-persisting golden clarity, to Matt Clark, and prayed earnestly for himself, although not on his own behalf. He prayed rather that God would give him the strength to fight if he could, to die if he must, but, above all, to reveal nothing, to compromise nothing, to put no one at new risk. The intensity of his prayer astonished him, and he found that his confidence rose and then soared into an emotional certainty that the Almighty would stand with him in life, in death, and in unequivocal fact, beyond each.

And so, for long minutes, Matt found himself absorbed completely in prayer the depth and height of which he had never before experienced . . . and coursing through his mind and spirit came the refrain, in background and in foreground, simultaneously consuming his mind and uplifting his soul: *My life for theirs . . . my life for theirs . . . for Mr. Belton . . . and for Rebecca . . . and for Luke . . . and for Dr. Chapel . . . please . . . please, Father . . . my life for theirs. . . .*

And then at length—he knew not how long he had prayed thus, motionless in the metal chair—he opened his eyes and ears and tried to grasp something about his surround. He saw only the dirty wall opposite him. And he at first heard nothing.

But in seconds he began to hear distant sounds, their meaning uncertain to him. Metallic scrapings over cement flooring . . . a diesel engine, deep and throaty, coughing to life, and then dying away . . . the faint mutterings of coarse men . . . a variety of other noises that, though unidentifiable, added to the impression of a busy, if hostile, environment, and one that brought men, machines, and, assuredly, weapons of many kinds, increasingly near to him. And a shudder ran downward through him, this time specifically from his throat to his abdomen. He tensed. He knew with utter certainty that they were coming to him now. It was now to be his turn.

He was to be tested, tortured, beaten, executed. This was to be the way in which death would come to him . . . death . . . after fewer than three decades of living . . . death in a small, unadorned, filthy enclosure with floors of cold cement . . . his body, momentarily still alive but soon to become a dead body, sitting in a plain folding chair, his limbs and torso encased in bindings of some sort . . . the enclosure, the bindings, his body soon to be the scenes of crude violence . . . and then, once the violence at length began, this enclosure, these bindings, this body—all three—to be covered gradually with the detritus of slow, tortuous death: not just his blood, but, also to be spattered throughout this hideous space, bits and pieces of hair and bone from his skull, shreds of clothing and skin from all over his body, fragments of his teeth, slivers of his fingernails . . .

And suddenly fear leapt into his brain and, like a small explosion, scattered in all directions every vestige of that holy confidence—that blessed certainty—that had so thoroughly inspirited him during his desperate prayers for the detective and for the courage to sacrifice himself for his friends. But this time . . . this time when the counterattack arrived he was not unprepared. He found that, for the first time, he was able to greet the onslaught of fear and doubt less as the outcome of *ambuscade* by superior and irresistible force than simply as the arrival of old acquaintance, at once familiar, completely unwelcome, and yet fully expected. And so he steadfastly refused to immerse himself in the fear that so determinedly sought to overwhelm him.

Yes, pain was coming. Certainly, torture was at the door. And of course, death stood just behind both.

No matter. He knew the Truth. He knew what obedience to that Truth would require of him. And so he fixed his mind first on his Creator and Redeemer, then on the faces of his friends, and finally on the Enemy and what that Enemy sought to do . . . to him, to Rebecca, to the children everywhere. . . . And in that attitude he waited, knowing that, whatever else might occur, there were no more decisions for Matt Clark to make. All decisions were made.

He drew a deep breath and looked down at his feet.

And in that instant he felt a sharp discomfort originating somehow from behind his eyes, seemingly deep inside his brain. Puzzled, he raised his eyes from the floor and found that, as he raised them, the discomfort was diminished. Allowing his gaze to drop toward the floor again, he found that the discomfort had mysteriously returned, insistent . . . And so he raised his eyes again, this time higher . . . and then higher still.

Chapter Eight

SHE WORE A LIGHT BLUE SUMMER SUIT WITH, AS ALWAYS, A pair of scruffy white tennis shoes. And at 11:00 that Tuesday morning, she quietly pushed her office door closed from the inside, walked back through her office to her desk, and dialed Sid Belton's phone number. She listened impatiently while the paired ringing sounds in her ear continued for ten seconds . . . twenty seconds . . . thirty seconds . . . Finally, she thoughtfully replaced the receiver and confirmed the number she had written down. She dialed again, allowed only four paired rings this time, and hung up.

Eleanor Chapel did not know Sid Belton well, but everything she had learned about him from her reference checks the previous afternoon led her to a sense of considerable surprise that he was not there to answer his telephone at their prearranged time. They had both been so clear. He would return to his apartment after his early morning trip to his former precinct office by 10:30. She would bring her second meeting of the morning to a close by 10:45.

And she had exciting news for him. Her first choice of newspaper editor had not only made himself immediately available to accept her call at 8:10 that morning, he had become more animated than she had ever before heard him when she explained the nature of her call. He had agreed within minutes to put his top writer-reporter on the plane to Baltimore-Washington International Airport on Thursday morning. The reporter would be prepared to meet Eleanor Chapel and her colleagues in Annapolis shortly after noon that day. And he would place her at their disposal for as many as forty-eight hours—possibly even longer—if necessary for full completion of the assignment. Further, the young reporter was someone whom Eleanor Chapel knew well by reputation.

The reverse was true also. Dr. Eleanor Chapel had, long ago, won the universal respect of millions of Christian people within the Southern Baptist denomination and beyond. As one of the country's best known Old Testament scholars, writers, and speakers—though without Cameron Stafford's political attachments and influence—she could make a persuasive telephone call to leaders not only within the Baptist organization, but within American Christendom broadly. As a rule, she gave the fact of her preeminence almost no thought. But on this particular June morning, she had acknowledged to herself that there were times when such preeminence could be convenient.

Now she sat down at her desk, the office door still closed, and mulled this new nondevelopment. Her assignment, for the moment, was finished. And nearly thirty-six hours stretched before her until the scheduled meeting Wednesday night at the detective's apartment.

Eleanor Chapel was not a particularly patient woman. In this instance, she had wanted the detective to know that her part in the arrangements had been completed and had hoped that he might have another assignment in mind for her in the intervening hours. She had cleared her calendar not only for the rest of the day, but for the rest of the week. This was one of the few times in the school year that she had freedom to introduce major alterations in her schedule on short notice. If the semester or summer terms had been underway, there would have been little chance of making rearrangements of any magnitude.

She stood, walked away from her desk, and gazed out her second-floor office window, which overlooked Broadway. She hated wasting time. She watched pedestrians walking briskly through the rising heat of the day, most of them purposefully striding along the wide sidewalk, carrying books or book bags or briefcases. The professor sighed, reached a decision, and turned to pack her own briefcase. She would dial the detective's number one more time, and if he still did not answer, she would go to the seminary's library to begin her latest research project on the book of Micah. She smiled to herself. Micah was one of her favorite books. How blessed she was to be called to spend an entire adult lifetime immersed in something she loved as she did the Old Testament.

She closed her briefcase, snapped it shut, and lifted the receiver. She dialed again, waited longer than she needed to, knowing that in such a tiny apartment three or four rings would always be sufficient, and hung up. Lifting her briefcase, she walked to the door, closed and locked it behind her, and headed for the north stairway. When she reached the bottom of the stairwell, she took one step forward and prepared to pull open the interior first-floor door. And there she stopped, her hand extended toward the door.

Eleanor Chapel believed that the Holy Spirit had special ways of speaking to each individual soul. It was obvious to her that Rebecca Manguson had been divinely selected as an appropriate and worthy recipient of messages of extreme power and import, sometimes communicated in supernaturally dramatic ways. But she also knew that even someone specially chosen, like Rebecca, undoubtedly received, day in and day out, hundreds . . . no, over the course of years, thousands upon thousands . . . of much more ordinary divine messages and responses. Simple prayers simply responded to.

The most emphatic replies to her own prayers, along with other kinds of "redirections from Heaven," as she spoke of them, had, for decades, often come in the form of divine responses "thrown at her brain." She liked the athletically supernatural image as her best means of thinking about how it felt to be redirected by the Holy Spirit. She could be walking along, her mind on some mundane piece of business, and suddenly a thought would materialize in her mind from out of nowhere. Yet it was not really from nowhere. It was an answer. Or a fresh perspective. Or an instruction. It was God. It was God's favorite way of ministering to, and guiding, Eleanor Chapel. God chose to favor a Rebecca Manguson—if only occasionally— with visions. But with her, He simply threw messages at her brain, anytime, anywhere, under any circumstances.

Now she remained motionless, her hand nearly, but not quite, touching the interior door handle. A thought had been thrown at her and had lodged itself in her brain with such force that her hand would move no further.

And finally, slowly, her hand fell to her side. She continued to stand motionless at the bottom of the stairwell. The stairwell was empty and quiet. She attended carefully to the thought . . . the new thought so force-fully thrown at her brain. And suddenly the conviction was overwhelming. Her hand moved involuntarily to her mouth and her eyes closed briefly as she murmured the words, "Thank you, Father."

Quickly she turned, climbed the stairs, and retraced the path to her office. Entering hastily, she closed the door noisily behind her and went to her desk. She opened the briefcase and removed her small black address book. In quick succession, using the telephone numbers that had been exchanged early that morning in the detective's apartment, she dialed Sid

Belton's number again, then Matt Clark's, and, receiving no answer at either apartment, the hotel to which the twins had moved the previous day.

She reached the hotel operator, who put her call through to the Mangusons' room. Luke answered somewhat tersely. "Yes?" he said.

"Luke, this is Eleanor Chapel. Is Rebecca there with you?"

His voice mellowed immediately. "Yes, Dr. Chapel, of course. Mr. Belton would have it no other way, you know. Would you like to speak to her?"

"No . . . I mean . . . I'm glad to reach either of you." She took a breath. The idea flitted swiftly through her mind that she was about to make a fool of herself. And she would seem the worst kind of fool. A nervous, eccentric old woman. She shook her head and squared her tiny shoulders. Fear never exercised any real influence over Eleanor Chapel. And it would not now.

She shook her head again. That overwhelming conviction that had placed her in its grasp at the foot of the stairwell was no illusion. Now she took another breath and opened her mouth to speak.

"Dr. Chapel? Are you all right, ma'am?" asked Luke.

"Yes . . . yes, I'm fine. Luke, I'm calling because neither Mr. Belton nor Matt Clark will answer their telephones. In Matt's case, it may mean nothing. It may simply mean that he has already departed for the airport, as by now he should have. But in the detective's case, I am certain that it does . . . It does mean something."

"You say you are certain that it does, Dr. Chapel? Can you tell me why?"

"The minor reason, Luke, is that he and I had a telephone appointment at eleven o'clock sharp this morning. He did not answer then, and he does not answer now, almost twenty minutes later." She hesitated again, but only momentarily. She took another breath and resumed.

"The larger reason . . . is that . . . something turned me around on the stairwell five minutes ago. Something sent me back here to my office. Something told me to attempt to reach each of you in turn. Something is telling me that . . . that . . . that we are needed, sir. The detective needs us now. And I know it."

"Dr. Chapel, give me just a moment, please."

She waited while Luke covered the receiver with one hand and spoke with his sister. "Dr. Chapel," he resumed after a moment, "we're going to get a taxi now and stop by the detective's apartment to see if anything is obviously amiss, and then we're coming to the seminary to get you."

"Coming to get me? Oh, no, Luke. It's not that I'm in any danger . . ."

"Dr. Chapel, please listen to me. We are *all* in danger. Rebecca and I do not want you to leave your office building until we arrive there to pick you up in our taxi. Please. You must let us do this."

Having rapped several times on the door of Sid Belton's apartment on 151st Street, Luke and Rebecca walked back down the stairs and knocked on the door of the building superintendent. They explained their concern to him.

"Oh, I think the detective can take care of himself about as well as anybody I know," said the wizened superintendent. "Not to worry."

As he began to push the door shut, Rebecca stepped forward and placed her left hand inside the doorframe, preventing the door's closure. The old man looked quizzically down at her hand, then back up into her face. She did not smile as she spoke. "Sir," she said evenly, "we have come a very long way. Mr. Belton is one of our closest friends in the world. You must allow us to look into his apartment. We must know whether or not he is all right. Please. The last thing we would do is to cause him harm. Or to allow anyone else to cause him harm."

Something in her mien led the superintendent to hesitate. After a long moment, he asked, "How do you know the detective? If you were plainclothes police officers, you would have shown me some identification by now."

Rebecca responded with a brief statement of their involvement with Sid Belton, beginning the previous summer. When she finished, the old man flashed a gap-toothed smile up toward her face. "Well, young lady, nobody could make that up," he said, shaking his head. "Come with me. I'll take you upstairs."

The three of them stepped into Belton's apartment and the twins knew at a glance that the detective had not returned to his home after escorting them through the alleyway to 150th Street early that morning. Each coffee cup remained exactly where it had been. The chair in which Belton had sat remained at right angles to the desk under which it had been positioned when they had arrived the previous evening. The kitchen chair that had been used by Rebecca was still in its place in the living room, off to one side of the cushioned chair from which Matt had spoken to the group.

Rebecca had no way of knowing what kind of housekeeper the detective was, but her experience with him in England had taught her that this was a tidy man. Like her brother and "the kid," his military background dictated that things once moved must forthwith be returned to their places when the purpose for their dislodgment had been fulfilled.

Followed by the superintendent, Rebecca crossed the living room and looked in at the kitchen. Nothing had been touched since she had said goodbye to Matt just ten hours earlier. A quick glance in the bedroom completed the tour. They turned to their host. "Thank you, sir," said Rebecca. "We're satisfied. You've been very kind to allow us into the apartment."

"Well?" he replied, "do you think he's gonna be okay?"

She smiled. "We're going to make certain of that, sir. You'll see Mr. Belton again soon, I'm sure."

Standing on 151st again, beside the waiting taxi, Luke turned to his sister before they stepped into the cab. "Rebecca, you realize we have nowhere to start on this. We've no clues at all. Something must have happened to him, and maybe to Matt, just after we drove away from the alleyway this morning. But for the life of me, I can't think of a reasonable first step, to say nothing of a second and a third. How do we move on this? Where do we begin?"

Rebecca was dressed now in her Nike waffle-sole running shoes, a pair of full-length, off-white tennis warm-up trousers, and one of the dark blue, short-sleeved Big Apple tee shirts that Luke had bought for her during a quick shopping expedition the day before. Now, she shook her head, the freshly gathered ponytail dancing down her back in shimmering rhythm with her response to his question. "I can't imagine, Luke. We've nothing to go on. And if there is nothing to go on, we may simply find ourselves forced to collect Dr. Chapel now and, tomorrow night or Thursday, move on to Maryland. The only thing we can do now is to retrieve Dr. Chapel and get her back to our hotel room. That much we can do. That much we *must* do."

As the taxi maneuvered south on Broadway toward the seminary, Rebecca turned to her brother, a puzzled frown forming a single crease across her normally unlined forehead. "What do you think happened this morning, Luke? How would Dr. Stafford—or someone else—have known to go after Mr. Belton?"

"Well," he replied thoughtfully, "I can only think that if I were Cameron Stafford, and had all my confidential files locked in that storage room, and had planned to move the whole lot to Maryland later this week, I'd be pretty unlikely to leave my bookstore unguarded. Certainly not unwatched.

"Since Matt had to move along that second-floor ledge that he described for us, and not once but twice, and since he eventually descended to the street by means of the outside fire escape . . .

"I can easily imagine his being followed to the detective's apartment, Rebecca. And once there, I can imagine arrangements being made rather quickly. Matt was with us for less than an hour, I'd say, but that's enough time, if you're Cameron Stafford, to get something organized, don't you think?"

"I do," she nodded, "but I don't know why they should allow you and me and Dr. Chapel to leave the apartment unmolested, and then do something vile to the detective . . . and perhaps to Matt . . ." Her voice trailed off.

Luke replied immediately. "I shouldn't imagine that they *allowed* the three of us to leave, dear. I should think they were not quite quick enough to try for us. They bagged what they could."

They rode in silence until the taxi approached 120th Street, whereupon Luke indicated the spot at which the driver should pull over to await Eleanor Chapel's arrival. The taxi stopped and Luke, sitting on the right, rolled down his window and, moving forward in his seat, placed his forearm along the top edge of the window opening. Then he slowly made a fist with his right hand. The huge muscles in his forearm rippled in the noonday sunlight. In that position, he remained, waiting.

Eleanor Chapel looked down from her office window as a taxi pulled to the curb just in front of the building. The right rear window descended, and as she watched, a man's forearm appeared in the window and its hand slowly closed itself into a fist. She picked up her briefcase, hurried to her office door, locked it quickly, and actually trotted to the same stairway she had used earlier. This time, at the foot of the stairway, she turned away from the interior door that led into the first-floor corridor, pushed open the heavy exterior door, and stepped outside. She reached the sidewalk and began to hurry toward the taxi, some one hundred feet from her and facing in the other direction. She could see the backs of Rebecca's and Luke's heads through the rear window. They obviously expected her to approach from the other direction.

As she scuttled rapidly toward the car, her well-worn tennis shoes a blur of motion, she saw in the corner of her eye a hooded figure beginning to cross the sidewalk from the shadows of her building. The figure wore a sweatshirt, despite the intense heat. The hood of the heavy, faded green garment was pulled up over the side of the figure's face. She could see nothing of the face and was not certain that the figure saw her at all. Her stomach muscles tensed, and she found herself wishing that Rebecca or Luke would turn around and see her. She moved closer to the street, but the figure adjusted its shuffling movements to complete its interception of her. At the last moment she stopped, the hunched figure directly in her path. She tried to see its face, but it tugged its green hood down further over its features. The hand that tugged at the hood was a very dark brown, and noticeably smooth-skinned. The thought passed through her mind with startling swiftness. "This is a young man. He is not homeless." And then a different kind of thought threw itself forcefully at her brain: "He is not a threat." And then: "Attend to him."

She reached into the side pocket of her suit and removed the small, thin coin purse that she carried within easy reach, partly for this exact purpose. Placing her briefcase on the sidewalk to free both hands, she pulled a dollar and several quarters from the purse and extended her hand toward his. He responded in kind, his palm up, and she placed the money into the palm. As she did, she saw that a folded slip of paper was positioned between the second and third fingers of the hand. She glanced up, but the face remained hidden behind the hood. As she pulled her hand back from his, she felt upward pressure from the hand, pressing the upper corner of the slip of paper into hers. She closed her hand over the paper, placed the tiny missive and her coin purse in a jacket pocket, and looked up again. The figure was already beginning to shuffle off in the direction from which it had come. She looked up at the taxi. She saw both faces now looking at her, and she lifted her briefcase from the sidewalk and moved quickly toward the waiting car.

As the taxi moved away from the seminary and university neighborhoods and began its forty-block trip north to the Mangusons' new hotel, Eleanor Chapel, having crawled over Luke to the center of the rear seat, removed the slip of paper from her pocket and unfolded it. Turning first to Rebecca, she asked, "Did you happen to see me give a little money to that man just before I got to the car? The man with a green hood pulled up over his face?"

"Yes," answered Rebecca, "Luke and I both had our hands on the door handles, prepared to get out of the taxi and come to you, just in case he turned out to be something other than what he appeared to be. But then we saw you give him something and he moved on."

"Well," she replied, now turning to Luke, "that became a two-way transaction. He gave me something, too." And with that she finished unfolding the slip of paper, stared at it momentarily, and then showed it in turn to her companions. Each saw that the message, if it were indeed a message, contained but two words and a number. The words were printed large and in pencil, and the number was barely readable: DANIEL 5. PIETA.

Rebecca and Luke looked at her inquiringly. After a moment, Eleanor Chapel shook her head. "I cannot imagine what we should think of this. A man who, I think, was a young African-American, and who, I also think, may not have been homeless or begging at all, just gave me a piece of paper containing pure encryption. What on earth is happening here, young people?"

Since neither had an answer to the question, nor had Eleanor Chapel expected one from them, silence consumed the next fifteen minutes of travel. During that time, all three minds grappled full force with the conjunction of events: a likely attack in the early morning hours at the detective's apartment just after the three of them had departed; and now an undecipherable message delivered by a man who may or may not have been homeless, and who may or may not have originated the message himself.

The Old Testament scholar was not the only one on the back seat of the cab familiar enough with the fifth chapter of the book of Daniel to know at least the general outline of the events described therein. But what the well-known "handwriting on the wall" passages in that Old Testament drama might have to do with the Pieta—which, after all, could be any depiction of the dead Christ in His mother's arms—was anyone's guess. And, beyond that, the same could be said of a half-dozen other issues: what, for example, might either of those—the handwriting on the wall or the Pieta—have to do with Eleanor Chapel or Sid Belton or Matt Clark? And what might any of this—the Scripture, the sculpture, the people—have to do with the MMHCC and Cameron Stafford and the impending Texas trip, or with the Texas files that Matt had examined in the bookstore vault? Or perhaps with the movement of all the MMHCC files to Maryland? Or with the MMHCC meetings later in the week in Oxford . . . The permutations flashing through their minds were overwhelming.

Finally, as the taxi neared the hotel, Eleanor Chapel broke the silence. "I have no idea whether or not this note has anything to do with us at all, but, if it does. . . ." Here she paused so long that the twins both began to think that her mind had moved on to something else.

"If it does," she resumed, "suppose the detective was accosted after we left his apartment . . . and suppose . . . suppose he somehow had the opportunity to scribble a couple of words on a slip of paper . . . and suppose . . . suppose he somehow got instructions to one of his former colleagues to have the note delivered to me in the most inconspicuous possible manner. . . .

"If we, for the moment, entertain those possibilities, then the reference to the Pieta might be to the rendering of that sculpture that is located in the detective's own church: in St. Patrick's Cathedral. And if we allow the simplest possible allusion from Daniel 5, just the 'writing on the wall,' rather than the countless other routes we could follow from that chapter. . . ."

Here she looked up, turning her face first to Luke and then to Rebecca. "Then perhaps . . . just perhaps . . . we should be on our way to the cathedral. To St. Patrick's. And right this minute. Not later today. Now."

She paused and again looked first at one and then the other of her companions. Seeing a nod from Rebecca and a shrug from Luke, she said first to herself and then to the driver, "We've been going north for twenty minutes, in the direction exactly opposite the cathedral. . . . Sir? Sir? We need to go to midtown instead. Can you get over to the parkway and take us down to Fifth Avenue at Fiftieth Street? We need to get to St. Patrick's Cathedral, and as quickly as you can safely get us there, please."

At 1:15 the driver pulled the car over to the curb beside the cathedral. Long before, the three had decided that Eleanor Chapel would enter the cathedral alone and proceed to the sculpture, shadowed at some distance by Luke. Rebecca, conscious of her promises to the detective regarding her public visibility, would remain in the car with the driver, circling the block for as long as necessary.

The Old Testament professor had been in St. Patrick's many times before, and more than once for no purpose other than to view the magnificent sculpture. Now she entered quickly, realized immediately that the 1:00 weekday mass was still in progress, and moved softly and reverently, hands clasped in front of her waist, down the right-hand aisle until she reached a point about halfway to the pulpit, from which the priest was still speaking. She entered an empty pew, pulled the red leather-covered kneeler down into position, and knelt, her compact frame comfortably straight up and down, her elbows on the back of the pew in front of her. She was a lifetime Baptist, but she loved the act of kneeling, and indeed, had happily done so in Catholic and Anglican churches all over the world, in her scholarly and recreational travels.

She completed a short, private prayer of gratitude and looked up. The congregation, numbering perhaps two hundred for this, the cathedral's seventh service on this Tuesday, was now in the process of receiving the bread and wine, processing down the main aisle. She watched them happily. There were few things she liked more than to see her Christian sisters and brothers enacting the sacrament, regardless of the form it took. She closed her eyes again in prayer.

Luke stood at the extreme rear of the church, in a position that allowed him to keep his eyes on Eleanor Chapel, and at the same time to have a broader view of much of the vast space encompassed by the cathedral. It was an odd sensation, being able to see everything that was happening, and yet at the same time to sense such a profound silence. It was as though the worshippers actually glided, rather than walked, moving soundlessly from their pews to the altar and back, as though floating through fields of heaven.

Luke knew that the strange message delivered to Eleanor Chapel might have nothing to do with the cathedral, or with the cathedral's particular rendering of the sculpture, or with Sid Belton. But Luke knew, too, that he himself was still unable to arrive at so much as a starting point, a first step to take, in a search for the detective. And so, for him, this trip to St. Patrick's represented a nearly desperate hope—but nonetheless a legitimate hope—that the slip of paper handed Eleanor Chapel constituted a genuine clue of some sort, and that her necessarily hasty interpretation of its meaning was at least close to the mark. If neither were, in fact, the case, then he saw nothing for it except to move forward on their MMHCC plan without the detective and, maybe, without Matt, as well. And that would mean going to Maryland at half strength and with none of the additional intelligence that the detective and Matt would presumably have been able to supply as a result of their efforts on this day and the next.

Luke was suddenly roused from his musings by the words of benediction that marked the end of the mass. He fastened his eyes on his colleague, and watched her rise gracefully from her knees and begin to move swiftly forward in the distance, around the side of the pulpit and the high altar. After a moment, he began to follow her slowly and at a distance of some two hundred feet. In just seconds, however, he lost sight of her completely, as he had expected. This was partly because of her size, but more because the cathedral's design did not provide an unobstructed line of sight from his position, along the right-hand aisle, to the passageways that led eventually to the altars alongside the sanctuary itself. He quickened his pace, his eyes moving from side to side and near to far with the seasoned discipline of one trained to distinguish friend from foe at the earliest possible moment.

As Luke neared the south transept and steered his irregular course toward the sanctuary, Eleanor Chapel, alone in the teeming crowd, arrived at the stunning sculpture of the dead Jesus in His mother's arms at the foot of the cross. Two worshippers, both women, leaned across the heavy wooden railing that protected the Pieta, each praying earnestly, each with one hand touching the foot of this magnificent representation of their crucified Lord and Savior. A dozen more worshippers and tourists had already begun to cluster around the statue, now that the service had ended, while dozens more, many of them tourists taking the self-guided tour, made their way slowly past in the prescribed counterclockwise circuit of the cathedral.

Eleanor Chapel glanced in both directions and realized she had no idea why she did so. If anyone other than Luke were watching or following her, she would have not the slightest idea how to recognize such, nor, she acknowledged, would she know how, or whether, to alter her course of action. She took a breath and made her way through and around those clustered nearest the sculpture. Moving to the right of the statue, she glided beyond the tight knot of worshippers and viewers. From her new angle, she could see behind the Pieta, the rear of which was anchored within a foot or two of the cathedral wall. Pilasters, placed at intervals along this portion of the cathedral, interrupted her view of the gleaming white wall that formed the backdrop for the equally white forms of the Christ figure and His mother.

She moved closer to the rear of the Pieta, her eyes cast down. Near the edge of the wooden railing, as it ended perhaps three feet from the wall itself, she stopped. Then she took one final step forward, now touching the railing with her fingers, and peered behind the statue, her eyes tracing the marble ledge that rose near the floor, then higher, to her own eye level, then higher still. And there, just inside the nearest pilaster, at a height of six to seven feet, she beheld a white envelope, hardly visible against the whiteness of the marble, apparently affixed to the wall with transparent tape. She stared for a moment in disbelief. She realized now that she had not actually expected the most obvious decryption of the odd message to yield this . . . or anything. And yet there it was. Before her eyes, behind the Pieta, the writing was on the wall.

She knew it would be impossible to retrieve the envelope inconspicuously. She was not even certain she could reach that high at all. But she studied the ledge and the height of the envelope, assured herself that the thing could be done, reminded herself that looking ridiculous was not something about which a sixty-ish woman wearing tennis shoes and a suit should concern herself, and stepped forward. She reached the bottom edge of the envelope from the floor, standing on her tiptoes. It yielded. She pulled it to her and turned to depart. Glancing to her right as she moved back along the passageway, it seemed to her that no one took the slightest notice of her, or of what she had done. This was, she reminded herself, New York City, where the unusual and even the bizarre were so commonplace as to be normal. She put her head down and, clutching the envelope, descended the two short flights of steps that had brought her to the sculpture, passed the sanctuary and the south transept, and headed back up the aisle down which she had passed five minutes earlier. She did not see Luke, but she was certain that he was watching her from a vantage point of his choosing.

And so he was. He had lost sight of her for perhaps two full minutes, but had arrived within easy view of the statue at about the time Eleanor Chapel had moved from the knot of worshippers and other viewers to a position near the rear, and to the side, of the Pieta. From his position, and Luke realized, from nearly any position other than the purposeful one that she had gained, the envelope that she had just secured so readily was quite invisible. The cleverness of its placement encouraged him. This had been contrived with some care.

Now that the professor held the missive, he trailed her closely. The distance between them was now no more than fifteen feet as the two made their way back up the side aisle. Only one person walked between them, and so Luke saw clearly the brief interruption in Eleanor Chapel's rapid progress toward the main doors. Near the rear of the cathedral he saw her slow, hesitate, and then actually come to a full stop for perhaps two seconds, appearing to look sharply to her right. And then she moved on, instantly regaining her swift, clipped stride.

Luke followed her glance and saw, kneeling in the fourth or fifth pew from the extreme rear, a neatly dressed African-American man of perhaps thirty. He wore a medium blue, long-sleeved shirt, with starched collar and a subdued red tie. His eyes were closed in prayer. As Luke passed his pew, he saw, draped with apparent carelessness over the back of the pew and falling down across the seat, a dirty, rumpled sweatshirt. Its color was long-faded green.

Two steps past the pew, Luke stopped and looked back at the man, etching the profile into his brain. After several seconds, just as he prepared to turn away, Luke, who was rarely surprised, saw the man turn his head quickly. Looking not directly at Luke but to one side of him, obviously holding Luke in the periphery of his eye, the man nodded his head slightly, then turned again to the front and bowed his head. Luke paused only for an additional instant, then turned, glimpsed Eleanor Chapel's slight form exiting through one of the main doors, and followed.

During the long taxi ride north on the Henry Hudson Parkway, speeding alongside the broad waterway, little was said. The passengers were aware that they had reached the point at which their taxi driver's presence must act as constraint on their conversation. Each, however, in turn, removed the material from the white ten-by-thirteen-inch envelope and leafed through its contents.

Large-scale maps labeled "Brooklyn" and schematics of large buildings passed under each pair of eyes. On several of the schematics someone had drawn laboriously, in red pen, an interlocking series of arrows, dotted lines, and Xs to indicate what seemed to be recommended points of entry and egress, together with several likely sites for . . . what?

They held their tongues until, after more than half an hour of racing along the parkway and dodging through intersections along upper Broadway, they reached the Mangusons' faded brick hotel. They paid the driver, walked up to their floor, entered the twins' plain but clean room, one furnished with a double bed for Rebecca and a sofa bed for Luke, and spread the documents on the floor. Then, sitting together on the colorless, threadbare rug, they prepared to review each document systematically.

But first, Luke turned to face Eleanor Chapel. "Dr. Chapel, talk to me about the man in the pew. Tell me everything you're thinking about him."

"Oh Luke! I have been bursting to tell you both. And I am so pleased you saw," she responded, eyes wide with excitement. "Did you get a good look?"

Luke nodded. "Yes, but I'm afraid he saw that I was examining him."

Here she turned to the mystified Rebecca, reaching out spontaneously to touch Rebecca's long-fingered, muscular hand with her small, deeply veined one.

"Dear," she began, "you saw, from the taxi, the man on the sidewalk in front of the seminary. You saw him give me the note earlier."

Rebecca nodded. "The man in the green sweatshirt? Yes, of course."

"That same man was actually in the cathedral, if you can imagine! He was wearing an expensive blue shirt and red tie, kneeling near the very back. But he had placed that filthy green sweatshirt over the back of the pew. And it was obvious that he had done it to signal us . . . to make clear to us who he was.

"And Rebecca . . . I actually know him!"

At this, Luke's head jerked up in surprise.

"Yes . . . he is a professor in the psychology department at Columbia. And, beyond that, he is a member of my own church! I admit I have never spoken with him at Abyssinian. But I see him there on Sundays, and occasionally on Wednesday nights. I have gotten to know him a little this year because he has collaborated with Cameron Stafford on the MMHCC project. He was often in the seminary hallways and offices last year. Usually, when I see him, he is with Cameron, or on his way to or from Cameron's seminary office. His name is Dolby." She nodded her head in affirmation of her own words. "Dr. Ellis Dolby."

She smiled, the skin around her blue-green eyes crinkling. "I just knew, back there on the sidewalk, that that was the hand of a young man. I knew it . . . yet I did not really believe it until I saw that awful sweatshirt."

Rebecca and Luke stared first at Eleanor Chapel, and then at each other. After a silence, Rebecca spoke, measuring her words. "So . . . we are to understand that one of Dr. Cameron Stafford's own colleagues from within the leadership ranks of the MMHCC . . . and a member of Columbia's psychology department . . . and a member, with you, of the congregation at Abyssinian Baptist Church in Harlem . . . posing as a homeless person . . . directed you to a place where he could provide you secretly with these materials . . . presumably because he did not want to be seen handing you this packet in public . . . nor to entrust the packet to the campus mail service?"

Eleanor Chapel nodded her head.

"And . . . we are to understand further that, once he had given you the encrypted message on the sidewalk," Rebecca continued carefully, the inflections in her voice marking her incredulity, "he immediately traveled to the cathedral, posted the materials behind the Pieta, and took his place for the one o'clock service . . . confident that you would decipher the message and come posthaste to the cathedral . . . yet not so quickly as to arrive before he could affix the envelope to the wall?" Rebecca nodded her head slowly, raising her eyebrows at Eleanor Chapel for confirmation, though the professor had been providing confirmation all along, nodding her head with every phrase Rebecca spoke.

"And," she resumed cautiously, her voice still expressing her skepticism at her own summary, "he took his place in the cathedral in such a way that you would see him and, especially, his disguise? He wanted to be certain that you knew who was providing you these documents?"

"Yes, Rebecca, yes!" Eleanor Chapel exclaimed, still bubbling with excitement. "But . . . I must tell you . . . these materials themselves . . . these maps and charts and arrows and markings . . . I have no idea . . ."

Rebecca reached for two of the documents and pulled them closer. She looked at them again for a moment, then turned them around so that her companions could see them well. "I'm convinced, Dr. Chapel, from what I think I gleaned while studying these documents in the car, that your colleague—Dr. Dolby, is it?—knows exactly where the detective has been taken, and is showing us with these maps and diagrams how we can find him. And I am nearly as sure that these diagrams of buildings are of those very same warehouses in Brooklyn to which Dr. Stafford was attempting to take Matt and me on Friday, when I was given my first vision on the way into the city from the airport.

"I think Ellis Dolby is telling us that the detective—and Matt, too, for all we know—has been taken to those warehouses. And I think that these hand-drawn arrows and dotted lines, in all likelihood, represent Dr. Dolby's suggestions to us as to how we might rescue him . . . or them."

She looked up. Eleanor Chapel's head was still nodding, and the elfin smile was spreading across her face as her excitement continued to build. "Yes! Oh, Rebecca! Can we save him? Can we save *them*? Can we do something? Can we do it now?"

Rebecca's eyes swung to her brother's. He evinced none of the professor's excitement. He shook his head slowly from side to side. "Tell me why, Dr. Chapel . . . tell me why, Rebecca . . . tell me why this Dolby person would do *any* of this. If he has been active in the MMHCC all along, why would he invite us to go into the same area to which Cameron Stafford attempted to take Rebecca and Matt earlier? What's to suggest that these are not precisely the same lyrics played to a new and more subtle melody? We know they desperately want to get their hands on you, Rebecca. This would certainly be a supremely clever way to capture you, don't you think? It has all the trappings of authenticity . . . a simple yet coded note delivered dramatically and clandestinely on the sidewalk in front of the seminary . . . a packet of materials placed cleverly in the detective's own church, St. Patrick's Cathedral . . . and all of it done by a person whom you, Dr. Chapel, know as a colleague and fellow church member. It's as amateurishly clever as any ruse could possibly be. And I don't like it."

Eleanor Chapel's face fell. She turned her eyes to Rebecca. "But . . . the detective could be in such danger . . . and this may tell us how to help him . . ." She stopped and looked down at her hands, shaking her head in bewilderment and deeply felt disappointment.

Rebecca leaned over and touched her arm. "Dr. Chapel, you don't know my brother. If you did, you'd stop worrying right now."

Eleanor Chapel looked up, first at Rebecca and then at Luke, whose eyes had narrowed as he stared reproachfully at his sister. The professor turned back to Rebecca. "Why is he looking at you that way?"

Rebecca laughed. "Because he knows in his heart what is about to happen, Dr. Chapel." And she laughed again, her response unfathomable to the senior professor of Old Testament.

"He will begin," Rebecca continued, "by insisting that, since this could very well be a trap, we cannot respond. We can, at most, he'll suggest, contact the police in hopes they may decide to act on this information. Then, almost immediately, he will retract that suggestion, realizing that, as has been the case in the past, we cannot expect the authorities to take action on information obtained inexplicably, and in this case, proffered by people two of whom are not even citizens of this country, and one of whom is acting on the basis of *visions* that she claims come to her from supernatural sources. No, he'll conclude, we cannot hope to obtain assistance from police at this stage.

"Then, within another five minutes," she went on, her gray eyes gazing knowingly at her brother, "he will stand up, square his shoulders, and announce that he will go alone to the warehouses and free the detective . . . and, of course, Matt, too, if he is there.

"And then I, ever the annoying sister, will point out that his chances of succeeding alone are poor. His chances of succeeding with me as his . . . well . . . assistant . . . are much better. And then he will sulk and pace for fifteen minutes before he finally relents.

"And then, Dr. Chapel, Luke and I will be on our way. And the next time we see you, we'll have Mr. Belton with us, and perhaps Matt, as well."

She smiled. "It's true, isn't it, Luke. That's just how it will go.

"And I've just saved you fifteen or twenty minutes of agony. Let's skip over all that and get our plans made. We've no time to waste."

Luke raised his palms toward her. "Just a minute, Miss Know-Everything. I'm not as easy as all that." As he spoke to his sister, a faint smile flitted across his lips, but his eyes remained tense.

And then the smile faded. He turned to Eleanor Chapel. "Dr. Chapel, from what you know, by reputation, of Ellis Dolby, what are the chances that he is, in effect, a spy? What are the chances that he has come to realize that the MMHCC is as corrupt, and as dangerous to America's children—and eventually to the world's children—as any allegedly 'educational' project could be? What are the chances that he, knowing that you have opposed the MMHCC from the first, has come to view you as his link to goodness and sanity and, perhaps, to the defeat of his own project? What are the chances that he was among those informed of last night's session at the detective's apartment, that he knows we three were present there, and that he knows the detective, and Matt, perhaps, were captured and taken to these warehouses? And what are the chances that he has quickly come to view you—and us, too—as his route, first, to effecting a rescue, and second, to beginning to undercut the MMHCC project itself?"

Luke paused, looking down. When he raised his eyes again to Eleanor Chapel's, his voice was husky with emotion. "It would take an extraordinary man," he said slowly, emphatically, "to come face to face with the Evil that is laced throughout this project, and then to have the courage to look his own death in the eye, and finally to begin to work against Dr. Stafford and his forces . . . something they will regard as high treason."

He paused again, not taking his eyes from hers. Then he resumed, even more deliberately. "Could he possibly be that man, Dr. Chapel? Could he be? Or is it more likely that he was chosen by Stafford and the others to make this contact with you in order to lure Rebecca and me into what could be a most effective—and most lethal—trap?

"What do you think, Dr. Chapel? What are the chances that this is a Christian man who is now ready to give up his life for the faith . . . for the children . . . for the parents? Tell me, Dr. Chapel. What do you think?"

There was another lengthy pause. Eleanor Chapel studied her hands as they rested in her lap. Finally she looked up, and when she did, she fixed Luke Manguson with an even gaze touched with a hint of anger. When she spoke, the emotion in her high, musical voice easily matched his own. The sentences came deliberately from her lips. "*What I think*, sir, is that our two Christian colleagues, our brethren, are in danger. What I think is that they may be undergoing torture as we sit here comfortably talking in our hotel room. What I think is that the Holy Spirit has already been in active communication with us about this evil that we face. What I think is that God Almighty is on the side of the righteous. And what I think is that there is nothing else whatsoever to think about."

The petite Baptist and the muscular Anglican stared at each other, their eyes locked. The seconds passed. And then, ever so slowly, an expression containing equal parts admiration for his adversary and reluctant acquiescence to her clarity and conviction began to play across the young man's chiseled features. The change became visible not just in the hint of a smile on his lips, but, perhaps even more clearly, in the relaxation around and in his eyes, which had been narrowed to hardened slits for the last several minutes of the discussion.

Unsure of how to read his expression, Eleanor Chapel turned her bright eyes in Rebecca's direction, the fine lines of her gray-flecked eyebrows forming the question. In response, Rebecca leaned forward and placed a strong hand over both of the professor's. And then she whispered, smiling gently, but with the clear suggestion of threat in her low, soft voice. "We shall have them here soon, dear. You'll see. We shall have them here very soon."

Chapter Nine

AT LUKE'S INSISTENCE, ELEANOR CHAPEL AND REBECCA had remained out of public sight that afternoon while he moved swiftly to prepare for the incursion into Brooklyn's warehouse district. He had first secured a room for the professor, one adjacent to his and his sister's. The two rooms shared a connecting door that the three of them agreed to keep open at all times.

He had then made the rounds of neighborhood shops. His stops had included a small hardware store, two clothing establishments, a pharmacy, and an Army-Navy surplus clothing and equipment store. Upon his return, he and Rebecca had worked out every detail of that night's operation. Contingencies were layered into their plans in an effort to prepare for as many of the enemy's counteractions as possible. As nightfall approached on a sweltering June Tuesday, they felt ready.

Eleanor Chapel's role that afternoon had been to secure transportation for the movement into Brooklyn. She herself, a lifetime user of public transportation, owned no vehicle, but with the determined help of an assistant pastor at her Abyssinian Baptist Church, she had eventually succeeded. She had been able to meet some, not all, of Luke's transport specifications. The loaned vehicle was indeed, as he had demanded, fast, maneuverable, and dark in color. It was not, on the other hand, large enough to carry four people, nor, to say the least, was it the inconspicuous, domestically manufactured sedan that he had specified.

And so the young pastor found himself that afternoon struggling to drive a jet black, seven-year-old Porsche 993 Turbo Cabriolet through the streets of Manhattan. He had picked up the high-performance vehicle at the home of the generous church member whom he had approached at Eleanor Chapel's behest, and had driven, haltingly but directly, to the church. Hours later, after receiving her call that all was in readiness, he drove the roadster from the church to the hotel. He had been asked to be prepared to wait there with the professor for what they assumed would be several more hours, during which time the twins would attempt their rescue of the detective . . . and, perhaps, of Matt Clark. The pastor would then drive the Porsche back to the church member's home, regardless of the time of night or morning.

The wealthy church member, a rising African-American star in a midtown law firm, had been assured by the assistant pastor that the cherished Cabriolet would be driven that night by an extremely skilled European driver who had handled high-performance automobiles many times before. And that was true. The pastor did not think it necessary to add the fact that the driver would be a woman, nor that her driving experience with such vehicles was mostly, up to that moment, behind the wheels of right-hand drive autos proceeding along the left-hand corridors of roadways throughout England and Wales.

The pastor acknowledged to himself that his conscience had protested mildly in regard to the second of his two omissions. But only mildly. When a person with the reputation of an Eleanor Chapel asks one to arrange an extraordinary thing, he told himself, one makes the assumption that truly large issues must perforce hang in the balance. He did not know her well, except by her illustrious reputation, but that was enough to know that he could trust her with his life. And so, he told himself, if not quite convincingly, that if the Porsche's attorney-owner knew either everything about this situation, a manifest impossibility, or, alternatively, if he knew almost nothing about the situation, he would trust Eleanor Chapel's reasons for asking, and he would trust her judgment in selection of driver. It was the intermediate condition, the just-enough-knowledge-to-be-dangerous condition, that the pastor wished to avoid, both with the attorney and, truth be told, with himself. And so he satisfied himself with a deliberately superficial acquaintance with the crisis and with reporting to the car's owner that modest dollop of truth.

Shortly after 11:30, hours after nightfall in New York City even under the extended daylight conditions prevailing in early June, the young pastor rapped softly on Eleanor Chapel's hotel room door. Luke sprang to his feet, crossed into her room through the connecting doorway, placed his hands around the professor's small waist from behind, and lifted her up until her eyes were even with the peephole. She looked, murmured, "Yes," and, her feet having been returned carefully to the floor, stepped aside for Luke to open the door.

She then conducted brief introductions. All were in agreement that the pastor displayed admirable composure at the sight of two people so obviously dressed for combat. Their faces were streaked with bootblack. The man's clothing was military, dull green in color, and without insignia. The woman wore a dark blue tennis warm-up suit. Their caps were billed. Their footwear comprised blackened running shoes with blackened shoestrings. The woman, tall and athletic in appearance, her long, jet-black hair pulled into a tight ponytail that protruded through a slit in the back of her cap, wore a U.S. Marine drill sergeant's swagger stick on one side of her belt and a black rubber-covered flashlight on the other. She was otherwise unencumbered. The man, not quite as tall as the six-foot woman but of astonishing breadth of shoulder and chest, carried on his belt three military-issue cloth pouches of differing size and shape containing, presumably, either tools or weapons. Across his shoulder and chest he wore a leather harness that, in the configuration for which he had opted on this occasion, supported two holsters, each containing still more hard-ware. The pastor, standing relaxed with the self-confidence of one who knows who he is and Whom he serves, found himself nonetheless staring at Luke's accoutrement.

"I'll explain more, Reverend," said Eleanor Chapel with a small smile, "as soon as they're on their way. They're anxious to get started, you understand."

Had the pastor been invited to inspect Luke's pouches, sheaths, holsters, and harnesses, he would have found no firearms. He would have found an array of tools and instruments designed to open, to penetrate, and to detect. And he would have found an assortment of knife blades, each of them constructed so as to fit into a single heavy, universal handle that was carried in one of the holsters that was, in turn, fitted to the shoulder harness. And had the pastor gone beyond the mere inspection of paraphernalia to examine the man himself and his background, he would have found not only, as with the man's sister, a respected educator of young people, but a former Royal Navy officer with extensive training in the arcane specialty of boarding hostile ships. And he would have come to understand that anyone selected by his Navy as boarding party specialist would have undergone exhaustive training in hand-to-hand combat of the sort that can at times turn a firearm into an unneeded and unnecessary nuisance.

The pastor and the professor stood together in the hotel room, talking softly and listening at the open window for almost ten full minutes after the twins' hasty good-bye. In response to his whispered question, Eleanor Chapel replied softly, "Luke explained to me that Rebecca always takes some time studying a vehicle's controls, indicators, and mirrors before she reaches for the ignition switch to start the engine. He says she could be a Grande Prix driver if she chose, but has always preferred to concentrate on her vocation . . . and on her tennis. In any case, your parishioner's car is in good hands, Reverend."

"I hope you're right, Dr. Chapel," replied the young minister. "I'm fairly sure those two are not on their way to the opera."

Forty-five minutes after starting the Cabriolet's engine in far uptown Manhattan, after having followed a circuitous route to the target in order to assure herself of the fact that no pursuers were engaged, Rebecca cut the motor in a Brooklyn alleyway just two blocks from the warehouse street. She and her brother sat silent with the windows down, listening.

Satisfied, Rebecca reached to her belt, unsnapped her flashlight, pulled a small, dark-blue volume from a side pocket in her warm-up jacket, and bent forward toward the floorboard of the roadster. Luke immediately leaned down toward her, his eyes closed. Turning to a well-marked page in her compact Anglican *Book of Common Prayer*, Rebecca whispered the "prayer to be said before a fight at sea against any enemy." She spoke the words slowly, concentrating on the act of praying, rather than on the act of reading. At the midpoint of this prayer, so familiar to a Royal Navy officer, Luke, eyes still closed, whispered in unison with her the phrases he had come to know by heart:

> . . . Stir up thy strength, O Lord, and come and help us; for thou givest not alway the battle to the strong, but canst save by many or by few . . . hear us thy poor servants begging mercy, and imploring thy help, and that thou wouldest be a defence unto us against the face of the enemy. . . .

Rebecca finished the reading. The two of them continued to pray silently for some time. Then she returned the prayer book to the side pocket of her jacket, squeezed her brother's hand, and after he returned the gesture to signal the end of his own prayer, she stepped from the car. Luke rose from the opposite side of the roadster, adjusted the pouches, sheaths, holsters, and straps that encircled his torso, and joined her in the shadows of the deserted warehouse against which she had parked. Together they looked skyward, assessing the moonlight. There was a half-moon above them and, as predicted by the weather service throughout the day, the night was cloudless.

"More light than I would have preferred," Luke murmured, more to himself than to Rebecca, as they turned and moved in the direction of the East River, she following him at no more than arm's length. Rebecca turned her head to look behind them every fifteen to twenty steps, as he had instructed her. At the westernmost end of the warehouse, they halted. Luke dropped to the pavement, pulled an implement from a pouch at his belt, and moved it along the concrete until it extended, resting on the pavement, two inches beyond the corner of the building. Peering intently into the compact, long-handled mirror, the reflecting surface of which formed a forty-five-degree angle with the handle, he studied the alley into which they were to move next. Satisfied, he retracted the device, inserted it into a slot at his belt, and rose to his feet. He turned the corner and broke into a gliding run, Rebecca following closely and easily at his shoulder. The twins' long-practiced heel-to-toe running mechanics rendered their heavily cushioned Nikes noiseless at this measured pace.

At the next corner, Luke repeated the extended-mirror maneuver, led Rebecca across a loading area that brought them to a second row of ware-houses, and continued at the same gliding pace to the far, or southwest, corner of the final row. There Luke used the viewing device a final time. They were now positioned to move to the entryway indicated on Ellis Dolby's charts.

Rebecca, supremely prepared and exhaustively rehearsed by Luke, had no need to communicate vocally with her brother, nor he with her. She continued to check visually in any direction in which Luke was not looking at a given moment. When he moved from the final warehouse corner toward the target doorway, Rebecca remained so close to him as to be able to rest her hand lightly on his shoulder at every moment.

As they closed on the entryway, she saw that, as she had expected, they were now in the narrow street into which Cameron Stafford had steered his venerable Buick a very long four days previous. They were entering the street from the opposite, or western, end, but she had no doubt that it was the same alley. She could now see in the moonlit distance, against the high face of the warehouse, the enormous overhead garage door from which the ancient flatbed truck had emerged to block the alley on that adventurous Friday afternoon.

Her attention now turned back to Luke. He had dropped to one knee and was examining the heavy padlock that hung from a hinged clasp protruding from the rusting metal door. She saw him nod to himself, reach into one of his sheaths, and remove a powerfully levered pair of bolt cutters. In just seconds, with Luke's strength and the cutters' leverage, the thick padlock hung useless. He returned the cutters to their sheath, slid the padlock quietly from its clasp, stood, and grasped the handle tightly. Lifting and pushing equally so as to dislodge the tight-fitting door with as little noise as possible, he felt it yield with only a small metallic complaint. He stopped the door when it had created a three-inch space, moved his eye briefly to the crack, then opened the door far enough to move his head into the space. Seeing only blackness, he slipped inside. As he moved his torso through the doorway, Rebecca moved with him, her shoulder and arm pressing lightly against him in balletic synchrony. He turned, pressed the door quietly back into its frame, and crouched in the suffocating heat and darkness of the uninsulated structure. Rebecca's hand rested gently on his forearm to ensure that both knew the other's exact position.

There they waited, motionless, allowing time for their eyes to adjust. After two full minutes, Luke whispered, "We'll need the light."

Rebecca already held her hooded flashlight in one hand, and, at his words, squeezed his forearm as a signal. She then flicked the switch, completed a single, rapid, counterclockwise sweep of the cavernous space in which they crouched, turned the toggle back to the "off" position, and in well-rehearsed concert with her brother, took five swift steps to her right as he quickly moved the same distance to his left. Thus, within seconds of

Luke's decision to illuminate, they had obtained a glimpse of the section of the warehouse into which Ellis Dolby had directed them, extinguished the flashlight beam so quickly that a guard would hardly have had time to switch off the safety on a handgun or rifle, and then created enough separation from each other and from the original flash point that a pistol or rifle shot aimed at that point would have struck nothing but metal. Having stopped, they each counted to thirty. Only then did Luke, his right hand following the warehouse wall, creep silently to his sister's side, moving steadily until he encountered her upraised hand against his chest.

Still silent, they began to move across the broad expanse of the warehouse's first section. Rebecca's hand remained lightly on her brother's shoulder. The Dolby diagrams had been committed to memory by both. The momentary illumination by flashlight had confirmed the diagrammatic accuracy of Ellis Dolby's documents: the warehouse row comprised six sections measuring two hundred by two hundred feet each. This was the westernmost section.

The flashlight sweep had revealed a floor clear of obstacles. Indeed, this first section appeared completely void of contents.

By moving directly across two hundred feet of concrete floor, they knew they would arrive at a spot roughly twenty-five feet from the ladder that they sought. According to the diagrams, the ladder would take them to a catwalk that ran the entire length of the warehouse row, just under a quarter mile from end to end. The catwalk had been placed some forty feet above the concrete floor, almost two-thirds of the way to the sixty-five-foot-high flat metal roof.

They reached the north wall and turned right. Luke moved quickly toward the invisible ladder with his left hand brushing the surface of the north wall. Rebecca's left hand remained in constant contact with his right shoulder. Luke reached the ladder, felt for his sister's hand, and pulled her hand forward until it touched the same chest-high rung on which his own hand rested. She grasped the rung with both hands and awaited his signal. When she felt his hand against the small of her back, she immediately started up in the blackness. She climbed silently and steadily for what seemed, in the dark, an impossibly long time. She had the odd sense of being miles above the concrete floor, but forced her mind steadily to agree to the dimensions that she knew were accurate. Forty feet and forty rungs from the floor, her hand encountered not another rung but a flat, corrugated metal surface.

She felt immediately for the vertical supports that she assumed would rise from either side of the catwalk's access point, found them, and pulled herself onto the catwalk. She quickly moved to the right-hand side of the opening, then rose to one knee. Once more she raised a palm in the direction from which her brother would come to serve as barrier for him in the darkness.

Then they stood together on the catwalk, prepared to move eastward along the north wall, high above the warehouse floor. They aligned themselves as they had while on the floor, Rebecca's left hand resting gently on her brother's right shoulder, while his left hand brushed along the warehouse wall. Ellis Dolby's notations had indicated that the first three sections from the western end of the warehouse, together with the fifth and sixth, were deserted. When they reached the metal door dividing the first section from the second, Luke found the handle, pulled cautiously, and felt the door yield readily. They moved through it, left it wide open behind them in case a running retreat became necessary, and continued their high-wire progress into and through the second section.

They repeated this process after two hundred more feet of travel along the catwalk. As they moved into the third section, looking ahead, they saw light for the first time since entering the building. At the wall dividing this final deserted section from the fourth, their goal, they saw around the edges of the door a dim, rectangular outline of light. They halted while Luke made final preparations.

Though they could see the outline of light at the eastern end of this third section, they still could not see each other. Rebecca knew, however, what her brother was doing. She knew that he was removing the largest of the knife blades from its sheath and inserting it into the universal handle, then placing the huge implement—or weapon, if necessary—into the "ready sheath" at his belt on the right side. She heard the metallic click of blade into handle, then the faint snapping sound of the guard strap securing the knife in its sheath. And she knew then that he was ready. She briefly fingered the club at her own belt, snapped its leather security strap, and returned her left hand to his shoulder.

They quickly traversed the remaining two hundred feet to the final door and stopped. Now that they were at the door, faint traces of artificial light from warehouse section four illuminated their darkened faces and forms. In this thin light, they reached into their side pockets and removed black leather gloves to conceal the white skin of their hands. Then they examined each other's already blackened face and neck as well as they could in the semidarkness.

Luke pressed the small button on the side of his watch to illuminate its face. It read 0130. It was Wednesday morning.

They nodded to each other in acknowledgment of their mutual readiness.

Luke stepped to the door handle and pulled and lifted cautiously. They knew that, with no illumination at their backs, the door's slow, slight movement would not be likely to attract the attention of a person on the warehouse floor forty feet below and one- to two-hundred feet across the warehouse. Luke slowly pulled the door toward him to create an opening of perhaps fifteen inches. Then he dropped to the catwalk, curled his body around the slightly open door while Rebecca prevented its further movement, and slithered through until he lay entirely within the weak light of the fourth warehouse section. Rebecca followed, replicating his movements, taking a position on her brother's right. There they remained motionless for some time, listening.

From what seemed a great distance they heard the intermittent, indistinct conversation of bored men. The position they now held, high in a shadowy corner of warehouse section four, was so remote and so weakly illuminated that Luke began to realize that only if this were a genuine trap could these men possibly detect their presence. His level of trust in Dr. Ellis Dolby and his documents was ratcheted up another notch, though Luke's congenital wariness remained firmly in place, pending the accumulation of a great deal more evidence in support of Dolby's conversion from leader to opponent of the MMHCC.

Finally, he whispered in Rebecca's ear, "Let's get a visual."

He crawled past her far enough so that they could both move their blackened faces to the catwalk's edge without interfering with each other's efforts. He looked down beyond his feet to her face, nodded once, and, together, they removed their billed caps, slid their faces to the edge, and observed purposefully for a full minute, moving only their eyes during the entire time. Then Luke pulled back, brushed Rebecca's shoulder with the toe of his shoe, and saw her move carefully back to her original position. He continued to slide away from the edge until he had created space for her to crawl up beside him. He lay now with his back against the north wall. In seconds she lay beside him, her face near his. In this position, their caps still in their hands, Luke whispered his final action decisions into her ear, the side of his face resting against her hair as it had when, as children, they had sneaked through the tall grass near their home, pretending to surprise and capture the jungle animals of their youthful imaginations. She listened carefully, responding only with nods of her head.

"We'll go with the first option from Plan Y, Rebecca," he said softly. "Do you think you'll be able to see my signal from the other end of the catwalk in these shadows?"

He waited while she raised her head, looked carefully at the far end of the catwalk, which was cloaked in shadows at least as heavy as those that now covered them, and nodded once.

"Good," he whispered. "The flatbed first, then, and the Buick second?"

Again, she nodded. "Okay," he said. "Questions about the power box?"

He waited while she rolled onto her right side and looked up at the two breaker switches on the wall above the catwalk. She shook her head and rolled back onto her chest.

"Ready, then," he whispered. "Let's get these people back home."

He placed his hand on the back of her neck and squeezed gently. She reached back with her right hand and covered his, returning the squeeze. Luke then reached to his waist, removed two small screwdrivers, placed them in her left hand, pulled his cap back onto his head, and inched forward. Rebecca slipped the tools into a side pocket in her jacket, replaced her own cap on her head, carefully fitting her ponytail into its slit, and resumed her prone position, watching as he began the interminable, two-hundred-foot journey on his stomach.

For the first thirty seconds of his maneuver, she could hear the small, scraping movements of Luke's belts and sheaths as they dragged along the catwalk. But the humming, whirring noises from two huge overhead fans muffled these incidental signals so effectively that, by the time he had completed a fraction of his journey, she could hear nothing except the indistinct murmurs and occasional boisterous guffaws of the men below.

The twins' visual inspection of the scene below them had revealed the movement, just as they peered over the catwalk's edge, of as many as two dozen men exiting a pedestrian doorway into the alley on the far side of the warehouse section. The group's departure had nearly emptied the cavernous space. Six men, apparently guards, remained. Two of these chatted idly, leaning against a gray limousine, drinking beer from brown bottles. Three others, at first standing near the rear of a white van, seemed to be making preparations for some kind of assault. The van appeared to contain a variety of weapons, or tools that could be utilized in that way—implements such as heavy iron crowbars, steel claw hammers, long-shafted screwdrivers, foot-long wrenches—and the three gave the impression of making choices for themselves from among this arsenal. The red lettering on the sides of the white van announced that it belonged to the Aristotelian Bookstore of Manhattan. A sixth guard, while the twins observed, stepped up into the same ancient flatbed truck that Rebecca had encountered on Friday, tested the reluctant diesel engine for several seconds, then switched off the motor and dropped to the cement floor. Turning to remove what was almost certainly an automatic rifle from the cab, he then proceeded swiftly to the far corner of the warehouse section.

There he stood alone near the pedestrian exit; the door now closed behind the departing group. This pedestrian doorway was positioned just fifteen feet from the extreme southeast corner of the warehouse. The armed guard now stood next to the first of a string of five small offices or cubicles, each seemingly made of plywood and lightweight lumber. The row of cubicles extended south-to-north from a point near the pedestrian door to one about halfway to the back, or north, wall along which the catwalk stretched at its forty-foot height.

Altogether, four vehicles were present. Their alignment from the near, or western, side of warehouse section four was, first, the old Buick that Rebecca had briefly commandeered on Friday; the decrepit flatbed that had blocked the alley that day; the white Aristotelian Bookstore van; and, finally, the gray limousine. Section four appeared to have but a single door for vehicles. That was the oversized one some seventy-five feet directly in front of the flatbed truck.

The gray limousine was parked near the row of plywood cubicles, and nearly at a right angle to them, as though it had been backed into position for the purpose of unloading something—or someone—from its trunk, and into one of the cubicles. The five cubicles had no ceilings, and were, in effect, mere partitions providing a dash of privacy for those who might work therein at desks with typewriters, telephones, and file cabinets. From Rebecca and Luke's original observation point at the northwest corner, looking across more than two hundred feet of warehouse section four at the distant row of offices, the twins had been unable to see inside any of them, despite the height of the catwalk and the absence of ceilings over the plywood cubicles.

Ellis Dolby's red-penned markings had indicated that the fifth of these small offices, the cubicle nearest the back, or north, wall of the warehouse, might hold a captive. Dolby had marked that office with a large "X" and with arrows indicating suggested routes to and from the tiny space. The automatic-rifle-wielding guard, meanwhile, was positioned near the first, or front, office.

Based on Dolby's indicators, the twins hoped that Sid Belton was sequestered in the fifth, or rearmost, office. If so, this would place Belton in the office nearest the catwalk and furthest from the armed guard.

The ladder near Rebecca's feet was one of two in this section. The other stretched to the floor from the extreme opposite end of the catwalk. In another ten minutes . . . perhaps fifteen, guessed Rebecca . . . Luke would be in position there. He would be able, they assumed, to see from that vantage point directly down into the fifth office cubicle where the detective might be imprisoned . . . and able as well to verify the accuracy of the schematics that showed the five offices were not built into the eastern wall of the section, nor flush with it, but with a six-foot space creating a corridor between them and the wall.

Furthermore, they hoped, Luke would be able to see well enough into the other four offices to confirm their preliminary count: one rifle-bearing guard and five other men, three of whom were armed with heavy tools useable as weapons, and two others who might, or might not, be armed. To Luke, even a single minute of actual on-site reconnaissance comprised the essential element in any successful rescue. The fact that this would-be rescue took place in a warehouse, rather than on the high seas, changed nothing about his assumptions.

And so Rebecca waited, watching her brother's slow progress along the catwalk. But her mind had already turned to her own impending responsibilities in the rescue attempt. Once she received Luke's signal, she knew, they both would be in constant motion—and in continuous danger—from that instant until the engagement came to an end . . . one way or the other.

Matt Clark, prompted by something at that moment wholly unde-fined, yet, in an odd way, nearly as insistent as Monday morning's overt supernatural intervention, had slowly and deliberately raised his eyes from the concrete floor at his feet to the base of the five-foot plywood wall opposite him. He had stared at the baseboard, puzzled. His eyes had at first returned to the floor at his feet. But then, prompted yet again by a strong sensation of discomfort seemingly behind his eyes themselves, he had lifted his gaze still further, now to the top edge of the cubicle in which he sat. Seeing nothing but badly painted wood, he lowered his eyes back to the floor only to find the same sharp, insistent discomfort originating from somewhere deep behind his eyes and within his brain. And now, alerted fully by the persistent signal from within, he raised his eyes yet again, stared at the top of the plywood wall, and then, the discomfort mounting again, adjusted the focus of his eyes both to distance and to semi-darkness. Thus, for the first time since his awakening in his makeshift prison, Matt looked above and beyond the tiny, ceilingless office in which he sat. Gradually he fixed his eyes on a distant catwalk, and at once the discomfort left him. The catwalk was fixed high above the warehouse floor and ran the length of the north warehouse wall opposite him. Squinting to see into the dim shadows, he began gradually to make out the indistinct figure of a man, a man dressed in dark clothing, his face apparently blackened, gloves covering his hands. Matt stared, disbelieving. And in a flash he knew. It could be only one man.

As he stared, the man slowly lifted an arm and pointed directly at Matt. The dark figure held that position for several seconds, then pointed downward, leading Matt's eyes to find and trace the shadowy line of a fixed ladder that appeared to lead all the way from catwalk to warehouse floor. The figure then gestured, a dramatic, jabbing motion with its hand conveying to Matt its intention to descend the ladder and move to the corridor between the office row in which Matt had been placed and the eastern wall of the warehouse section. Then, as quickly as it had materialized, the figure lowered its arm and retreated into the blackness of the corner formed by the intersection of the north and east walls. In that position the figure was practically invisible.

His heart racing, Matt forced himself to lower his eyes. He thought for a moment. He thought both about the prompting—the discomfort behind his eyes that had driven him to search out the figure on the catwalk—and about the figure itself. And he smiled.

After a moment, he turned his head to the left and looked at his guard. Standing near the doorway to the cubicle, facing partially away from him, the guard held an automatic rifle in both hands and looked steadily toward the exterior pedestrian door. Matt looked down. They had trussed him loosely and badly, using but one knot on a single, eighteen-foot length of clothesline. Nevertheless, applied in this instance to a man with the use of just one of his hands, the truss had proven effective enough. The quarter-inch plastic clothesline encircled his right wrist, which was drawn up behind the chair back, perhaps four or five times, looped twice around his chest and the straight-backed chair in which he sat, then passed under the seat, and finally around the chair legs to encircle both of his feet at the ankles. The ends of the line had been brought together and tied along the left side of the chair, midway between his right wrist, pinned at the midpoint of the chair back, and his left ankle, drawn back against the chair's left leg. Out of kindness or carelessness, his captors had allowed his atrophied left arm to hang free at his side. Now, looking down and to the left side of his chair where the clothesline's knot hovered a foot above the concrete, he examined this arrangement with newfound interest.

Matt had assumed that his captors' temporary lack of punitive interest in him—or, at least, their placing the detective ahead of him in their execution schedule—was the result of his having been merely a target of opportunity. While Matt knew that he had doubtless been responsible for leading his shadowers to the apartment in his thoughtless haste to reach Sid Belton, he knew, as well, that Cameron Stafford's hastily formed mission had certainly been arranged in the expectation of capturing Rebecca, Luke, the detective, and for all he knew, Eleanor Chapel. Those four would be regarded by Stafford as the dangerous ones. For as generous as his mentor had been to him, Matt knew that Stafford regarded him as an unexceptional intellect, a young man with a certain presence and personality, but without Rebecca's astonishing versatility and genius; without her brother's breathtaking physical prowess and special combat training; without the detective's extensive worldwide information network, shrewdness, and analytical experience; and without Eleanor Chapel's encompassing wisdom and reputation within academe. And Matt understood all of that to be a fair and objective assessment of his capacities as compared with those of his colleagues.

Added to that assessment was Cameron Stafford's firsthand knowledge of the ease with which Matt had been swayed and influenced and pulled into the MMHCC ranks, bespeaking a weakness which no doubt had led Stafford to hold him in contempt from the very first. Given all of that, Stafford could hardly have concluded otherwise about him. The other four were indeed the dangerous ones. Matt was, in comparison to the others, a cipher.

And Matt had not seriously entertained the idea of a rescue attempt by the Mangusons. He did not see how it would be possible for them to obtain any information whatsoever concerning his and the detective's fate. They would have no means that he could even imagine of gathering pertinent clues about their disappearance, and he knew, it could take a long time indeed—perhaps as long as two or three days—for them to become certain that there had been a disappearance at all. And so he expected the twins and the professor to move on, using the information he had been able to reveal to them in the detective's apartment, to expose the MMHCC and its methods as well as they could without the detective's assistance or his. They would follow the movement of the bookstore's second-floor files to the Maryland shore and disclose them to the Christian media. They would accomplish the main goal: exposure of the MMHCC, first, as the force for Evil that it was in its very core, and next, as the aspiring perpetrator of Evil in schools throughout the country and eventually the world. His colleagues would have no alternative. And so there would be no rescue. And he would bear no resentment. He would feel, as he felt now, only gratitude that he had been forced from the wrong side to the right side in time.

In that state of mind, expecting violent death by bludgeon to begin at any moment, Matt had at first been disbelieving at the sight of the figure on the catwalk above him. And yet there it was. And now that he had come quickly to grips with the truth—that a rescue was in the making—he knew that the figure on the catwalk would be coming down soon . . . very soon . . . to wreak the sort of havoc that only Luke Manguson could wreak on those unfortunate enough to get his attention in this way.

And he knew something else, as well. Rebecca would be with him. Somewhere in the cavernous warehouse, he was certain, she was present.

Matt thought quickly about what Luke would do. Certainly he would have with him his array of knife blades, an array Matt had had occasion to see once before. Now that he had fixed Matt's position and had seen that Matt was bound, he would be at his side with one of those blades in minutes—or, maybe, in seconds—and would be slashing through the cords that bound him. Maybe, thought Matt, he could speed the process somehow.

Matt studied the knotted clothesline. The knot was a simple one. It was small and loose, and its ends fell almost to the concrete floor. The distance from his useless left hand to the knot was perhaps three inches. He glanced quickly at the doorway of his cubicle and saw that his guard had stepped away. Shrugging his minimally functional left shoulder, he began to set up a tiny pendulum movement of his left arm and hand. As he did, he found himself blushing with embarrassment at the lack of discipline that had led him to abandon the physical therapy regimen that had been prescribed by his doctors. He was not completely without muscle and nerve in the shoulder, arm, or hand. But when he had given up on his grandiose plan of restoring the appendage to its original state, he had given up so fully that he simply surrendered all attempts to send any kind of signals to the left arm, under any circumstances, ever. And so it had withered more and more completely as the weeks and months had passed.

He watched his left hand swing back toward the knot that bound him. After a half dozen attempts, he saw—and, indeed, felt faintly—his left little finger make contact with one of the loose ends of the plastic line. Three swings later, he willed his left thumb and index finger to close, and to his surprise, they weakly seized the thin plastic line. Sweating from the effort, he gritted his teeth and, his second and third fingers joining the first against the thumb, he heaved his shoulder up and forward, jerking his head to the right as he did so. When he turned back to look down at his left side, he saw that his hand no longer held the line. But he also saw that the knot had dissolved. The ends of the clothesline hung limply, coiled along the concrete. Quickly he looked up again at the doorway. The guard remained out of sight. Then he looked up and refocused his eyes to peer into the distance at his rescuer. At that instant he saw Luke, on one knee, raise the huge blade of a knife, not in Matt's direction, but in the direction of someone who was apparently so far to Matt's left that he . . . no, Matt thought, *she* . . . was not visible at all from where he sat.

At that moment blackness descended.

Matt immediately began to struggle with his bonds, fighting with his feet and strong right hand to extricate himself. He knew Luke would be coming, and he wanted to keep him from coming all the way to this office. It was the one furthest from the catwalk, and the one nearest the armed guard. In seconds he fought free of the restraints, stood, and, in the darkness, stepped toward the corridor on his right. In his mind an image formed of a powerful figure running toward him in that corridor, a ten-inch blade upraised before him.

If Matt could have seen in the darkness, he would have observed Luke, in a flash, placing the knife in his teeth, leaping to the near ladder, and, with his prodigious strength, clamping the outside rails of the ladder between the palms of his gloved hands and the insteps of his rubber-soled shoes, and sliding down the ladder as though it were a firehouse pole. Matt would have seen Luke hit the floor five seconds after his signal to Rebecca, then turn and sprint for the corridor between the five small offices and the east wall of the warehouse section.

But he could see nothing. He felt to his right for the doorway that faced the small corridor and moved immediately into it, feeling for the warehouse wall. As soon as he touched it, he advanced twelve steps, dropped to one knee, held his breath, and listened. In seconds, as he expected, he heard the faint, rubber-soled footsteps coming swiftly his way. He knew the knife would be up and out front, and so he turned his face to the left and into the wall, pressed his torso against it, extended his right hand across the corridor at knee level, and the instant he felt Luke's knee, whispered, "Luke!"

Although the time lapse between the hand-to-knee contact and the subsequent whisper of a name would have been so small as to defeat a handheld stopwatch, Matt felt the blade slap into his exposed right forearm while the single whispered syllable still hung on his lips and in the air. But it was the flat of the blade, and its cold contact with his skin lasted only another fraction of a second. And in still another fraction, he heard Luke's voice, quiet, but not whispered. "Hold on," it said.

With his good hand, Matt quickly reached for Luke's belt in the darkness. But, given the low crouch in which Luke ran and maneuvered, Matt reached too high and his hand met something that he knew instantly could only be the detective's body. Luke had, he realized, already raced into the office where the detective lay. He had hoisted the lightweight body across his shoulders as easily as if it were a summer raincoat, secured it by seizing a wrist and an ankle with his left hand, and, holding the knife in his right, he had come to free Matt.

Matt slid his hand lower, found Luke's belt, gave a sharp tug, and then was nearly jerked from his feet by the power of Luke's rush, back in the direction from which he had come. Stumbling, holding on desperately in the total darkness, Matt ran as well as he could. It soon seemed to him that they had run further in a straight line than was possible, given his impressions of the dimensions of the warehouse. But then he heard a slight metallic impact of raised knife against the back wall. He then was nearly pulled from his feet again as Luke pivoted to his left and began to tear along in the darkness, running west along the back wall of section four, now, presumably, directly under the catwalk. Occasionally Matt could hear men's voices, not sounding alarmed, but calling to one another in the darkness. He could not make out what they said, nor did he try. He was fully occupied with the physical demands of running through the blackness of the warehouse, holding on to the human locomotive that had come to rescue him.

They continued in their new direction for only a few seconds. Luke suddenly stopped and apparently dropped to one knee. The lights had been off, Matt estimated, for perhaps ninety seconds. It had seemed forever.

Matt found himself breathing heavily, now that they had stopped, kneeling against the north wall. Then he heard Luke's low voice. "Be ready. They'll find flashlights eventually. And they may realize they can send someone up one of the ladders and get the master switch engaged.

"If the lights come up now," he continued rapidly, "or if the flashlights find us soon, we'll try for the doorway to our right, out of section four and through the other three sections to the doorway to the street."

"And if they don't?" whispered Matt.

"We want a vehicle," the reply came.

At that moment, perhaps three minutes after the lights had been extinguished, Matt heard a remarkable sound just as he saw two flashlight beams knife through the darkness, well to his left, near the row of offices. When the sound became louder and unmistakable, he saw both flashlights direct themselves toward the source of the noise. And so he recognized, weakly illuminated, the ghostly, fragmentary shape of the old flatbed. Incredulous, Matt watched as the rusted cab, diesel engine knocking violently, lurched toward the front wall of the warehouse, dragging its elongated trailer behind it like some prehistoric creature freshly awakened and now in great ill temper.

Had he been able to see into the flatbed's cab, he would have seen, moments earlier, a dark-clad woman climbing up the short ladder to the passenger-side door, then using her hooded flashlight to illuminate the exposed tangle of wires under the dashboard. He then would have seen her cross-wire the ignition switch to start the motor and, manipulating the clutch pedal expertly, slam the machine into first gear. Next, he would have watched as she drove the drill sergeant's swagger stick against the accelerator pedal, wedging the handle of the stick against the driver's seat. And finally, as the huge machine lumbered forward, engine noise building in a throaty, terrifying crescendo, he would have seen her slide quickly back to the right-hand door, drop to the concrete floor, and sprint away from the monstrous vehicle. What he did see was the massive, screaming eighteen-wheeled bulldozer-carrying flatbed truck, gaining momentum, headed directly toward the center of the enormous—and closed—overhead garage door.

As Rebecca slid back across the floorboard of the lurching vehicle that she had just set into ponderous motion, she heard men's voices beginning to shout in her direction. Dropping to the concrete and sprinting away from the truck, she saw over her shoulder two flashlight beams probing the darkness. Using the enormous length and bulk of the flatbed to shield her, she ran straight for Cameron Stafford's vintage Buick. In the faint reflected light from the wild sweeps of the two flashlights, the Buick's hood glinted dully.

It was enough. She flew to the car, opened the driver's side door, leaped in, and immediately smashed the dome light with the butt of her own flash-light. She placed the hooded flashlight on the seat beside her and switched it on, then manipulated one of the screwdrivers Luke had given her before they had separated on the catwalk, using it, as she had with the truck, both to expose the ignition wires and to cross-wire the switch. The primitive General Motors engine roared to life at the moment the flatbed, having drifted slightly to the left in its nearly seventy-five feet of travel since Rebecca had left it, finally plowed into the south wall of the warehouse, partially smashing through the garage door and partially ripping through the metal wall itself. It ground through tin, sheet metal, wood, and glass as though the door and the wall were made of tissue paper. The truck lum-bered through, completely unaffected by the puny obstacles, its accelerator firmly jammed against the floorboard by Rebecca's club. It continued steadily through the door and wall and out into the alley, dragging shards from the splintered surfaces along with it, a grating, scraping, screeching, rending horror of noise attending each revolution of the mighty wheels.

Rebecca shoved the Buick's automatic transmission lever into its low-gear setting and felt the Buick, its engine idling rapidly enough to drive the vehicle slowly forward without the accelerator's assistance, jump sluggishly into forward motion. In the dim but ample light suddenly streaming into the warehouse through the monstrous hole in the south wall, she could now see well enough to aim the nose of the old car just to the left of the jagged opening. She tapped the accelerator once and, dropping her head below the steering wheel and preparing to exit via the passenger side, deftly snapped on the car's headlights and kicked the high-beam floorboard pedal with her left foot.

From his position along the back wall of the warehouse, crouching under the high catwalk, Matt watched and listened in bewilderment as the diesel grumbled to life and appeared to drive itself toward and then entirely through the south wall. But he could not attend carefully to this phenomenon, for, as soon as the truck's raucous motor came to life, his attention was consumed not only by flashlight beams and shouting voices, but by Luke's hasty placement of Sid Belton's limp form on his shoulders.

Saying only, "Take the detective to the van when you can," Luke had disappeared. But before Matt could so much as form his next thought, he saw the Buick's headlamps suddenly illuminate an area just to the left of the shattered warehouse wall, and within seconds, heard the terrifying and unmistakable sound of an automatic rifle in action. In concert with the fearsome weapon's own continuous report came the devastating sounds of shredded glass and splattered metal as rifle bullets destroyed the Buick's windows and slammed into its sculptured fenders and doors. As the onslaught continued, bullets riddled the wounded auto's left front and rear tires. Tilting to its left, its hubs beginning to crunch into the concrete floor, the faded, dying relic crawled to a stop, its still-idling engine no longer able to overcome the resistance generated by its crippled left-side wheels.

During its six-second burst, the automatic rifle had announced its own location both audibly and visibly. The abrupt cessation of fire, Matt guessed, had less to do with the guard's having become satisfied with his results or having run out of ammunition than with Luke Manguson's arrival at the spot.

Matt tried to focus. He desperately needed to assess the situation on the battlefield, despite the surreal visual conditions. The faint light that entered the warehouse through the newly created hole in the front wall was intersected weirdly by the still-functioning headlights of the wrecked Buick. In this strange black-and-white world, Matt could make out the silhouette of the bookstore van, some one hundred feet away and directly in front of him. He could also see the outline of the limousine, positioned to the van's left and quite near the offices in which he and the detective had been held. And he could also see dimly at least a half-dozen ghostly forms, some running, others crouching either in the open or near the limousine. At that moment no flashlights were operating, since none of the guards was foolish enough to wish to call attention to himself while in proximity to automatic weapons fire. With the rifle silenced, the warehouse had gone quiet except for the low mechanical purr of the bullet-riddled Buick engine and the still more distant noises of the flatbed beginning to grind itself against the abandoned structures on the opposite side of the alley.

"Take the detective to the van when you can." Those were Luke's orders. In Matt's mind, this moment seemed as good as any to make the attempt. He shrugged the slight form of the detective forward against the back of his neck, looped his right arm behind the detective's knees and, reaching across his own body, grasped the nearer of Sid Belton's wrists in his right hand. Matt took in a deep breath, exhaled, and started forward. With 145 pounds on his shoulders, he found that he could not actually run as Luke had been able to do under the same conditions but could maintain a rapid, long-striding, walk. The vast warehouse seemed eerily quiet after roaring engines, clattering rifle fire, and shattering glass. Now, though his eyes darted left, right, and forward, Matt could distinguish nothing except the van's rectangular bulk directly in his path. As he neared its still-open cargo doors, he suddenly flinched and dropped to a crouch as a form flew past him from behind and to his right, leaping into the van through its rear doors without seeming to slow. It moved to the driver's seat, and having switched on a hooded flashlight, appeared to be working at the ignition wiring. "Rebecca," he thought to himself. He rose from his crouch, completed his hasty journey, and deposited his burden carefully on the cargo floor of the van just as the motor sprung to life. Matt moved into the cargo hold and pulled the detective's broken body carefully forward.

From that moment, the action seemed to accelerate still further, multi-plying itself so quickly that Matt found later that he could not reconstruct events in an orderly way. But some things he could remember. First, the warehouse lights came up, altering the visual landscape in an instant. Before Matt's eyes could adjust, two men had opened the driver's side door of the van, reached in, seized Rebecca, and dragged her violently from the truck.

Matt leaped forward through the cargo space and arrived at the open driver's side door of the van to see Rebecca being held by both men some fifteen feet away. He saw that she was dressed in her dark tennis warm-ups, her face blackened, her hands gloved, her ponytail drawn through a slit in her billed cap. She was held tightly by the guards, one of whom held a twelve-inch screwdriver to her right cheek. The metal end of the screw-driver was jammed so violently into her cheek that a small river of blood already coursed down the side of her face. The grim threesome faced the front of the warehouse, and when Matt followed their eyes with his, he saw, another sixty feet from them, the momentarily quiescent automatic rifle. Under it, face up, blood running down his face from a broken nose, lay the guard who had crippled the Buick with a long burst just seconds earlier. His weapon was now held by Luke Manguson, and its muzzle seemed to point directly at his sister.

One of the guards was shouting at Luke. "Drop it! Drop it now! I'll put this damned screwdriver all the way through her pretty face. I'll do it!"

Then, from a great distance, high up on the catwalk and at its oppo-site, or western, end, Matt heard another shout. "You heard him! Drop it, Manguson!"

Matt turned his head, moved to his right to the passenger seat of the van, and looked up toward the far end of the catwalk. There he saw another of the warehouse guards, this one holding a second rifle. The man stood in front of the master power switches, one of which he had obviously just activated to illuminate the warehouse section. Before Matt could turn his head to look back toward Luke, he saw, to his further amazement and confusion, a second figure emerge on the catwalk. Dressed entirely in black and wearing a ski mask that covered its face completely, it stepped through the door immediately behind the guard. In its gloved hands it carried what Matt identified even at 150 feet as an ordinary baseball bat. The figure, unhesitating, charged awkwardly at the rifle-aiming guard from behind and, carrying the bat as though it were a jousting lance, drove its barrel into the back of the man's unprotected skull. The guard fell forward onto the catwalk as if shot in the head, crashing onto the metal surface face down, right hand and arm hanging over the edge. The weapon, tumbling wildly, fell forty feet and clattered to the concrete floor, discharging one round of ammunition harmlessly into the back wall of the warehouse.

Matt spun his head back to the left just in time to hear and see Luke Manguson unleash a burst of automatic rifle fire, aiming just over Rebecca's captors' heads. At that instant, Matt saw Rebecca, seizing on her guards' terrified response to the bullets whining past them, swing her open right hand up and back over her shoulder, driving her palm upward, into, and through the nose of the guard who held the screwdriver pressed into her face. In almost the same motion, she dropped and twisted to the floor, rolling away from the guards, toward the van. Luke then fired two more short bursts below and to the near side of the guards, effectively turning them away from the van. The bullets ricocheted behind them as they ran, glancing off the concrete floor. As the guards fled toward the northeast corner of the warehouse section, a gloved hand high on the catwalk slammed the handle of the master lighting switch back down to the "off" position. Darkness fell again on warehouse section four.

With Matt behind the wheel, the white van maneuvered laboriously through the darkened warehouse, headlamps off. Luke had stationed himself in the front of the van with Matt, kneeling between the passenger-side seat and the dashboard, his shoulders facing the rear and the captured automatic rifle's barrel resting on the window opening. Luke had made clear to Matt that his final rifle bursts, aimed through the semidarkness at the right-side tires on the gray limousine, had exhausted the weapon's ammunition. The rifle's presence, however, they both knew, would continue to influence the guards' behavior.

Matt, who had not attempted to drive since his disabling injury, found the vehicle unwieldy and struggled to dodge through and around the debris. Spinning the wheel left and right with his good hand, he passed behind the ruined Buick and picked his way through the glass and metal clutter inside and outside the flatbed truck's physically catastrophic exit through the front wall. He then turned sharply right into the alley, avoiding the rear of the still-twitching flatbed trailer, and made for the western end of the street.

In the van's ample but inhospitable cargo area, Rebecca hovered over the crumpled detective, whispering to him steadily. She could now see in the faint light provided by moon and street lamp that his face was a mass of contusions, that his right arm had suffered compound fractures, and that his right hand had been severely burned. She had immediately probed his anterior carotid for a pulse and had felt none. Still she whispered to him, telling him she was there, telling him that his work was not finished, telling him that they needed him.

Luke directed Matt through the two right turns that led them back to the alley in which the borrowed Porsche waited. As Matt slowed, Luke called back to his sister. "Let me have the Porsche's key, Rebecca. You stay with the detective in the van. I'll follow you and Matt back to Manhattan."

Her response was quick and sure. "No, Luke. One of us has to go back to the warehouse. You know why. And you know who has to drive that Turbo. Put the rifle away and come back here and tend to the detective. There can't be any hurry, in any case, to get to the expressway now. The guards have no useable vehicle remaining. They have no way to pursue us. Come here and talk to him while I take the Porsche back to the warehouse."

Alarmed, Matt began to protest. "What? Go back? Why? We've got to get out of here. There's still at least one weapon back there in the warehouse, and just because you shot out two of the limousine's tires before we left, Luke, doesn't mean they can't get another vehicle and . . ."

Luke raised his palm toward Matt, glanced sharply at him, and Matt fell immediately silent, embarrassed. Matt knew he had no real understanding of the tactical situation. And he knew that the twins did, and he knew from experience that they were superb decision-makers under fire.

Luke turned back to his sister. "All right, go," he said simply. "We'll head for the expressway. We'll get to Dr. Chapel as fast as we can. She can advise us about where to take Mr. Belton."

Rebecca turned, swung the rear cargo doors open, and then turned back and bent low over the broken man, her ponytail cascading over his battered face. "Don't you *dare* die, Sidney Belton," she said emphatically, no longer whispering. "I shall hold it very much against you if you do. Do you understand me?"

As she raised herself from him again, all three heard a muffled, guttural response. "Yes ma'am," it said indistinctly. "I . . . don't want you . . . mad at me."

Time stopped.

Rebecca stared, speechless, at the crumpled form. Then she moved.

"Oh!" she cried out. "Oh . . . thank you! Thank you!" As she fell back beside him, she found laughter escaping her lips, completely unbidden, while at the same time tears sprang to the gray eyes and immediately rolled down her face and onto his. "Luke! Matt! He's with us! Oh! He's with us still!"

Matt, profoundly surprised that anyone could have lived through the beating he had unwillingly heard, and unexpectedly moved by the mere sound of the detective's voice, switched off the van's engine and followed Luke quickly into the cargo area. In an utterly spontaneous gesture, both men went immediately to their wounded comrade and, kneeling, placed their hands on him.

Semiconscious, Sid Belton found himself dimly aware that five hands rested on his body. He found himself equally aware, and almost in the same physically perceived way, that three prayers were being offered for him at the same time. His skin tingled at each point of contact. He felt suddenly warm.

An independent observer at that point, regardless of artistic bent or background, might well have been struck by an urge to sculpt, so dramatic yet stationary were the forms, a woman and two men in prayer, their hands placed with such obvious caution and purpose on the fourth figure's horribly damaged and disfigured body.

The three held their positions over the motionless detective for perhaps a full minute. Then, without overt signal, the two men rose, turned, and began pulling insulation and packing materials together to fashion a more comfortable resting place for the detective. After working quietly for several minutes, Matt stepped from the cargo doors and looked up and down the alley. At one end of the street he saw the dim interior light of a telephone booth. He put his head back inside the rear of the van and addressed himself to the twins. "Suppose I telephone Dr. Chapel from the public phone at the end of the alley? That way she can begin to make her contacts and set arrangements for emergency treatment."

"Oh, good!" responded Rebecca. "But she's not at her home, Matt. We brought her to our hotel today. And don't be surprised if a man answers. One of her pastors is with her. You have the number memorized?"

Matt moved toward the distant telephone in his loping run, pinning his left wrist to his body with his right hand, while Rebecca turned again to the detective. She placed her hand gently on the side of his face, moved her lips closer to him to whisper more words of encouragement, and then realized he was trying to speak again. She placed her ear near his mouth, holding the ponytail away from his face with one hand, and was able to make out the words, spoken as low moans. "There's . . . a service revolver . . . in my ankle holster . . . It's loaded. Take it with you, ma'am. Take it."

She sat back, reached to the detective's feet, pulled up one trousers leg and then the other, and found the weapon. She unsnapped the strap on the ankle holster, removed the small handgun carefully, and, crouching low in the cramped van, moved forward and handed the revolver to her brother. He examined it quickly, moved the safety mechanism off and then on, and returned it to her. "Yes," he said. "Now, go, Rebecca. We'll move out in five minutes."

As she accepted the firearm from him and turned to go, she felt her brother's powerful hand on her upper arm. She turned and found him staring hard at her face. He pulled her slowly back to him and, with his free hand, turned the right side of her face toward the weak moonlight drifting into the van from its open rear doors. His eyes widened. "Rebecca!" he exclaimed, astonishment in his voice. "You're cut! Your cheek has been slashed! You're bleeding!"

She pulled away from him angrily. "Stop it!" she hissed, surprised at the vehemence of her own response. "We have *work* to do, Luke." She slid out the cargo door and trotted quickly to the Porsche. Once there, she hesitated, one hand on the door handle. After a moment she turned and retraced her steps slowly, thoughtfully. Finally, she stood just behind the van's rear bumper and looked deep into the shadowy cargo compartment at her brother. He sat frozen, devastated by her furious reaction.

She spoke softly to him. "Luke . . . Luke, I'm sorry. I think I was reflexively angry because . . . well . . . compared to this. . . ." Here she leaned into the van and gestured to the silent form of the detective, *"this* is nothing," she said, touching her face. "And you know, dear, if it had been Matt, or any man, you'd have had no real interest in a facial cut. You'd just think of it as another battle scar . . . something to be proud of, even. And I didn't want you to be . . . well . . . quite so stricken simply because your . . . your pretty sister is not going to be so completely pretty anymore.

"But I'm fine, dear. You know how facial cuts bleed. It won't be so bad as it looks right now, I'm sure. I'm fine. Really. And I love you very much."

She turned away, paused, then faced him again. "By the way, Luke. You'll remember that Matt doesn't have a driver's license? He really shouldn't be driving the van."

He stared at her for a long moment, detected the shadow of a smile on her face, and realized that his sister had decided to elicit laughter from him before she departed. He screwed his face into a faux glare and said, "You can't reprimand me one minute and make me laugh the next. I'm a full thirty minutes older than you, you know. I want a little respect from my baby sister!"

And they both laughed quietly from the depths of their lifelong love for each other.

Moving quickly, having restored Luke to himself as only she could, Rebecca slid behind the wheel of the Porsche. She cranked the eager Turbo, moved the shift lever into first gear, and executed a lightning U-turn, retracing the route back to the scene of the warehouse struggle. In her rearview mirror, as she whipped the roadster into its first turn, she saw Matt racing for the van. "Good," she thought to herself. "The detective will be on his way in seconds."

She stopped the car and turned off the rumbling Turbo about seventy-five feet from the final corner. Leaving the key in the ignition, she lifted the detective's revolver from the passenger seat, switched the safety mechanism to the "off" position, and walked quickly back to the alley that had seen so much action in the handful of days since her arrival in New York. Fifteen feet from the corner she stopped and listened. As she prepared to move forward again, she heard the sound of a pebble, inadvertently kicked. She placed her back flat against the wall and, shifting the revolver to her left hand, aimed the muzzle slightly downward at an angle designed to destroy, with one shot, the knee of an armed adversary if one were to materialize carrying its own firearm. Her brother had taught her well.

A moment later, she observed a figure moving hesitantly around the corner of the building. In the moonlight she recognized the dark ski mask that Luke had described when he had told her in the van how the rifleman on the catwalk had been disarmed. A second later, the figure's gloved right hand emerged. The hand carried a three-foot-long club, the device she knew the mysterious assailant had used to render the catwalk gunman unconscious.

By the time the dark figure, its peripheral vision limited by the ski mask, realized Rebecca was there, it saw, at the same time, the revolver in her left hand. She saw it freeze and heard a small, timorous gasp from under the mask. The heavy wooden club dropped noisily to the pavement, and the figure quickly raised its hands to its shoulders, palms open to Rebecca.

"No!" it whispered desperately. "Please, Miss Manguson. No!"

Slowly, she lowered the revolver to her side. She moved her right hand to the weapon and slipped the safety mechanism to its "on" position. Then she looked up at the hooded figure, its hands still raised, and to the figure's astonishment, smiled, the caked blood on her cheek subtracting nothing from the quality of her beauty. And then she spoke softly, gently to the terrified figure before her, a mischievous note rising in her voice. "Dr. Ellis Dolby, I believe? I should think, sir, that you have earned a ride home tonight."

The figure gasped again. For several moments, its hands remained raised and at its shoulders. Then its head dropped to its chest and its hands briefly covered its eyes, hidden within the mask. Its shoulders began to shake, and Rebecca realized that the sounds she heard were sobs. As she took a step to move to its side, she heard its voice. Its whisper was so soft that she took a moment to realize that the figure was not addressing her at all.

"*Thank You, Lord,*" the whisper said. "*Forgive me my cowardice . . . I am not brave . . . like this woman You have sent to help me . . . Thank You . . . for giving me . . . sufficient strength . . . to be of help to her on this night. . . .*"

CHAPTER TEN

"YES, OF COURSE," REBECCA WAS SAYING TO HER bespectacled passenger as she maneuvered the Cabriolet onto the approaches to the Queensboro Bridge over the East River and into Manhattan, "I did indeed return to the warehouse for no purpose other than to find you.

"Did you think," she continued, glancing at him and smiling, "we would be so callous as to become beneficiaries of all the risks you've taken, without being willing to take a small risk on your behalf?

"And, believe me, Dr. Dolby, the risk of retrieving you," she noted, "was quite small. We were confident that the guards would not be searching for you. As far as we know, only Luke and Matt were in position to see you on that catwalk. None of the guards—one already disabled by Luke, two under fire from him, and two hiding somewhere behind the offices—could see how your man was silenced. Luke and I fully expected to find you making a quiet exit along the pathways shown by your own diagrams."

After a moment, Ellis Dolby, adjusting his thick, wire-framed glasses out of long habit, replied thoughtfully, "I admit I've not been thinking too clearly. I got a taxi to bring me to the warehouse area of Brooklyn hours ago and hadn't really considered how I'd find another one, in that part of town and at this hour of night, to take me back home. I just knew I had to be at that warehouse in case there might be some way for me to contribute. I can't tell you how foolish I've felt tonight, carrying this baseball bat around. But it's the only thing I own that could possibly be used as a weapon. And, frankly, I didn't really imagine that I'd be able to use it to hit somebody. But when I saw that that guard was going to fire at you and your brother, something just took over my body, and I found myself rushing at him like a crazy man. I mean, a *crazy* man. I'll never understand how I did that. I've never hit anybody in my life with anything, much less with something as lethal as a baseball bat. I do hope the gentleman suffered no more than a slight concussion—or less—at my hands."

He paused and looked over at the Porsche's driver as she worked their borrowed automotive masterpiece up and down through its lower-range gears. "You know, Rebecca," he said hesitantly, "that cut on your face is a terrible looking thing. Should we be stopping at an emergency room?"

"I want to get to the hotel as fast as I can, Ellis," she replied with a touch of impatience in her voice. "We don't know the extent of the detective's injuries. We do know they are far more serious than mine."

"Yes, of course," he replied apologetically. "Sorry." He paused again, then asked, "And what about the police? I felt I couldn't go to them because . . . well . . . I was much too afraid."

He looked away from her, shamefaced. "I was afraid they would ask a lot of questions of me . . . and that I would actually become one of their chief suspects, not just in the kidnapping, but in the larger scheme. I've been in an agony of indecision for months now, seeing that I'd allowed myself to get involved in such terrible things, Rebecca. I know I must be legally complicit in any number of . . ."

Rebecca interrupted him with a touch of her hand on his arm. "It's time to stop thinking that way, Ellis," she said with more emphasis than she intended, realizing as she heard herself speak that she sounded as though she were addressing one of her students. "You've taken great risks today: finding a way to communicate on a public sidewalk with Dr. Chapel, providing us with the information we needed to plan the rescue, even helping us to extricate ourselves during our most difficult moment in the warehouse. And yet you're still on the 'inside' of the MMHCC. Think of it, Ellis. Just think of it for a moment. What you've done is wonderful!

"And," she continued, "once we get Mr. Belton back to health, you'll see that he'll make certain the authorities understand the value of what you've done. And it must be the detective himself who makes all contacts with the police, Ellis. If any of us were to attempt that now, we'd be trying to induce them to move against some of the most respected individuals in your entire country, and without a shred of effective evidence. My visions would—and should—count for nothing in a law enforcement context. Our only hope, really, is to get to the internal documents that you're already familiar with, the ones that Matt was able to review last night at the bookstore, and to show them to Dr. Chapel's media contacts. That's the only real chance we have to draw law enforcement into the fray, and even more important in the long run, shift the weight of public opinion."

"But," protested Dolby mildly, "what about the plain fact of their kidnapping two people? And then the beating and torture of one of their captives? Can't we involve the police by that route? Or . . . or no . . . I see," he corrected himself. "I see . . . if we move on that front, in that way, rather than moving against them by means of the documents Mr. Clark found, we lead Dr. Stafford to an immediate cover-up of all that he has done so far. He would have the files destroyed before you would have a chance to reveal those documents to the media. Dr. Stafford would pull back from all his planned illegalities—the bribes, the fraud, the extortion, the whole machinery he'll use to ensure victory—before his people act on any of those plans. And that would mean they could just go forward, largely unimpeded, with the main scheme, pushing it through state legislature after state legislature, just on the strength of their *legal* lobbying tactics. The MMHCC project might become even more successful . . . even more destructive to the children . . . if it were stripped of all its excesses.

"We need," he continued, not waiting for Rebecca to respond, his voice waxing nearly to its full-blown lecturing volume, "to expose their criminal and murderous *intentions*, as reflected in those documents, in order to expose and discredit the whole gang and, by indirection, the project itself. And the documents provide the only *real* opportunity we have at hand."

"Yes," she replied quietly.

They rode in silence for several minutes, crossing the island of Manhattan from east to west at midtown.

Rebecca glanced at her companion. "This must have been so hard for you, Ellis, alone with this burden for so long."

He swallowed hard and looked away again. When he turned back to her, his eyes were filled with tears. "I'm sorry. I know you must think I'm a child. . . . I've known you for about thirty minutes and already you've seen me cry twice. . . . But you can't imagine how lonely it's been, and how desperate I've felt. I didn't even disclose my fears to my pastor, to say nothing of the police. Mostly I've just been terrified. I've been afraid for my career, if you can imagine. And I've been even more afraid for my life. And, in my best—or worst—moments, I've been afraid most of all for my soul.

"But," he continued, still struggling with his composure, "when I heard Dr. Stafford and others beginning to talk about you, Rebecca—the moment Matt Clark asked Dr. Stafford to help him find accommodations for you at the seminary—I began to think there might be hope, if only I could think of some way to reach you. They're afraid of you, you know. They would do anything to corrupt you or, failing that, to kill you." He looked at her. "But you know that, of course."

Then, turning away, he continued with his previous thought. "And then I found out from them that Dr. Chapel had been contacted by Detective Belton—yes, they knew about that right away, somehow—and I began to imagine that Dr. Chapel might provide me a means to reach you. And when they captured Mr. Belton and Matt last night . . . well . . . I knew that I had to act this very day . . . I had to reach you through Dr. Chapel immediately . . . or nothing would matter any more. It took a sense of complete desperation to lead me to act, Rebecca. I'm not a brave person. I'm not a good Christian. I would have made a poor martyr."

She glanced at him again as, downshifting expertly, she turned from Central Park South into Columbus Circle and then right onto Broadway, heading north toward the hotel. "Ellis," she said somberly, "may I ask you to think about something quite seriously? You have managed to save the lives of four people by your actions today and tonight. And more important by far, you're in the process of helping us prevent something, if it were to succeed, that would place in jeopardy the souls of hundreds of thousands of young people. *Hundreds of thousands*, you must realize. You've taken great risks on behalf of a godly mission. You'll be taking still more.

"And so, Dr. Ellis Dolby," she concluded slowly and with emphasis, "in view of that . . . let's have done with 'I'm not a brave person,' shall we? Let's just decide to have done with it . . . permanently."

He stared at her for a moment and then threw his head back and laughed aloud, long and hard, a raucous, high-pitched cackle that brought a bright smile of surprise to Rebecca's face. And then, turning his head again to look at her, he said simply, "Well, Rebecca . . . sure . . . okay."

He then looked away from her again, nodding to himself thoughtfully. After a moment, he spoke softly, more to himself than to her, "You know, I think maybe I *will* 'have done with that,' Miss Rebecca Manguson . . . I think maybe I'll just 'have done with it,' once and for all."

Then, turning again to her and raising his voice over the engine's finely tuned whine as she accelerated through the Porsche's versatile third gear along Broadway at West Seventy-Second Street, he asked, smiling, "Will that do it for me, then? If I just stop thinking that I'm not a brave person, will I then be brave? I'm a psychologist, you know. It sounds a little simplistic."

Working the clutch with her left foot and dropping the shift lever into fourth, she replied without moving her eyes from the roadway, and to his discomfort, without returning his smile, "Complexity is no virtue, Dr. Dolby. And complexity is never, in itself, an indicator of truth."

As she braked and downshifted for a traffic signal at a nearly deserted intersection, she added, "I'd suggest, if I may, that you just stop using those terms at all. Instead of laboring to be brave . . . or intelligent . . . or suave . . . or any of the things our societies—yours and mine—seem to value so much, why don't you just have a go at doing your duty?"

She glanced at him, still unsmiling, and nodded. "You've done your duty—done the things that God required of you—throughout this day, you know. And that's what Luke has tried to do. And that's what I've tried to do. You can see that it seems to have been quite enough.

"So," she concluded, "let others wrestle over bravery and cowardice and a thousand other labels for God's human creatures." She looked at him and, finally, he noticed with relief, smiled. "Just do your duty, Ellis. Submit yourself to Him. In the end, there is only one label worth having."

Rebecca opened her eyes and looked sleepily about her. She lay on the floor in Eleanor Chapel's hotel room—the three young men had slept in the room she and her brother had originally occupied—with her head on a sofa cushion and her body wrapped tightly in the thin blanket she had found in a bottom drawer of the room's small chest. The room was dark and hot.

She unrolled herself from the blanket and sat up. In the faint light provided by the softly luminous face of the bedside clock-radio, she could see the outline of Eleanor Chapel's diminutive form and could hear her breathing, whispers of air traveling rhythmically in and out of her body.

Rebecca peered at the clock and saw that it was not yet 5:00 A.M. She had been asleep no more than an hour, despite being a good sleeper under most circumstances. Why, she wondered groggily, had she awakened?

The answer came as soon as the question had been posed; the room immediately began to remove itself from her senses. The wall dimly visible opposite her suddenly appeared to her eyes far away . . . a hundred miles . . . a thousand miles. The sound of her companion's breathing now came to her from a great distance . . . seeming to echo impossibly across high, remote ranges and over deep, uncharted chasms. Even the feel of the threadbare blanket on which her hands still rested was transformed under her fingers, seeming to recede uncannily from her touch, as though pulled from her by angels perched around the far edges of the universe. Indeed, the room seemed to her to have become as large as a universe . . . and as rich . . . and as threatening . . . in its possibilities. Awe consumed her, filled her with equal parts love and fear, and she clasped her hands against each other in front of her chest, sitting fully erect, gray eyes now wide, muscles tensed, struggling to breathe.

As on other occasions, the vision formed and completed itself with startling clarity directly in her line of sight, outlines sharp and bright. First she saw, appearing more massive and architecturally muscular than she remembered from Sunday's altar-rail vision, an outdoor arena. Light in color, it sailed majestically above her from her low perspective, which seemed to be the grassy surface around which the structure rose. This time she saw that the arena was filled with spectators, tens of thousands of people seated before her and arrayed in two layers, with the lower deck topped by a soaring upper deck or balcony that seemed to reach to the sky. Once more she could see that words appeared in huge block letters, apparently written across the facing wall of the upper deck. But once more she could not decipher them, and for the same reason as before: the centerpiece of the vision forced her attention away from the arena's more distant background and toward the grassy surface immediately before her. And there, again, were the children . . . children by the tens of thousands . . . children of all ages and of every ethnicity . . . each child holding a book from which it read, silent and intent. And as before, as she watched, the children began to change. A thick, choking bank of low cloud or fog blew itself through the arena and in and out among the children and, as it did, each child, as before, began to deteriorate, to diminish, to grow weak, fragile, ill.

Here her first vision, on Sunday, of children and arena had ended. But this time, as Rebecca remained unmoving on the hotel room floor, her back rigid, her eyes wide, the vision held itself steadily before her for some time, the children weakening, failing, falling, while she continued to gaze, again horrified, at the otherwise stationary scene. But then her attention was gradually directed elsewhere within the field of vision provided her. She began to sense that, near one extreme boundary of her perceptual field extended, on the grassy surface itself, very near the opposite end of the arena, a platform of some kind had been erected. On its raised surface a dozen adults seemed to move slowly as though in formal procession. As she strained to grasp the nature of the procession, the vision began to fade from her view. But before it was extinguished entirely, the low cloud or fog bank that had pervaded the arena's surface suddenly and with impossible swiftness swirled toward the platform and concentrated itself around and above it, the density of cloud seeming to blot out the sunlight and obliterate the ceremonial procession.

And as the vision faded to black, as swiftly as thought, two additional phenomena thrust themselves upon her. One was a prickling sensation at the back of her neck, a sudden awareness of something behind her and yet also within the confines of the envisioned arena, something that threatened Rebecca Manguson herself, something that prepared to move directly and catastrophically against *her*. The second phenomenon was, once more, the certainty that a command was attendant. And once more she knew the nature of the command that painted itself into her brain. And once more the command held but two words: *Prevent this.*

Seconds passed. Slowly, she felt her muscles turning to water, and she slumped gradually to the floor on her right side, a soft moan escaping her lips as she did. Yet even as she began to collapse, emptied, she forced her mind back into the dream in an effort to recapture every detail, and to play again the visionary sequences before her internal eye.

While she fought weakly through her exhaustion to bring memory into focus, a series of small, inarticulate sounds—less than moans and more than sighs—escaped her throat so easily that they passed from her unnoticed. And so she was startled to feel the small, veined hands on her head and shoulder, and the warm breath on her neck, and the light, soft tangles of unbound gray hair falling against her ear. The voice whispered urgently, "Rebecca . . . Rebecca . . . what it is, dear? Can you talk to me? Can I help you?"

Rebecca, using all her available strength, slowly lifted one hand to Eleanor Chapel's cheek and felt a surprisingly strong hand grasp her fingers and hold them tightly. And she found that, though she tried, she could not speak or return the gesture.

And so the two women remained until, after several moments, Rebecca felt a gentle flurry of movement against her as the senior professor of Old Testament worked to cover the shivering young woman with the thin blanket and, where it would not reach, with the warmth of her small body. And there she held her until she felt Rebecca's muscles relax still further and heard finally the measured breathing of a woman emptied . . . and filled.

A half hour after sunrise, the twins, Matt Clark, Eleanor Chapel, and Ellis Dolby sat on the floor with coffee or juice in the larger of the two connecting hotel rooms. This was the room originally occupied by the twins and now used by the three men. Matt had just completed his summary of the kidnapping and of his experiences in captivity, insofar as he had been conscious to perceive and thus remember anything about those drugged, chaotic hours. He ended his account with Cameron Stafford's heavily escorted departure from his cubicle.

As he paused to consider how to broach the episode with Edward Jamieson, his mind was suddenly filled with dread at the necessity for him to communicate Jamieson's explicit threat toward Rebecca. And so he was at length interrupted, the others under the pardonable impression that his account was complete. He sat silent as the conversation continued without him.

Throughout this, Rebecca sat erect with her back touching the wall separating the two rooms, a glass of tomato juice resting on a saucer on the floor to her right. Her left hand was entwined with Matt's right, a delightful fact that had stamped a smile on his face at the session's beginning when he had realized that her hand was extended toward him, inviting him to sit beside her. Now, his report only partially finished, it was some time before he could focus on anything but this contact with her hand and his fear of reporting the Jamieson episode.

But finally he forced himself to attend. Eleanor Chapel was speaking. He made a concerted effort to listen.

"And the doctors are quite optimistic," she was saying, characteristically bright-eyed, despite the hour of morning and the brevity of the night. "It's so wonderful to have such talented friends as these two physicians, healers who can minister to the detective in their own outpatient surgical center, and even place him overnight in the center's guestroom. He has three or four broken ribs, unspecified internal injuries, a broken right arm—broken in several places—awful burns on his right hand, and the horrid face and head injuries. But, all said and done, they seem more than satisfied with everything except the severity of the concussion. They'll be watching him closely during these forty-eight hours. Then, if they're satisfied that he's out of danger, we can bring him home . . . I mean, we can bring him *here* . . . here with us." The elfin face brightened still further, and then, a new thought appearing to have arrived, fell quickly. Her brow furrowed and she made a small fist with one hand.

"However," she continued, "when I finally reached the plastic surgeon—another trusted friend—at her home and talked her into coming to attend to Rebecca's facial wound, I found her to be most unsatisfied. She took nearly twenty stitches. Then, she talked with me outside the room before she left at about 4:00 A.M. She's a cosmetic surgeon, you know, and she's accustomed to making facial scars virtually disappear. Since Rebecca's face was cut by a large screwdriver, not a knife, and because Rebecca was twisting to escape her captors when the gash was made, I'm afraid the surgeon thinks it's likely to leave a rather conspicuous and somewhat jagged scar. I think she's personally offended by it."

At this, Rebecca actually laughed aloud, causing four heads to turn in confused surprise. "I'm so sorry," she said, "I don't mean to make light of this, but it's only a *mark*, you know. An *irregularity* where there wasn't one before."

She leaned toward Eleanor Chapel and patted the older woman's knee. "It's not that I'm unappreciative of your getting a preeminent physician to help me, Eleanor. I just can't seem to view this wound from the same perspective as . . . ah . . . some others do. Really, I just want the detective to be well. I can't think of me right now."

She turned her head full left to face Matt squarely and then turned still further, partially facing the wall behind them, completely exposing to his view the ragged, uncovered tracks of the neat black sutures that snaked in a shallow "V" across her lower right cheek. "I'm going to be scarred for life, my dear," she said brightly. "Do you think you'll be able to manage satisfactorily?"

Matt's mind reflexively placed her cheery question in wondrous, thrilling juxtaposition to the phrase she had chosen to introduce it: "For life," she had said to him. "For life."

He smiled at her, entranced as always. Then, chuckling audibly, he said with a mischievous note in his voice, "Well . . . I may need to think that over for, say, seventy-five years. Yes. Yes, I think I'll probably need to examine your face on a daily basis for at least that long. Then I'll let you know. How does that sound?"

Luke Manguson observed this exchange with warm pleasure, smiling as Matt gave his playful response. He had liked Matthew Clark from the moment, a year previous, he had seen how Matt had looked at his twin. He knew the look. It bespoke the kind of all-consuming love that he wanted to observe in any man with whom she might consider a long-term relationship. He had seen many men "fall in love" with his sister. Most were simply smitten with her physical elegance and athleticism. This was more than that, he knew. Much more. And the fact that their parents had been lifelong friends provided a commonality in their heritage that Luke considered a God-given coping stone, as did Rebecca herself.

Luke moved his eyes from Rebecca's wound to Matt's left arm and hand, trailing lifelessly on the rug beside him. The fact that Matt had placed himself between Rebecca and the automatic rifle fire that would certainly have taken her life that wild night at the edge of the Pembrokeshire cliffs had only served to cement Luke's own, thoughtfully unspoken view: this union had been decided upon in the Beginning. Now, he looked with love upon them both, as they sat holding hands and gazing into each other's faces. Luke was certain beyond question that Matt Clark would look at her scar, if indeed he ever came to notice it at all, as just one more component of her exquisite beauty. It would be, after all, not only part of her, but, as well, part of their common history, just as was Matt's shattered shoulder and arm. Matt would no more shy away from her scar, nor even conceive of such an action, than she from his damaged limb.

Luke watched as his sister smiled once more at Matt, squeezed his hand, and raised the hand to her lips. Then, holding his hand against the left, unmarked side of her face, Rebecca turned her eyes to meet Luke's. She paused, smiled at him, and then, somewhat to his surprise, addressed him on a completely new topic. "Luke, I had a second vision this morning." She glanced over at the clock on the nightstand. "A little over two hours ago. Apparently I was noisy enough in response to awaken Eleanor. She covered me up afterwards, as I was somehow very cold."

Suddenly her colleagues' sleepily indulgent torpor vanished; each was removed in a flash from the quiet warmth that had filled the room during the lovers' exchange. The atmosphere grew immediately electric as Rebecca began to recount the new vision, laying her emphasis on its new component: the platform-like structure at one end of her visionary arena, the structure's surface traversed by adults in a vaguely glimpsed processional. She described carefully the lightning-like movement of the ground cloud from its poisonous presence in the midst of the assembled children to the area around and above the platform itself. She tried to find a vocabulary that could transmit adequately her sense of the cloud's ominous prospect, as it blocked the sun itself and assailed the platform with its choking, concentrated vapor.

"And just now, in the telling," she concluded, "I realized that the cloud's movement to the platform somehow did not diminish its effects on the children in the least. I can't say just how that was clear to me. But I'm certain that, if anything, the threat to the children was actually *increased* by the attack against the adults on the platform . . . Oh! I wish I could do this better."

With a quick movement of both hands, Ellis Dolby adjusted his thick, wire-framed glasses, his sudden movement causing the others to glance his way. They were surprised to see him grimace. "What is it, Ellis?" asked Eleanor Chapel, the member of the group best acquainted with him. "Are you all right? Does Rebecca's . . . gift . . . disturb you?"

He did not reply right away. Then he shook his head thoughtfully and said, "Rebecca's reputation precedes her. Members of Dr. Stafford's inner circle view her as their foremost opponent within the ranks of what they refer to as their 'spiritual enemies.' They don't, of course, speak in terms of her being chosen to carry divine messages. They characterize her as delusional. I don't actually know how many of them believe her to be 'chosen' by God, and thus, see themselves as—I assume—'chosen' by God's enemies. Dr. Stafford sees it all quite clearly, I finally came to understand. But I don't know about the others.

"As for me, the more I became immersed in the project, and the better I got to know Dr. Stafford and his senior colleagues, the more fearful I

became that this 'spiritual enemy' to whom they so often made reference—
this Rebecca Manguson—was anything but delusional.

"In any case, I managed to startle myself a moment ago by remembering something I should have told all of you as soon as she and I arrived
here last night. It's just that . . . there was so much going on . . . and with
my mind still so . . . well . . . disabled . . . by the warehouse episode . . . I
didn't think of it."

They looked at him expectantly.

"It's obvious," he began, "that the dying children in the vision represent
the young victims of the MMHCC project in which I have played a part for
so long. And it's obvious that Rebecca is instructed to *prevent this* . . . to
halt the project . . . which is exactly what the MMHCC fears."

He stopped and adjusted his glasses again, glancing uncomfortably at
the others. He cleared his throat and, taking a deep breath, continued.

"Yes, that much is clear. But this new component that she described
reminds me . . . It reminds me that there has for some time been a mysterious ingredient in Dr. Stafford's plans . . . an ingredient about which I
know nothing, nor, I think, do others within the MMHCC junior leadership
ranks who, like me, were previously included in everything that he
developed. I don't know what it might be, but he and three or four others
have been working on a feature of the plan that is being held secret from
the rest of us. I've had a bad feeling about it for weeks. The basic design
and purpose of the MMHCC is horrible enough, even before you stir in the
criminal 'extras' that Dr. Stafford has been fashioning.

"This new thing—whatever it may be—is likely to be as monstrous, I
fear, as any other piece of this diabolism. It could be worse, though I don't
know how."

He paused and again adjusted his glasses, shaking his head slowly, his
eyes on the floor. "And what this private Evil may have to do with Rebecca's
newly dreamed . . . ah . . . platform . . . inside the arena . . . I don't know.
The two things may not be related. But somehow I doubt it."

He looked again at his four colleagues; each appeared to be lost in
thought. Still again he adjusted his eyeglasses with his trademark two-
handed, thumb-and-index finger lifting motion, pinching the wire arms of
his glasses and snugging the plastic bridge into the intersection between
nose and eyebrows. Then, with some hesitation, he asked, now almost
formally professorial in his demeanor and phrasing, "Can you—any of

you—posit a theory . . . an hypothesis . . . regarding the arena that Rebecca describes? The progressive, insidious damage to the children, each child immersed in a textbook, seems transparent in its import. But why an arena at all? What has this kind of structure to do with the children?" He looked from face to face.

"Does the arena," he continued, "simply represent the idea that the people of the United States, and eventually of the world, will become onlookers to this disaster? That the national populace will comprise, figuratively, the audience, as the project plays itself out in schools across the country? That the people of the nation will become involuntary witnesses to the project's effects upon America's youngsters? And if so . . . or if not . . . what about the two visions' undecipherable block letters on the second deck's façade? Surely it must be of critical importance that the explicitly verbal portions of these visions be read, interpreted, and acted upon by our group?

"Do we have a notion regarding how each of these pieces fits together? In particular, does the arena have anything to do with the core message? Does the arena have anything to do with this newly transmitted, presumably 'secondary' message? And what *is* this new, presumably secondary message? Or is the new message—the mysterious platform filled with adult figures and quickly covered by the deadly cloud—in fact the primary message?"

The ensuing silence grew long. Finally, somewhat to his own surprise, it was Matt Clark who spoke. He had for some time been looking to his left, in the direction of the room's only window, his right hand still entwined with Rebecca's left, his fingers absently caressing hers. When he spoke, he did not turn his head away from the window, even though it was she whom he addressed.

"Rebecca?" he said softly.

"Yes?"

"If I spoke words that were, in fact, those that are written on the façade of the arena's second level . . . do you think there is a chance you'd recognize them? Might you have *recognition* memory where you don't have *recall* memory?"

She looked down for a moment, thinking. Then she replied, still looking down. "No," she said tentatively. "No . . . I don't think I actually saw the words at all during either vision. I only saw that there *were* words, or phrases . . . I could see them out of the corners of my eyes, so to speak. But

I don't even know if the words were written in English, Matt, much less what words they were."

Silence returned.

Matt turned his face to hers. "Could we try it?"

She looked up at him and smiled. "Of course we could. But how could you possibly . . ."

"Let me give this a try. I'll give you a moment to reestablish the vision—in memory—in your mind. Then I'll . . . I'll just try."

She smiled again willingly and nodded, turning her eyes back to the floor in front of her, then closing them to concentrate. He turned his head back toward the window, away from her, and was silent again. Their hands remained clasped, his fingers still caressing hers gently. His mind seemed to be far away, just as was hers, as they both struggled to remember: she, her visions; he, something else. Then, after almost a full minute of new silence during which the others waited patiently, he spoke softly, still facing away from her.

"Tarawa."

"What?" she replied, not looking up or opening her eyes.

"Tarawa," he repeated. "T . . . A . . . R . . . A . . . W . . . A."

Though his face was turned from her, he could feel through their conjoined hands that she had no recognition of the word.

Moments passed. Then, still facing the window, he spoke again.

"Peleliu."

Silence. And more silence.

"Rabaul."

Nothing.

"Bougainville."

Her head snapped up, eyes open. He felt the swift change in the muscles of her hand, and he turned his face to her. Her eyes, gray and wide in amazement and confusion, met his.

Then he spoke again, looking steadily into her eyes.

"Belleau Wood," he said.

"Midway . . .

"Coral Sea . . .

"Iwo Jima . . .

"Okinawa . . ."

She was nodding slowly, recalling, seeing.

And then, after another five seconds of silence, he spoke one final word. "Guadalcanal."

"Oh!" she cried out in certain recognition. "Oh! Yes! Yes, Matt! What *is* it? What *is* it? What *are* they? How could you have *known*?"

He smiled. And, at the same time, he shook his head in wonderment at the utter mystery of the Holy Spirit's having, still again, infused this Englishwoman's mind with words she did not know, with images of places she had never seen, with meanings the implications of which she knew nothing.

Still looking into her eyes, Matt replied, "Your arena is Navy-Marine Corps Memorial Stadium in Annapolis, Maryland. It's the arena used by the Naval Academy's teams. The façade of the second deck lists in block letters the names of the United States Navy and Marine Corps' great battles."

He paused, then continued. "Annapolis is situated, I'd say, about thirty miles by water—and a good deal further than that by land, using the Chesapeake Bay Bridge—northwest of Oxford, where the MMHCC will be holding its sessions, Rebecca . . . where the files that I studied at the bookstore will be moved today."

The group entered another extended silence, working to process this new revelation, straining to connect the disparate parts of what they knew must somehow constitute a whole. Then Ellis Dolby's voice, low and soft, pushed itself almost unnoticed into and through the perplexity that filled the small room. His voice was less than a murmur, and it cast itself among them timidly, as though a modest choral prelude to a mighty processional awaiting its cue. It found the four of them waiting, a tiny congregation, holding its breath to see who—or what—might be preparing to move down the aisle into their midst.

"If we understand the vision only in part," he whispered urgently, "how can we move against the Evil? How can we even recognize the Evil? How can we *prevent this*, as we are commanded?

"Help us, Rebecca," he sighed, almost inaudibly, looking at her intently through his thick glasses. "Help us."

Pulling her left hand from Matt's grip, she drew her knees slowly to her chest with both hands. She closed her eyes once more and bowed her head. And then she covered her face with both hands.

"I can't," she whispered. "I don't know what to think."

Then, dropping her hands from her face, she looked up at her brother. "And Luke," she added, no longer whispering, "there was still another new element to this vision. I don't want to tell you . . . but I know I must.

"As the vision faded, I knew something was behind me . . . something within the arena . . . and I knew that its purpose had nothing to do directly with the children, nor with the procession at the opposite end of the arena. It had to do only with me, Luke. It was coming for me, and for me alone."

Beside her she heard a groan from Matt Clark. His right hand moved swiftly to his temples, and he groaned again. After a moment, he looked up to find Rebecca's face near his, her hand clutching his upper arm. "There is something else," he said haltingly, "about my warehouse experience . . . something else I must tell you. . . .

"After Dr. Stafford's exit, another man remained to speak with me . . . He said his name was Edward Jamieson . . . He seemed somehow *higher* than Dr. Stafford . . . And he said . . . he said that he would become Rebecca's nightmare . . . and that . . ."—and here Matt looked down and groaned softly again—" . . . and that . . . they would execute her . . . they would execute her in front of tens of thousands. . . ."

Chapter Eleven

NOON APPROACHED, HOTTER STILL. ELEANOR CHAPEL, HER energy unflagging in the heat even after two fitful hours of sleep, had departed the hotel midmorning to be at the detective's bedside, and to ensure that the privately negotiated security arrangements for him were in place. Despite the impracticality of involving the city's police force at this stage, she and her medical confidantes had acted immediately on the need to provide continuous protection for the detective. Merely sequestering him in a private guestroom adjacent the physicians' outpatient clinic was not enough.

Upon her arrival at the clinic just after eleven o'clock that morning, Eleanor Chapel had found the security arrangements excellent, the detective sleeping comfortably, and at the foot of his bed, a cot awaiting her. Grateful, she allowed herself to lie down, and in seconds she slept soundly.

Back at the hotel, competing church bells tolled twelve o'clock in raucous disharmony, but Luke Manguson and Ellis Dolby heard nothing. They were engaged in a concentrated effort to recapture their own lost sleep, having gone to bed as soon as the morning planning session had concluded, and Eleanor Chapel, observed by both men until she stepped onto the bus, had begun the twelve-block ride to the clinic where the detective lay. Now, as the bells fell silent, the two of them continued to sleep undisturbed, though during times of real danger Luke was never deeply asleep in the usual sense. The slightest untoward close-range sound—a lock being manipulated, a doorknob turning—could find him instantly on his feet, his hand on an always-present knife, ever ready to stand between his sister and danger.

While he slept, Rebecca and Matt sat together in Eleanor Chapel's room. The connecting door between rooms remained open, and the pair conducted their conversation in whispered tones so as not to awaken the sleepers. The room's only chair was drawn up near the side of its only bed.

Matt, in the chair, leaned forward toward Rebecca, while she sat on the bed with her back against the headboard. She sat erect, with her knees drawn up against her chest, just as she had sat on the floor throughout much of the morning session. The fingers of her left hand toyed with the ends of her now unbound hair, which she had pulled forward over her right shoulder.

"So," Rebecca whispered, "Ellis will meet tonight with Dr. Stafford and the other senior MMHCC people? And then Ellis will proceed as planned tomorrow—on Thursday—to follow the files, and Dr. Stafford, to Oxford?"

"Right," said Matt simply.

Barefoot and wearing white tennis shorts and a blue tee shirt against the oppressive heat of the small room, she sat forward and crossed her long legs at the ankles, her hair falling into her lap as she did. Continuing absently to curl isolated strands of hair around the fingers of her left hand, she reached with her right hand for his.

"And what," she asked, "will Dr. Stafford do about you, Matt? He knows by now, surely, that you and the detective have been pulled from his grasp, and he certainly knows that Luke and I were the ones who engineered the rescue."

"He expected you to try, of course," Matt replied quickly. "He *wanted* you to try. He did not expect you to succeed. He expected you by now to be in his custody. He expected us all to be in his custody.

"As for me, he has never been very much interested, you know, Rebecca, whether I was working as his assistant or, starting just two days ago, as his antagonist. He won't give much thought to me.

"He'll simply punish the warehouse guards for failing to capture or kill you, increase the security for the Oxford meetings tomorrow and Friday, and, no doubt, place greater emphasis than ever on the criminal aspects of his project: especially the bribery and extortion components. I've finally come to realize that, whenever he's threatened or thwarted, he just gets nastier. He loses that precise political compass that serves him so well at most other times. I realize now that he begins under those conditions to make mistakes of excess.

"The thing I learned—*one* of the things I learned—from you and your family last year," he continued, "about a certain kind of . . . um . . . advanced

Evil . . . is that under pressure it simply reaches deeper into its essential repertoire. It can't do otherwise. It finds itself compelled to fight back by ever more grotesque means, because those are the means it owns and understands, even when those tactics threaten to become self-defeating. It finds that it must use methods that are compatible with its fundamental nature. And so this kind of Evil—Dr. Stafford's kind—spawns greater Evil because that's what it understands."

"My family and I taught you that, Matthew?" she said, glancing at him out of the corner of her eye and smiling quickly at him in the way that always turned his legs to jelly and sent his heart racing. Then she looked down at her lap where her left hand continued to toy with her loosely arrayed hair.

He saw how the bandage on the right side of her face moved when she smiled, then returned to its original shape when the smile left her. He hoped she would always remain as unconscious of the bandage—and, soon, of the developing scar that it concealed—as she seemed now.

"Well, good for us," she concluded brightly. "Good for Mum and Dad and us twins for teaching you something, lieutenant!"

Matt smiled at her, delighting in her resilience, her happiness, her strength, her eyes, her arresting dialect. He loved to hear her say the word "lieutenant," pronouncing it "leftenant." He loved *her*.

Then she turned serious again. "But it's obvious when you think about it, isn't it?" she continued. "That which is Evil at its inception—but not yet technically criminal—steadily creeps toward criminality in response to certain types of barriers and pressures. Evil strips itself naked in order to become more and more itself. Under any sort of real threat, it disrobes more rapidly, more completely.

"And without that tendency . . . that marvelous consistency . . . that locked-in rigidity . . . we wouldn't stand a very good chance, Matt," she said, again looking down at her lap where her left hand continued to work carelessly with strands of her shimmering hair. "Since we are bound by God's laws, we can't just do anything we like in order to stop Dr. Stafford. We have rules to observe."

She smiled at him. "God has rather exacting specifications regarding the timbre of our decisions, you know. Otherwise, my brother, Old Testament warrior that he was born to be, would be free to hunt these people with machine guns and grenades and worse, rather than to limit himself to

defensive strategies and rescue missions and document-disclosure expeditions. The dividing line between the two is really quite spectacular, if one
will just pay attention."

She glanced away, then looked at him again. "And what about Ellis,
Matt? Is he going to be all right? Do you think they'll suspect . . ."

"I can't see how Cameron Stafford is likely to be suspicious of Ellis. But
it's possible, Rebecca. For all we know, Dr. Stafford could have had him
followed at any point. Even Ellis's wonderful sweatshirt disguise may not
have worked as we believe it did. You've said he first approached Dr. Chapel
right there on the sidewalk in front of the seminary. We just can't know."

Still holding right hands, they began what she thought was a comfortable silence. Then she felt something in the muscles of his hand, looked at
him carefully, and saw that Matt, his eyes on the floor at his feet, was
blushing. She started to ask the question, then thought better of it, and
slowly pulled her hand from his. He looked up.

"This is a mistake, isn't it?" she asked somberly. "It's not fair for me to
be sitting here on the bed in shorts and a tee shirt, holding your hand. I'm
sorry. We ought to be in the middle of a two-mile run together. I find hiding
in this room to be my least favorite activity. I wish we could start for
Maryland right now."

A burst of uncontrolled laughter suddenly escaped Matt, and he
clapped his right hand over his mouth in an effort to avoid waking the men
in the adjoining room. "Good grief, Rebecca!" he whispered, when he was
able to shunt the laughter aside. "Good grief!"

Smiling cautiously at his mysterious response, she whispered, "What is
it, Matt? Why 'Good grief, Rebecca!' Why on earth was that so funny?"

He shook his head, still quietly convulsed. "Well . . . let's see, Rebecca,"
he said. "It seems to me that, all in the space of about fifteen seconds, you
decided that I was thinking . . . ah . . . well . . . you somehow looked at me
and knew . . . ah. . . ."

She leaned toward him, now stifling her own bemused laughter. "I knew
that you were starting to think about kissing me, dearest. Is that what you're
trying so miserably to talk about?" she murmured sweetly, small laughing
sounds escaping her throat despite her efforts to hold the noises at bay.

He rolled his eyes and looked away. "Well . . . as a matter of fact . . ."

She swung her legs off the bed and stood up in front of him, and he sat
back in his chair in surprise. She walked around his chair, reached down,

took his good hand in hers, and pulled him to his feet. Then she reached up with both hands, cupped his face, and kissed him gently and carefully.

It was, he thought to himself later, the tenderness of the kiss that struck him more than anything except for the complete surprise of it.

And then, after what seemed to him both an eternity and a millisecond, the kiss was over, and she playfully pushed him back two steps until she forced him to sit down on the edge of the bed. She picked up the chair and moved it ten feet away from him. Taking a seat, she looked at him happily and said, "We're healthy young adults, my darling. We must learn to be more circumspect than to sit alone . . . holding hands . . . sitting on a bed . . . in a bedroom. This is courtship, you know. We're supposed to be out . . . walking together, or running together, or dining together, or going to a theater together, or sitting or kneeling together in church, or . . . and here's the part we *must* do as soon as our . . . our orders . . . have been fulfilled . . . talking about the future. I'm as convinced as ever that there is an 'our future,' Matt. God pulled you back from a precipice on Monday morning. He continues to drive us together. It seems quite clear. We just continue to find ourselves in such *maelstroms* that we can't reach the point of even beginning a normal sort of courtship. That time will come, though, and soon enough, I think."

He looked down again at the floor in front of his feet. Again he felt color creeping into his face. But this time he knew that, despite the kiss, her beauty was not driving this second unwanted change in his appearance.

She leaned forward in the chair, looking at him closely from across the small room. "Matt?" she said incredulously, "Are you . . . you seem . . . are you actually *angry*?"

He shook his head. "No," he said, angrily. "Yes . . . I don't know."

She stood and crossed the floor. She hesitated in front of him, then knelt beside the bed at his feet, placing her hands on his knees, her eyes peering inquisitively at his face from closer range. "What is it? Please. I don't understand," she said quietly, confusion in her low voice.

He raised his hand to his temples and rubbed his forehead with thumb and fingers, closing his eyes tightly. "Give me a minute, Rebecca. Please," he said.

She dropped her hands from his knees and sat back slowly on her haunches, waiting, still watching his face closely.

After a moment, still massaging his temples and still looking down at his feet, he began to speak, at first haltingly. "You captivated me the moment I first saw you, in England . . . last summer. I tried to speak . . . I tried to speak to you while we were there . . . about our . . . about our relationship . . . but you gave me only Ecclesiastes . . . and you were right. But then . . . even then . . . you let me . . . you let me court you . . . and you let me get close . . . and you let me kiss you."

He swallowed, looked up, and extended his right hand to her face, caressing her hair as it fell across her cheekbones and down over the front of her blue tee shirt. "And you let me save your life. And you saved mine. And when I recovered, I set about preparing myself for a life with you, preparing to teach. I told myself that it was vocation, like yours. And it may have been. But you were always foremost in my thoughts . . . not teaching itself, as a profession . . . not even Christianity itself, really. Just you."

He paused, dropped his hand from her face and hair, and letting his eyes fall to the floor again, resumed speaking in a low voice. "And that was my mistake, of course. I let go of the . . . of the . . . divine quality . . . in . . . in our love"—and here he blushed so deeply that she again leaned forward and placed her hands on his knees, though this only accelerated his physical discomfort—"and started to think in terms of some kind of 'career' under Dr. Stafford's tutelage and guidance and mentorship . . . and in the process got lost . . . completely lost.

"And that led directly, as I should have seen from the moment I allowed myself under his spell, to my losing you, just last week, after that . . . that . . . willful blindness . . . that corruption . . . that tumbled out of me on the park bench."

Suddenly flushing again with anger, he jammed the knuckles of his fist upward into his forehead in frustration. "Ahhh!" he said in inarticulate fury. "He *knew* that's what would happen. He *planned* this! He wanted me for his assistant for no reason other than to provide himself a means of involvement when you eventually came to New York . . . Ahhh!" he said much too loudly, again pounding his forehead in a rage that, after a shocked moment, led her to spring forward from her knees and envelop his head and neck with her arms, shielding him.

Seconds passed. Gradually she relaxed her grip as she felt his muscles go limp in her grasp. Then he began to speak again, his face now buried deep in her neck and hair. "And then you left me, as was required of you. And then . . . thank God . . . He forced me back to the common ground . . . to

His common ground . . . the foundation that He provided for us almost from the start . . . and you accepted me . . . I think."

He paused, waiting. Their faces still touching, he felt her nod immediately.

"And now we're just as we were a year ago: courting, but courting through a crisis a thousand times larger than the courtship itself could possibly be."

Reaching up to her neck with his good hand, he moved her face away from his just enough to be able to look into the wide, gray eyes, his hand in her hair, her arms still loosely around his neck.

"But we are not as we were before," he continued, speaking now in a stronger voice, no longer conscious of the sleepers in the next room. "You've said you can't look at my arm and hand without feeling our oneness, Rebecca. Have you thought about your wound, and how you got it?" He moved his fingers around to the near side of her face, to her bandage, touching the skin above and below it with his fingertips.

"You're marked now, just as I am. We've been marked on each other's behalf. We're bound together in ways that no fiction writer would dare portray. And our marks are permanent, Rebecca," he said, moving his hand back to the left side of her face and pushing her hair away from her cheek.

"Rebecca . . . Rebecca . . . our parents have been best friends for decades. You and my mother have been given the gift of visioning . . . of seeing . . . of receiving . . . And I was brought to Christianity last summer by the two of you.

"Rebecca! What if you and I are destined by God *not* to have a normal courtship? What if these extraordinary events *are* the courtship? What justification can there be for our continuing to think that 'the time will come' when we will have leisure time to go out to dinner . . . to the theater . . . even to church? Rebecca! *This* is the time. It can't be otherwise!"

They stared into each other's eyes, each surprised by the intensity of his declaration. After several moments, she cupped his hand with her own, turned her face into his hand, and kissed the palm that had caressed her cheek. Then she rose from her knees, turned from him, and stepped to the window. After another moment, she turned back to him and, still standing, looking to him like a queen in bare feet, shorts, and tee shirt, asked quietly, "What do you want, then, Matt? If you're right about . . . about all that you've said . . . then what?"

Not taking his eyes from hers, he stood, stepped to her, and took her left hand in his right. He lifted her hand to his chest, much as she had done with his at the airport just days earlier, and smiled into the unforgettable eyes that had spoken to his soul from the first moment. "Then this," he said, and, still holding her hand, he slowly, athletically, deliberately dropped to his left knee.

Looking up into her startled face, he said, his voice now low and soft, "Rebecca Manguson . . . I, Matthew Clark, fledgling, unformed Christian, propose that we establish our intent to marry . . . that we pronounce our . . . our engagement . . . our *engagement* . . . to be in effect as of this moment . . . that we ask our parents' formal blessing on this mutual commitment . . . and that you accept this . . . this . . . my grandmother's engagement band, as a symbol of the promise . . . of the promise of oneness . . . that this step holds for us."

Stunned by his own words, he searched for and found sufficient presence to move his right hand, still holding her left, so as to extend the small finger of the hand toward her. Unable to remove the ring himself, he moved it into her hand, and her fingers took it hesitantly. Using both her hands, she carefully slid the ring from his finger and then waited for him to take it back from her. When he did, she shyly extended the third finger of her left hand toward the ring, looking on with utter amazement at the transaction of which she was a part. He moved the ring onto her finger, and seeing it fit perfectly, looked up into her eyes in hopes of seeing something there that would match the almost desperate commitment that he knew was in his.

But he saw something quite different in her face. He saw that she was troubled. Her eyes were on the ring and on their joined hands, but the eyes expressed no joy. She looked at him and shook her head slowly. Then she placed the fingers of her right hand on the ring and prepared to remove it.

Still on one knee, he watched the movement of her hand and knew what it meant. His good hand moved away from hers and to his temples, massaging his forehead with thumb and fingers, looking down at the floor in front of her bare feet.

She gripped the ring and stopped. Jumbled thoughts raced through her mind. This was not the way she had imagined things. She did not yet know him in the way she wanted to know him before taking this step . . . if, indeed, the step should ever be taken at all.

And vocation. What of her vocation? For her, vocation had been primary for some time. And it remained so, or so she thought.

And what of his vocation? Did he in fact feel vocation as she did? This . . . this *engagement* proposition, coming from nowhere . . . was altogether premature . . . and premature for more than one kind of reason.

And yet . . . and yet she sensed that she could not gainsay a single word in all that he had just articulated in his declaration to her. He had spoken a comprehensive truth.

When, indeed, would their courtship be normal? How, indeed, could she continue to insist that these vortices into which they were repeatedly cast did not comprise God's intended courtship for the two of them?

While he continued to look down, still kneeling, still massaging his temples with his right hand, she looked upward. She, like this man's mother, was chosen to receive Supernature in ways that others would never know. But, in Eleanor Chapel's apt phrase, even a Rebecca Manguson most often found the Holy Spirit's messages simply "thrown at her brain," whether in prayer or while walking down the street or while standing in front of the girls in her London classroom or . . . as now . . . standing in front of a man whose proposal hung in the air . . . and whose maternal grandmother's ring encircled the third finger of her left hand. Still grasping the ring with the fingers of her right hand and still looking upward, she opened her mind and waited. And the wait was brief. In mere seconds, there it was, thrown at her brain, unmistakable, admitting of no objection and of no argument. *Accept this, and be glad.*

She looked down. She was surprised to see that tears had been falling freely from her cheeks and onto her hands. And suddenly she knew joy. A surpassing joy that filled her heart. And she fell to her knees before him and opened her arms to him . . . crying . . . laughing . . . almost singing. . . .

And betrothed.

Yes . . . by God's grace . . . *betrothed!*

CHAPTER TWELVE

Dear Rebecca,

It's after midnight, and I think you and Dr. Chapel are asleep. I know Luke is. His breathing is somehow rough when he sleeps. Sort of like a horse snorting. Well, no, not exactly like a horse snorting.

Anyway, I'm not asleep. I can't stop thinking about you. I know I'll need to get dressed in about four hours to get ready to catch the train to Baltimore, and maybe I'll sleep a little on the trip.

But now I can think only of you and us and how it might be.

When I get too wrapped up in imagining a future together, though, I get pulled back. Something "thrown at my brain," as Dr. Chapel would say. I get reminded that our engagement—our engagement!!!—doesn't mean that our lives are suddenly going to become "normal." It only means that we've given ourselves up to something we're convinced is His intent for us: to be one flesh.

It gives me goose bumps to write that. Even to think that. I find myself wondering how I can possibly be worthy of you. How can I possibly be the one that God intends for someone as, well, as unbelievable as you are? I don't understand it.

But every time I go too far in that direction, I step back and say to myself that He intends it and that's really all there is to say. He will no doubt continue to force me to be a better person and to be more worthy of you than I am now.

Or maybe that's not even the way to think about this. Maybe it's not an issue of worthy or not worthy of you. Maybe it's just an issue of my providing you with something He wants you to have for the rest of your life: a man . . . in addition to, and different from, your brother . . . a man who loves you and becomes your partner and companion in everything you do. And—and this thought drives me to my knees—the father of your children.

Maybe that's all.

And if that's all, then, with His help, I can do it.

It was a lot of fun to speak with our parents yesterday, wasn't it? Both moms were crazy with joy and crying so hard they had to put the dads on the line. And then both dads were so struck dumb that we didn't have anybody to talk to for five minutes. Hilarious. Absolutely hilarious!

Well, I'll see you this afternoon in Rock Hall. Please drive carefully in that Porsche. We've got speed limits, you know. And you never can be quite sure how your foreign driver's license and passport will be viewed by the highway patrol officer who has had to chase you down.

I know, I know. Fine words from somebody who doesn't even have a driver's license!

I'm rambling now. I just don't want to stop talking to you. Actually, I really do want to stop talking to you. I really want to walk into your room and lie down beside you. I want to listen to you breathe while you sleep. I want my eyes to be on you until they close to join you in sleep.

Well. I'll stop.

Please know that I love you, Rebecca.
Always,
Matt

She smiled and folded the letter, then slipped it into the back of her prayer book to reread later in the day. The time was nearly nine o'clock. She was alone in the hotel room. Matt would, about now, be getting off the train at its BWI stop, preparing to meet the reporter. Ellis Dolby would be on his way to Oxford with Cameron Stafford by car, but she knew that they would have no way to know his whereabouts until they actually linked up with him—or failed to—in Oxford. Eleanor Chapel had returned to their hotel room at midnight, slept for five hours, and then departed before dawn at the same time as Matt, getting the first bus toward the clinic. And Luke was already out, foraging for the equipment and provisions they would need for the expedition to Maryland.

Her morning devotions complete, she sat on the floor and began to stretch in preparation for an hour-long session of calisthenics and rope jumping, in place of a high-risk run through the streets. She smiled to herself at the thought of Eleanor Chapel's success in securing yet again the marvelous roadster that had been reluctantly loaned them for the Brooklyn warehouse incursion. Loaned a second time with as much reluctance as on the first, the black Cabriolet was no more what Luke had wanted this time—something plain, with ample passenger space—than in the case of the Brooklyn rescue effort, but they were in no position to be selective. The Porsche would do fine, she thought to herself.

Eleanor Chapel had also, working from the detective's clinic the previous afternoon and evening, altered the logistical arrangements with the reporter. Matt would now rendezvous with her at BWI airport, and with Matt's having no driver's license, the car would be rented in her name. The two of them would drive south to Annapolis, east across the Chesapeake Bay Bridge, then, in a near-complete circling movement, east, north, and, from Chestertown, west and finally south to the spit of land jutting toward the bridge from a distance of twelve miles, designated on maps as the town of Rock Hall. The tiny village reportedly comprised a handful of stores and several dozen homes, together with three small-craft marinas. The editor with whom Eleanor Chapel had been working by phone throughout the week had been able to make arrangements with a friend who was proprietor of Swan Creek Marina. Rebecca, Luke, Matt, and the reporter would rendezvous there midafternoon, and amazingly, be given unlimited use of the proprietor's two-year-old, twenty-six-foot, twin-outboard motorboat for the Thursday night foray southward under the Bay Bridge and on to Oxford. Luke's specifications had been met nicely with the twenty-six-footer. He had wanted speed and, especially, a craft with a small surface-search radar set. The marina's proprietor had promised both in his conversations with the editor.

Rebecca sighed to herself as, sitting on the hotel room floor in hurdler's position, she reached forward to touch the toes of her right foot, gradually letting the weight of her own torso force herself downward until her rib cage actually rested on her right quadriceps. Her thoughts were on the young reporter. The woman came highly recommended by her editor, whose judgment, in turn, was trusted completely by Eleanor Chapel. Rebecca found herself hoping the woman was neither fragile nor volatile. Whatever she might be like, she would need extraordinary composure in the face of a concentration of power and Evil strong enough to disorient and intimidate almost anyone. Yet, in the end, everything would depend upon this woman, her editor's choice for the most dangerous assignment his Christian periodical had ever undertaken.

Still in the full-stretch hurdler's position, Rebecca closed her eyes and prayed for this woman whom she would meet in several hours. She prayed that God would give the reporter the strength and the will to face the Enemy with the confidence and self-assurance granted to those who know themselves to be Christ's own.

She was in midprayer when she realized that, even more so than for the young reporter, her prayer must be on behalf of Ellis Dolby, who was, while Rebecca prayed alone in her hotel room, at that very moment insinuating himself into the layers of Evil that encased Cameron Stafford. Forming a picture of him as she prayed aloud, she found a smile forming on her moving lips. Perhaps Ellis Dolby's built-in nervousness would stand him in good stead. How could he appear more nervous than usual, when his everyday demeanor bespoke nervousness in the extreme?

She prayed for his success . . . and for his obedience.

She prayed that he would do his duty.

Matt Clark stepped off the New York-to-Washington train at BWI and walked to the shuttle bus that would transport him to the terminal. His thoughts were on the details of the upcoming thirty-six hours.

With the detective *hors de combat*, the burden of logistical preparation had fallen on Eleanor Chapel. However, Matt thought to himself, the void created by the detective's convalescence had been filled, in some ways even more effectively, by Ellis Dolby. Through him, the group had even fuller access to Cameron Stafford's plans and intentions than it could possibly have obtained through Sid Belton's Maryland-area connections.

Ellis Dolby had known a great deal. He had known that the town of Oxford, situated on a small peninsula that extended from the tip of a larger one—the horn on the rhino's nose—would, in response to the wishes of the conference planners, shut down its ferry and its one highway to all nonresidents except for the MMHCC leaders. He had known that the MMHCC's coffers had readily yielded sufficient funds to rent almost the entire town for two days, effectively reimbursing the several dining rooms and small bed-and-breakfasts for the guests they would presumably not be able to serve. He had known that every room in the only establishment boasting more than a handful of guestrooms, the stately and historic Robert Morris Inn, had been rented by the MMHCC for both Thursday and Friday nights. Only its dining room would be open to the public.

Further, Ellis Dolby had known that water traffic in and out of Oxford's marinas would be restricted just as were the ferry and highway access points, with docking available only to residents. And he had in hand and in mind the agenda for each of the series of minutely organized ninety-minute sessions that were to be led personally at the inn's meeting room by Dr. Cameron Stafford. And, finally, he knew his own responsibility in the sessions: personally to handle the logistical circus, including photocopying the pertinent MMHCC files and readying them for distribution to each participant at each session. His role was also to collect that same material at the conclusion of the sessions and to take all but the originals to the shredding machine that Cameron Stafford had ordered sent to Oxford from the university.

And, in regard to what Ellis Dolby had *not* known, there was the stunning bit of news that Dolby had never so much as heard of Edward Jamieson. This astonishing fact lay in the midst of the data, an enormous puzzle at the very center of all the other mysteries. And Matt's physical description of Jamieson brought no glimmer of recognition to Dolby, either.

Matt turned all this over in his mind as he stepped from the shuttle bus and, an overnight bag slung over his shoulder by its carrying strap, entered the BWI terminal. He checked the monitors for the arrival gate, walked to concourse B, passed through the security checkpoint, and after a short walk, arrived at the gate. His timing had worked well, he thought to himself; the flight was due to arrive at the gate in just twenty minutes.

He sat down and, placing his bag on the floor and his well-used leather document carrier on the empty seat beside him, pulled from it Eleanor Chapel's photocopied notes regarding the person whom he would meet in minutes. The notes, jotted hastily during her initial conversation that week with her editor friend, were simple.

April Johnstone—early thirties—best investigative reporter—two awards for Christian journalism—graduate of Southeastern Baptist Seminary in Christian education—average size—short brown hair—glasses—quiet—tough—very tough—completely fearless.

Eleanor Chapel's other notes pertained to logistics, and Matt passed over them quickly. He hoped this "very tough" young woman would not be irritated that he had been sent to accompany her. After all, without a driver's license, he was of no practical use in getting the two of them from the airport to Rock Hall. But Eleanor Chapel and the editor had agreed that whatever background information Matt could supply during the drive would constitute time well spent. And, more important, they agreed that Matt might well, during the drive, begin to form an opinion regarding the extent to which this young woman might succeed or fail in the deadly storm that now formed itself over the tranquil village of Oxford.

"How long you been here, ma'am?"

"I've been here almost the whole time you've been in the clinic, Detective. I went back to the hotel for a few hours each night . . . but just for a few hours."

He pondered this piece of news for a moment, then asked, in his low, raspy voice, speaking more slowly than usual through the array of bandages and temporary support structures that interwove his face, jaw, and cranium, "How come, Eleanor? I've just been lyin' here like a bump on a log. The staff people and the security people are around all the time, I think. What were you doin' here? I don't get it."

"Well," she said, seeming annoyed, "some of the time I was praying for your recovery, Detective."

"You coulda done that from anywhere."

She looked down at her hands. "Well, some of the time I was talking to you, and some of the time I was reading to you."

"Readin' to me? Talkin' to me? Whatd'ya say to me?"

"I read from C. S. Lewis," she said, picking up a worn paperback copy of *Till We Have Faces* from the foot of the bed. "This is a wonderful story, and I thought it might entertain us both, and at the same time teach us something."

"Yeah? How was it gonna teach me somethin' when I was out like a light?"

"The mind does wonderful things, Detective. Your extended unconsciousness did not mean to me that your mind could not receive messages. God has made us more complicated than that."

"Hmm. And whatd'ya say to me when you weren't readin'? When you were just talkin' to me, whatd'ya say?"

"Oh, nothing," she said, slapping the book into her lap in irritation at the detective-like interrogation. "I just prattled on to hear myself prattle. It kept me awake when I grew tired of reading."

The detective, his head propped on two pillows, bandages covering not just his head and face but an assortment of other anatomical components, considered this last. "Just prattled on, huh?"

"Yes."

"So, that means you didn't say anything to me about . . . uh . . . let's see . . . likin' my mind a lot . . . or thinkin' I'm really a good person . . . or bein' pleased that you're gettin' to know me pretty well . . ."

"DETECTIVE!"

Her exclamation was punctuated by his bark of laughter, an incongruous sound followed by a groan and a movement of one hand toward his damaged ribs. She was on her feet and at his side in a flash. "Numbskull! Incorrigible reprobate!" she said through clenched teeth, her small face reddening with anger part feigned and part genuine. "You are a deceitful lout! How dare you eavesdrop on my solitary conversations with you!"

Groaning softly with the effort, he reached for her hand, and she allowed hers to be taken. He rolled his head to one side, far enough to permit his hardened, deep-set black eyes to encounter the dancing, accusing blue-greenness of hers. "You kept me goin', ma'am," he said quietly, the teasing tone now absent. "You kept me goin' when I couldn't get any kind of grip on anything . . . didn't know what was happenin' with me . . . didn't know whether I should be tryin' to get better or . . . you kept me goin', Eleanor.

"Oh . . . and for what it's worth to ya', ma'am . . . I'm pleased that I'm gettin' to know you pretty well, too, but, I gotta say, you must have a couple of screws loose to get mixed up with me and the kid and the Manguson twins. Trouble sticks to us like flypaper. Y'know what I mean, ma'am?"

"Yes," she said evenly. "I've known it would require a multitude of loose screws to get mixed up with you from the moment I saw that car of yours."

After a short silence during which she continued to stand beside the bed, her hand in his, she asked, "Can I get you something, Detective? Are you as comfortable as your injuries will allow? Shall I read more from Professor Lewis?"

For a moment, he did not reply. Then he said, not looking directly at her, "Eleanor . . . my . . . ah . . . research . . . into your background . . . told me you've been a widow for a long time. Would you . . . would you tell me what happened? I know I don't have any right to ask, but . . ."

"I'm pleased to be asked, Detective," she replied quickly. "I've never had any reluctance to talk about my husband. He was a dear man, and good to me always. But we were married only two years before he went overseas. He flew Thunderbolts over Europe. He's buried at Arlington. I take the train to Washington twice a year to visit him at the cemetery."

"He flew a P-47? Man!"

"Yes."

"I've read that flyin' that thing was like tryin' to break a bronco!"

"Well, I can't tell you much about that. He didn't talk to me about his flying, really. We always had other things we wanted to say to each other . . . and to ask each other."

"Sure. Didn't mean to get caught up with the airplane, ma'am."

"I love it that you got caught up with the airplane, Detective. If *he* had been talking to you, I'm sure the two of you would have had great fun with that conversation. It's just that our own conversations tended in different directions."

"Did you expect to have children, ma'am? I know I'm pryin', but . . ."

"You know, prying is asking questions about something that someone does not want to be asked about. It makes me happy that you're asking.

"Of course, we expected to have children. We looked forward to starting our family after the war. But when he came home to Arlington, I really had no interest in starting over with someone else, Detective. I just pitched myself into graduate studies and launched a career.

"No, not a career, actually. A vocation. I felt called to do what I have done, from start to finish. And I'm not finished yet, either."

"Vocation," he mused. "That's the way Miss Manguson talks about her teachin'. I wish I had thought about things in that way when I started on the force, but I was really just lookin' for a job that had some excitement in it, after I got outta the service. And it gave me that, sure enough."

"The fact that you did not think of it as vocation does not in the least mean that you were not called to do it, you know."

There was another pause. And then she asked him a new question, displaying a tiny hesitation that he noticed instantly, as he, in fact, unfailingly noticed everything.

"Detective," she said, "why . . . are you a bachelor? Why have you not . . .?"

He barked again with his throaty laugh, and once more clutched his broken ribs in consequence. "Eleanor," he said, holding his side for a moment and then taking her hand again, smiling up at her, "look at me. I'm not much of a catch, you know. I'm short and homely and I do dangerous work and . . ."

She raised her hand quickly to stop him. "That wasn't an invitation to speak about your shortcomings, Detective. I'm not interested. You've made choices with your life, and those choices appear to have excluded the development of relationships of any depth. Why? Why such choices?"

He looked at her. "Well, ma'am . . . right now . . . I'd hafta say . . . I really can't imagine . . . Right at this particular moment . . . I can't even begin to imagine."

And then Sid Belton witnessed something he never expected to see. He saw Dr. Eleanor Chapel, internationally famed professor of Old Testament, Union Theological Seminary, drop her eyes and blush like a schoolgirl.

Chapter Thirteen

MATT STARED ADMIRINGLY AT THE HUGE BLACK OUTBOARDS. "Twin Mercuries, I see. Think we've got enough power, Luke? Should I toss in a couple of paddles for more speed?"

Luke laughed as he continued to clamber around the gleaming, black-hulled twenty-six-foot Blackfin runabout as it nestled portside-to against the Swan Creek Marina's evenly planked pier. "Maybe you should toss in a couple of petrol tanks, lieutenant. These motors must get all of a half mile a gallon."

As Luke spoke, a family of swans sailed majestically past the dormant engines of the *River Runner*, as if to provide avian validation of the marina's name. The eight-member swan family was observed in its watery parade by four *homo sapiens*, each of whom suspended feverish preparations on board the rakish vessel just to watch. The adolescent flotilla, parents proudly positioned in the vanguard and the rear, paddled silently into the distance.

"Amazing," said Rebecca reverently.

"Yes," answered Matt, standing just behind her shoulder.

"They're completing their voyage while they still have enough daylight," noted Luke approvingly. "Let's follow suit; I want to get into open water and down near the bridge before nightfall. Rebecca, will you make ready to cast off at half past the hour? We'll be set by then."

Precisely on time, the massive outboards, throbbing in ominous concert, propelled the *River Runner* out of the marina's narrow confines and into the channel. Inevitably, both men were taken back in their minds to the almost magical quality somehow present in every nautical sortie: the familiar thrill of the last line parting, the vibrant shudder of vessel underfoot, the sibilance of a sculptured prow slicing through a pliant medium. Now they turned their heads and watched once more as a harbor fell behind them. Then, together, they swiftly began to orient themselves to their chosen course. In practiced harmony, they identified promontories and man-made landmarks, assessed the weather-driven condition of the surface, searched for water-borne traffic, familiarized themselves with the radar set and its display console, and formed a clear image of their route.

April Johnstone sat quietly in the stern, her materials in her lap. She peered through thick eyeglasses at a sheaf of notes that she had freshly extracted from her briefcase. She did not look up, either at the scene through which they passed or at her comrades.

She had been pleasant enough to Matt when the two had rather easily identified each other at the BWI gate. And he had found her businesslike during the drive from the airport to the rendezvous point on the eastern shore, at times feeling as though he were the interviewee for a background story on Cameron Stafford.

At the marina, privately to the twins, who had arrived in the Porsche roadster just after he and April Johnstone, Matt had said only that she had driven the car well enough and seemed eager to start. Beyond that, he could report only that she seemed to be exactly as advertised by her editor: tough and competent.

And that would have to be enough, Matt noted to himself. She seemed no one's ally and no one's friend. And there had been something in the way she had made reference in the rental car to Cameron Stafford, something in the way she formed her questions about him and the MMHCC, that had led him to suspect that her feelings toward Stafford were anything but dispassionate. She appeared almost animalistic, filled with deeply rooted antipathy, at any mention, her own or Matt's, of Stafford's name. She struck him as a strange creature, and yet he trusted her somehow to do this job and to succeed with it, no matter how difficult and dangerous it might become. And he certainly trusted Eleanor Chapel's judgment of the editor and, thus, of his choice of reporter for the mission.

Now he nodded to himself in quiet satisfaction as he glanced over his shoulder at the taciturn young woman, her nose still buried in her notes, short brown hair whipping wildly around her face in the twenty-five-knot wind generated by the craft's slapping, shuddering flight across the moderate chop raised by wind and current. She would do fine, he thought to himself.

The sun dropped under a low cloud and perched, resting on the low hills of the western shore, a bright, stationary orange ball providing fair warning that the day was officially over. Its warning given, it vanished precipitously into the indistinct landmass north of the bridge's Annapolis-area approaches. Darkness followed quickly as Luke, switching on the cockpit's superb map lighting system, again verified their channel positioning and began to align the irregularly pitching bow with the eastern span's looming mass of steel and asphalt. For a Royal Navy officer who had repeatedly conned Her Majesty's warships through confined waters scarcely wider than a ship's beam, this was, from a technical navigation standpoint, child's play. But Luke lined up the *River Runner* with the buoys and the Chesapeake Bay Bridge's own markers with a steady intensity that brought a smile of admiration to Matt's face. Navigating the swift craft though a yawning, seven-hundred-foot-wide channel at night, a simple matter in one sense, was something to which Luke Manguson would bring the full range of his nautical acumen and skill. Darkness on water nearly always transformed simplicity, not necessarily into difficulty, but into a measure of uncertainty. And so Matt found it a pleasure to be in the hands of such a professional seafarer.

With visibility unimpaired by fog or rain and with numerous navigation aids at hand for Luke's use, Matt stepped away from the radar console—its display expected to be very much needed during the run-in to Oxford, and always of importance should visibility deteriorate—and, his good hand on the brightwork of the port handrail, moved to the stern. There the women sat several feet from each other, their orange life jackets creating the odd illusion of bulkiness where, in fact, inside each there was mostly sinew.

He sat down beside his betrothed, smiling at that very thought, and placed his arm around her shoulders. He saw immediately that she was shivering in response to brisk wind and sinking temperatures. He stripped off his windbreaker and wrapped her in it. She turned her face into his chest. He rested his lips in her hair and thrilled to the oneness he felt with this woman. And he wondered, thinking first of the steel savagery of the screwdriver's path through the soft skin of her face, then of the mangled wreckage that remained of his own shoulder, what new wounds the two of them might find themselves accepting on each other's behalf before the *River Runner* could rest again with the swans.

"Eleanor? You awake?"

"No."

"Yes, you are. You're antsy as a rabbit. I can hear you thrashin' around down there. You've been tossin' and turnin' for half an hour, I'd say, maybe more."

He had easily persuaded her not to go back to the now-empty hotel room for the night. But he had hit a stone wall in his efforts to induce her to shift the furniture in the clinic's small guestroom. She had haughtily refused to move her flimsy cot alongside his hospital bed, stating her position as if it were the conclusion to one of her brilliant forty-five-minute lectures: "Sleeping at the foot of a convalescing adult's bed is Christian ministry. Sleeping *beside* a convalescing adult's bed is ridiculous. You don't need me beside you, Detective. You just need a presence in the room. I'll be that for you, and happily, but don't think I'm going to line up beside you as if we were goofy pubescents at a slumber party."

Though he had found the allusion unfathomable, he had had no difficulty grasping the import of her message.

Now, hearing his words in the dark, she sat up and looked in his direction, peering over the footboard of his metal-framed bed.

"Someone can thrash around and yet be asleep, you realize, Detective."

"Yeah, but not you. You're awake."

"I'm certainly awake now."

"So, now that you're awake, talk to me."

She sat for a moment, glaring vaguely at him in the near total darkness. Then she sighed resignedly. "All right," she said, less grumpily, "I'll ask you a question. Where, exactly, do you think they are, right this minute?"

"What time is it? I can't see a clock."

"It's almost midnight."

"Well, if they left about sunset like you said Luke wanted to . . . and if he runs that boat at, maybe, fifteen miles per hour or so . . . hmmm . . . well, I figure they're probably goin' ashore in Oxford just about now . . . Yeah . . . I'd say they're probably already there, Eleanor."

"And are they all right, Detective?"

He smiled in the darkness. "Are you kiddin' me? You put Luke and Rebecca Manguson, backed by Almighty God Himself, up against those tinhorn, two-bit thugs, and you wanna know if they're all right?

"I'll say this. If there's anybody in the world you wouldn't wanna be during the next forty-eight hours, it's Dr. Cameron Stafford, Eleanor. It's Cameron Stafford and anybody else that's got anything to do with him. That dirtbag and his MMHCC crowd are gonna find themselves standin' naked as jaybirds on a fifty-yard line. Know what I mean, ma'am? Know what I mean?"

"What on *earth* are you talking about?"

He laughed once, grabbed his rib cage in pain, and sighed.

"Go to sleep, Eleanor. Somebody may get hurt, but I doubt it's the twins or the kid. And the MMHCC is dead meat. I *know* you know what I mean by that."

"April! April! Wake up, dear. It's a nightmare. It's just a nightmare."

The luminescent face of the clock on the nightstand in their room, upstairs in the quaint, rustic Oxford Tavern and Inn, showed quarter past three o'clock, as Rebecca leaned over her roommate's kicking, moaning form and shook her gently by the shoulder. Suddenly, with a gasp and a start, April Johnstone sat up abruptly.

"Ohhh," she said softly, covering her face with her hands. "Ohhh, I'm sorry. What was I saying? Was I saying anything?"

Rebecca sat on the edge of the bed and rubbed the young woman's back. She did not reply to her question, waiting for the nightmare to clear.

After a moment, April shook her head. "I'm sorry I woke you, Rebecca. I'm all right now. I'll go back to sleep. Thank you for helping."

Rebecca did not move from her side but continued to knead the tense muscles in the reporter's shoulders. After some time, she spoke softly, her words measured. "April, you were shouting Dr. Stafford's name. Repeatedly. And twice you screamed 'No! No! Please stop!'

"What did you see in your dream, April? Please talk to me. I need to know what you saw. Please."

Rebecca, dressed in a light yellow summer nightgown, rose and stepped back to her own bed. She sat down on the edge of the bed and waited expectantly. It became clear to her new friend that the question was not going to be dropped. An answer would be required.

At length, in a quiet, pained voice, April Johnstone spoke, still holding her face in both her hands, sitting cross-legged on her bed, resting her elbows on her knees. "He . . . Dr. Stafford . . . came to my seminary several years ago to give a guest lecture . . . actually, several guest lectures . . . on contemporary theology. Our student association invited him and organized the visit. I was the program chair.

"Actually, we had hoped to get Dr. Chapel to come, but her schedule wouldn't allow it that semester, and Dr. Stafford was the only other 'big name' that seemed to stir up the students' interest. So, he flew to North Carolina and I was the person who met him at the airport and took the responsibility for getting him around. I found him alternately obsequious, overbearing, or truculent, depending upon his assessment of the person in whose company he found himself at any particular moment. His lectures were brilliant, I suppose . . . but I just found him . . . horrible . . . just horrible. Horrible to be with and horrible to watch.

"Then, the next day, when it was time to start back to the airport, he asked to drive the school car that I'd been given, saying he wasn't comfortable being driven by a 'girl.'

"So, he drove."

She stopped, raised her face from her hands, and looked at Rebecca for the first time. The look on her face was so embedded with grief—an *old* grief, thought her listener—that Rebecca almost cried out in surprise.

Then the young reporter, turning her face away, began to speak again, now barely whispering. "We were on a narrow two-lane highway, the kind that has twists and turns and small houses and little farms scattered along the way. We came around a curve and surprised a little brown and white dog. It couldn't have been much more than a puppy. Belonged to some child, I'm sure.

"Dr. Stafford swerved onto the road shoulder and drove right for the little thing. It saw us and tried to dodge away, but Dr. Stafford swerved again so that it had no chance. It was scrambling away, looking over its shoulder at us as we bore down. I'll never forget the sound. . . ."

She swallowed hard. "When I looked over at Dr. Stafford, I saw . . ."

Rebecca stood quickly, stepped back to the other bed, and, sitting down, placed her hand on the distraught woman's knee. "What?" she said softly. "What did you see, April?"

"His face . . . was like a demon's mask, Rebecca," she whispered. "I've never seen Evil so . . . so . . . so *perfect*. It was *pure*. It was his *essence*."

She raised her hands and covered her eyes. And she groaned and spoke indistinctly through clenched teeth. "It's as if the experience poisoned me, Rebecca. I haven't been the same, since. And it's been almost four years, now. I find myself hating him . . . positively *hating* him . . . and then I find myself overcome with guilt. And it has only become worse with time . . . not better.

"And when my editor assigned me to this story, I didn't know what to say. I didn't want to do it, but I felt I had to. I felt I was being given a chance to get back at him, somehow . . . not just for killing the puppy . . . not just for being so *glad* that he killed the puppy . . . but for being what he is! I know what he is, Rebecca!

"But I don't know how to be, anymore. I'm so eaten up by him that sometimes I feel that I should not even have the right to call myself a Christian. I don't believe in Christianity any less than I did before . . . but I'm so *terrible* now . . . I'm such a *terrible* person on the inside. And I keep dreaming the thing over and over: I see the little dog, and I see our car chasing the poor thing, and then I see its little face and its terrified eyes . . . and I hear myself screaming Dr. Stafford's name . . . over and over, screaming his name."

And she began to sob uncontrollably, her shoulders heaving.

And then suddenly she felt herself enclosed by strong, feminine arms, and she heard Rebecca's voice in her ear. "April . . . April . . . Why do you think you were the only person at your seminary who saw the Evil that he was . . . and is?

"Why do you think you've been asked . . . after such an experience . . . to face this man again . . . in fact, to face him later this very day? Actually, to face him in just hours . . . this very morning? Why do you think it's you?"

She paused, holding the sobbing woman tight to herself, then continued, her voice strong, insistent. "If, as you've said, you don't believe in Christianity any less than you did before . . . then you believe that the Holy Spirit is active with us continuously . . . every day, every moment."

And she paused once more, feeling the woman's sobs against her chest.

"So, why? Why would the Holy Spirit have brought you—not one of the other seminarians at your school, but only you—to that experience . . . and now to this one? Why not someone else? Why not someone else?"

Rebecca allowed the question to hang in the air, remaining quiet, continuing to hold the agonized woman in her arms. And gradually, exhaustion beginning to overtake her, the young reporter's sobs grew weaker as the minutes passed, transforming themselves into intermittent sighs, and finally into sniffling, irregular gasps.

At length, Rebecca stood, leaned over the bed, fluffed the pillow, and said quietly, "Here, April. Lie down. Sleep. God is with us. God is with you. You've been chosen to help us confront one of the great Evils besetting this planet at this moment in God's time. You were chosen for this . . . long, long ago."

April Johnstone, no longer crying, lay down and closed her eyes. Rebecca pulled the sheet up to her roommate's chin. "I'll wake you in a few hours. Much depends on you today. Evil has *not* stained or contaminated you in any way that sets you apart from the rest of humankind. Each one of us has that very stain. And each one of us has been . . . died for . . . exactly for that reason.

"What sets you apart, my dear, is that you were chosen to see this particular Evil long before the rest of us. This isn't revenge, today, for the murder of the little dog. The murder of the little dog, and its aftermath in your soul, has prepared you for this day. You've been toughened, you understand. You've been steeled. You've been made ready for Dr. Cameron Stafford. And you've been made ready for death . . . or for life . . . in whatever form and in whatever frame each may come to you.

"And just one more thing I want you to remember. He will no longer be your nightmare, April. From this point forward . . . it is we . . . you and I . . . and Luke and Matt and Ellis . . . and Eleanor and Mr. Belton . . . it is we . . . who will have become *his* nightmare. Yours is finished."

Chapter Fourteen

APRIL JOHNSTONE, WEARING A WHITE SLEEVELESS BLOUSE, knee-length khaki shorts, and brown loafers without socks, took her seat in the casual-dress dining room at the Robert Morris Inn. "Thank you," she said with a relaxed smile to the hostess who seated her and gave her the luncheon menu. She placed the burgundy cloth napkin in her lap, her menu on the table, and, pulling her thick glasses down near the end of her nose, looked over them through the tall window at her left elbow. The town of Oxford's only north-south artery, Morris Street, ran tranquilly past, just twenty-five feet from the window. No traffic, pedestrian or vehicular, interrupted her view up the street toward the entrance to the ferry landing, nor, visible in medium distance, of the broad expanse of the Tred Avon River.

She lifted the menu from the table to eye level and opened it, but allowed her glasses to remain well below her line of sight. She looked just above the top of the menu. Her view of the entrance to the dining room and of the hallway behind it was unobstructed. At that precise moment, she saw a slight, bespectacled, African-American man walk past. The good photographs she had been provided in preparation for the assignment left no doubt as to the man's identity. She noted that he carried a large sheaf of papers.

She looked down at the menu, but her mind was elsewhere. This came as no surprise. What did surprise her was that her mind insisted upon revisiting, not the nightmare that had so dramatically interrupted her sleep, not the long-ago encounter with Cameron Stafford, not even her confession to Rebecca of the hostility and guilt that had undermined her sense of worthiness to be called Christian, but, unaccountably, the chain of events just prior to the nightmare: the voyage south to Oxford. It had been a voyage to which she had attended very little in her planning, and yet, in the doing, one that had filled her with the most profound sensations, both of comfort and, especially, of fear.

In those hours before the dream, and the salvation from the dream that Rebecca's words—and strong arms—had brought, the reporter, fearless in the face of adversaries she understood, had found herself surprisingly discomfited at the prospect of a night voyage over a large body of water. Embarrassed, she had struggled to display the same aplomb that she saw in her companions.

Then, oddly, she had found that something in Luke's bearing and quiet confidence had calmed her to an extent she would not have imagined possible. She had even begun to enjoy the southerly passage down the channel, well before the boat had passed under the twin spans of the Chesapeake Bay Bridge. But her anxiety had resumed when the boat turned east, passed around the southern tip of Tilghman Island, and moved steadily away from the main channel. As expected, navigation became difficult for the two men as they steered the boat into the dark, constricted waters, lined with inlets and river mouths, that formed the waterway to Oxford. The men's intensity and apparent uncertainty had unnerved her to such an extent that she had finally lain down in the footwell, feigning sleep. From that position, she had listened as they discussed radar bearings and distances to various identifiable points of land, and, following two premature turns, she had felt their relief in her very bones as they talked excitedly of finding, at last, the half-mile-wide mouth of the Tred Avon. Entering the river cautiously, they had passed, from a comfortable distance, the handful of streetlights that marked the tiny town. But the reporter had found her heart in her throat from then until the moment, hours later, when her Cameron-Stafford-induced nightmare came to an abrupt end, and Rebecca led her to a place in her soul that she had been unable to find for four interminable years.

She had been pleased that Ellis Dolby's warnings about the marinas and vehicular approaches to the town had led them again to rely upon her editor's limitless network of friends to secure docking for the boat and lodging for the night. However, the location of the privately owned pier that had been made ready for them required them to circumnavigate the town, heightening her anxiety still further, to the point finally that it seemed to approach genuine terror.

At one point, having risen to her knees from the boat's deep footwell, she had been transfixed by the sight of the Robert Morris Inn, a mere two hundred yards off the starboard beam at their point of closest approach. She knew Cameron Stafford himself was there, just across two thin slivers of water and roadway, perhaps standing at a window and staring directly into her eyes. It had been at that moment that she had leaned over the side and vomited energetically into the river, Rebecca holding her forehead and comforting her with assurances that the voyage was near its end, and that what Rebecca called her seasickness would soon be a thing of the past.

Though she was not actually to become sick again, she had experienced another wave of nausea when, upon reaching the mouth of Town Creek, Luke had throttled back almost to idle, to limit the trademark growl of the twin Mercuries. But in the silence of those enclosed waters, the engine noise had still seemed to the reporter like a continual peal of thunder in an electrical storm. She sensed Cameron Stafford's nearby presence, and imagined his striding along the Oxford streets to meet their vessel and to consume it with the fire of his hatred.

But Luke had moved them quickly into their berth, shutting down the engines just minutes after midnight. A short walk through the dimly lighted streets had brought them to the small inn whose innkeeper had been asked by their benefactor to accommodate them in every way he could. She had by then found herself so exhausted from the unremitting anguish that she had ignored Rebecca's efforts at conversation and reassurance, and had crept to her bed fully clothed, slipping off her shoes and pulling the covers up to her chin.

Almost immediately after her head had touched the pillow and her eyes had closed in sleep, it had seemed to her, the nightmare had come.

Now, as she stared, unseeing, at her menu, in the very building in which Cameron Stafford presided over still another MMHCC session, Rebecca's words formed again in her mind: "Why do you think it was you, April? Why not someone else?" And, again and again: "Your nightmare is finished."

She realized the waitress was at her side. Pushing her glasses quickly into reading position, she ordered the first salad her eyes found. The menu and the waitress departed abruptly, and she found herself feeling utterly naked, without protection of any kind . . . and the man who had for four years been her nightmare was just a few feet away down the main hallway, seated in the corner conference room. He could, she knew, materialize before her at any moment.

Panic welled and, instead of fighting it down, she closed her eyes, bowed her head, and gave thanks for the food that she was about to receive. A calmness descended rapidly, blessedly, over her, and grateful, she reached down to her soft leather document pouch, removed a section of that morning's *Baltimore Sun*, checked the pouch's secret—and presently empty—compartment, and returned it to the floor, allowing it to lean against the wall at her left side. She scanned the newspaper headlines absently, processing little, continuing to focus on the presence that had returned to her as she had said grace, a presence she had felt almost continuously in her waking moments since Rebecca's stunning declaration: "Your nightmare is finished."

Her salad arrived almost immediately. She consumed it deliberately, continuing to scan the newspaper as she did, toying with her food between bites. Eventually so little remained of her salad that she decided to yield to the waitress's third request to remove the plate and to bring the small dessert menu. Then she repeated the procedure, dabbling with a tangy lemon tart until, finally, some ninety minutes after she had arrived, there was only coffee before her. She drank two cups, used the ladies' room, returned, and asked for a third.

Suddenly Ellis Dolby appeared at the doorway.

Ignoring her presence, he entered the dining room from the hallway that connected the conference room with the office, strode purposefully toward the rear dining room where the bathrooms were located, and while walking briskly past a vacant table perhaps fifteen feet from her, casually placed a thin packet of documents on the polished table surface.

Seizing the document pouch from the floor beside her, the reporter quickly placed the newspaper inside its main compartment and was on her feet. She crossed the dining room, retrieved the loose documents at a near run, then turned and followed Dolby into and through the rear dining room, entering the ladies' room just seconds after the door to the men's room had closed behind him. Once inside, she removed the newspaper, folded the document pages once, slipped them into the pouch's hidden compartment, one which actually formed a false bottom inside the case, sealed the compartment, reinserted the newspaper in the main section of the document carrier, and returned swiftly to her table. She hurriedly asked for the check, left cash on the table, and headed for the doorway that led to the inn's main door. She made the assumption that Ellis Dolby had exited the men's room while she was still in the ladies' room.

She passed into the hallway and walked rapidly toward the exit. Suddenly she stopped. "Stupid!" she said under her breath. She had removed fifteen dollars from her coin purse, and then in her haste, had left the purse on the table with the money. Her driver's license and other identification—including her reporter's credentials—were in the purse. Wheeling abruptly, she collided hard with Cameron Stafford.

Each fell back a step.

She caught her breath and waited for the color to drain from her face. It did not. "Excuse me," she said with an equanimity that, she knew instantly, could have been provided only by the Presence within. She stepped around him, reentered the dining room, and, ignoring her table and the coin purse that sat conspicuously atop it, returned to the ladies' room. There she counted to sixty, strode back through the dining room, again without going near her table, and once more turned toward the main exit to the inn. Cameron Stafford had not moved, except to turn around to meet her.

"Excuse me, miss. I know your face from somewhere," he said matter-of-factly. "Where have we met before?"

She looked at him quizzically as though vaguely struck by the familiarity of a face. Peering at him thoughtfully, she removed her glasses and met his gaze. After a moment, she said, "You remind me of someone I've seen in newspapers or magazines. Are you a famous person?"

He smiled. "Yes."

Then, after a moment, he said evenly, "May I see some identification and the contents of your document case, please? We're holding some rather high-level meetings here today, and we want to be careful that our materials do not find their way out the door. We also need to ensure that only residents of the town are present." He extended his hand in what he may have regarded as a friendly manner.

"Why, no," she replied, just as evenly. "The document case is my property, sir, and as you see, I have no identification on my person."

The smile faded. He lifted his hand and beckoned without turning his head. From behind him two muscular gentlemen appeared at his side. "Sir?" said one gruffly, looking first at Stafford and then at April Johnstone.

"Inspect the packet," he said curtly.

Standing impassively, she allowed the men to lift the case from her unresponsive hand. They unzipped the pouch, removed the newspaper, looked inside, and saw nothing. One of them turned, opened the pouch fully for Cameron Stafford's review, then returned the newspaper to its place. He zipped the pouch and extended it to the reporter.

April Johnstone accepted the case wordlessly, looked steadily at Cameron Stafford, and said quietly, "May I go now?"

He smiled thinly and stepped aside. When she reached the front door, she opened it wide and looked back down the hallway. All three men were watching her intently. She had the impression that Stafford was about to give the two an order. She paused and stared directly into Cameron Stafford's eyes.

Then, a half dozen steps behind them, she saw Ellis Dolby pass out of the dining room and turn away from the men, toward the office. Glancing over his shoulder and seeing all three men were turned away from him, he quickly held high a small coin purse, then slipped it just as quickly into his pocket.

April Johnstone, a faint smile now on her face, nodded courteously toward Cameron Stafford, turned, and was gone.

As the door swung closed behind the reporter, Cameron Stafford turned his head and glimpsed the figure of Ellis Dolby as it disappeared into the office. Thoughtfully, Stafford turned again to his two colleagues, spoke briefly to each, and watched one follow in Dolby's footsteps, down the hallway, while the other strode quickly to the front door and onto Morris Street.

The reporter walked at a deliberate pace south on Morris Street toward the Oxford Tavern and Inn where her three colleagues awaited her. The street was deserted, with just two vehicles—a new Mercedes and an old Ford pickup truck—waiting in front of one of the locally owned grocery-and-sundries that sat roughly at midpoint on the town's north-south axis. The walk from the Robert Morris Inn to the tavern was perhaps a half mile, and she refused at any point to look behind her. She simply strolled, document pouch under her arm.

As she approached the tavern, passing just in front of the Episcopal church on her right, she heard a faint, indeterminate sound, and turning her head, saw a movement from deep behind the church. There was Rebecca, positioned so that, at that moment, she could be seen easily from the intersection of roadway and church driveway, but, from either direction along the street, she was screened from view by the church and its outbuildings. The reporter saw Rebecca's quick hand signal and knew precisely what it indicated. She had been followed, just as they had assumed she would be.

She knew her role in this contingency, though not that of her colleagues. Without hesitation and without looking toward Rebecca a second time, she walked past the front porch of the small tavern from which, she felt certain, Luke and Matt watched from the second-floor shadows. She continued without change in her leisurely pace for three short blocks. Approaching a neatly lettered wooden sign indicating the Pier Street Restaurant and Marina to her right, she turned in that direction, walked the remaining one hundred yards to the site, stepped onto the deck of the outdoor seating area, and asked for a table on the water. She was escorted to one of the heavy wooden picnic-style tables and took her seat, facing away from the street and parking lot through which she had just walked, the only pedestrian or vehicular approach to the restaurant. Despite having no money with her, she ordered a glass of iced tea, and with a flourish, removed the newspaper from her document pouch.

Soon she sensed, rather than observed, the arrival of one of Cameron Stafford's henchmen. And she sensed, as well, that he had taken a table not far behind her, also alongside the water, blocking her exit from the outdoor seating area. And she sensed, too, that she would not be in possession of her document pouch with its precious evidentiary material—the material that would provide the public indictment of the MMHCC and establish the astonishing perversity of its means and methods—for more than a few more minutes unless she acted immediately. But act how?

Rebecca's words, uttered in the wee hours of that same morning, came mysteriously to her mind. "Much depends on you today . . . You've been toughened . . . It is we . . . who will have become *his* nightmare. Yours is finished." And suddenly, as in the Robert Morris Inn just twenty minutes earlier, she felt a strange calmness, an almost eerie serenity, again enfolding her spirit.

And then, in a flash of insight that washed over her in a cleansing wave, so overwhelming that, had she been standing, she knew she might have been driven to her knees, she became somehow certain that her life's work was at its end. She caught her breath and found herself fighting back tears. Where had this come from? What could it mean? Was her own death truly at hand? Was she to die now, having brought the child-saving documents from the Enemy's lair?

The sudden tightness in her chest fought against the continuing serenity in her spirit. And she recognized the conflict: this was the joy and anticipation of immortality now unexpectedly face-to-face with the terror and fear of death. This was the exultation of Heaven's promise tested by proximity to her own murder. She drew a deep breath and closed her eyes. Was she ready?

To her surprise, she realized that she was smiling. How, she thought to herself? And why?

And she knew. She knew that she had done her duty, that she had acted in obedience. She had done His will for her, as she had been led to understand that will. She had . . . what had the apostle written? " . . . Fought the good fight . . . finished the race . . . kept the faith." And she found herself smiling more broadly, almost laughing aloud, and shaking her head in amazement as another of the apostle's phrases came to her, truly thrown at her brain, unbidden but joyously welcome: "For me to live is Christ; to die is gain."

And she *felt* in the core of all certainties that her mission on earth had reached fruition. The calmness grew deeper. The serenity grew more profound within her. She felt somehow that she could simply close her eyes and surrender to eternity right then. And happily. Without a vestige of fear.

And yet . . . her charge had not yet been completely fulfilled. Certainly, the critical documents were in her possession, but they remained in great jeopardy. She would give herself up to save them . . . to save the children from the ravages that would be visited upon them. But how? She searched her brain desperately for another answer. It came from an unexpected source.

She felt the waitress at her elbow, leaning down to place her tea on the table. She saw the woman's hand linger next to the glass, and she realized then that a small slip of paper extended from under the napkin on which the tea glass rested. The waitress quickly moved away, and the reporter unobtrusively slipped the paper from under the glass.

Sliding the note to the edge of the table just in front of her chest, she unfolded it with one hand and read the three sentences, written in graceful feminine script: "Use the ladies' room. Bring the documents. Come now."

Leaving the newspaper on the table with her tea, she tucked the document pouch under her left arm and, walking as casually as she could, entered the restaurant's interior dining room and found the restroom at the rear of the building. The waitress watched her pass down the hallway, enter the ladies' room, and, in no more than thirty seconds, emerge with the woman who had given her the note. The tall, athletic brunette, dressed in running shoes and white tennis shorts and shirt, her hair gathered in a tight ponytail that fell far down her back, smiled at the waitress and pressed five dollars into her hand for the iced tea and the assistance.

Then she led the reporter through the rear service entrance and turned left, away from the pedestrian and vehicular approaches to the restaurant. The two women, walking close to the wall, passed around the building to its north side and half walked, half ran past an outbuilding to a small boat slip at the mouth of the inlet that led to the Pier Street Marina. There they quickly boarded a strange, unwieldy-appearing rubber raft, scarcely large enough for the two of them. Rebecca pushed off, sat carefully in the stern, and pulled the starter rope on the raft's compact outboard motor. It sprang to life with remarkably little noise, and keeping the restaurant building between herself and the outdoor seating area where Stafford's security guard sat, she maneuvered the unstable vessel across the mouth of the inlet and then north along the shoreline, hugging the rocky shore. Some fifty yards north of the inlet, she accelerated as much as the small motor would permit, turned sharp left away from the shoreline, and, using all the speed the outboard could muster, headed for the center of the Tred Avon. In just seconds, the strange craft merged with dozens of other small boats, many of them crewed by children participating in one of the town's regularly scheduled sailboat regattas. She held a westerly course through the teeming confusion of wind-driven, oar-driven, and motorized boats—none of them appearing to move in the same direction as any of the others—and, in minutes, cleared the center of the channel, making steady progress toward the western shore of the river. Not long after leaving the congestion, she changed to a southerly course, and hugging the far shore, steered toward the mouth of the Tred Avon.

From the Oxford shore opposite her, four pairs of binoculars watched her as she drove the tiny vessel determinedly toward the passages to the Chesapeake. Her brother and her fiance, each tense and silent, standing at the rear windows of their second-floor room at the tavern, held two. A third pair was held to his eyes by the security guard who had followed the reporter from the Robert Morris Inn. Now in desperate fear, quite literally, for his life, he sat stock still, frozen in terror and confusion, at his table alongside the water.

The fourth pair of field glasses was held by Cameron Stafford. No more than one hundred feet from the horrified security guard, and unseen by him, standing alone in the restaurant parking lot beside an elongated gray limousine, Stafford stood erect, a small smile playing across his lips. He stooped, looked in the car, and spoke to the driver. The driver lifted the limousine's telephone from its receiver and dialed a number.

As the underpowered, square-bowed raft had cleared the center of the river and its wild sailboat, motorboat, kayak, and canoe traffic, the reporter had turned her head to the side and called over her shoulder above the confusion of small noises: the purr of the miniature outboard, the slap and splash of water against the rubber sides of the raft, the intermittent rise and fall of a whistling wind. "Rebecca," she had shouted, "where did this boat come from?"

"My brother arranged for this," she called back, "before you left for the Robert Morris. We knew that if you were followed, it wouldn't do just to have you pass by the tavern and seat yourself on the deck at the pier. We knew we would need to get you away from there straightaway. Luke and Matt had already prepared the boat—checked for leaks, filled the petrol tank, tested the steering—by noon and took it down to the water. After you and your shadow had passed, I waited for you both to reach your tables, then ran behind the tavern to this funny thing, drove it to the restaurant side of the inlet, and came in the service door.

"The waitress was lovely about helping. I wish we had a better boat, but there was no way to arrange for anything of that sort. The tavern's proprietor actually keeps this in his garage with his lawn equipment."

The reporter took a moment, then asked, her voice rising over the wind, "Where are we going now? Not much further, I hope?"

"We'll be heading for Tilghman Island. We passed near it last night. We'll put to shore at one of the piers along its eastern side, and then we'll just wait there for Luke and Matt. They'll need nightfall to go in and get Ellis Dolby out of the Robert Morris, you know. You and Ellis have got the documents for us, and now we can't leave him with those people a second longer than necessary."

Rebecca had paused at that point to survey the river traffic behind them, and observed closely by the men on the Oxford side, had maneuvered the cumbersome raft gradually nearer the far shore of the river. After some ten more minutes, satisfied with the raft's position, she called out, "It's going to take us nearly two more hours, I'm afraid, to get to Tilghman in this little thing, April. And once we're there, we'll still have quite a long wait for the boys. I've brought money and this little knapsack with your light jacket and mine. We'll be able to get something to eat at one of the inns, and we'll leave the raft tied up in a spot where Luke and Matt and Ellis can see it, using the boat's searchlights."

As they began to move out of range of the field glasses that had followed them to that point, they fell silent, feeling abrupt changes in water conditions as the clumsy vessel began to wallow and pitch alarmingly. Rebecca knew that the tidal action from the bay would begin to make itself felt against the sluggish current of the Tred Avon and the stronger flow of the Choptank River, near the confluence of the three, but she had not expected the conflicted waters to affect her lightweight craft quite so dramatically. She struggled to hold course.

The next half hour was filled with a quiet tension while Rebecca tacked vigorously back and forth, plowing first into the extreme shallows to find purchase for the miniature engine and propeller, then, encountering underwater vegetation, rocks, or both, back into the swirling confusion of currents, fighting toward the tip of the promontory. At long last, the fragile craft cleared the point of land that marked the true, geographical mouth of the Tred Avon, and Rebecca set a straight course for Tilghman Island, across more than seven miles of open water that Luke expected to be far quieter than those she had just transited.

The women had not spoken for some time when Rebecca called out, "I think we're all right now, April. These waters are out of the currents, even though they're also more open. Do you think you can lie down and rest a little? You must be exhausted from all the tension . . . and the night- mares . . . and the lack of sleep . . . and two whole hours under the same roof with Cameron Stafford."

The reporter turned her head again, and calling over her shoulder, said, "I think I might be able to curl up in this foot space, at least enough to rest my back and shoulders. I won't be able to sleep, but it would be absolute heaven to change my position and relax for a few minutes."

Rebecca, holding her course firmly, watched her new friend carefully begin to turn herself around so as to face the stern. April Johnstone moved slowly, mindful of the raft's inherent instability, and as she prepared to fold herself into the small space in the footwell now just behind her, looked up at Rebecca and smiled. The smile transformed her, thought Rebecca. April Johnstone now seemed, to her eye, absolutely beatific.

Rebecca returned the smile with her own, then watched in confusion as her friend's face changed, first to a look of puzzlement, and then to something quite indescribable. She realized after a moment that the reporter's gaze was fixed on something behind the raft, visible over Rebecca's shoulder.

Before she could turn her head, Rebecca heard the change. Shattering the tranquil auditory world which they had entered upon rounding the point, one in which birdsong and bird call became more pronounced than the distant, diminishing sound of machinery, there came suddenly that stupefying scream unique to the most powerful of inboard marine engines. Turning her head quickly, Rebecca saw the enor- mous, preposterously high bow of the racer flying directly toward the raft, now no more than 150 yards away. At more than fifty-five miles per hour, impact with the fragile raft would come in fewer than six seconds. She wheeled around, shouting, "April, jump!" But she was too late. No sooner had she shouted her friend's name than she saw and felt an upraised forearm smashing her in the chest, sending her flying backward over the raft's toylike motor and into the water, her body covered as she hit the surface by that of April Johnstone.

Wetness and blackness and hellish noise and the scent of eternity were, all at once, upon them both.

Chapter Fifteen

FROM THE TAVERN'S SECOND-STORY WINDOWS, LUKE AND Matt watched through field glasses until the raft, long since a mere speck of black against a field of blue, finally disappeared from view near the mouth of the Tred Avon, almost two miles to the southwest. They busied themselves immediately with preparations for their own departure, still hours away, then napped fitfully until the proprietor awakened them, as they had asked, at six o'clock. Luke was intent on preparing the *River Runner* for departure before nightfall.

They rolled out of their beds, collected their gear, and followed the tavern owner down the back stairwell and out the door to his waiting station wagon. Then they lay down in the rear cargo area, out of sight of chance passersby, while he took them on the short drive to the secluded boat slip at Town Creek where they had made fast the night before. Thanking the proprietor for his unquestioning and enthusiastic assistance throughout the visit, they clambered aboard the vessel and completed all preparations by seven o'clock. Then they reclined from opposite directions in the footwell just forward of the twin outboards, their heads sharing a knapsack for a pillow, and read, rested, and napped until nightfall. As nine o'clock approached, they began final preparations.

The Mercuries responded to a touch of the starter, and Luke backed the powerful craft out of its slip and into the broad creek, cranking the wheel to the left to swing the stern left, then back to the right as he shifted gears, first into neutral, and then into forward. Nudging the throttle just enough to gain steerage, Luke moved the sleek vessel into the center of the widening channel, brought the bow toward the right side of the waterway, and, just five minutes after starting the engines, entered the Tred Avon under a moonless night sky.

Using both the channel buoys and the small surface-search radar as aids to navigation, he brought the boat far out into the center of the river, well away from the Oxford shore, before he turned downriver and pushed the throttle to midrange. At a brisk fifteen knots, they moved across the north face of the town and, through their binoculars, studied the lights still blazing from the Robert Morris Inn where Cameron Stafford, Ellis Dolby, and a cast of prominent American educators, publishers, politicians, and business luminaries had completed a long and productive day, a sumptuous evening meal, and, by now, were off to their rooms, perhaps to pack for their journeys home on Saturday morning, certainly to sleep.

Luke maintained his position river center until he had cleared the town's northwest point, then he came left to steer a southerly course straight toward the Tred Avon's mouth where Rebecca and April Johnstone, in the motorized raft, had crept slowly from their sight hours earlier. But he held the new course for only sixty seconds. Suddenly he turned sharp left ninety degrees, switched off the running lights, and, still at speed, steered a course close across the face of the Oxford Yacht Club. Throttling back, shifting into neutral and then into reverse, he backed the engines down and skillfully slid the craft in among the high pilings of the ferry slip. Matt leaped onto the landing and, using his good hand and arm with seasoned efficiency, secured the craft fore and aft while Luke snugged the boat against the underside of the ramp, starboard side-to, and cut the engines.

In just seconds, the two men had circled back to the clubhouse and taken position in the darkness, crouching together against the southwest corner of the building. From that position they could see across the darkened parking lot to the Robert Morris Inn, both to the main structure, two hundred yards away and on their left, and to the somewhat smaller annex, just one hundred yards away and directly in front of them.

Ellis Dolby, in charge of logistical arrangements for the MMHCC meetings, had placed himself in a first-floor room in the annex. He had given Cameron Stafford a second-floor room in the main building, a short walk away from the annex, in the same structure that housed the inn's dining room. Luke's basic plan for Dolby's evacuation called for Dolby to leave his room sometime between 9:30 and 10:00, and, if unobserved, to move straight to the yacht club's parking lot. The three of them would then race back to the ferry slip, board the *River Runner*, cast off immediately, and make a high-speed retreat down the Tred Avon. Once they had rounded the promontory that marked the river mouth, they would tack, at low speed, across seven miles of largely unmarked shallows to Tilghman Island's eastern shoreline, following the route taken by the women in early afternoon. There they would retrieve Rebecca, the reporter, and the precious document packet that April Johnstone would be carrying with her.

Contingency plans abounded, as always when Luke Manguson was in charge, and for a number of reasons. They could not know in advance whether or not Ellis Dolby would, in fact, be free of his duties and his mentor by 9:30. They could not know exactly what the security precautions and dispositions would be, once the conference had ended and its participants had retired for the night. They could not know whether or not the room arrangements, detailed so carefully by Dolby beforehand, would remain intact once the participants had actually arrived in Oxford. Above all, they could not know whether or not Ellis Dolby would continue to be regarded as trustworthy by the MMHCC leaders.

After all, the fact that the Mangusons had found the Brooklyn warehouse and rescued Matt and Sid Belton suggested at least the possibility of a traitor within the upper levels of the organization. In addition, the warehouse guards and their supervisors would by now have concluded that a third person played a role in the attack that freed the two captives. The armed guard on the catwalk could not have rendered himself unconscious, and the twins were on the warehouse floor at the moment he was struck. Ellis Dolby, Luke and Matt knew, could very well by now have become a suspect in Cameron Stafford's eyes.

These and other uncertainties—including their necessarily inexact foreknowledge of the motorized raft's location along Tilghman Island's eastern shore—had led Luke to establish with Rebecca a one-hour target rendezvous window, rather than an exact hour and minute. The *River Runner* would arrive at the island, if possible, between quarter 'til midnight, on Friday, and quarter 'til one on Saturday morning.

And so they waited in the darkness, checking their watches from time to time. While one of them looked in Ellis Dolby's anticipated direction of escape, the other checked continually for security patrols from any other quarter, including from the direction of the river itself.

Matt was calm. He, like the Manguson twins, had made peace with extreme danger long before. There had been a time in his life when this peace had been based entirely on his sense of fidelity to the military units within which he had served. He had, throughout his five years on active duty, avoided pushing his mind too far in the direction of that concept's constraints and limitations.

He had settled for a minor but workable truth—one that would permit him to function responsibly—despite his certain knowledge that that truth was seeded in barren soil. He knew, but would not then acknowledge, that without belief in a Creator and in a moral law that intersected the creation at every point, there could be no nourishment for his cherished sense of fidelity to his comrades, and in the end, no real peace with danger, no true peace with death. The concept was utilitarian to the point of nonsense, allowing no distinction between a group with noble purpose and one with vile purpose . . . or one with no purpose at all. Fidelity to comrades as an ultimate good sought to deify any group purpose whatsoever, simply because it was a *group* purpose. It was a shallow religion suitable for those whose desperation to confer meaning to danger and death placed them in position to accept the most convenient fiction available.

Now he was a different person, and ironically, found himself as a civilian facing danger greater than he had known during any of his five years of active military service. The new Matt Clark was acutely aware that his sense of peace in the face of danger—in the face of death—had become, and now, was once again, based in something that had come to sustain him at all times and under all circumstances. Danger, he now knew from intimate experience, did not and could not alter the fundamental conditions of life or of death. Danger presented him, quite simply, with one more opportunity to do his duty, to act in obedience to the Holy Spirit's leading. And this duty was, in fact, not in any important way unlike his duty to be compassionate, to be generous, to be courteous, to be civil. In the face of danger, he had finally realized, the response called for by God's moral law and the Holy Spirit's impulse was not different in substance from any of those other responses.

It had, as did they, its own name: and that name was courage. But its larger name was duty.

And its stronger name was obedience.

Ten o'clock came and passed.

At quarter past the hour, on Luke's unspoken signal, the two men moved promptly into the first of their contingencies. They moved rapidly across the parking lot, turned right, and crept to within yards of the river just south of the point. Then, aided by indirect illumination provided by the annex's spotlights, they jogged across the grassy expanse fronting the elaborate, antebellum-style structure and turned left toward the building. In just three minutes from the time they began the movement, they stood beside Ellis Dolby's room under the high, south-facing windows. Without pause, Luke stooped and interlocked his hands at knee level while Matt placed his foot gently into the cup thus provided. Then, his good hand on Luke's shoulder, Matt stood on the human step, while Luke straightened his back and raised his hands and Matt's two-hundred-plus pounds to chest level. Matt turned his head and from his new elevation looked into Ellis Dolby's room. After a moment, he tapped Luke's shoulder, and, in agile concert with Luke's lowering movement, stepped down and back onto the grass.

Matt gestured, and in response the two moved away from the building and into the shadows. There they crouched, and Matt whispered briefly into Luke's ear. Then they stood and shook hands slowly, Luke's left hand covering their clasped right hands. Joined in that pose, three hands together as one, they bowed their heads, closed their eyes, and prayed silently.

The room's only door opened onto a porch. The screened door from the porch, in turn, faced the evenly mowed and manicured yard across which they had just run.

Their hands empty, the two men strode rapidly from the shadows to the near corner of the annex, moved along the flagstone pathway that traversed the front of the building, and drew open the screened door. They crossed the porch without apparent concern at the floorboards' squeaking, groaning announcement of their approach, paused while Luke took his position in front of Matt, and stopped at the door to the guestroom itself. Luke knocked once, turned the door handle, and pushed hard.

The door swung open and the two stepped quickly into the room.

Four heads turned toward them. Two faces showed surprise and alarm. One was impassive. The fourth appeared confused by the intrusion.

The latter face was Dolby's. Blood ran from his swollen mouth and his eyes displayed a type of fear that Matt recognized at once. It was the fear of yielding . . . of betraying . . . of disclosing . . . and as Matt stared at the small, battered professor, he saw, first, recognition, and then, hope, pass across his desperate countenance.

Matt smiled at him and nodded.

The impassive face was Cameron Stafford's. He turned immediately to the two security guards and held up both palms, stopping the movement that each had begun toward his sidearm. Then he turned to face the visitors. "Good evening, gentlemen," he said cordially. "I've been expecting you. I was quite certain that your female accomplices had not come to Oxford unescorted.

"And I was confident that you would come for your criminal partner rather sooner than later, since you must have known that I would be unlikely to oppose you physically . . . that is, violently . . . that is, with gunplay . . . when the inn is filled with an array of such distinguished guests as have honored us this day and evening with their presence."

Here he looked down at Dolby, the only one seated, and added, "Professor Dolby, you should probably take this opportunity to exit now. Your future has been decided this week, and I must emphasize, *not* in your favor.

"Good-bye, Ellis," he said with contempt.

At this, Dolby, who was not bound, struggled to rise, staggered, and fell forward. Luke was there, catching him by both shoulders, bringing him upright, then passing him into and under Matt's right arm, which quickly encircled and supported his unsteady colleague.

Luke turned back to Stafford. Speaking in his low, clear voice and precise Oxford dialect, he addressed the MMHCC leader. "You referred to Dr. Dolby as our 'criminal partner.' And you are correct, of course. We had no one's permission to cut through a padlock or to enter your warehouse, just to name two of our trespasses. And if we are to be called to account for such actions, we'll stand ready to accept our punishment.

"It will have been worth it, sir, if we can prevent you and your colleagues from ruining the minds and souls of children across this country and around the world. We know Whom we serve, Dr. Stafford, as, I'm altogether certain, do you."

Stafford's face changed, and suddenly Matt saw traces of the same deranged personality that had confronted him in the Brooklyn warehouse fewer than seventy-two hours earlier. Perhaps alcohol had had nothing to do with what he had then seen and experienced. . . . Perhaps this was something else entirely.

The suddenly beet-red, swelling face, visibly pulsing at the temples, teeth bared like a cornered animal, spluttered at Luke. "Silence! Silence, you insolent hireling! You and *your* pathetic colleagues, both cowering behind you like the ciphers they are, have neither the intelligence nor the will nor the courage to do *anything* about us and what we seek! If your little band of zealots possessed even an ounce of those qualities, you would have crashed into our midst this morning and made every conceivable effort to tear the meeting asunder by any means that you could devise. You would have endeavored to destroy the MMHCC *absolutely* in the name of whatever you consider worthy of sacrifice.

"But look at you! *Look* at you! You stand here with *nothing*. You are going to walk out this door in sixty seconds, having accomplished *nothing* other than to retrieve—and with my *permission*, if you please—this pitiable excuse for a psychologist. Whatever being you may think you honor and obey, I can only say that that curious being seems to hold no power over anything or anyone, and judging from the likes of you three and your women, has not one soul in its service capable of lifting a finger, with the slightest effect, on behalf of its allegedly divine purposes!"

Luke responded quietly and without hesitation. "We are required by that very Being to Whom you refer to operate within constraints that you do not acknowledge, sir. We are bound by a moral law . . . the same law . . . the same ethical framework . . . you seek to remove from our children."

Stafford paused. He seemed to Matt to be struggling to regain something like the composure that was normally his. The room was quiet. Other than his brief verbal response, Luke had not moved, nor changed his expression of quiet, almost analytical, attentiveness.

Stafford looked down for a moment, still fighting to regain control of his emotions. Appearing to succeed, he looked up, first, at Luke, then, at Matt. Clearing his throat, he proceeded in a lower voice and at something resembling his usual, measured pace of speaking. His face gradually resumed its normal appearance of dignified, scholarly benevolence.

"Judging from the equanimity in your collective demeanor, it occurs to me that perhaps the two of you are unaware, as is Dr. Dolby, of the . . . ah . . . tragic accident that befell your . . . your women . . . early this afternoon?"

Seeing no response, he continued. "Yes. Yes, it seems that some sort of racing craft—one of those huge inboards, I'm given to understand—was careless enough to . . . ah . . . to run up and over the little rubber boat that someone had been so thoughtless as to loan them." He paused dramatically. "Yes. Yes, it seems that the propeller . . . the marine propeller . . . how can I break this to you gently . . . the propeller actually . . . chewed its way . . . chewed its way through everything . . . yes . . . chewed its way through the raft, its little outboard motor . . . the reporter . . . the novice reporter . . . from that little Christian tabloid . . . and . . . yes . . . yes . . . through your beloved . . . your beloved Miss Manguson herself."

He paused to allow the words to hang in the air. Luke's face showed nothing. Matt stared at his mentor, repelled. He found he could not breathe. Then he felt Ellis Dolby's arm move up and around his waist in physical support, as their roles suddenly reversed, Dolby now the comforter.

At length, satisfied that his words had stunned his audience into silence, Stafford picked up a new theme. "Of course, upon reflection, you'll agree that the tragic end to which your women have come simply means that your overall scheme has produced outcomes that are all of a piece. You have failed at everything, and in every way.

"Yes. For example, we have held our MMHCC meetings here in Oxford quite successfully. Your efforts interrupted nothing, provided no distraction, produced no diversion from our business.

"And yes. For another example, your attempt to steal confidential documents from our perfectly legitimate organization has failed spectacularly. You have no extant documents and no extant photographs of documents. You have no physical evidence of anything . . . of any kind.

"And yes. For a third example, every single one of our plans for the future remains firmly in place, wholly unchanged by any of your countervailing efforts. We shall move forward on the same broad front that has been envisioned all along, without a single missing component, completely unaffected by your laughable penchant for the futile and the quixotic."

Here, he turned to Matt. "And yes. On a different but related topic, Matthew, your heretofore promising career with the MMHCC now lies, I'm afraid, in ruins. As does, I think you'll find, any other career you might attempt in this country, and just perhaps, in any other country as well."

He paused for a moment, looked each man thoughtfully in the eye, then continued. "But perhaps none of this is getting through. Perhaps each of you is still caught up in some sort of reverie regarding the boating incident to which I alluded earlier. Perhaps some flicker of light glows, however faintly, within your minds and hearts, some ember of hope that I have simply invented a story of ultimate tragedy in order to add to your distress."

Here he turned to the security guard on his right and motioned with his hand. The man stepped quickly into the bathroom and returned carrying a large, clear plastic bag. At Stafford's gesture, the man held the bag high for the three men to see. It contained wet, shredded clothing, most of it saturated with blood, and a waterlogged pair of blue Nike running shoes.

Stafford smiled at Luke. "I should think some of this material might look familiar to you, Lieutenant Manguson? You'll note especially the shoes?

"Really, gentlemen," he continued, "I think you should just carry the unfortunate Dr. Dolby home. Here, at the end of the day, so to speak, you've got nothing to show for your miserable efforts.

"Oh, you can go to the police with some tales about kidnapping and rough treatment, but, in the end, it's just the word of several petty, nondescript, undistinguished young people against that of some of the most reputable people in America. The documents you tried to steal are disintegrating at the bottom of the Chesapeake Bay, of course; you have nothing whatsoever by way of evidence to support any claim you might make. And you'll never know precisely, beyond the description I have already provided, what happened to young Miss Manguson or to that reporter you duped into complicity in your schemes.

"Now go back to New York—or, in your case, sir, to London—and recognize that you've no chance against the MMHCC, or for that matter, against any large-scale effort our side may ever choose to make. We'll get what we want, and we'll get it quite legally."

Here he laughed. "And, should there be occasions on which we choose not to remain completely within the law, you'll have no evidence to support a charge to the contrary.

"In short, we shall always win."

Here he laughed again. "And if you should somehow annoy us, we'll simply arrange to have you killed without a trace. You see? Nearly always legal, and where not, never leaving any sort of evidentiary trail.

"You should just all go away now. Who knows? We may even choose to allow you to live. For a while."

Now he turned to face Matt more directly. And he smiled knowingly. "There is something you should know about your deceased fiancée, Matthew. Had she not met her . . . ah . . . demise so unfortunately this afternoon, she would have been . . . ah . . . just as unfortunate, though in a different way, not long after, perhaps as early as tomorrow morning. She had no chance. None whatsoever."

And now he smiled again, the wicked smile of absolute triumph. Of triumph undiluted by compassion for the vanquished. Of triumph that knows only that victory has been achieved, that victory is total, and that those defeated are, in consequence, unworthy of sentiment.

At this, for the first time, Matt saw Luke's muscles begin to tense. The change began in his hands, which became fists, and rippled up through his forearms and biceps. Luke took one step toward Cameron Stafford.

Matt moved and spoke quickly, leaving Ellis Dolby's side and coming to a stop when he reached Luke's shoulder. His voice was strong and clear. "No, Luke," said Matt quietly. "No. Don't do it.

"Rebecca is alive. She is *alive*. If she were not, I would know it. If she had died this afternoon, I would have felt a change somehow. I was praying for her . . . thinking about her . . . continually . . . from the time she rounded the point until we moved this evening to prepare the boat. I was in prayer throughout the time of this accident he claims to know about . . . I would have felt something, Luke . . . I know I would have felt something."

He paused and glanced at Stafford, then back at Luke.

"And this man in front of you isn't worth it. I don't know what has actually happened this afternoon with Rebecca and April, but I know, despite what he claims right now, this man has lost everything: his plans, his organization, his fame, and his respect. I don't know how, but I know that he has."

Here Matt turned his face back to Stafford's. "And as for his soul . . ."

Leaving the sentence unfinished, Matt touched Luke's shoulder, and the two men turned and left the room without looking back, Ellis Dolby following close behind them.

Fifteen minutes after the young men had departed the Robert Morris Inn, Cameron Stafford climbed the stairs to his room in the main building, above the dining room where April Johnstone had toyed with the last meal of her life. He unlocked his door, stepped inside, and found Edward Jamieson sitting on the room's small sofa.

Jamieson did not rise.

Stafford closed the door, signed heavily, and turned to his guest. "What is it?" he said tersely, facing Jamieson from just inside the door. The younger man, in wordless response, rose and, his gaze locked onto Stafford's momentarily confused countenance with a mixture of disgust, contempt, and perhaps—just perhaps—outright hatred, moved slowly and, thought Stafford, menacingly, to a stance so near to Stafford that the older man fell back a half step. Stafford adjusted his glasses in a gesture designed to disguise a sudden nervousness, or, in truth, a rising, almost palpable, fear.

At length, it was Jamieson who spoke.

"Did you personally interview the imbeciles who drove the boat?"

"No."

"Do you have *any* evidence that the women are dead beyond those shreds of clothing you've been waving around?"

"All three men—each one with long experience in my service—said that there were pieces of a body . . . of a corpse . . . in the water . . . floating just below the surface."

"Pieces of *a* body? A corpse? *One* dead woman?"

"They assumed the other was chewed into such small pieces . . . or that it was so deeply slashed and sliced . . . that it sank to the bottom."

"And you believed that story?"

"They said there was no other possibility. They had watched the water's surface continuously from the time of impact until they departed the scene a quarter hour, or more, after. It's not an unreasonable explanation."

Jamieson wheeled and strode back to the small sofa. He turned and sat down immediately, leaving Stafford with his back to the door.

Jamieson stared long and hard at the older man and then asked evenly. "And the document carrier?"

"That was not recovered, nor did I expect it to be. I looked in it before the reporter left the inn. It may have had some sort of secret compartment—perhaps a false bottom—but it certainly was not waterproof. There is no possibility of its floating to the surface. It will simply disintegrate. The documents themselves would by now already have become little more than unreadable pulp. It's only ordinary paper, you know. I don't know why you place so much emphasis on . . ."

"Fool!" shouted Jamieson, leaping to his feet and advancing in swift strides to a position so near Stafford that their chests nearly touched. Stafford, the door at his back, could retreat no further. He pulled his head back as far as he could, but Jamieson simply leaned forward until the men's faces were but inches apart.

"Your blunders are not only monumental, they are too numerous even to count!" he hissed, spittle exploding into Stafford's face with each hard consonant. "And now we have arrived at the very *denouement* without the slightest assurance that the stolen documents—stolen from *you*—are not in enemy hands . . . without the slightest certainty that Miss Manguson— the *only* really worthwhile target—is dead . . . and with the three young men—including the pathetic espionage agent—free to create whatever mischief they like."

Stafford tried to pivot away from the onslaught, but Jamieson, younger and quicker, pressed his chest into Stafford's and forced him back into the door itself. Jamieson then reached around Stafford and slammed his hands against the door on each side of the older man, his forearms enclosing Stafford like pincers and preventing any further attempt at escape.

Jamieson's peculiar and devastatingly malodorous breath, coming now from his open mouth, poured into Stafford's nostrils and sickened him. He felt his knees weakening.

But that was not all . . . and Stafford knew what was coming. He closed his eyes behind his glasses, trying to shut out the spectre, but elimination of the monster's visual image did nothing to help him.

And gradually, as Jamieson, panting in fury, continued to cover Stafford's face with his breath and with hot, moist expectoration, Stafford began to lose consciousness. Or, perhaps more accurately, he began to *change* consciousness. He began to feel the physical weight of Jamieson's Masters' driving downward physically, invisible, irresistible . . . driving downward upon his head and shoulders . . . supernatural forces descending unopposed upon him.

And Stafford began slowly to fall, and to fall in an exaggerated parody of collapse, his arms and hands extended outward to catch himself long before he neared the floor. As this movement began, one which Jamieson recognized instantly, he had, quickly and athletically, turned his body sideways to allow the forced descent. And then he had knelt quickly over the now prostrate form of Cameron Stafford, still exhaling toxins onto the back of the straining man's neck.

Stafford pressed his hands against the floor, trying to fight the inexorable pressure, but he succeeded only in inviting still greater compression onto his back, shoulders, and cranium. His forehead ground itself into the edge of the synthetic rug near which he had collapsed, and he groaned against the effort and the incomprehensible and supernatural weight of the Master's contempt.

And then, suddenly, blessedly, he lost consciousness.

When, minutes or hours later, he awoke, he looked up from the floor where he had fallen to find Edward Jamieson, an odd-shaped briefcase in one hand, preparing to depart. Jamieson seemed to look down upon him from a great height. He spoke to the still-prone Stafford, his voice now calm, unemotional.

"Get out of the way, if you please," he said pleasantly enough. "I must get on the road for Annapolis."

Stafford half-rolled, half-crawled to the side, his muscles responding vaguely to his brain's commands.

Jamieson stepped past him, then looked down at him again. "What do you expect from your portion of this morning's agenda?"

"What do you mean?" he responded heavily. He shook his head to clear it of the fog into which he had awakened. "Yes . . . of course . . . I expect it to go forward like clockwork. All is in readiness, just as it has been from the first.

"There is no need for the slightest concern. . . ."

He stopped. Edward Jamieson had not waited for his reply.

The *River Runner* made the eastern shore of Tilghman Island just after one o'clock on a warm Saturday morning, following a dispirited retreat in moonless blackness from Oxford and the Robert Morris Inn. After Cameron Stafford's brazen monologue, there was little for the three men to say or do. It seemed obvious that Stafford saw no reason to pursue them, or to interfere with their retreat in any way. He considered his triumph complete, and with Rebecca dead, had attained one of his leading perennial objectives, while at the same time his MMHCC conference had gone exactly as planned.

Luke had admitted to his partners that he had been fooled completely. As they made preparations to cast off, he had said ruefully, "Never did it occur to me in planning for this night, Matt, that, if Dr. Stafford suspected Ellis of anything at all, he would allow him to leave like this. Never did that cross my mind until we were outside Ellis's room and you saw that he was interrogating him in such an accessible place, and with such minimum levels of security. It begins to look as if we could simply have escorted him out of the inn during broad daylight any time we chose. I am truly embarrassed. I did not see this coming."

Dolby had responded, speaking with difficulty through his swollen and lacerated lips. "No, Luke. No, he saw right away, this afternoon, that I was working with April Johnstone. I had retrieved her purse in the dining room, and he caught me carrying it.

"He made me his prisoner at that point. And as soon as the banquet ended this evening, he began the interrogation. I don't think he would have let me go earlier without a fight. I think he had just that moment decided . . . just as you arrived . . . that I was of no real use to him."

Luke had nodded bleakly at this, still unconvinced, but at that point the business of navigation had begun to absorb both Luke and Matt. The extended silence that ensued provided time for Dolby's mouth to swell still more, and for the caked blood to dry hard on his lips.

Luke and Matt, their rescue of Dolby accomplished, suddenly had no other danger-laden tasks facing them. And so, as the *River Runner* eventually cleared constricted waters, reached the mouth of the river, slowed, and turned west, their minds raced almost in tandem back to Cameron Stafford's assertion that the women had been killed. Neither man wished to take seriously Stafford's allegation, but the image of the bag containing the bloody clothes and running shoes returned relentlessly to each man's mind.

Luke had attempted to keep the story at bay psychologically, tucked into the "secondhand allegations" corner of his mind. But it refused—and refused obstinately—to remain there.

Matt had tried to sustain himself with the memory of the sudden certainty he had experienced as he had moved to stop Luke's threatening motion toward Cameron Stafford: that ringing, clear confidence that, had Rebecca been killed, he, because he had been in prayer for her throughout the afternoon, would have been led to sense her transformation from life to death to eternity. But he knew that that confidence had been borne aloft on fragile wings. And as the freshness of his earlier certainty faded with the diminishing brightness of the lights of the town, certainty transformed itself into doubt. And then doubt into terror. No longer could the unutterable be excised. It lurked there, ruthless.

He found his good hand beginning to tremble. Tears pooled in his eyes, occasionally overflowing. His teeth clenched intermittently. A choking sensation came again . . . and again . . . and again . . . to his throat.

Meanwhile, Ellis Dolby's mindset regarding the women moved in still another direction. He, like Matt, tried not to believe Cameron Stafford's claim. But the rationale for his skepticism about Stafford's story was rooted in the Holy Spirit's obvious, to him, choice of Rebecca Manguson as special agent, operating on the planet in ways simply not possible for other Christians. The idea that God would 'allow' her murder in the midst of her efforts to carry out a divine charge was incomprehensible to him.

Dolby knew that he held the advantage over Rebecca's brother and fiancé in adopting this rationale. His relative absence of emotional involvement with Rebecca Manguson allowed his more complex, more dispassionate approach. And yet, he, too, found the macabre beginning to permeate his mind.

He tried to face the fear; he tried to drive it away. Each time, it crept back stronger than before.

He dared not show this expanding, consuming fear to his companions. He knew that Rebecca was the love of the two men's lives, each loving her in sharply differing ways, yet with equal depth, and almost, with a kind of desperation. And so he kept his face to the wind and his shoulders squared to the bow while the image of the sack filled with blood-stained clothing and blue running shoes passed repeatedly in front of his mind.

Forlorn, grimly fatigued, they soon switched on the *River Runner's* port spotlight as Tilghman Island loomed off the port bow. They played its beam first on one small pier and then another, as they motored slowly, south-to-north, along the length of the island's eastern shoreline. At pier after desolate pier, nothing met the probe's silent inquiry except an occasional bright-colored but empty boat. They completed the run, then reversed course and traversed the island again, northern tip to southern extremity, now using the starboard spotlight, seeing the same nothingness.

At some point, as the quarter hours crept by one after another, Ellis Dolby muttered clumsily through his swollen and blood-caked lips, "Y'know, there was somethin' about th' plastic bag that Dr. Staff'd showed us that didn't fit exactly. Did eith'r of you have that thought?"

"No," said his companions in sullen unison.

Dolby, seemingly undeterred, continued despite the joint one-syllable rebuff. "There really was somethin' about that bag that didn't ring true. I just can't f'r th' life of me think what it might've been."

Since no question had been asked, not even a one-word response was offered him this time. And so the three men stood doggedly at the starboard rail, Luke's left hand on the wheel, staring into the blackness of Tilghman Island, refusing to yield.

Inside himself, Matt's heart was dissolving. From time to time he felt himself on the verge of physical collapse.

Luke, on the other hand, fought to regain and maintain the distant mental perimeter he had been working to erect. A world without Rebecca would not be possible; he had never known such a world. And he would not let that world approach his rational awareness unless he saw something more compelling than clothing and shoes. His heart was not breaking. His heart was wrapped in a continual prayer for her, a prayer he had begun hours earlier. And nothing else was allowed to approach and to remain. Only his prayer, silent, repeated, desperate: "Father, please . . . keep her whole . . . keep her well . . . keep her here . . . take me first."

At half-past four o'clock, the night's blackness as yet unrelieved, Luke turned to Matt. "We're running low on petrol, Matt. We'll need to tie up at one of these small marinas and refuel as soon as someone opens it for business."

They pulled in and made fast at the next opportunity. Exhausted, they covered themselves with tarps and the little spare clothing they had on board. None slept . . . and one cried.

Not long after seven o'clock, well after sunrise, Luke heard an automobile engine, the squeak of brakes, and doors being opened and closed. The shop owner had arrived.

Luke roused his comrades and they followed the cheerful proprietor into the marina's store. Luke and Matt handled the refueling while Ellis Dolby bought a Saturday morning newspaper and began idly to read. As Matt completed the transaction and Luke prepared to step on board to get underway, Dolby suddenly exclaimed, a chirping, indecipherable noise that led his companions to look sharply in his direction. Frozen, they stared at him.

He wore an unreadable look of emotional distress on his face, and he did not respond to their demands for explanation. Finally, sighing heavily, miserable, irritated, and yet concerned, Luke and Matt strode to their friend's side and looked down at the newspaper's headlines. Dolby indicated a heading that ran across the page, below the fold, on page one. Suddenly, both men snatched the paper closer to their faces, read rapidly, and, grabbing Dr. Ellis Dolby from each side by his upper arms and actually lifting him from the deck, they ran for the *River Runner* as fast as they could go.

Chapter Sixteen

REBECCA, SMASHED IN THE CHEST BY APRIL JOHNSTONE'S forearm and shoulder, instinctively filled her superbly conditioned lungs with air as her friend hurled her violently backwards, over the raft's tiny engine and into the water. Her senses were next assaulted by the unearthly roar of a supercharged Rolls-Royce Merlin engine, designed to power Second World War fighter planes and now, adapted to marine inboards, passing two feet over her head. This eardrum-shattering sound was followed by the scream of a marine propeller, its underwater protective arm removed, as it chewed its way through flesh, bone, metal, and rubber, producing the sickening image of blood pulsing and swirling into the gray water as the reporter was ripped and sliced to pieces within inches of Rebecca's face.

The otherworldly disaster imprinted itself fully in her shocked brain and nervous system during the half second that passed between the propeller's first contact with her friend's skull, the instantaneous death that it brought, and the subsequent shredding of the corpse by the furious, churning screw. And for long seconds thereafter, floating motionless just under the surface, Rebecca stared at the mangled ruin suspended before her.

She could not think.

She could not move.

Then, in a flash, she forced into her mind the only words—the only promise—that would allow her to transcend the paralysis: " . . . *sown a natural body; . . . raised a spiritual body.*"

She quickly reached down, untied and then loosened the laces of her blue Nike running shoes, kicked the Nikes off her feet, spun around in the water, and with sweeping breaststrokes and long, scissoring kicks of her powerful legs, she torpedoed underwater in the direction opposite the racer's course. The seconds flew past as she drove herself relentlessly forward: ten seconds . . . twenty . . . thirty . . . forty . . . Her lungs had long since begun to demand air. She refused their demand and continued. Fifty seconds passed. Sixty seconds.

Suddenly, in the watery distance she saw something solid . . . dark . . . vertical. At the same time, she realized that the water was becoming extremely shallow, perhaps not eight feet in depth. Altering her course slightly, she stroked toward the mysterious shape, lungs rebelling, muscles screaming. She reached the cylindrical, telephone-pole-sized wooden object, circled it quickly, and, her legs delivering one more powerful kick, propelled herself directly upward. She broke the surface, gasped, and, fighting her desperate need for more oxygen, allowed herself to drop straight back down under the surface, the vertical post squarely between her face and the course traveled by the murderous vessel.

Almost as soon as she sank under the surface again, her feet touched the sandy bottom. Now holding the sides of the barnacle-encrusted post loosely, she allowed herself to float slowly to the surface, and her face just clear of the water and almost in contact with the rough wood, began to take in the air in deep, grateful gasps. After several more moments, turning her eyes upward in response to some unidentified impulse, she was startled to see two pairs of eyes staring directly down into her own.

She blinked in momentary disbelief. And then, in defiance of every emotion that had consumed her in the long moments since the disaster, she broke into a wide smile. Her slender, upright wooden refuge from the murderers was, she saw, a support for one of the Chesapeake Bay's ubiquitous platforms constructed explicitly for *pandion haliaetus*—the osprey—the bay's majestic and indomitable raptor.

"Why, hello," she said softly to the two curious adolescents perched ten feet above her, as they peered over the edge of their nest at the intruder. "Thank you, both," she added. "I promise not to be any trouble."

Returning to the horror at hand, she first steeled herself for what she expected to see and then moved her face slowly to the side of the post, peering intently with one eye toward the spot from which she had fled. She saw the racer, perhaps a quarter mile away, idling slowly back toward the carnage, its several occupants obviously looking for signs of life . . . or, preferably, from their viewpoint, for signs of death . . . in the water.

For fifteen minutes, the sleek vessel circled the area, always 50 to 150 yards from Rebecca's position. Periodically, one of the crew would reach into the water with a boat hook to lift flotsam from the surface. Watching this grisly activity, she was suddenly overcome by the full weight of April Johnstone's sacrifice, and she found herself beginning to retch into the water, struggling to remain quiet while the racer circled in lethal proximity to her hiding place.

Finally, the monstrous engine roared to near-instantaneous crescendo, and the racer headed back in the direction of Oxford at stunning speed. Treading water easily, Rebecca adjusted her position in the water to keep the post between her face and the rapidly disappearing menace. And soon a deathly quiet was restored, and she knew she was alone once more.

Still holding fast to the post, she closed her eyes and prayed for the friend with whom she had shared the final moments of life. Her prayer included a brief, but deeply embarrassed, thanksgiving that she had herself been spared through the actions of this woman whom she had known for all of twenty-four hours.

"My life for yours," she said to herself, remembering.

She and Matthew Clark had experienced that very transaction just one year earlier. But for the two of them, it had been a balanced transaction, a mutual exchange. Now, here it was again, but without symmetry. And great tears of regret and gratitude and self-accusation sprung to her eyes and flowed down her cheeks, mingling on her face with the bay's wetness, merging then with the living waters that had become a liquid shroud for the torn corpse of April Johnstone.

"You were mine to protect," she murmured. "My job was to save you, April, not the other way round. You were mine . . ." And she sobbed, disconsolate, the only other sounds those of the gentle splash of moving water against the post to which she clung and the occasional flapping of the young ospreys' mighty wings as they jousted playfully in the nest above her.

Gradually, she pulled her mind back to the present. She shook her head to help push her grief to the edges of consciousness and brought her breathing under control. Treading water slowly, holding onto the life-saving support, she looked up from time to time to smile at the bustling osprey youngsters. Then it occurred to her that the raptor parents, perhaps not far from the nest, would not take lightly a human presence so near their children.

In any case, she knew it was time to go. The battle was far from over.

Taking one more deep breath, she asked aloud for the Holy Spirit's presence and protection, and pushed away from her thin refuge. Turning in the water, she began to swim strongly toward the promontory that she and her friend had so recently rounded. The bottom came gradually up to meet her, and after no more than fifty overhead strokes, she began to wade. And she knew with bitter certainty that Cameron Stafford would have been dismayed, a half minute later, to see Rebecca Manguson, very much alive, as she stepped from the mingled waters of bay and river and onto the sand.

She had not yet formed a plan. She knew her approximate location with respect to waterways, but she knew almost nothing about the landfall that she had reached. This was the peninsula opposite Oxford's, a peninsula that jutted south toward the promontory near which she stood.

The area seemed from the shore to be as it had appeared from the water: a desolate expanse filled with inhospitable vegetation, insects, and wildlife, few roadways, and fewer homes. She stood in the midafternoon summer sun in her wet shorts and tee shirt, barefoot, thick hair dripping, ponytail still intact. She searched northward along the general line of the irregularly shaped peninsula. She could see nothing but distant stands of trees, marsh grass, and sand.

She turned west to face the open water and considered the predicament. She needed to communicate with Luke and Matt. She needed to tell them that April was dead, and that she herself was unhurt. She needed to alter the rendezvous arrangement for that night. She needed to tell them, above all, about the document pouch and its contents.

She knew that, if there had been roads near the promontory itself, and if she were still in possession of her running shoes, she could easily have run to the nearest substantial town, St. Michael's, in perhaps a little more than an hour. But she had mounting reservations about making any attempt at all by land, given the uncertainties introduced by rugged terrain, bare feet, and absence of information regarding the location of homes, of villages, and of Cameron Stafford's forces. Overland success would depend ultimately upon chance meetings with supportive individuals willing and able to help her.

To the west, Tilghman Island lay seven miles away in the sun-soaked distance. The water was shallow, compared with the bay itself, with insignificant currents and, at the moment, little surface action . . . the very reasons Luke had selected that route for the raft's escape. But she had never attempted a swim of that length and could not even form an estimate of the time such a crossing might take. If she could succeed, the rendezvous arrangement would be intact. She could await the men's midnight arrival on one of the small piers that dotted the eastern side of Tilghman. Any other choice seemed to invite either failure or, in the case of returning to Oxford, almost certain capture. Still facing the water, she clasped her hands in front of her chest, bowed her head, and prayed for guidance, for her brother, for Matt Clark, and for Ellis Dolby. And then she prayed for strength. Without further hesitation, she raised her eyes to the distant strip of land and strode once more into the water.

As soon as the water's depth permitted, she settled into a comfortable sidestroke, generating propulsion mostly with her legs, lying first on one side and then on the other. The nettles were numerous and disconcerting. The small jellyfish-like creatures' sting was more annoying than painful, but she had not expected to encounter so many of them. She steeled herself to ignore them and swam on efficiently, checking her position frequently by aligning herself and her course with the promontory behind her and the apparent midpoint of Tilghman's long, gray shape in the distance.

An hour into the swim, the June sun was past midpoint in its steady descent to the western horizon. Fatigue approached, not so much in her muscles as in her spirit. She began to feel isolated in a way that frightened her. She was more than two miles, perhaps, from the promontory, with nearly five miles still to swim. She was far from any regular water traffic route and could hear nothing except the sound of her own movement through the water.

Suddenly, she stopped, treading water, and said aloud, softly, "The Lord is my shepherd . . . He leadeth me beside the still waters . . . I will fear no evil: for thou art with me . . . ." And, starting again to swim, this time using the breaststroke, she began to play the psalmist's words of comfort over and over in her mind, in rhythm with her steady cycle of stroke and kick.

And thus, imperceptibly, the last traces of debilitating fear and isolation dropped steadily into the background of her awareness. And Rebecca knew—and felt—that she had not been left comfortless.

After two seemingly interminable hours, she was well past the halfway mark in her journey. As the sun began to inch down toward the western shore of the bay, she became aware of a new sensation in her laboring muscles. She recognized the signal, the harbinger of true physiological exhaustion, the implacable fatigue so familiar to the long-distance athlete. She had experienced the phenomenon as a runner during more than one of those twelve- to eighteen-mile runs she had at times undertaken during her tennis off-seasons. Having on those occasions faced the outright muscle failure brought about by endurance efforts that exceed the body's repetitive muscle-contraction capacity, Rebecca had no doubt that it would be possible to drown from this kind of fatigue. And so she first debated, as she swam on, the technical question of stroke selection. In response to her own arguments, she turned onto her back and began a tentative backstroke. She at first found some relief, but the relief was fleeting.

Turning onto her side again, she looked toward the island. It seemed actually further away now than when she had looked a quarter hour before, when she had first turned onto her back. And she was now, regardless of stroke, struggling to swim efficiently, since any kind of arm stroke and every type of leg action deteriorated quickly into a parody of well-coordinated propulsion.

And so, somewhat dispassionately, she began to contemplate the end.

Rebecca Manguson knew death as it can be known, among the living, by those who have come most fully to understand eternity. She did not, therefore, associate her own death with fear or with personal loss, but with deep regret that her parents, her brother, and now, her betrothed, would be stricken by the fact of her transition.

She knew exactly how to proceed. She knew, first, as a Christian. And she knew, as well, as one who had faced ultimate danger repeatedly in her life. She knew precisely how to accept the approach of death not only without complaint, but with more than a little anticipatory joy. And she knew in just the same way how to enact the full paradox: the refusal to give in to any threat as long as the slightest resource remained to be tapped, whether the threat were physical, psychological, emotional, or, as had been the case before in her life, the actual face of the Enemy.

Isolated, an infinitesimal speck in one sense, the center of God's universe in another, she actually smiled. It was all quite simple, in the end. One's responsibility to the Almighty was to live and to serve in obedience. To live and to serve for as long as living and serving were possible, knowing that the outcome ultimately would be consistent with His will. It could be no other way.

Taking up her most reliable stroke again, she turned from one side to the other for perhaps the fiftieth time. And this time, as she did, she looked briefly behind her and fleetingly glimpsed something: a minute interruption in the flatness that had met her gaze for nearly two-and-one-half hours of continuous swimming. After several strokes, puzzled, she glanced back a second time, and saw it yet again, a tiny irregularity on her distant horizon.

She stopped, began to tread water, and focused her eyes on the small fleck of indistinct whiteness. Improbably, it did not move to either side of her line of sight. It simply grew slowly—agonizingly slowly—larger, and yet larger, with each passing minute. She remained in position, treading water slowly, conserving her remaining energy, yet no longer thinking of fatigue. The speck began to take on shape, and within minutes, she knew that a small, white-hulled cabin cruiser was headed straight for her, as though her position constituted some kind of landmark on an established navigational track. Yet she knew that she was far from any boat channel, stranded, in fact, in the center of an immense liquid desert.

Nonetheless, impossibly, the substantial craft continued its course, plowing unwaveringly toward her, holding as steady as if she were its only destination. She found herself consumed with awe.

And she at length saw that, unless she actually swam to one side or the other, she would once more, in the span of just three hours, find the prow of a vessel riding directly over her. Sidestroking painfully, she moved slowly to her left, to a position perhaps fifteen feet off the vessel's starboard bow, and waited. The cabin cruiser's moderate speed of advance did not slacken as it approached, and she realized that, not only had she not yet been seen, but that she was, in fact, below the helmsman's line of vision. As the boat drew abreast her, she filled her lungs to shout, "Help," found the word did not fit her condition as she saw it, and instead called out, "Here! Here in the water! You've come for me!"

Almost immediately the single outboard's powerful drone was cut to a discrete, throbbing rumble, and first one, then two, then five surprised faces quickly appeared in the stern, looking in disbelief at the source of the unexpected declaration. Then one face vanished, apparently returning to the helm, and Rebecca heard the mechanical clicks and notchings of gears being shifted, first, into neutral, and then, after a moment, into reverse.

Gradually, the gracefully delicate, medium-length Chris-Craft halted itself, paused, and began to inch back toward her. Simultaneously, Rebecca began a slow breaststroke toward the square sternplate which announced to her welcoming eyes the name of her rescuer: the *Rectory*, and just below the name, the homeport, *St. Michael's, Maryland*. Then she realized that three of the faces crowding the stern were those of children, each wide-eyed in astonishment and excitement. As the vessel, still growling in reverse, lumbered finally to within a few yards of the swimmer, the helmsman throttled back and then cut the engine entirely. The boat came dead in the water a scant ten feet from her.

Rebecca turned her face to the left, watching while a slight, middle-aged woman extricated a boat hook from the port gunwale. And then she heard a piping voice in the new silence: "Mommy? What's happened to that lady's face?"

The lady in question answered promptly, smiling at the child and glancing reassuringly at the child's mother, whose own face reflected acute embarrassment at her young daughter's question: "I have a cut on my cheek, dear," said Rebecca, "with lots and lots of stitches. The doctor sewed me up like a rag doll!"

She awoke with the sunrise and took several moments to remember where she was and how she got there. "Saturday morning!" she thought to herself. "Is it possible that I left London a week ago?"

Answering herself in the affirmative, she cast her mind swiftly back through the kaleidoscope, pausing at the scenes she cherished: the detective's appearance in St. Luke's churchyard; her brother's emergence from the shadows the following morning just yards from that same spot; she and Matt Clark, together in the Manhattan hotel room, crying and laughing on their knees; the telephone calls to their ecstatic parents on the other side of the Atlantic.

Sitting up in bed, she looked out the second-floor window of the rectory as the morning sun brightened the rooftops around her. She smiled, remembering the most recent of the surprises.

Imagine, she thought to herself, the rector of Christ Church in St. Michael's, on his family's first trip on board the old, but nicely reconditioned, gift from parishioners grateful for his years of service, arrowing straight to her position just as she reached her extreme physical limits. She envisioned once more the enigmatic smile that had played across his face when she had asked what had led him to a spot so far removed from any boat channel, and so far off course from the most direct route he might have followed from Cambridge, on the Choptank, to St. Michael's.

"Yes," he had said simply, "What, indeed?"

As soon as Rebecca had been taken on board the *Rectory*, the rector's wife had quickly taken her below to the tiny sleeping quarters and had left her alone with dry underclothing, a pair of her own cutoff jeans, and a long-sleeved sweatshirt. Then, once Rebecca returned topside, she had been fed the leftover sandwich from the family's noontime picnic and a great deal of bottled water. Only then had the impatient children been given unfettered access to their mysterious visitor.

On arrival in St. Michael's, Rebecca's first disappointment had been her failure to reach Luke and Matt by telephone from the rectory. She had tried to establish contact with them before they had left the tavern and inn in Oxford, but she had been able to speak only with the tavern's proprietor, who explained that he had already taken them in his station wagon to the *River Runner*, after they had insisted on preparing the boat for its sortie while daylight still remained.

Her second disappointment had been the unsuccessful midnight rendezvous with the men. Though she had chosen not to explain her circumstances fully to her rescuers, she had told them enough so that they saw the importance of driving her around the St. Michael's peninsula and thence across the short bridge to Tilghman Island a half hour before midnight. While a parishioner's teenage daughter stayed with the three sleeping children, the rector and his wife had taken their guest to a pier situated near the northern extremity of Tilghman, and there the three of them had waited, searching the dark waters that Rebecca had earlier attempted to cross.

No boat had emerged from the blackness.

After waiting nearly three hours, they had driven back to St. Michael's and the rectory, unaware that the *River Runner* was by then approaching the jetty on which they had waited, its twin Mercuries pushing slowly toward the northern end of the island. Twenty-five minutes after Rebecca and her hosts' departure, the men rode miserably past the then-barren pier.

Now Rebecca rose, washed her sunburned face, rubbed lotion into the countless red and raw marks from the nettles' stings, and knelt at the guest bed for her morning devotions. Her long-treasured Anglican prayer book had been lost in the collision, and she used the Bible that sat on the guestroom nightstand, first, for her readings, and then, in part, for her prayers.

She refused to dwell on the possible fate of Luke, Matt, and Ellis Dolby, and not because she felt any certainty that nothing terrible might have happened to them. She knew they might all be dead, horribly wounded, or captured and undergoing torture at that very moment. But she also knew that a dozen alternative explanations existed for the failure of the midnight rendezvous, many of which had nothing to do with their being incapacitated in any way.

And she knew that her duty included a sustained focus on their charge. Pursuant to that charge, she had telephoned Eleanor Chapel in New York just after seven o'clock in the evening, soon after her failed attempts to reach the men in Oxford. The effort to reach Dr. Chapel had been successful, and to Rebecca's surprise and delight, she had learned that the detective had been released from the clinic, and for several hours had been resting comfortably at the hotel, happily watched over by the professor.

And to Rebecca's immense relief, Sid Belton had insisted, his words relayed via Eleanor Chapel, that he would travel to the Oxford area immediately in order to assist in the murder investigation that Rebecca planned to initiate as soon as the detective thought it feasible. While he doubted that a simple murder charge could be sustained, he saw fine opportunities for charges of conspiracy to murder, manslaughter, and lesser offenses. He wanted FBI involvement from the start, and he wanted to be present at every stage. And he had induced Rebecca to laugh aloud when, in response to Eleanor Chapel's demand that she accompany him every step of the way, he had responded loudly that the only way he would arrive in Maryland without her would be for her to affix a mailing label to his forehead and send him there by truck.

Now, dressed again in her hostess's shorts and sweatshirt, and wearing a pair of the rector's gleaming white, and ill-fitting, running shoes, she walked downstairs and, hearing no one, turned into the small family room. Just as she sat down in a cushioned rocking chair, she heard a soft thump against the front door and, looking out, saw that the Saturday morning newspaper had been tossed onto the front porch by the delivery boy. She quietly pulled open the red paneled front door, pushed open the lightweight screened door that covered it, and retrieved the paper. Struck by the freshness of the morning warmth, the tranquility of the narrow neighborhood street, and the lush beauty of the rectory's trees and grounds, she sat down on the porch swing and, after several moments of gazing gratefully around her, opened the newspaper and scanned the front page, her eyes moving slowly from the top, above the fold.

Turning the paper over, now reading below the fold, her muscles suddenly tensed. She caught her breath as she read—and reread—the headline that stretched across the center of the page: FIRST LADY TO SPEAK AT USNA GRADUATION CEREMONIES TODAY IN ONGOING CONTROVERSY. Heart rising to her throat, Rebecca raced through the article, knowing what it would say before her eyes brought confirmation.

Nearly 1,000 United States Naval Academy first classmen will graduate today in ceremonies to begin at 10:00 A.M. in Navy–Marine Corps Memorial Stadium in Annapolis. The First Lady of the United States, her husband a USNA graduate, will be the commencement speaker.

The First Lady is expected to focus her remarks on her increasingly public opposition to the Matheson Mental Health Curriculum for Children. With the MMHCC poised to unleash a full-scale, nationwide effort to persuade all 50 state legislatures to adopt its elementary reading program, her newly public stance has generated a well-coordinated series of forceful responses from a number of MMHCC leaders.

Columbia University and Union Theological Seminary's Cameron Stafford, among the most prominent spokespersons for the MMHCC, was quoted earlier in the week as having labeled the First Lady's efforts "the worst kind of meddling by non-elected citizens who leverage their spouses' visibility to criticize efforts in the public interest about which they know less than nothing." He went on to characterize her efforts as "beneath contempt," but "consistent with this administration's religiously warped antipathy to anything that offers our citizens—in this case, our children—the chance to develop worldviews most strongly supportive of democracy, equality, decency, and prosperity." Stafford noted yesterday that his remarks had been taken "totally out of context."

Neither the First Lady nor the President has chosen to respond to the MMHCC's criticisms of her earlier statements regarding the project.

Also in attendance at the graduation ceremonies, and participating in the awarding of diplomas, ensign's stripes, and second lieutenant's bars, will be the Chief of Naval Operations and the Commandant of the Marine Corps. The President himself is not expected to appear.

Attendance at the event is limited strictly to the families of the graduates, military personnel, and others by invitation. A reception for the newly commissioned Navy and Marine Corps officers and their families will be held in Bancroft Hall on the Naval Academy campus following the commencement activities.

Twenty minutes from the moment she dropped the newspaper onto the porch at her feet, Rebecca cast off, and the *Rectory*, the minister of Christ Church at the helm, backed from its slip in the town marina. Its aging-but-reliable outboard engine immediately at full throttle, the craft sprang from the marina and headed for the approaches to the Chesapeake Bay. Once clear, the rector set his course for Annapolis and Navy–Marine Corps Memorial Stadium.

Chapter Seventeen

AS SOON AS THE *RECTORY* HAD CLEARED THE WATERS OF the St. Michael's marina, Rebecca went below. In the tiny sleeping quarters, she exchanged the cutoff jeans and sweatshirt for yet another loaned garment from the diminutive wife of the rector. The bright pink, short-sleeved dress, its hem reaching almost to midcalf on its owner, barely covered Rebecca's knees. The dress's shoulders, the seams of which hung nearly two inches off its owner's slight frame, Rebecca found almost impossibly constricting. The frayed white pumps, salvaged from the rectory's secondhand store during the frantic scramble induced by the newspaper's thunderclap, were too tight for walking but would do for sitting.

Since she had no notion of what to expect on her arrival at the stadium, she settled for the idea that she would go barefoot, carrying the pumps, until she arrived at . . . her mind could not finish the thought. She only knew that the divine charge—*Prevent this*—had been associated in each vision with this same arena, that some kind of ceremony had been depicted, that there had been imagery suggesting threats both to dignitaries occupying a dais and, metaphorically, to children who decomposed before her eyes. And she knew that her last vision had added the element of a threat from somewhere behind her, yet also inside the arena, and that this final, physical threat was aimed not at the dignitaries, nor at the children, but specifically at her.

Now, as she tried to stand long enough to adjust the fit of her dress in the jarring, slapping, shuddering cabin, her visions' images floated, vivid and insistent, through her mind. And so she saw again in her mind's eye the thick, choking bank of low cloud blowing in and out among the children. She saw again the same fog bank swirling toward the dais,

seeming to blot out the sunlight and to obliterate the ceremonial procession there. She remembered that the threat to the children had actually
seemed to increase in response to the attack on the adults on the platform.

And now she felt again her sudden consciousness, in the final vision,
of something behind her, something poised and prepared to move lethally
against her, something coming for *her*, and for her alone. And she remembered Matt's reluctant, groaning allusion to someone named Edward
Jamieson, someone who forecast his role as Rebecca's nightmare,
someone who stated authoritatively that she would be executed in front of
tens of thousands.

And then Rebecca, shaking her head in an effort to clear it of these
manifold threats, purposefully brought into her mind once more the
command: *Prevent this . . . Prevent this.* And pushing the avalanche of
impending and predicted catastrophe away, she clung to this single, over-
arching command. *Prevent this . . . Prevent this.*

And now, sighing audibly and shaking her head again, she forced her
attention onto the fact that this was a graduation ceremony. Her appearance, presumably, would matter. She reached down, squeezed the pumps
onto her feet, and stood, swaying expertly against the boat's motion.

The tightly constricted cabin had no mirror, but as she looked down at
herself, dispassionately considering the look of the borrowed pink dress
and white high-heeled shoes, she acknowledged that, from the neck down,
she might well give the impression of a woman on her way to observe and
celebrate a family member's graduation day. She would need to do something about her hair, and she knew, something about her face. She had
seen how quickly the rector's children had been alarmed by the still-raw,
V-shaped cut and the stitches that emphasized its stark, irregular path
across her lower right cheek.

Retrieving a hairbrush and a first-aid kit from the all-purpose bin that
she found bolted against the cabin's forward bulkhead, she set to work.
After fifteen minutes of vigorous brushing of her still-tangled and matted
hair, and after careful, tedious reconfiguring of four different, varying-
sized bandages, she climbed the four-step ladder to the main deck where
the rector held his course for Annapolis. She asked him to pass candid
judgment on the condition of her hair, once again flowing straight down
over her shoulders and back, and on the flesh-colored bandages that now
covered the track of her wound.

"My candid judgment is that, if you'd had an Easter bonnet, you would have been picture perfect at our sunrise service. The bandages do call some attention to themselves, of course, but not in any way that would get more than a perfunctory glance. I should think you'll pass readily for some proud midshipman's sister or girlfriend."

Then he corrected himself. "I should have said you *could* pass for a sister or girlfriend, if you just had some identification that suggested such, and above all, a ticket for admission to the ceremonies.

"There will be military security at the stadium. What are you going to do, Rebecca? And what can I do to help?"

She looked out over the sharply pitching bow of the lightweight cabin cruiser, and beyond, to the Chesapeake Bay Bridge shimmering in the early morning sunlight. "I don't yet know, sir. My brother has always done the planning whenever we have needed to execute any kind of 'tactically problematic mission,' as he might say."

She smiled as she thought of how much Luke relished contingency planning. "Without him," she continued, "I'll just need somehow to place myself in the midst of the ceremonies. I can't imagine how I'll do it, sir. But my charge leaves no doubt about the outcome I am to attempt."

With that, she turned to him and asked, "How much longer, do you think?"

The minister checked his chart briefly, looked up, and replied, "I think we'll reach the mouth of the Severn River in less than half an hour, Rebecca. We'll have to reduce speed at that point, but, even so, we'll pass the Academy on our port side and arrive at Dorsey Creek just a few minutes after that. A little maneuvering under the bridges, and once we've passed under King George Street—the Dorsey Creek Bridge—I expect to be able to put you ashore just over a mile . . . no . . . maybe a mile-and-a-half . . . from the stadium."

He looked at her. "You know that I don't understand much about what you're charged with attempting, Rebecca, but I'd be remiss if I did not say that I'm experiencing great conflict about helping you do something mysterious and, it would appear, dangerous, and without involving our police departments in any way. The only thing that keeps leading me to continue to do your bidding is the plain miracle of our finding you yesterday during your swim. I was led to steer almost two miles off course, into near-shoal waters at some points, with no idea as to why. I've never felt anything exactly like that, and believe me, I'm no stranger to the Holy Spirit's special leading.

"It's so obvious to me that we were sent to pick you out of the water that I'm holding my normal judgments and decisions in abeyance. I can only hope I'm not being an irresponsible, foolish accomplice in something that should be placed in the hands of the authorities right now."

She nodded soberly. "Yes," she replied, "it's not fair to you, is it? I've involved your whole family in something that I understand very little myself, and I've asked you to trust that my experiences of the Supernatural have been authentic. And I can't give a bit of reassurance, sir. Not a bit.

"I can only state again the obvious. Law enforcement authorities would not—could not—take action on the basis of things dreamed by an Englishwoman who arrived in the country a week ago. I *have* alerted the authorities—at least, I've alerted someone who will notify the authorities appropriately—about something terrible that happened yesterday, sir. One of the phone calls I made last night from your home was to that purpose. But I have no way to persuade law enforcement officials to intervene in something that, my visions alone have made clear, is about to happen this morning."

She smiled. "I can't thank you enough, sir, for saving me, and for helping me now. I'm going to go below again, if you don't mind, and begin my prayers. There are others for whom I must pray right now."

She looked back, one foot on the first rung of the ladder. "You'll call me when it's time?"

The *River Runner*'s massive twin outboards screamed through the Saturday morning stillness along the eastern side of Tilghman Island. The three men were grim. Here, in the midst of their increasingly desperate search for Rebecca and the reporter, they had found the newspaper's account of the First Lady's address, and like Rebecca, knew immediately that this was the reality around which Rebecca's final vision had been built. The action required of them was obvious; they must reach the stadium before ten o'clock. That gave them just over two hours. What they would be called upon to do on arrival, none of them could guess. They simply knew that there they must be.

After the scramble to get underway, they had been unable to focus upon the stadium and the violence that might await them there. Each man, each in a different way, was consumed with thoughts of the two women. Where were they? Were they, in fact, dead? Each found it in a certain sense preposterous that they were making flank speed for Annapolis, while Rebecca and April Johnstone were . . . somewhere . . . somewhere *here* . . . in *these* waters . . . or on *these* islands and peninsulas that they were leaving behind in their rush to Annapolis.

Matt felt himself increasingly faint. He moved to the starboard railing, and holding onto it with his good hand, sank to one knee on the vibrating, unpredictably shifting, fiberglass decking. Placing his shoulder against the gunwale, he leaned against it heavily and sighed. He brought his right hand to his temples and began to massage his head. Suddenly he realized that he was screaming. His scream was a mixture of animal rage and inexpressible desolation. Luke and Ellis Dolby spun around and stared at him. Then Dolby crossed from the port side and knelt beside Matt. Leaning close to his ear, Dolby said indistinctly through his blood-caked, swollen lips, his voice just below a shout, yet barely audible above the roar of the outboards: "She *lives*. Y've said so. Y'know it's true. *Believe* it, Matt."

Together, the two men turned their backs against the gunwale and sank to side-by-side sitting positions on the deck, both now holding their heads in their hands. Luke, at the wheel, stolidly kept his eyes forward, steering the closest possible course around the southern tip of Tilghman. Suddenly Luke wheeled around again in response to still another shout from one of his shipmates. This time he saw it was Ellis Dolby. Dolby was on his feet, screaming in much the same fashion that Matt had just done, his eyes wide, his face contorted in an expression that Luke could not recognize.

Literally jumping up and down, Dolby began shouting to his comrades. His unrestrained excitement, his continuous leapings into the air and crashings back to the deck, the wild flailings of his arms, his efforts to shout at the very top of his voice, and the painful stiffness in his now thoroughly misshapen, blood-encrusted lips, all combined to lead him to slur his words in helpless frustration. "Th' bg! Th' bg! Dt'r Stf'd's bg! H'r sh's w'r *unt'd*! Th' w'r *unt'd*!"

Luke and Matt stared at him, uncomprehending.

He stared back at them. Gyrating in frustration, he shouted, "N'tw'ts! Dbl' n'tw'ts! Wh't y' th'nk? Y' th'nk sh' w's *wearing* h'r sh's like th't? Y' th'nk h'r mrdr'rs fish'd h'r sh's out 'f th' bay, an' th'n *untied* 'em b'fore th' threw 'em in th't bg?"

Seeing no light bulbs, Dolby shouted for a final time, now standing relatively still and slowing his words, trying laboriously to enunciate with as much care as he could muster. "Ahhhggg! Triple . . . nitwits! *Rebecca . . . untied . . . her . . . shoes . . . after . . . the . . . crash!* She . . . took . . . 'em . . . off . . . so . . . she . . . could . . . swim . . . better! She . . . wasn't . . . *wearing* . . . 'em . . . untied, and th' murderers . . . didn't go . . . to th' trouble . . . of *untying* 'em . . . before tossing 'em . . . into that bag! Rebecca needed . . . to swim away . . . from the crash . . . Rebecca untied . . . her own shoes! I *knew* somethin' . . . was funny . . ."

He was unable to finish the sentence. Suddenly, first Matt, and then Luke, leaving the wheel momentarily unattended, swarmed over Ellis Dolby, laughing, shouting, pounding him on his back, on his shoulders, on his head, forcing him down to the deck, pummeling him happily until, laughing uncontrollably, he shouted again, "Okay! Okay! I surrend'r! Don't beat me . . . any more! Somebody . . . needs . . . to drive th' thing!"

Matt and Luke stood. Luke stepped back to the wheel, and then he turned and looked back at his mates. The ecstasy from Dolby's insight remained on all three faces, but only for seconds. Then the smiles gradually faded, and each pair of eyes turned away from the others' and looked out somberly across the water.

Each was remembering, now . . . remembering April Johnstone.

The *Rectory*, its throttle back at one-third, grumbled slowly past Santee Basin and Dewey Field, then turned left into the restricted waters of Dorsey Creek, passing Rickover Hall and Nimitz Library on its port beam. At 9:30 on the Saturday morning of graduation, no activity was visible on the campus of the Naval Academy from the waters that framed its grounds. The young woman in the pink dress and white high-heeled shoes and the middle-aged cleric at her side stood erect behind the small cabin cruiser's windscreen giving thanks: she, for the visions that had led her to understand that she was required to be here, now, at this place; he, for the inexplicable promptings that had led him to chart such a strange course toward Tilghman Island the previous afternoon.

In the minister's mind, the Holy Spirit's action had been apparent through more than the spectacular navigational phenomenon. He had felt led to do—and not to do—other things in the past few hours for which he had no ordinary explanation. He had, for one thing, refueled the *Rectory* immediately upon arrival in St. Michael's, something he had never done before with any craft. Then he had set the vessel in a slip that would allow immediate release from the pier itself and from the marina's constrained waters. And, that morning, he had *not* left home early, as was his long-standing habit, to make his Saturday hospital rounds.

None of this could he have explained while it was occurring. All of it had been, he saw, orchestrated with the greatest care.

Now, barely maintaining steerageway, he eased the vessel under the footbridge connecting the main campus with Hospital Point, then, two hundred yards further, under Hill Bridge, a sleek concrete structure that the *Rectory*'s windscreen cleared by less than two feet. Another two hundred yards further, he took the vessel carefully under the narrow center span of Dorsey Creek Bridge, with King George Street's automobile traffic rumbling steadily above them.

Between the two vehicle bridges, the *Rectory* passed Hubbard Hall on the right, with its three jutting piers designed to accommodate the Academy's racing crews and their shells. The minister knew Annapolis and the campus well enough to know that, should he put his charge ashore there, she would find herself in restricted areas, almost certainly to be detained by military police for some time. And she had neither passport nor any other identification.

Once under the third bridge, the rector spun the wheel to the left.

Making a quick 180-degree power turn, he brought the *Rectory* starboard side-to against the pier that serviced the boathouse for St. John's College, whose campus skirted the creek. "Rebecca," he said quickly, "it's twenty-five minutes 'til the hour. I had hoped we could make it sooner."

He took her right hand in both his own and squeezed it. "Godspeed, my daughter," he said, clearly making the phrase a prayer and not merely a sentiment. "I trust the Holy Spirit will guide your every step. Go!"

She stepped to him, hugged him for a brief moment, then, gripping her white pumps in her right hand, moved behind him to the stern. She placed one bare foot on the gunwale and, without hesitation, jumped to the pier. She walked three steps toward the college's boathouse and then, without consciously deciding to, broke into a run. She wheeled left at the boathouse, climbed to the sidewalk bordering King George Street in five running, climbing strides, and turned left again to cross the bridge. Looking over the bridge's rock-and-cement railing as she ran, she waved to the rector.

And then she was gone from his sight.

Suddenly she found herself running hard, and she slowed slightly, knowing that the minister's estimate of the distance was only that. She decided to pace herself for a fast two-mile run. If it turned out shorter, all the better.

She tried to look carefully at the roadway in front of her feet, aware that any sharp object or sufficiently irregularly shaped rock could disable her in her barefoot flight. Her long strides worked the hem of the pink dress up high, so that it rode well above her knees. She forced her mind away from the embarrassment that she would normally feel under such circumstances and focused only on the roadway, on her stride, on her breathing. Clear of the bridge, she angled across the street to find a continuous sidewalk, then ran up the long hill to the end of King George Street. Following the minister's instructions, she swung left and followed the roadway's right-bending curve through a residential neighborhood and finally to an intersection that brought her to a halt. She recognized neither the locale nor the street names from the rector's description.

There, at the corner of Annapolis Street and Melvin Avenue, she stood, confused. Had she run too far in this direction? Should she have turned earlier? Should she retrace her steps? Would that simply take her further from the stadium? If she were near it now, why were there no signs?

She drew a deep breath and prayed: "Father, I cannot help if I cannot reach the field. I need You now, too. Please. I haven't time for a mistake."

On the verge of deciding that, with time running out, she must select a direction and begin running again, she heard a man's voice from across the street. "Ma'am," he said gruffly, "are you lost? Can I help you?"

Rebecca saw that the man had stepped to the front door of a small delicatessen or grocery store. She also saw other men crowding to the door behind him. The thought occurred to her that she might look like good sport to them, standing there in her too-short pink dress, holding her white pumps, breathing hard, clearly alone.

She was not in the least afraid. But she had no time for sport.

"Please," she called to the man. "I must get to the stadium *now*! Will you help me?"

He smiled casually. "There's no football game this mornin', honey. Why don't you join me an' the boys right here for a little breakfast?"

She knew he bore her no ill. But she fixed him with a long stare, unsmiling, waiting, demanding an answer with her whole being.

Suddenly, he dropped his gaze and, glancing back once at his friends, scurried across the street toward her. As he neared her, he pointed to her left. "Down there, ma'am," he said. "Can you see the second traffic signal down there? That's Highway 70. You gotta get across that highway. Then you'll see the stadium on your left. You can't miss it, once you're at the highway."

She murmured her thanks and in two seconds was in full stride. She flew past one intersection without slowing and, in another half minute, arrived at the multilane highway that connected Annapolis with the main east-west thoroughfare leading, in one direction, across the Bay Bridge. Impatiently, she waited two full minutes—an eternity with the hidden blessing of allowing her muscles and lungs a full recovery for the desperate running that remained—before she had clearance through the high-speed traffic. Then, in a flash, she was across the highway and making straight for the stadium.

Seeing that the parking areas on the near side of the complex were not fenced, she sprinted directly for the looming structure, now flying between row upon row of parked vehicles as she neared the high chain-link fence that surrounded the stadium proper. As she closed on this perimeter, she heard the midshipman marching band in full force and sensed the festive mood that emanated from the crowd on this brilliant June morning. She also glimpsed clusters of Marine and Navy military police, their armbands reading MP, dotting the parking lot, and especially, the open gates to the east-side stands.

Slowing so as to ascertain her position while running, and so as to reconnoiter more effectively, now breathing very heavily, she saw as she turned to follow the fence what appeared to be a single strand of electrified wire running across the top of the ten-foot-high chain link. She followed the strand with her eyes as far into the fence's curving distance as possible. She saw no interruption in its flow around the stadium.

Latecomers to the ceremonies, hurrying through the parking lots, stared at her as she flew by them in the pink dress, black tresses flowing behind her, white pumps in her hand. Three teenage girls in one group broke into spontaneous applause at the astonishing speed, elegance, and power they saw before them.

Circling the stadium counterclockwise, she quickly arrived at the west-side stands and saw that the unclimbable, electrified fence was, along its 140-yard straight-line length, interrupted at intervals by combination vehicle and pedestrian gates, all but two of which appeared to be closed. She verified at a second glance that the electrified wire did not run across any of these gates, all of which seemed to have an identical design. Each gate was perhaps nine feet high and comprised a series of vertical steel rods. The individual rods collectively made up a pattern tracing a shallow, symmetrical U-shape across the top. In a flash, she guessed that, at the center point of each gate, the rods were closer to eight than to nine feet high.

The entirety of this recognition took but an instant. So, however, did the realization that, though eight-foot gates of this type were readily scalable for Rebecca Manguson, military police in impressive numbers waited on the other side as far as she could see. And surely Secret Service agents were there, too. She would be taken into custody the instant her bare feet touched the concrete within the perimeter. And so she flew on, past the two open gates and beyond.

Desperate now, nearing the extreme end of the west-side perimeter, she heard the band music stop. She had attended a sufficient number of her brother's Royal Navy ceremonies to know what that meant. The color guard would be moving onto the field. This small unit of ensign-bearers would march to the center-front of the field, present arms, and, at that point, the national anthem would be rendered by the midshipman band. She could wait no longer.

Halting at the southwest corner of the fencing, her chest heaving, the bodice of the pink dress now soaked completely through with perspiration, she saw that the ground outside the stadium sloped down to the right from where she stood, to the vehicle entrances at field level, well south of the perimeter. The right-angle corner formed by the perimeter just before it started to follow the downhill grade was, she saw, the site of a final set of pedestrian-vehicle gates, this set locked and secured just as tightly as were all but two along the entire west side of the stadium. Looking through the vertical bars and past the handsomely lettered signs on each—"Class of 1927" on one, "Class of 1925" on the other—she could see in the distance that no one, military police or other, on the interior of the fence seemed to be looking in her direction. She had reached perhaps the most obscure, least observed spot in the entire complex.

Rebecca tossed the white pumps to the pavement and attacked the gate just as she had a similar barrier at St. Luke's churchyard in Greenwich Village just a week earlier. Then, she was dressed for running; now, she was climbing barefoot and wearing a dress. Had she been asked, she could have described something of the damage the metal bars were doing to her hands, knees, shins, and feet, to say nothing of the fabric of her borrowed dress.

But her mind was elsewhere.

She dropped to the gravelly surface, moaning softly as the pebbles punched into her feet. Momentarily on all fours, she sprang up and, after six running strides, she stopped in a small archway and looked far down onto the bright emerald field of her visions. She gazed from the top of an impossibly steep cement stairway that ran, not through the stadium seats themselves, but *beside* the lower deck of the west stands and directly onto the playing surface. The wall framing the southern edge of the stands, now just to her left, blocked her view of the field as a whole, and more important by far, blocked the spectators' view of Rebecca.

The stadium was silent as a church. She breathed a prayer, eyes closed, and then sprang forward. Twisting her hips and shoulders to the left to increase the lateral surface available for her flying feet, she descended at a run, observed only by a scattered handful of people, most in the crowd having been seated at the north end of the field, near the dais. Thus, the spectators, far away from Rebecca's end of the field, screened from her by the south wall of the arena, and riveted by the precision of the color guard as it neared the First Lady and the other dignitaries, did not turn their heads to the south end of the stadium to see the slight figure as it approached the grassy field.

Her torn dress now flapped loosely around her thighs. Small streams of blood flowed down her lower legs from the cuts and abrasions on her knees and shins, while the soles of her feet bled in a dozen places.

After a descent that seemed to her interminable, she reached the soft grass and floated, silent and unseen, behind two MPs stationed facing the dais, their backs to the woman in pink. Now, once more accelerating, she sprinted easily and gracefully to the exact center of the south end of the field, stopping just behind the football goal posts. There she stood and faced the length of the stadium.

A tiny pink figure in a vast arena, Rebecca Manguson searched the field. And in the precious seconds before the onset of the violence that she considered inevitable, she found the memory of her visions bleeding into the reality of what lay before her. There was the same grassy surface on which the envisioned children had sat in compelling metaphor, reading silently to themselves. There was the same envisioned periphery, high above the children, the concrete façade on which dark blue block lettering had recorded the names of thirty-one Navy and Marine Corps battles. There was the same envisioned dais at the far end of the field, now a hundred yards from her, on which the dignitaries had stood, waiting.

But here, now, no longer seeing through a vision, she stood watching the graduating class of midshipmen, splendid in white uniforms, standing at attention, their backs to her, on each side of a broad corridor in the bright distance. And striding steadily away from her, passing rapidly through that corridor in the stark silence of the hushed stadium and stilled marching band, the six-man color guard of midshipmen approached the dais.

And suddenly there was no periphery. She saw through a kind of illuminated tunnel. She could see nothing at all except the color guard, and she felt herself now observing the backs of those six marching midshipmen in a kind of bold, almost telescopic relief. The color guardsmen wore white, black-billed officers' caps, navy blue jackets, white trousers, white gloves, and black shoes. Each of the four interior color bearers carried an ensign, with the United States flag on the right. The two outside members of the unit carried military rifles, the right outside midshipman with his weapon at right shoulder arms, the left outside midshipman with his weapon at left shoulder arms. All eyes in the stadium were focused on the six underclassmen as, in perfect formation, they silently approached the First Lady of the United States.

And now Rebecca knew. These men were not midshipmen. These men were assassins.

In a lifting, soaring run, the woman in pink started forward.

And as she did, she felt a prickling sensation at the back of her neck. And she knew in her soul that, while death for the First Lady of the United States lay in Rebecca's path, eighty yards directly in front of her, death for Rebecca Manguson approached just as quickly and just as surely . . . but from behind.

Luke Manguson's watch read 9:39 when he threw the *River Runner's* shift lever into neutral, then, seconds later, into reverse, and began to nestle the sleek boat against the weathered wood and rubber surfaces of the Annapolis city dock. As soon as Matt had secured the lines fore and aft, Luke cut the engines and leaped onto the dock, running hard and looking for a taxi. Within three minutes, he had brought a cab around to the dock, and Ellis Dolby, earlier given all the cash the men had on hand and ceremoniously appointed Chief Financial Officer of the group, had negotiated the docking fee with the harbormaster.

Now the three men, squeezed into the taxi's back seat with Dolby crushed between the broad shoulders on each side of him, tried to calm themselves while the driver struggled to free the cab from an unexpected maze of Saturday morning traffic. Finally Luke and Matt could stand it no longer. At almost the same moment, waiting at the third traffic signal they had encountered in three minutes, their hands went to the door handles.

"Listen, mate," said Luke to the driver, "we've got to run for it. Bring our partner here to the stadium as quick as you can. It's straight ahead, right?"

The driver turned his head and looked back at Luke. "You're *really* in a hurry, huh? Don't get out. Double the tip, and I'll get you there faster than you can run. But you gotta pay for the speeding ticket if I get caught, okay?"

With that, the driver began to roar past the motionless traffic, first on the right, occasionally with his right wheels on the sidewalk, then on the left, actually forcing some oncoming vehicles to the side of the road. Ellis Dolby, his head down, closed his eyes and muttered maledictions at the driver, at his two friends, at the whole idea of risking their lives now in order to risk their lives again in just moments, in order to . . . what? He knew that one of his many weaknesses was an inability to remain focused, whenever conflict approached, on goals that had seemed perfectly rational when put forth in the safety of a planning session.

And then he thought of the Brooklyn warehouse and his baseball bat, and of Rebecca's counsel to him on the drive back to Manhattan that night.

He chuckled to himself and looked up. The taxi was careening through a ninety-degree turn to the left, attracting enthusiastic protests from the horns of the drivers across whose paths the cabbie was taking them. When the vehicle righted itself, and Dolby, straightening his glasses, was able to see out its windows, there, to his astonishment, on the immediate right, was a stadium.

The car came to a halt in a squeal of rubber. Luke looked at his watch. It read precisely ten o'clock.

While Dolby paid the driver, Luke and Matt bolted from each side of the car and sprinted up the driveway toward the south end of the stadium. The vehicle gates were closed and guarded, but they saw that two broad, sweeping pedestrian walkways rose from the field-level vehicle entry gates toward the entrance levels for the west and east stands, high above field level. Luke gestured to the right, and Matt lowered his head and drove up the hill toward the east stands. Luke wheeled left and, his powerful legs churning like small pistons, sprinted upward toward the west stands. As the two men separated, they heard the midshipman band strike the final notes of its pregraduation medley, and they knew that the color guard would now be advancing onto the field. And so they knew that they were almost certainly too late.

Luke reached the top of the long grade and came to an abrupt stop. Not twenty-five yards from where he stood, two pedestrian-vehicle gates faced him. On one gate were the words, "Class of 1927," on the other, "Class of 1925." At the base of the gates, lying haphazardly on the pavement, was a pair of white high-heeled shoes. He was instantly certain that he knew why they were there.

Had anyone observed Luke Manguson's attack on the gate, the overriding impression might have been that an extremely determined man was attempting to force his way directly through the vertical iron bars, rather than to climb over them, so violently did he drive himself into them. But in a phenomenal display of strength and agility, he converted horizontal force to vertical force in a lightning series of moves and, more quickly than one could possibly see how it had been done, he was dropping to the other side. Without the need to gather himself, he landed on both feet, wheeled, and sprinted to a small archway that, he realized quickly, overlooked the playing surface itself, far below him.

He saw that the long, cement stairway falling away from his feet led directly onto the field, descending alongside a wall that marked the south end of the west stands. He raised his eyes to the field itself and caught his breath. There, standing just behind the football goal posts at the extreme south end of the playing surface, was a tall, slender, barefoot woman in a bright pink dress. Even from this distance, he knew the woman at a glance.

Luke closed his eyes. "Thank you," he prayed. "Thank you, Father."

And then he opened his eyes and flung himself at the precipitous flight of steps, taking them in fours and fives all the way to the bottom. As he leaped down the final half dozen steps to the grass, he stumbled briefly, righted himself, and sprinted forward. But at that precise moment, so did his sister.

Seeing Luke's gesture, Matt wheeled right to begin the long sprint upward toward the east stands. But after a half dozen running strides he suddenly brought himself to a halt. What had he glimpsed as he read Luke's hand signal? What had registered in his brain in the split second that he focused on Luke's right hand, just before he pivoted, put his head down and raced to his right? What could possibly have flitted, against every conceivable possibility, across the extreme periphery of his line of sight?

And he knew.

The athletic, pink-clad form had disappeared from view almost before he had had the chance to sense its presence. The lightly running figure, apparently barefoot, had vanished from sight in front of the athletics dressing room facility that lay midway between the vehicle gates, near where he stood, and the athletic field's south goal posts. The goal's two uprights, the tops of which he could see over the low roof of the building, soared toward the sky perhaps twenty yards from the front of the dressing facility.

And so he stood frozen, his mind racing.

That had been Rebecca, of that he was certain. And what had she said in her last vision? That a threat materialized from *behind* her, from *inside* the arena.

And what had Edward Jamieson said to him in the Brooklyn warehouse? That he—Edward Jamieson—would become Rebecca's nightmare. And that she would be executed in front of tens of thousands of people.

The deadly pieces were in place.

Matt shifted into action. He spun around and headed back toward the south vehicle gates, reaching as he did for his wallet. Sprinting toward the gate, he attracted the immediate and unfavorable attention of both the military policemen who stood guard there. The senior of the two, a marine gunnery sergeant, unsnapped the flap of his holster and placed his hand on his sidearm.

Holding his U.S. Navy Reserve officer identification card far forward and in front of his chest, Matt spoke quickly, addressing the stern-faced, broad-chested sergeant. "Please allow me to pass, sergeant," he said urgently. "There is some kind of threat . . . a threat to the people on the field . . . from inside the teams' dressing facility." And he gestured desperately toward the unimposing brick building just inside the vehicle gates.

The sergeant stared at him, utterly unmoved. One hand remained resting on the still-holstered pistol.

"I've got to get in, sergeant," Matt pleaded, still holding his identification card in front of himself. "I'm unarmed. You can see I'm unarmed. Let me through, and come with me. Please, sergeant. Draw that weapon and come with me. We've got to get in there *now!*"

Matt's officer rank impressed the sergeant not at all. Where security was at issue, especially with the First Lady of the United States present, something far beyond a reserve officer's identification card would be necessary to lead him to step aside. The sergeant looked Matt evenly in the eye, placed both hands behind his back in informal parade rest position, and said simply, "No, sir, lieutenant. Sorry."

At that moment, Matt saw both military policemen look sharply at something behind him and turned to see Ellis Dolby rolling, convulsed, across the grass beside the vehicle driveway, making strange gurgling, choking sounds and thrashing wildly with legs and arms as he spun in incoherent agony along the grass. The two marines, unhesitating, moved as one to assist the stricken man, while Matt, having taken three steps to follow them to the aid of his friend, suddenly realized what he was seeing and stopped, turned, and raced through the vehicle gate and into the arena.

To himself he thought as he ran, "How on earth does Ellis *think* of these things?"

Matt ran straight for the near door of the team dressing rooms. The building was utilitarian, a low, dull brick structure that provided home and visiting teams easy access to the playing field. For a graduation ceremony, Matt assumed, it would be empty and unused . . . perhaps locked, as well.

But he also knew that just on the other side of this building stood Rebecca Manguson. And he knew that this structure, and this structure alone, was situated both behind her and yet inside the arena.

Matt hit the door at a run and felt it yield immediately, but only for a few inches, brought to a halt by a small chain-and-lock device. He stepped back, lowered his right shoulder, and drove into the door a second time. His thrust tore the chain from its four-screw anchor in the doorframe, and he fell forward, staggering into a darkened corridor. As he did, he heard a voice shouting from close behind him, and he knew that the burly marine sergeant was coming for him, and coming in a state of extreme ill humor.

Matt's entrance into the building had been noisy. He had slammed into the door twice, the second time with enough force to rip a metal anchor plate, rattling and clattering, from its wooden frame. And now the sergeant's booming shouts echoed down the bare concrete corridor into which Matt had burst.

He knew that his arrival had been thus broadcast to anyone and everyone inside the building, and so was not surprised at the sound that came suddenly to his ears: the sound of heavy, metallic hardware— weaponry, he had no doubt—as it dropped hastily onto hard cement flooring. In response, he turned to his right and ran toward the sound, flying through two empty dressing rooms with the marine at his heels. He stopped abruptly at the communal showering room that occupied the extreme northeast corner of the building. As he did, the sergeant laid rough hands on Matt's right arm, prepared to bring him roughly to the floor if necessary, but, his gaze following Matt's, the marine stopped and stared.

On the bare floor of the shower room lay a high-powered, large-calibre rifle, fitted with silencer and professional-quality telescopic sight. Beside the rifle lay its compact carrying case, revealing such a firearm's only purpose: an assassin's weapon, readily disassembled to travel in a leather-covered, innocuous-appearing, though oddly shaped, container the size of a briefcase.

Just above the weapon and its case was a frosted, opaque window, raised perhaps five inches from the sill. Both men saw at a glance that a gunman on one knee would have had a clear field of fire at anything or anyone on the entire length and width of the playing surface. Such a gunman would have been able to fire unobstructed at someone standing a mere twenty yards away, under the south goal posts. And he would have been able to fire, equally unobstructed, at someone a hundred yards away, standing on the dais.

And if the gunman considered his to be a suicide mission, he could have shot once—perhaps twice—and then, since escape would be impossible, could have taken his own life. Once he had reached his firing position at this window, he would have been supremely confident that he could not be stopped. And yet he had been stopped.

Suddenly the two men heard, in close sequence, two new sounds. The first was the sound of a door slamming hastily shut on the other side of the building. But in the millisecond that passed before they would both have begun to run toward that unmistakable sound in pursuit of the would-be gunman, they heard a second.

It could only be described as the sound of a collective gasp, of thousands of people pulling in their breath sharply, as one, in horror at what they were seeing. And both men, forgetting the would-be assailant in their instantaneous and overwhelming concern—in Matt's case, for the woman who had been the nearer of the gunman's targets, and in the sergeant's case, for the woman who had been the farther—ran across the small room and crouched, peering down the length of the football field, stricken equally by what they saw developing and by the impossibility of their being able to intervene.

The Secret Service agent in charge of the First Lady's four-man security detail furrowed his brow and took a step nearer the President's wife, whom he never allowed more than a few paces from him in public settings.

The young woman in the pink dress, racing toward the north end of the field, was obviously no threat to his charge. He took three seconds to look each member of his security detail in the eye, shaking his head quickly at each. He did not want them to make the slightest movement toward their weapons. The last thing he wanted in a situation like this was for one of his agents to put a bullet in the chest of some midshipman's headline-seeking girlfriend.

Then he noticed that, angling in from the side, a young man appeared to be pursuing the woman. "Oh boy," he thought to himself. "She wants to get on television and this guy—maybe her brother—wants to keep the family from being humiliated by exactly that. Should be interesting."

But he took a second step nearer the First Lady and squinted closely at the muscular young man as he closed on the dais from, now, roughly sixty yards. The agent concentrated on the man's hands. They were empty. So were the woman's. As long as they stayed that way, he thought to himself, this was likely to remain pure comedy.

In the foreground of the agent's vision, he noticed the color guard coming to a halt thirty yards in front of the dais and saw the two midshipmen on the outside begin to bring their rifles from shoulder-arm position to port-arm position. At the same moment, he saw, behind them, the woman in pink slowing and appearing to hesitate, now just ten yards from the color guard.

As Rebecca started forward, she knew only that her eyes had lost all peripheral vision, and that only the counterfeit color guard unit was now visible to her. But she was also aware, as she lifted into full sprint, that in her mind's eye she was racing between row upon row of children. And as she flew past them, she saw in her mind that each child, first by the hundreds, then by the thousands, and finally by the tens and hundreds of thousands, looked up at her, attentive, surprised. Their troubled, fragile faces seemed to be brightened, strengthened by the sight of her. Some of the children began actually to rise from the grass, to raise their small hands in salute, to wave at her in unspoken gratitude. And soon they all stood. They stood by the thousands and tens of thousands and hundreds of thousands. They stood, hopeful. Quiet. Expectant.

And so she ran, the dress in tatters and soaked all through with perspiration, her dark hair flying straight out behind her, her lower legs and feet bloody. And suddenly every eye in the stadium, starting at the south end and rippling toward the north, shifted from the color guard and the dais to the woman in pink. And, seconds later, to the young man who seemed to pursue her down the center of the field. The Naval Academy graduates, facing the dais, saw her and her pursuer only from behind, once the two had flown past them. The members of the color guard could see them not at all.

As she closed to within thirty yards of the color guard . . . then twenty . . . she slowed, still seeing only the six men, and yet, seeing nothing on which to act. At ten yards she came to a near halt, while behind her, her brother, pounding down the center of the field, closed on her like a runaway freight train.

And then it happened.

As the color guardsman on the left brought his rifle to port arms, he quickly dropped to one knee, brought the stock to his right shoulder, and sighted the barrel of his weapon at the forehead of the First Lady of the United States. The movement was so swift and practiced that, even though Rebecca had never, in her hesitation, come to a complete halt, and even though she accelerated toward him as soon as he dropped to his knee, and even though she hurled herself through the air, flying over his right shoulder, as he sighted down the barrel, he squeezed the trigger and the first round exploded from the muzzle before she could stop him. But in the fraction of a second that passed between the contraction of the muscles in his trigger finger and the movement of the trigger itself and the snap of the firing pin and the detonation of the powder in the round and the projectile's spinning exit from the rifle, Rebecca's left hand slammed into the barrel from above as she dived over the rifleman's shoulder. The bullet, its intended path minutely altered, left the muzzle and burrowed deep into the turf after traveling twenty-five yards in its downward sloping flight, plowing into the grass and soil just in front of the dais.

On the right of the color guard formation, the second assassin was, in one sense, more fortunate. Despite Rebecca's momentary hesitation, her brother had not yet overtaken her when she sprang forward. Without slowing, Luke veered to the right and drove straight for the other rifleman. But he arrived a full second too late. The bullet winged its way toward the platform as Luke's forearm smashed into the back of the assassin's skull, rendering him instantaneously unconscious, his weapon tumbling to the grass.

Luke rolled once, sprang to his feet, and charged the ensign-bearers, all four of whom had dropped their flags to the ground as their comrades had sighted their rifles. At least two of the four, Luke saw, were in the process of unsnapping their handgun holsters. Luke waded into their blue-clad line, felling the first two men in swift sequence with lightning-like, two-fisted, sledgehammer-heavy blows to their chins, cheekbones, and noses.

Simultaneously, Rebecca and the first assailant continued to writhe in the grass in strange hand-to-hand combat in which both adversaries concentrated more on gaining control of the firearm than on each other. Rebecca used all her strength in an effort to keep the muzzle pointed harmlessly downward. The gunman, kicking wildly at her face and chest, tried to wrest the barrel from her hands so that he could open fire again toward the dais. Just as he seemed about to succeed, and just as Luke's right hand smashed into the face of the second of the four flag-bearers, all eight combatants were swarmed under by an avalanche comprising military policemen, Secret Service agents, and, by the dozens, members of the graduating class of the United States Naval Academy.

A mere ten seconds later, in the electric calm that quickly ensued, all eyes around the stadium turned again to the dais, where lay, face down and motionless, her petite form now covered by two Secret Service agents, the First Lady of the United States. Those nearest the dais could see blood on her face.

Chapter Eighteen

ELEANOR CHAPEL AND SID BELTON DEPARTED NEW YORK City early that Saturday morning. They drove south through New Jersey and Delaware, then found Highway 301 and followed it toward the Chesapeake Bay Bridge. After nearly four hours of driving, nearing the bridge, they turned onto Route 50 and headed south for Oxford, Maryland.

Shortly after eleven o'clock, an hour following momentous events in Annapolis of which they were as yet unaware, they slowed as signs warned them of the twenty-five-miles-per-hour speed limit within the Oxford town limits. Just opposite the fire station where Cameron Stafford's security forces had maintained their roadblock until the MMHCC dignitaries' departure earlier that same morning, the detective turned to the driver of the dilapidated automobile, and in his raspy, guttural rattle, admonished her.

"Eleanor, you're still doin' thirty miles an hour. I'm not gonna bail you out if they throw you under the jail. Know what I mean?"

Keeping her eyes on the roadway, her feet just reaching the pedals with the front seat all the way forward and a cushion from the detective's living room sofa under her hips, she replied tartly, "Your Oxford colleagues are much more likely to throw *you* under the jail for bringing this atrocious automobile into their otherwise attractive little town, Detective. Is there any chance whatsoever that *you* know what *I* mean?"

He cackled delightedly in response, holding his broken ribs as he did. "No, no," he replied, "they'll just understand that this is how us big-city detectives travel when we're undercover. With any luck at all, the car'll probably win a prize of some kind. You know how small towns are always havin' contests."

"I was raised in a small town, Detective. I don't recall our town *ever* having had contests. I really don't know how you've been able to fool your superiors all these years into thinking that you know something about something. You seem to be filled to overflowing with misinformation."

He laughed again, clutching his side. "You're gonna be the death of me, Eleanor. I've laughed more in the last four hours than I have in the last four months. You're good for me, if you don't kill me."

Following Rebecca's telephoned instructions, Eleanor Chapel turned left at the Episcopal church, drove slowly past the small inn and tavern where Rebecca and her three colleagues had spent Thursday night, and turned again at the sign that indicated the Pier Street Restaurant one block to the right. She pulled into the parking lot, switched off the ignition, and looked at her watch. "It's quarter past eleven, Detective. Do you think your friends will be on time?"

"I don't know about the two local officers, or about your editor friend, Eleanor, but I can assure you the FBI men got here quite awhile ago. They're not foolin' around with this."

Slowed by the detective's injuries, they moved gingerly across the parking lot, stepped onto the deck of the restaurant, and asked the hostess to seat them with a group of five men, two of whom waved to them from a table near the water. As they approached, the men rose and advanced somberly.

Belton spoke first, addressing himself to the two FBI agents. "Boys, don't even *think* about slappin' me on the back or even shakin' hands. I got so many broken bones I could fall apart if you even gave me one of your *looks*."

With a tenderness that shocked and moved Eleanor Chapel, the two agents touched Sid Belton on his shoulders and, as though caressing the skin of an infant, patted the detective so gently and with such transparent affection and respect that her breath caught in her throat. Still addressing the two FBI men, Belton turned to her and said, "Dr. Eleanor Chapel, let me present two of the finest law enforcement officers I've ever had the privilege to know," and then he spoke their first names to her.

She shook their hands, and then stepped around the agents and warmly embraced one of the three remaining men, April Johnstone's publisher and senior editor. His eyes were red and his face was haggard, both from grief and from his all-night drive after receiving her urgent telephone call the previous evening. "I can't thank you enough, my dear friend," she said to him earnestly, "for all you have done for us this week, and now for making this awful drive, overnight, to meet with us today. We owe you everything."

She then orchestrated the remaining introductions, which included the two Oxford police officers, in part to make certain that all four law enforcement officials understood the role the publisher had played and would continue to play. The six men then moved to the table and stood behind their chairs, waiting for Eleanor Chapel to take her seat. She did not. Looking at Sid Belton, she waited for his nod, and receiving it, she excused herself. The men took their seats.

She walked quickly back into the interior of the restaurant and asked for the location of the ladies' room. Reaching it, she opened the door to the small, neatly appointed room, closed the door behind her, and locked it carefully. Then, following Rebecca's telephoned directions, she walked to the old-style toilet, said a small prayer to herself, and reached around and behind the upright tank.

And then she gasped and emitted an indistinct, choking sound.

Fumbling briefly with the strapping tape, she tugged at the tape's corners determinedly until the tape began to separate from the porcelain surface. Then slowly, delicately, she extricated April Johnstone's document pouch from its hiding place. She clutched the folder to her chest, and then, lifting it to her face, pressed her lips against the soft leather.

Returning quickly to the table where the six men sat waiting for her, she saw them rise as one, all eyes on the folder that she carried in both hands. She stepped around to the side of the table, and with some formality, placed the document pouch in the hands of the publisher. He stared briefly at the folder in his hands, then looked up at the five law enforcement officers. "Gentlemen," he said, struggling with the emotion of the moment, "we're set to go with our special edition on Monday. The secular press and networks will pick up the story later that day. You'll keep this under wraps until five o'clock Monday, then?"

They nodded in unison.

"Then let's go get your copies made, folks. The journalists will break the back of the MMHCC's agenda with the schools. The courts will jail the leaders and most of their henchmen. And the children . . . the children will get a chance."

Here he turned to Eleanor Chapel, his voice thick with memory. "And the last story of April's life will have been her best."

"My goodness," thought Eleanor Chapel, one day after she had handed over the document pouch to the publisher, the FBI, and the police, "this will be a Sunday luncheon to remember."

She looked contentedly around the elegant dining room at her colleagues as they inspected the antique furnishings and historic wall hangings in the family living quarters of the White House. All six of them had had to scramble to clothe themselves suitably for the occasion, and in the end, had been forced to accept the White House appointment secretary's repeated assurances that neither the President nor the First Lady expected them to find anything special to wear. The secretary had even promised that their hosts would be studiously casual in their own dress, in recognition of the extraordinary nature of the invitation, and of the battered physical condition of four of the eight participants, including the First Lady herself.

Eleanor Chapel, the scuffed gray-white tennis shoes stubbornly adorning her tiny feet, turned to the man who stood at her elbow, his arm almost touching hers. Sid Belton, still weak from the astonishing array of injuries he had sustained, and from the mostly liquid diet he had been forced to accept as a concession to the damage his face, mouth, and jaw had undergone, shifted nervously from one foot to the other. He found himself wondering how an ordinary person was supposed to know how to conduct himself in such a situation. If Eleanor Chapel were not standing beside him, he might just . . .

"Detective," she said quietly, sensing his discomfort and hoping to take his mind away from his social misery, "I've been thinking . . ."

She fastened her blue-green eyes on his. "If I understand what you explained to me last night after your meeting with the FBI and Secret Service people, that gunman in the dressing facility was, the FBI thinks, the primary assassin. Yes? And he was charged with killing, as his foremost task, the First Lady, and as his secondary task, Rebecca, Luke, or anyone else who appeared on the field intending to interfere. Yes?"

"Yes, ma'am. That's what they think."

"Which means we were wrong about the threat from behind Rebecca being a danger only to her, and not to the First Lady?"

"Well . . . either that . . . or the FBI is wrong."

"Hmmm. And, according to the FBI, the six-man color guard on the field comprised an elaborate backup, then, assigned to kill the First Lady if the field house gunman failed?"

Sid Belton nodded. "Yes, ma'am. That's what they think."

"And the field house gunman, they think, was going to commit suicide after he had killed the two women. Yes?"

Belton nodded again. "Yes, ma'am. That's what the FBI thinks, mainly because the guy couldn't possibly have gotten out of the stadium after trying either of those shots. That's what those FBI and Secret Service boys said to me last night, after they had studied the material Ellis and Miss Johnstone extracted from the sessions in Oxford, and after they had interviewed everybody who had been in position to see what happened at the stadium."

She pursed her lips and looked down, a small frown line creasing her forehead. She began to speak even more softly, and her companion leaned closer to hear the words, her high, musical voice scarcely above a whisper.

"But, Detective . . . if the man was prepared to lose his life in this . . . why would he drop his rifle and run away like he did? When he heard Matt and the marine sergeant crashing through the door, why would he not simply have fired at his targets immediately . . . and then gone ahead with his own self-destruction?"

She looked up at him. "Do you know what I mean? Or am I missing something obvious?"

His head still inclined close to hers so as to match her near-whisper, he shook his head. "No, ma'am . . . you're not missin' somethin' obvious.

"See, the FBI pictures this guy as a skilled hoodlum . . . a cold-blooded, veteran killer . . . a guy whose concentration wouldn't have been broken at all by the noise of Matt and the marine smashin' through the outside door.

"And if they're right . . . if that's how he was . . . then he'd have set his mind to follow his orders absolutely: to shoot the primary target—that's the First Lady—and then the secondary target—that's Miss Manguson, or Luke, or Matt, or, I suppose, me—and then himself.

"But the FBI thinks that when Miss Manguson arrived under the goal posts, she was positioned square in front of the rifleman . . . she was, without knowin' it, screenin' the First Lady with her body. So, they think, this dirtbag with the rifle saw he couldn't shoot the First Lady without shootin' Miss Manguson first, and they think, he saw that by the time he woulda shot Miss Manguson—and called attention to himself and his rifle by doin' that—and then sighted through that telescopic lens at the other end of the field, the First Lady woulda been swarmed over and covered up by four layers of Secret Service agents. See what I mean, ma'am?

"The gunman, the FBI boys figured out, woulda expected the *color guard* to screen his shot temporarily, since they marched down the center of the field, until they got close to the platform. Once they got close, he woulda known he'd be able to see over 'em, and woulda figured he'd get a clean shot at the First Lady, since she was standin' on that eight-foot-high platform.

"But then Miss Manguson first stood right in front of him, and then ran right down the middle of the field from one end to the other. They think she was still in the guy's way when Matt and the sergeant crashed through that door.

"So, the FBI figures he just couldn't get the shot he wanted. And when our boys busted down that door, they think the guy dropped the weapon and ran, because, first, he hadn't completed his mission, and, second, if he got out quick enough, he might be able to get away while everybody was focused on the action at the other end of the field, maybe, and live to kill these two people—and others, too, I guess—some other day.

"That's how the FBI and Secret Service boys look at it, Eleanor."

The blue-green eyes, unwaveringly fastened on his deep-set black orbs, still appeared troubled. She shook her head at him slowly. "But not you, Detective. You see it some other way, don't you?"

The lopsided grin appeared.

"Well, ma'am, that would be the picture of the absolutely rational human being . . . a guy who is almost hypnotically locked in to do a job a certain way . . . and when that way gets fouled up somehow . . . he *decides* to make his escape so that he can come back another day and complete the job, includin', I suppose, endin' his own miserable life."

He leaned even closer to her, his mouth very near her ear.

"But you're right . . . I don't believe it for a minute, Eleanor."

She smiled and raised her eyebrows at him.

"I'm doubtful, ma'am, about every bit of that theory.

"When I think about what kind of person this gunman was . . . I'm guessin' this guy knew how to use a rifle . . . sure . . . like almost anybody who ever served in the military . . . but was no expert assassin. I'm bettin' the MMHCC got this guy to agree to do this job by threatenin' his family. After all, that's their *modus operandi*. We've seen that from them for two years now. Physical threats to family members is one of their favorites, along with blackmail, extortion, bribery . . . sometimes within a person's family . . . sometimes not. . . .

"There are a lotta pretty good people, Eleanor, who, if they're convinced somebody is gonna kill or torture or even just publicly humiliate their spouse and their children, will sign up to do just about anything. But when the time comes to do the job, if a guy like that, who, after all, is probably a decent person—I mean, decent enough to be *in their way*, if y'know what I mean—if a guy like that gets roped into somethin' like this . . . well . . . he's just *hopin'* somethin' will come along to mess everything up, y'know?

"But . . . aside from that . . . aside from what kinda guy this was . . . I don't even agree with the FBI boys that he was interested in the First Lady. He wasn't interested in her at all. He was there to get Miss Manguson. And maybe Luke and the rest of us, too. But mainly her. *Always* her.

"The color guard was the assassination unit all along . . . and the only assassination unit. The guy in the field house was there to murder Rebecca Manguson. Plain and simple.

"See, the bad guys know who she is, Eleanor. They knew the chances of her bein' . . . ah . . . bein' *directed* to that stadium . . . were very, very good. They were *sure* she'd show up.

"And they've wanted her for *their* side . . . or, if not . . . dead . . . for a long time.

"And . . . if I'm right about that . . . *and* if I'm right about what kinda guy this was in the field house . . . well . . . just imagine you're him . . . you're there with your rifle . . . all set up to shoot somebody . . . and imagine you're prayin' that you won't really hafta do that . . . and imagine, all of a sudden . . . here's this young lady you're supposed to kill . . . pretty as a picture . . . right there in a pink dress . . . standin' right in front of you *with her back to you.* . . .

"Y'see what I mean, Eleanor? If you're that guy . . . you gonna pull that trigger? You gonna murder this young lady who's standin' twenty yards away from you, lookin' the other way?

"This is probably a decent human being, ma'am . . . aimin' this rifle at Miss Manguson's back . . . sweat pourin' down his face . . . maybe prayin' to God that he can still get outta this . . . closin' his eyes . . . maybe even pullin' his finger off of the trigger and wipin' his face . . .

"Imagine this guy's *end-of-the-world* relief when he hears the good guys—Matt and the sergeant—crashin' into his hidin' place, and realizes in a flash that he doesn't have to kill anybody at all. Why, when he hears all that commotion . . . he's probably the happiest guy in the world to throw that rifle down and run like the blazes. And by the time he blasted outta that field house door, on the other side of the buildin', I guess, from where Matt and the sergeant were, everybody was lookin' at Rebecca and all that action at the other end of the field.

"So that's what your plain old, ordinary, run-of-the-mill, New York City detective thinks really happened, ma'am. It's not as neat and sophisticated as the FBI's take on this . . . but . . ."—and here the lopsided grin returned to the battered and misshapen countenance—"I'm bettin' that that's exactly what happened on that field yesterday mornin'. It fits people . . . I mean real people . . . better than the other thing . . . better by far.

"Know what I mean, ma'am?"

Her small, shy smile appeared fleetingly, but then the puzzled look returned to her face.

He touched her arm gently. "What is it, Eleanor?"

"But what about Rebecca and Luke . . . and Matt and Ellis . . . in the eyes of the FBI, Detective?" she asked, speaking slowly and thoughtfully. "What does the FBI think about them? They were at the stadium, after all, because of Rebecca's *visions*. I've heard you say before that that kind of evidence can't be taken to law enforcement people. They would just think someone is crazy . . . or, maybe, that that same 'someone' is actually involved in the plot.

"So . . ."

And here she stopped, again looking upward at him.

"Yeah." He nodded again. "That's another good question, ma'am."

He looked down at his feet, obviously embarrassed. "Well, Eleanor, I didn't much wanna tell you about this part of my meetin' last night . . . but, since you've asked me to tell you . . .

"Y'see, ma'am . . . well . . . these FBI boys know me a little, see . . . some of 'em have been workin' with me for a long, long time . . . and when I explained to 'em in private about our deal . . . y'know . . . that the publisher gets to break the story tomorrow . . . Monday . . . and that they gotta understand that Miss Manguson and the three boys are the good guys . . . good guys who get their information sometimes through some pretty special 'back channels' . . . and that that's all they need to know about that . . . and that that's all they're *gonna* know about that . . . well . . . these FBI boys I've worked with . . . they just know that they'll have to be satisfied with that, ma'am.

"Now, the Secret Service was a little tougher. See . . . I don't know them, and they don't know me. But, as it turns out . . . this president and this First Lady know *you*, Dr. Eleanor Chapel. They know *you* and your reputation like they know the backs of their own hands. Those two are from Georgia, y'know . . . Southern Baptists, themselves . . . and serious about their Christianity.

"So . . . *my* . . . ah . . . well . . . reputation . . . such as it is . . . carried enough weight with the FBI boys to get past Miss Manguson's visions as a source for some of the evidence. And . . . *your* reputation, ma'am, carried more than enough weight with this president and his First Lady so that, on *their* instructions, the Secret Service boys backed off and just had to say, 'well, okay.'

"See what I mean?"

He looked at her closely. He saw that something still hovered in her mind. Something still called for an explanation to this capacious intellect.

"That man . . ." she said tentatively. "That Jamieson man . . . Edward Jamieson, wasn't it . . . the one that Matt talked about . . . the one who said he'd be Rebecca's nightmare, who said that she would be executed in front of tens of thousands . . . that man . . .

"I haven't heard anything about him, Detective . . . except for Matt's description of what he said in the warehouse. And Ellis said he'd never even heard the name before. And yet . . . Matt described him as the one who whispered in Cameron Stafford's ear after he tried to strike Matt . . . whispered in his ear as though he were Dr. Stafford's counselor . . . or mentor . . . or superior, somehow. . . . And then was the only one who stayed to interview—and threaten—Matt further.

"I mean . . . he seemed so *central* . . . such a significant personage in that group of MMHCC people at the kidnapping scene. What happened to him, Detective? What was his role at the arena yesterday?"

Sid Belton shook his head slowly. "Eleanor," he said, "the truth is that I have no idea who he was . . . or is . . . or what kind of role he played. He did seem to predict Rebecca's assassination in the stadium. He did seem to know that she would be there . . . and that she would be shot. . . . And, of course, that may mean *he's* at the center of every piece of this . . . that *he's* the Evil at the very heart of the Evil . . . that *he* set everything up . . . arranged the whole thing.

"And . . . if that's true . . . then he must be very, very highly placed . . . maybe in the government itself . . . to get that gunman into position in a stadium that must have had tight security in place as early as the day before the graduation ceremonies. And . . . maybe . . . to arrange for the midshipman color guard—those six kids are okay, by the way—to be bushwhacked under the stadium half an hour before the ceremonies and replaced by professional hit men. And . . . again, just maybe . . . to influence the numbers and the disposition of the Secret Service agents and, I suppose, even of the military police at the perimeter of the stadium at the exact moment of the assassination attempt. . . .

"He's just a mystery to me, Eleanor . . . a complete mystery."

He paused, and she laid her hand on his uninjured arm. Smiling shyly again, she said, still whispering, "It doesn't matter, Detective. We've known all along that cutting the head off this beast does not kill it. Evil will return . . . again and again . . . and humans will trade their souls for all the things they've always traded their souls for: power, influence, money, sex . . . family . . . cowardice. Humans' capacity to invent new sins has not advanced much since Old Testament times, you know."

She smiled and shook her head. "Human beings can be *redeemed* now. But they have to decide they *want* to be redeemed. And if they don't want to be redeemed . . ."

Her voice trailed away.

And then suddenly, before the six guests had even realized that their hosts had entered the room, the First Lady of the United States had run to Rebecca and had thrown her arms around her at the same time that her husband had done the same, first with Luke, and then with Matt. The two women held each other for a very long time, long after the President had moved from Luke and Matt to Eleanor Chapel, to Sid Belton, and finally to Ellis Dolby, shaking hands with each in turn, and commiserating at length with the latter concerning the spectacular cluster of cuts and bruises around his swollen and misshapen mouth.

Eventually the room fell silent, and all eyes returned to the First Lady and the young woman whom she still held tightly to herself. Gradually each observer realized that the older woman was quietly sobbing. The guests, taking their cue from the President's relaxed smile and loving gaze, joined him in staring happily and without embarrassment at the emotion-charged embrace, and indeed, began slowly to close the circle around the two until the eight individuals had become a rather small knot of mutual support and regard.

Both women's faces were bandaged heavily, as were Sid Belton's and Ellis Dolby's. Rebecca had received repeated blows and kicks to her face while grappling with the color guardsman whose shot she had managed to deflect. Navy doctors had taken a dozen stitches along her hairline, and had placed other bandages on the abrasions and smaller cuts on her forehead, nose, and mouth. And they had reworked the tattered, makeshift bandage that Rebecca herself had fashioned, while still on board the *Rectory*, to cover the stitched track made by the screwdriver days earlier.

The First Lady's bandages covered, first, a superficial bullet wound that had tracked down the left side of her face and had nicked her earlobe. On the other side of her face, smaller bandages covered abrasions and cuts suffered when she had been thrown to the platform by her protectors.

Her life had been saved by the barest of margins. In the two seconds of elapsed time between the first color guardsman's shot, deflected into the ground by Rebecca, and the second guardsman's shot, fired unobstructed in the instant before Luke arrived to render him unconscious, the chief of the Secret Service detail had been afforded the heartbeat of time that he required.

Between the two shots, he had sprung headlong at the First Lady, his arms rigidly outstretched, and making contact at shoulder level, had shoved her roughly to the deck. The four lateral inches that her head had moved at the instant of the agent's blow, before she began to fall, had made the difference between the second bullet's finding the center of her forehead, as it would have, and its grazing the side of her face and ear, as it did.

Safe, now, in her Pennsylvania Avenue residence, the First Lady tenderly released "the woman in pink," as she had referred to Rebecca during the hours before she could learn her identity. After dabbing momentarily at her eyes, she moved quickly to Eleanor Chapel and then to all the others, giving them each an enthusiastic embrace and a bright, heartfelt smile that gladdened their souls.

When all were seated and the President had blessed their food, a simple luncheon was served amid the elegant surroundings. Soon he was recounting proudly to his guests, over his wife's good-natured protests, how, after the gunfire, she had adamantly refused not only evacuation, but all medical treatment. He explained that, while holding a handkerchief to the side of her bleeding face, she had delivered a stirring commencement address, one that focused equally on the service to country that the newly commissioned officers would render and on the need to educate the nation's children in ways that would serve them meaningfully and morally throughout their lifetimes.

As the President completed his statement and a comfortable silence fell upon the group, the First Lady seized the chance to move the conversation in other directions. And so, as the quarter hours and half hours passed, the occasion began gradually to look and sound like any other family gathering over a good meal: two, three, and even four conversations often going forward simultaneously. It was in this relaxed, even joyous atmosphere that, as coffee and a small fruit dessert were served, Sid Belton caught the First Lady's eye. She smiled and nodded, glancing knowingly at her husband.

Rising painfully and walking slowly around the table to Eleanor Chapel's chair, and then asking for silence with his eyes, he waited while Luke, on cue, rose and, after asking the confused professor to rise, turned her chair completely around to face the detective. Her hand on Luke's arm, she circled the chair and sat down, frowning menacingly up at Sid Belton as he stood anxiously over her, fingering one of the numerous bandages along the side of his face.

"Eleanor," he began, his raspy voice trembling slightly, "I've spent my life by myself, thinkin' that no woman could ever stand to be with me for

very long, and thinkin' that . . . well . . . that there was no woman that I'd
ever want to be with for very long, either.

"I know now that I was wrong about the second thing.

"And I'm hopin' that I was wrong about the first thing, too.

"I know that you're the best Baptist on the planet, and that I'm a
mediocre Catholic. And I know that there'll be some things we gotta work
out about that.

"And I know that you're . . . well . . . a few years older than me. But I know,
too, that I'm a real old forty-seven-year-old and you're a real young sixty. . . ."

"Sixty-two!" she interjected proudly, her face brilliant with excitement.

"Yes, ma'am," he said, continuing, "and I figure it's obvious who is
going to have a certain amount of trouble keepin' up with who, as the
years go by."

He stopped and took a deep breath, lifting his dark eyes desperately
from the bright blue-green of Eleanor Chapel's, to the deep, quiet gray of
Rebecca's. At this, Rebecca rose and swiftly circled the table. She came
to a stop behind the detective and placed her left hand lightly on his
shoulder. Then, she said in a stage whisper, "You should keep right on
going, Mr. Belton. We think you're doing very, very well."

Amid the general hilarity that ensued—the President and First Lady
laughing loudest and longest of all—Rebecca steadied the groaning policeman while he struggled to drop to one knee. Once there, he began anew.

"Eleanor," he said, his voice shaking again, "you'd do me the greatest
honor of my life if you'd agree, in front of these . . ." and here he glanced
at the President and First Lady of the United States, and then at his
colleagues, " . . . in front of these friends, to marry me just as soon as we
get things figured out with the priests and ministers, and before I get any
older and more broken down than I am right now. There's nothin' that
could possibly make me happier, ma'am.

"I'm hopin' you'll . . . I'm *very much* hopin' that you'll. . . ."

"Oh, stop it!" she interrupted sharply. "Are you going to prattle on
indefinitely, or do you expect to come to a conclusion to this interminable
monologue sometime this afternoon?"

And here she smiled at him adoringly, her bright face seeming to light
up the entire room and all who sat, entranced, with her.

"Because if you ever do stop talking," she continued, "I'm going to
give you a 'yes' on one condition."

He waited, still on one knee, Rebecca's hand still firmly on his shoulder. "Yes, ma'am? And what would that be?"

"No more of this 'Detective' when I'm speaking to you, Sidney Belton. You'll be 'Sidney' to me, or you'll be single for the rest of your life."

She paused to let this revelation sink in.

"Now," she continued, "what do you say to that . . . Sidney?"

The lopsided grin emerged, and he replied quickly, "I say . . . I say that I like the sound of that a lot, Eleanor Chapel. I like that a whole lot."

Amid raucous applause from around the table, Matt slapping his good right hand against Ellis Dolby's thoughtfully upraised left, the professor shifted forward in her seat to receive the petite ring that Sidney Belton's undamaged left hand had managed to extricate from a pocket. As she raised a small hand toward his, Rebecca, her own left hand still on the detective's shoulder, turned her eyes to meet the steady gaze of Matt Clark. It was a gaze that she had come to expect, to recognize . . . and to rely upon.

She smiled at him, her gray eyes sparkling, and, as though by mutual agreement, both then looked in thrilled amazement at her left hand as it rested on the detective's shoulder. Together they feasted on the sight of his maternal grandmother's engagement band, nestled snugly and gracefully on the third finger of Rebecca's hand.

And for the moment . . . just for the moment . . . the world seemed good and safe and filled with promise.

Just then the President, breaking the fresh silence, spoke softly to the group. "You know, I don't see how it would be possible to write a better ending to this episode. I wish all stories could end exactly this way."

Several heads nodded with satisfaction.

One did not.

Eleanor Chapel turned slowly in her chair to face the President. He looked at her. Only a trace of a smile was on her lips, and the smile had the suggestion, not of agreement, but of mere courtesy.

Then, after a moment, she shook her head. Just a tiny movement. One that escaped the notice of most of the others.

And the President, after a longish pause, nodded his head. He understood.

Preparing to rise from the table, the President looked at his wife and smiled. "My dear," he said, "Dr. Chapel has just reminded me, with one of her *looks*"—and here he smiled broadly—"that this is no ending."

Then he stood, and all present stood with him, some more easily and quickly than others. After a moment, the President continued, "We can rejoice today, my friends, and indeed we do."

Here he turned his eyes back to Eleanor Chapel. "But nothing is finished, because nothing is conquered. The book is not closed. Other chapters yet remain."